PRIDE

BY LORENE CARY

Black Ice
The Price of a Child
Pride

Anchor Books

A DIVISION OF RANDOM HOUSE, INC.

NEW YORK

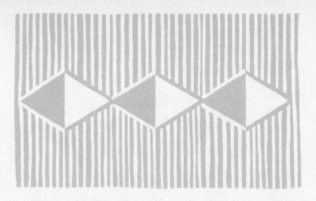

P R I D E

a novel

L O R E N E   C A R Y

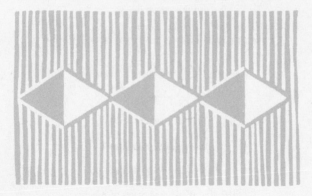

First Anchor Books Edition, February 1999

Copyright © 1998 by Lorene Cary

All rights reserved under International and Pan-American Copyright
Conventions. Published in the United States by Anchor Books, a division of
Random House, Inc., New York, and simultaneously in Canada by Random
House of Canada Limited, Toronto. Originally published in hardcover in the
United States by Nan A. Talese/Doubleday in 1998. The Anchor Books edition
is published by agreement with Nan A. Talese/Doubleday.

Anchor Books and colophon are registered trademarks of Random House, Inc.

"Portrait," from *The Black Unicorn* by Audre Lorde. Copyright © 1978 by
Audre Lorde. Reprinted by permission of W. W. Norton & Company, Inc.

The Library of Congress has cataloged the hardcover edition
of this title as follows:

Cary, Lorene.
Pride : a novel / Lorene Cary. — 1st ed. in the U.S.A.
p.   cm.
I. Title.
PS3553.A78944P76   1998
813'.54—dc21   97-23794
CIP

ISBN: 0-385-48183-7

Book design by Fritz Metsch

www.anchorbooks.com

Printed in the United States of America
10 9 8 7 6 5 4

To Robert C. Smith

and in memory of
Emily Hamilton

"Portrait"

Strong women
know the taste
of their own hatred
I must always be
building nests
in a windy place
I want the safety of oblique numbers
that do not include me
a beautiful woman
with ugly moments
secret and patient
as the amused and ponderous elephants
catering to Hannibal's ambition
as they swayed on their own way
home.
—AUDRE LORDE

Nobody sees a flower, really, it is so small—we
haven't time, and to see takes time, like to
have a friend takes time.
—GEORGIA O´KEEFFE

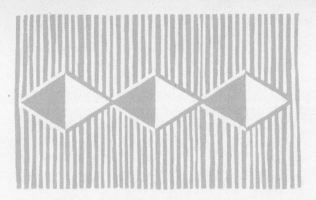

R O Z

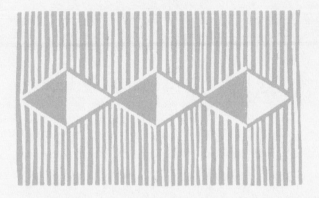

1

At this point in my life I don't think there's anybody I would have done a wedding for except Bryant. Maybe my son. My daughter we won't even discuss.

But once I took it on, though, you'd better believe that this wedding was going to be a very special affair, and classy too—even if the bride was pregnant and barely eighteen years old, and the wedding party put together couldn't have financed a used Chevrolet. I wanted to dignify and elevate their union, and show them what was possible. Hiram and I practically raised Bryant, and I refused to see him and his girlfriend stand up in some JP's office in their sneakers as if they didn't have anybody who was willing and able to do better. That's a terrible way to start out.

Plus, since they were getting married at our country house in Chester County, and since Hiram was looking toward Congress in a couple of years, this was my opportunity to invite a few of our neighbors and supporters out there. What that meant was that I had to keep a very firm hand on the proceedings. I told the kids they could bring their hip-hop music to the reception and all, but for the ceremony, at least, we were going to do this thing right.

Despite everything. Despite the fact that the bridesmaid arrived with her hair stuck out all over her head talking about her cousin was supposed to do it, but the cousin's boyfriend's house caught on fire, and the kids were staying over with him, so the cousin had to go get them, and now what was she supposed to do, and did we have a beauty shop out here she could go to?

Not hardly.

So I gave Audrey my car so she could drive back to the city to get my daughter Nicki's dryer. Audrey is my old, old girlfriend and Bryant's mother. We took him after she divorced her husband and went back to finish nursing school. When her drinking got bad we kept him. Bryant is like a son to both of us.

Audrey never did like Bryant's girlfriends and couldn't abide this one. She was not totally on board with the wedding, and she did not approach the hair dryer emergency like a team player.

"I got sober so I could watch my one son throw his life away for some big-face, big-titty, big-ass gold digger with a lisp? And then run my ass ragged because the maid of honor shows up to the train station with hair look like she had first-period gym? I don't think so, Roz. She'll have to march down the aisle with them nappy spikes lookin' just like that."

I would have sent my daughter, Nicki, but she was already upstairs trying to help take in the girl's dress where the bodice hung off her chest like it was pouting. I mean everybody had to pitch in on this one.

I wanted to light into Audrey point-blank, like: "Well, what the heck *did* you get sober for?" But at this point, better, I figured, just to stay positive, *period,* with everybody.

"You know what Hiram said, Audrey. With a girl like that, the boy's sort of livin' large." I had to laugh. It just made her madder.

" 'That tho thweet. Y'all tho funny. . . .' "

"She does have *some* ambition," I said. "I've talked to her. I can tell these things."

"What ambition? To marry my son, that's her damn ambition."

Audrey was right, but I wasn't going to give in. "She tells me she wants to open a manicure shop," I said.

"Oh, piss."

"Now, I'ma tell you again, since you seem a little slow on the uptake, Audrey: the dryer is in Nicki's closet, up on the shelf. And take this money."

"What do I need money for?"

"You always need money, Audrey; even if you don't need it, it's good to have. And take the cell phone."

Audrey calls me bourgie; she calls me all kind of names, but I don't care. You see who was throwing the wedding, don't you?

In fact, quiet as it's kept, if this had happened any sooner, Audrey would've been out of the picture altogether. It hadn't even been a year since she'd called us at three in the morning to come get her from behind some bucket-o'-blood bar where two men supposed to be giving her a ride took her in the alley and raped her. Hiram went and took her to emergency, where they examined her and brought in a rape counselor, advised her to get therapy and get sober, and released her. Didn't Hiram drive her straight to the city's detox and rehab center—which is right behind Betsy Ross's house, if you can believe that.

Then Hiram being Hiram, he strikes up a friendship with the young black guys who admitted her. He bought them breakfast and listened to their dream of creating a community-based rehab afterwork program. Hiram's put them in touch with Neesie's church and some funders, so it may actually happen. And Audrey's sober; that's the main thing. She's part of our lives again.

I walked Audrey to the car and repeated my instructions about the burglar alarm system to make sure she understood how to work it. She wasn't hardly listening to me.

"Here," I said, reaching into the car for my traveling pad and pencil, "I'll write it down."

"You know that yellow heifer tricked him," Audrey said.

Written directions or not, it was even money she'd set off the alarm when she got there.

"God knows I am trying to get this pulled off with some semblance of dignity and style. Will you help me, Audrey?"

"You know she got herself pregnant just so she wouldn't lose 'im."

What could I say? Bryant is like a throwback—steady and responsible to a fault—and I'd be willing to bet money that Crystal had to maneuver to get him to slip up. I'm sure Audrey was right again.

"My grandmother used to say, 'Who knows what goes on when two people close the door to their bedroom?' "

"They didn't have a bedroom. Probably didn't have a damn door."

Forty-five minutes later she called from the house to say: no dryer. So I ask Nicki, and she tells me that after she and the new Boyfriend-Who-Could-Do-No-Wrong went native with the dreads, she lent her dryer I bought her to some girl at her school who's on scholarship from Camden. Which means I can kiss that hair dryer good-bye.

"You should've asked me."

Asked her? Who bought the doggone dryer? "I know you're not talkin' to me," I said.

She shrugged and kept working on the dress. That boyfriend was a real pain in the neck. A know-it-all. Got her acting like she was a woman grown, and the fact of my presence was stunting her growth.

The maid of honor is sitting there looking me in the face talking about "That's all 'ight. She don't have to bother. With the little veil, ain't nobody gonna see. Plus I got gel."

I used every trick in the book to get Audrey to zoom out to the beauty supply place. I didn't care: guilt, shame, bribery. She called me names. I told her to take that money I gave her and buy a Gold-N-Hot hard hat and extra-strength perm, too. The bridesmaid's roots were pure steel wool—I swear to God—and steady whining.

"I told you just some gel take care of that."

Now, you don't want to be rude, because children these days take such offense, but I had to let her know very politely that there was no gel in the whole wide world could fix what she had crawling down the back of her neck.

"I have a plan for this evening, honey," I said. "And one part of that plan is for you to be as beautiful as we both know you can be. Will you work with me on this?"

My daughter, Nicki, rolled her eyes, but people respond to that sort of appeal. Besides, my other girlfriend Tamara kept popping her head in every half an hour saying, "Cut it. Just let me cut it down to the roots. I'm telling you, with eyeliner and Fulani hoops, you'd be *stunning*. Aesthetically, this could be a real turning point for you."

When we were kids Tam would tease you until you almost wanted to hit her, except she'd hit you back. All this poor girl could do was look at me with those big eyes like: please don't let that five-foot-ten woman with the dreads get near me with no scissors.

I told her to put on a sweatshirt and come trail around and give me a hand putting out the flowers.

The place looked gorgeous, if I do say so myself. It's an old farmhouse, built by a black caretaker on land given to him in the eighteen hundreds by the family he worked for. He built the front section, I understand, from local stone that he dug out of his own fields. In later years, his children and grandchildren added rooms, but then, I guess, the gene pool ran shallow, because they messed over the building and then messed up their finances so bad that we got the property for next to nothing. The one thing I'd expect that living out here would have taught them is the advantage of inheritance. White people out here hold on to their land, and they hold on to their money, which is why they have no debt and why everybody else in America is fighting over what's left.

I told her that this land has been under black ownership for more than a hundred and fifty years. And I explained to her about the original owner and showed her the gravestone that he carved every day for fifteen years before he died out of a piece of quartz shaped like a cross he found in the creek. Fifteen years, a little at a time. He finished the carving and died a month later. It's a wonderful story. If the family didn't have the sense to keep the place up, well, too bad. I have no qualms about making use of the history they threw away. Whether it made any effect on the bridesmaid, I couldn't say.

Since everybody knew the kids didn't have any money, and the bride's family didn't have a pot to piss in, I tried to keep the presentation humble. Tamara hooked up this "whole village" theme. Tam being Tam, she did it tongue-in-cheek. But, ironic or not, Tamara understands the spirit of a thing like this, or what the spirit ought to be, and then she can translate that into something tangible. Tamara must have made fifty phone calls to get everybody in the bride's and groom's families to donate Bryant's and Crystal's favorite dishes. Then she made up cards with *kinte* cloth around the edges and that person's name, like Aunt Clara's Uncanny Corn Pudding or Uncle Sonny's Hot Sauce, with a big circle with a diagonal line through it like the no-smoking signs, except for where they put the picture of a cigarette were the words CANDY ASS, which is what Sonny always says: "If you're a candy ass, don't eat this stuff."

Now, she did all of this, mind you, even though she personally thought that half the food was "uninspired" (her word) and that only two dishes were "truly extraordinary"—the yellow mustard hot sauce and the black-eyed peas and rice with smoked turkey butts. So she filled in with her own creations, which are fantastic. I tried to get her to make this thing I read about where you bake a ham on a bed of fresh-cut grass, but she launched into a diatribe against Martha Stewart and the taste police and Ralph Lauren ads, so I let well enough alone.

She baked a gorgeous wedding cake with lemon custard in the middle and butter-cream icing and tiny broomsticks and candied pansies and mint leaves cascading down one side, which was about as far into haute cuisine, she said, as she was willing to go.

It was plenty. That thing was exquisite. Tamara brought it down from New York in three cardboard boxes in the back of her little red Karmann Ghia and assembled it at the house. I mean, she outdid herself for this wedding.

I ordered twenty flats of purple and yellow pansies for the inside and outside of the house and, because it was Valentine's Day, red and white roses for the formal arrangements. The house is mostly muted beige and cream and yellow, so the color just popped.

Then there was the wedding party. I wanted little Empire-waistline dresses in red velvet with puffy taffeta sleeves for the bridesmaids. A classic look, young, but with style. But, no. Girl-friend had to have one of those black-and-white weddings. She thought it was *da bomb,* as the kids say. Well, you have to have a very good eye to pull those things off. And money.

And I'm sorry, but it was too late for white.

She wore it, though. Blue-white to hurt your eyes and shiny and tight. I always say: A place for everything and everything in its place—and that cheesy white satin dress was not the place for that big old pregnant belly and butt. God knows baby got back *and* front to begin with, which is why Audrey started calling her T&A.

By the time the deal went down, her three attendants dropped to one. To make a long story short, they were trifling. There's no excuse. The one attendant left was the pitiful girl who had brought us the original bad hair day—although she looked fine once we finished with her, thank the Lord—in a black off-the-shoulder dress. Despite Nicki's work, the pointed tips of the bodice stuck off her chest like some kind of crazy plumes. The shoes were so big, she wobbled. Somebody gave her the idea to wear some off-white stockings that went way beyond bad to comical. Child was so busy trying to do sultry, she ended up making herself look like a crow.

I tried to tell them that an evening wedding is not the same thing as a nightclub act. But the bride was marrying the most promising young black man she'd ever met, so, hey, she knew everything there was to know about everything. Put the *B* in bad taste, but how could she tell? I gave them like a Currier and Ives backdrop and they come on stage doing Heckle and Jeckle. Hurt your feelings if you think about it like that for too long.

So I didn't. I just sat up in the front in a red peplum jacket and—just to go along with the program—a black full-length straight skirt with a side slash, not to mention a long-line bra for control under the jacket, a long-line girdle for the skirt, and control-top panty hose underneath everything to try to control whatever was left. Dear God. My midsection was so bound up I could feel the gas pockets forming down in my gut before the service even began.

But they were happy. And I refused to be anything but. Bride's gown too white and too tight? The maid's dress too black and too big? Music out of a boom box while the groom's own mother could play piano like an angel? Hey, no problem. Therapist used to say I didn't have any boundaries with my kids, so guess what? I let them plan this whole mess by themselves. Don't come back to me ten years from now saying I made them do this or that, and they got the wrong start in their married life, and it's all my fault. I let them tack it up—some of it—to their hearts' content.

And they loved it. Or, as we used to say, they *loveded* it. All the kids, mine, too—my son, Hiram Junior, standing next to Bryant as his best man, and my daughter and her boyfriend, the so-called Afrocentric intellectual—I swear they acted like we were at the Penn relays instead of a solemn event. They put their hands up in the air and did those doggie hoots like the audience on the old Arsenio Hall show.

"They gonna make this thing into a fuckin' farce," Audrey said through her teeth. "It'th da bomb!"

I just put my head down and said a prayer.

When I looked up Arneatha was standing in front of the fireplace completely unperturbed. Arneatha can fall over her own shadow, she's so clumsy, but let her stand still somewhere and she exudes calm. I've seen her do it in a classroom: the peacefulness spreads right through the children. Bryant and Junior were so handsome in the tuxes Hiram got them, and Bryant looked so much like Audrey's father, I couldn't help remarking on it.

"Don't even say it."

Arneatha indicated with a finger that the bridesmaid should step back and give the bride room to squeeze in next to Bryant. The ring bearer started to have a fit because he couldn't see, so Junior scooped him up and held him in one arm for the rest of the service. When the wedding party was still and the guests were finally silent, Arneatha let out that beautiful voice. It is a voice that is rich and smooth, not overpowering, but intense. It's a gift and, when she wants to, Arneatha knows how to use it.

"Dearly beloved," she began, "we are gathered together here in the sight of God and the ancestors and in the presence of these witnesses to join this man and this woman in holy matrimony."

At the point in the ceremony where you can read something, the bridesmaid and Junior stepped forward. The ring bearer, who was spoiled rotten, wouldn't get down, so Junior shifted him to his left arm and read holding his papers in the right:

" 'There is no sweeter name than that of my friend, my love, my soul's companion.' "

Then the girl read: "For the Bible says: 'Rise up, my love, my fair one, and come away. For lo, the winter is past, the rain is over and gone; the flowers appear on the earth; the time of the singing birds is come, and the voice of the turtle is heard over the land.' "

Tamara leaned forward and whispered into my ear, " 'The voice of the turtle?' "

"And the Bible also says," he continued, " 'A faithful friend is the medicine of life.' "

Then the bridesmaid started to sing "You Are So Beautiful to Me." Her voice was husky and smallish, but right on pitch and from her throat, not all up in her nose like most of the children sing today. Audrey nodded her head. It was just right.

When she finished Arneatha went into her signature wedding

prayer: "Father God, we ask your blessings on these two people. They are so very young. We ask that you teach them how to care for and care about each other, knowing that in a marriage nobody gets his or her way all the time, knowing that in many cases, Lord God, you will ask that they rise to the occasion when they swear they cannot, and share when they feel they do not have enough, and give what they never got themselves."

I commenced to crying right on cue. Like a big baby. I'd been keeping up a good front, but I was exhausted, and Lord knows that like Audrey, I wished he'd held off a few years. And sitting there I had another thought: that of all the people in the room, Arneatha herself was the one who should've had the babies. It wasn't too late yet, but it almost was. We were becoming grandmas already.

Why else was I crying? I don't know.

"Dear God, help them build a life for themselves and their children. We don't fall in love, we receive love from God and we use it in our lives. We know what's in everyone's mind at this wedding, Lord. You've already blessed them with fertility. Teach them how to make love work in the home they will now build together."

I probably wouldn't have boo-hooed like that had it not been for the cancer. And, as these things go, I had it easy—I contracted one of the *good* cancers. The girls teased me that I had the rich white women's cancer with the 96 percent cure rate. But something like that rocks your world. It just does. And then there's the other 4 percent.

What I did, the minute I was diagnosed, was I decided to fight this monkey. To my mind, that means not giving in. I like life rich. Like the kids say: phat, large. I made up my mind to that a long time ago. I am going to eat my beef and my pork. Sorry. Pigs' feet is what kept our people *alive*. I mean it. That's why God gave Adam dominion over the animals. And I am going to put cream in my coffee. I will not let this cancer dictate my every move. I will not live in constant fear. I swear, I think that makes it grow more.

I didn't go to the cancer support groups the hospital sponsored because of the same reasons. I do not want to sit up in a room with a bunch of baldheaded white women talking about how scared we are that the cancer's going to come back. Arneatha told me I was missing an opportunity for spiritual growth, and I told her that I loved her dearly, but that I was growing just about as fast as I could take. I told her, I said: "I got *you;* what I need the group for?"

So, as Arneatha was saying that marriage is an honorable estate, she looked at me and it felt like the look she gave me in the hospital when I asked if she believed in heaven. "All I know," she said, "is that life is short, and that this is no dress rehearsal."

Jesus have mercy.

This is the real thing, I kept thinking, and it's already half over. Half a lifetime ago, I was standing up there myself. I wasn't but nineteen when I got married to a grown man— Hiram was thirty-one—and I knew precisely what I was doing. I'd worked at his bar for eight months. He'd been watching me, but kept his distance. So one day I pulled him aside and told him that I knew his political ambitions. I told him that I knew exactly the kind of wife he needed, and that I could be that wife. I told him that not many women could think as big as I knew he was thinking, and very few could live up to the vision. But I had imagination—and I knew how to stick. Then I stood there waiting for an answer. Thinking that I couldn't possibly be serious, I guess, he told me that he had a thing for blondes. What about that? Could I be a blonde for him? He said it kind of offhand. I *was* awfully young.

Now, I was not some poor, pathetic child slinking around the world dying to be a wife. I was on a mission—we all were, our set, our little pride, as one of our teachers at Girls' High called us, us four lionesses lying out on our rock in the sun, watching the water hole, just seeing what was going to turn up for us. That makes it sound like we were going to gobble up whoever came along, but too bad how it sounds. If you're a black woman with ambition—or man, for that matter—you better be aggressive and expect that somebody's not going to like you. Because we are supposed to be *sub*. Subservient. Subsistent. Substandard. Subliterate. Subordinate. Subdued. America doesn't want us off welfare. They want us *on* welfare, right where they can keep an eye on us.

Far as women are concerned, a lotta men want you to be sub, too. Not Hiram. Hiram expects you to be on equal footing, which is hard sometimes because he is larger than life. It's why people vote for him. Hiram walks into the room and people turn to see who it is. He disturbs the air.

So, there are women, inevitably. I didn't quite figure that in at nineteen, but then, you don't at that age. It hasn't been so bad, really. Nothing I could ever really point to specifically. No disrespect.

He has very strong principles across the board, and where it counts. It wasn't enough for him to own a bar; he wanted to move the drug dealers off his corner so neighborhood people could come in for a beer without being afraid. We had a couple of little light-bright old schoolteachers on the block, lived together in a perfect little house with green shutters—I swear they were lesbians—and he made us make a pitcher of iced tea for them so they could stop in after school on Fridays and have a glass with us. That sort of thing. He brought in a local DJ so people could dance outside the bar on Saturday nights and sold soda and water ice and roast beef sandwiches from a sidewalk table. You have never seen a bar like Hiram created. It was like the family barbecue that most of us wished we had.

So when he said the blonde thing, I decided not to take offense. I didn't go off about how here's another brother wants white women and all that. What I did, I took it as a challenge. Everything with him is a challenge, a competition. I said—to myself, that is—OK, Negro, you want blonde? I'll see you your blonde, and I'll raise you.

I went home and bought some Dusky Sahara-something-or-other and dyed my hair. Then I had my girlfriend, Audrey's cousin, give me a new cut and curl. I told her I wanted it bone straight, with just a bang at the bottom for movement so the highlights could catch the light, but short, sophisticated. And I'll tell you a funny thing—see, people think fashion and hair and all is frivolous, but how are we introduced to one another if not through our eyes?—when I picked up the mirror that night, it was as if the woman looking back was exactly who I was meant to be all along, as if that little girl with that rhiney red hair and freckles was the ugly duckling, and, now, I had become the swan. Blond swan. I swear. I decided who I was going to be for Hiram Prettyman, and I can look anybody in the face and tell them: I have lived up to it, too.

When Arneatha got to the part in the service about married people present renewing their commitment, I reached over and squeezed Hiram's hand. Twenty-one years. I remember thinking at that moment maybe that's when marriages, like people, came of age.

Arneatha told Bryant to kiss his bride, and, honest to God, he just went for it. Tamara leaned forward over my shoulder and said to me, "Remember you asked what he saw in her?"

And I have to say, until that moment I never could picture it. You don't, with your own children. Or at least I don't see them as, you know, sexual persons. Tam would. But then, she's the one went down on some little Negro at a house party—and we were only sixteen!—so I figured, consider the source.

Audrey saw it, too, which is why she always called the child T&A. Audrey does have a nasty mouth on her sometimes, and that's no more than the truth. In fact, when we had our big falling out fifteen years ago over Bryant—that time she said she was coming to get him to take him to the zoo, but she didn't, and he fell asleep right there by the front door, in his own chair, dressed up in the little blue blazer Hiram bought him—we got into the fight of our lives, and Audrey said some things to me that to this day I will not repeat. But God knows she has paid for it. For every drink she poured down her throat, she has paid a terrible price.

I can't forget, but I surely can forgive, and it's as if I had saved a place for her in my heart all along. Bryant will take longer, though. He gives her her due respect, but he is very, very cool. I can understand that.

Tamara slipped out to get the food and the toast going. I swear, she should've been a caterer. Caterers make good money. College professors do, too, but I have always thought that she was trying to prove something. She said as much herself—that the only thing her Jamaican parents wanted was money and middle-class respectability, even though they couldn't stand respectable, middle-class Americans. So, her compromise was to teach college, drive a thirty-year-old sports car, and stay single.

But if you watched her constructing that wedding cake, putting in straws between the layers to hold the thing together, and then piping the butter cream like they blow insulation into a crawl space under the shed kitchen, you would have seen her whole body come alive. I mean, she twisted and turned and maneuvered. Then she'd put a dab on her finger and come over to me and put her finger to my mouth. The butter and lemon and some drops of raspberry liqueur blended on my tongue like I never could have imagined.

"Tastes like spring, doesn't it?" she asked. "You said you wished we could've had a spring wedding. So, here's the taste of May. And look—"

She opened a mail-order box from out of the fridge and showed me purple-and-yellow pansies crusted all over with sugar.

"They're crystallized," she said. "They'll match the ones you put out front."

They were so beautiful I didn't know what to say. So she tore one, popped half in her mouth, half in mine, and then went back to cementing the top tier of the cake with butter cream.

Tamara may dog Martha Stewart, but I say, if you don't like what she's doing, go out and do it better. I told Tamara that I think, in the nineties, America's ready for a tall, gorgeous, dark-skinned woman with her own TV show on cooking. Oprah has prepared them. Audrey went for the idea so much that she called cable companies and got information about every public access channel in the Delaware Valley.

Tamara wouldn't take us seriously.

"Oh, I get it," she said. "I'd be like a cross between Martha Stewart and Grace Jones. That'll make 'em take notice."

OK, I told her. We only have but so many schemes to make one another rich and famous, and she already threw away Audrey's idea to do a line of divorce cards back when she was in art school and nobody else was doing them. Now even Hallmark publishes divorce cards. But why listen to us? I'm just the high school graduate who does charity balls and Audrey's the temp nurse. Like what do we know?

2

I stayed on Tamara like white on rice about the caterers, some former soup kitchen people Arneatha hooked up, and Tam stayed on them. By the time Arneatha finished the service, and the bride and groom walked between the two rows of family and friends crowded into our living room, the servers were waiting right by the big double doors with glasses of champagne on silver trays. Thank God.

Crystal's mother was trying to push ahead of everyone to get a glass. She was one of those fat women with little tiny hands and little tiny feet. Looked pumped up with air, like if you pricked her, she would pop. But then, once she got up next to us in front of the couple, she could hardly stand on those little football feet.

One of Bryant's old friends from the neighborhood made the first toast. But it wasn't about marriage at all. It was about "the brothers"; they were going to be there for one another. They slapped hands and grunted and shook their heads. Someone named Buck-Man sent a message from jail—"Stay strong and get along"—which was repeated solemnly as a prayer, and they vowed to stay in touch no matter what.

Then before I knew what was happening, three of those boys poured champagne right onto my brown-and-beige-and-rose

Aubusson-style carpet from China, and a half dozen more raised their glasses about to follow suit—for the boys who ain't here—like this is the movies. I didn't care that it was only a tablespoon each. That doggone rug cost more than what half of those Negroes earned in a year. I've been knowing all of those boys since they were toddlers, so I just shouted, "No, you don't," and they stopped.

Then came more toasts. The first was from the boyfriend of Crystal's mother. He looked like a James Brown impersonator; he had the hair, the walk, the half-boots with a heel, everything but the cape. The mother kept sending him to get her a chair, and he'd leave and then get waylaid glad-handing somebody or fetching some more champagne and come back without it. And she's teetering on them little football feet like a strong gust'll blow her right over. It was clear to see that the boyfriend had never been to a party where someone came up to him with a tray and offered him a new glass of whatever he was drinking. And assumed everybody was the same way.

"Hope they got plenty of that free wine in the back. This the kinda crowd where you say 'cheese,' and they all jump in line." He said it to Tam, of all people.

"Yalp," she said, "and she be the first one." She pointed to me.

He started to laugh, then caught a look at my face.

"Don't let her intimidate you," Tam said. "She's a native Ebonics speaker, too, although she pretends otherwise."

He did a little James Brown jig and laughed so hard, his flip shook up and down.

"This all your hair?" Tam asked.

"Yeah, baby. Why? You want some? Ha! Ha!" Caterer walked by and he almost made her jump out of her skin, yelling, *"Hit me!"*

As far as I was concerned his toast wasn't even as good as the kids': "I'll be brief, but you shouldn't. Hey!"

Crystal's mother grinned and giggled so bad, it was terrible.

"Hah! Hey, now! Hey! Get on the good foot!" the boyfriend screamed. "I'ma tell you what my father tol' me: Make it last, brother, make it *last.*"

Tamara sang into Audrey's ear. Even though I couldn't hear I knew it had to be her theme song:

> *"I'm a one-hour Mama.*
> *So no one-minute Papa*
> *Ain't the kind of man for me."*

The two of them snorted. All I could do was put my head down.

My one goal in life since I'd heard Crystal was pregnant was to pull off this wedding, and make it perfect. Now these fools were doing a nineties-style coon show, and our West Chester neighbor Brooke Phillips was laughing so hard his face and ears were all red. Phillips didn't know anybody there except us and our kids, but I sent him an invitation because he was the only person in the area to invite us over for drinks when we bought the property, and because he's active politically and a *very* good friend of the governor's. The wife is weird, but I take it she does what she's told, and usually, like tonight, he leaves her home and makes her excuses. They're Republicans, of course, but pro-choice, Rockefeller Republicans. And, most important, Phillips always has taken a keen interest in Hiram's career.

"Shut up," I said to Tam.

I could've kicked myself for trying to pull it off. This far into our political life I should've known better than to invite him. There's a reason people stay to themselves.

Then, just to top it off, some of Crystal's friends, all of them wearing black dresses and black lipstick and nail polish, made their own short toasts: "Well, you did it now; now you in the soup for real."

And, "You got 'im now, whatcha gonna do with 'im?"

And, "Y'all got more heart than I do—shi'."

They tossed their weaves together and made homegirl grunts and groans like they'd been dealing with the problems of the whole wide world for fifty-ahundred years.

"Ladies, ladies, excuse me," my son, Junior, said. He'd been waiting. I expect that Hiram asked him to go last, after the other young people. Junior had just finished applying to law schools a few weeks before, to please us, he said, although he wanted to get out and work for a while. We leaned on him, though. Once they get out, it's not so easy to get them back in.

"Bryant is my brother," he said. "And he's just about the most serious man I ever knew. So I know he's serious about this here. Crystal, hangin' out with this guy is just about the best thing I could wish on any young lady. But, if you should happen to have any trouble with 'im, you just talk to me."

They hugged and laughed. Junior had been watching his daddy for a lot of years—you could tell.

Then Hiram stepped forward and wished them long life together and health and prosperity, and told them to stay on the honeymoon. We all drank to that. It was perfect. I could see that he had been waiting for the right moment. Then he said to the group: "This is what we're all about, as a family, as an extended family, as a community, as a people. These two young people are making a new family, and they've pledged to love each other and work together, and we—all of us here—have pledged to help them. Isn't that what you said, Reverend?"

"That is what I asked," Arneatha said, "and everyone here agreed."

"I pledge my help here and now, Bryant. You've been like a son to me. You've brought joy into our home, and through your hard work and now, through your marriage and your child, you will add strength to our community. I'm proud of you, and I love you. We all love you, and we welcome Crystal into the family."

"Hear, hear!" Brooke Phillips held his glass up high. A year before, Hiram got him to make a big pledge toward Arneatha's little parish school. He loved Neesie and St. Augustine's School. He walked over and hugged Neesie and slapped Hiram on the back. Darned if his eyes weren't wet.

Audrey raised her glass, and Arneatha and I noticed at the same minute that she had a glass of champagne like everybody else. At every toast, she put it to her lips, but didn't drink. She licked her lips. Neesie ducked away from Phillips, zipped into the kitchen, banging into the swinging door, and reappeared with a can of ginger ale. I eased my way toward them from my side of the room. Crystal's mother was talking a blue streak about how headstrong Crystal had been, and how God told women to be obedient to their husbands, and the whole time Crystal's standing there with her mouth stuck out, looking no more than thirteen years old, I swear, and the young people weren't listening anymore.

When I got over to my girlfriends, Audrey was just staring at Crystal's mother. Then she handed her glass to Arneatha. "Make you want to slit your wrists, don't it?" she said.

Neesie went to put down the ginger ale, and was so busy trying not to get a water mark on the chest of drawers that she spilled the champagne all down her own leg.

Tamara came to tell me that the servers and the food were in place. I looked around for Hiram to announce dinner—we have given beaucoup parties and dinners over the years, and we've got a system down pat—but he and Phillips had stolen away somewhere. I did not want these people here all night, so I asked Arneatha to say grace so we could get going on the food.

When she said "Amen," they were on it.

"You going to play now?" Tamara asked Audrey. " 'Cause as soon as they scarf down this food, they're going to crank up those speakers and we will be wrapped in rap until dawn's early light. Promise."

"Nope. Not until dawn. Until two o'clock," I said. "Just like the bars. I want all of these people out of my house by two. I told Bryant. Even if I have to drive them to the train station myself."

"Train stops at one-thirty, Roz."

"Well, I'll give 'em money to share a cab."

"Roz, why won't you eat something? You know how crazy you get on an empty stomach."

"Are you kidding?" I said. "Many girdles as I'm wearing I'm lucky I can still breathe."

Audrey got up and went to the piano in the parlor. Arneatha looked after her. "You know, it really hurt her feelings that neither of her parents came."

"Did Bryant invite them or did she?" Tamara asked.

"What difference does that make?" I asked.

"Bryant doesn't care," said Arneatha.

"Much as she hates them on his behalf," Tam observed.

"You'd think she'd know them by now," I said.

"It's easier to say that when they're not your own parents," Arneatha said.

"I said it about my own mother."

"Everybody can't just get over things like you do, Roz," said Arneatha.

"You don't have to defend her against me. I get tired of tippy-toeing around Audrey."

Hiram and Phillips came toward us. Hiram gave me his arched-eyebrow look, opened the closet, put on a jacket, handed one to Phillips, and grabbed a couple of cigars out of the humi-dor on the hall table. I knew there had to be something substan-tial going on.

On the way to the patio, Hiram slowed down enough to talk to everyone as he went by. When he asked Tamara how things were going at her college, she said, in the most matter-of-fact tone, "I'm being forced out of the department, and they won't publish my book."

"You've written a book?" Phillips asked. "What's it about?"

I tried to catch Tam's eyes to let her know not to be rude. I could hear it coming.

"It's a book of art criticism and social commentary that can-not decide whether it's for a general audience or the academy. I treat the murder of a truly brilliant dancer-turned-performance artist. He was a gay black man who used drag in his act to examine the virulence of homophobia as well as the fascination with gender reversal in America at large and within the black community. I've been able to get gorgeous photos. When men see some of the pictures, they cannot believe he's a man."

"I'd like to see those photos."

"I'm sure you would." She looked at him with her eyes half closed, sort of challenging.

Hiram finished chatting up Crystal's mother and her boyfriend and took Phillips's elbow.

"Do you have a title?"

"I was going to call it *Eugene/Eugenia: Dragging the River of Life for the Body Politic,* but the academic press has no sense of humor. They have to undergo a humorectomy to get the job."

Tam plays with men's minds. I've seen her do it for years. She's very tall, very gorgeous, with that twenty-five-year-old's body, and they can't stop fencing with her. And the smarter they are, the more they go for it.

"Do you have a new title now?"

"Come on, Phillips, let's duck outside for a smoke," Hiram said.

"Say, hold on. I want to hear the title."

"Bend Over," Tamara said.

"I'm sorry?"

"Bend Over, Mr. Phillips, is the new title."

"She is so bad," I said, flashing every tooth in my head. "When it's her birthday I'ma give her a great big old bag o' dirt, I swear."

"C'mon, Phillips," Hiram said, exchanging a tiny eyeroll with me. "She's having a difficult time at her college."

Then Tamara said again what she'd never even mentioned on the phone all that month: "Not problems, Hiram. Just dismissal. I'm up for tenure, and I won't get it, and then I'll be dismissed."

I did not believe Tam, because she always teased, and because she seemed so unconcerned.

"Oh, listen," she said in that same deadpan tone. "Audrey's playing the piano."

Audrey had said she might play some old standard like "My Funny Valentine," but for some reason that night she never did. Instead she jumped instead into "Maple Leaf Rag." It was the song she used to play a long time ago, because the kids would do cartwheels to it and laugh. Back then, she used to get buzzed and hammer it out loud and fast and sloppy. Even I could hear wrong notes, and I don't know music. This time she played it lightly. It felt sad, but the kind of sad where you make a joke and keep on going.

Bryant looked up and listened.

"Hey, Bry, man," Junior said. " 'Member this? 'Member what we used to do when Aunt Audrey played this song?"

Junior stepped out of the buffet line and did two or three cartwheels right there in the dining room.

"Look at your tux, man." Bryant smiled a little.

Crystal yelled, "No, he di'n't!"

"Come on, Bry. 'Member? Synchronize."

Bryant said not a word, but in a few seconds, when Junior put his hands up, Bryant threw his up, too, and they did the cartwheel together, just like they used to in our dining room on Christian Street, hands touching the floor, feet up in the air at exactly the same time to Audrey's madcap playing. Crystal clapped her hands and laughed. Bryant stepped back in line and smoothed his cummerbund.

"You know," I said to Tam, "Junior and Crystal are like the only ones Bryant ever jokes around with. And Audrey just remembered that song from all those years."

"She's been practicing," Tamara told me. "Every night at my mother's place."

"Why'd she mess around with the toast?" I asked. "Like to give me a heart attack."

"It is her champagne. Do you believe in the whole disease concept of alcoholism? I'm never sure what she means when she says that. Is it a disease like manic-depressive is a disease? Or like diabetes?"

"What do you mean, it's her champagne?"

"She bought it. When Bryant and Crystal decided to have champagne at the wedding and no hard liquor, she told me she wanted him to have something nice. And I said not on my dime, because these kids wouldn't know the difference anyway. So she went out and borrowed her brother's car and bought the champagne and brought it over this afternoon."

"Oh, Lord, don't tell Arneatha."

"Don't be a ninny, Roz," she said. Tamara's been saying that to me as long as I can remember. I am not a ninny, but people sometimes think I am. "Besides, Arneatha's busy. Look. Hiram's African is moving in on her. I hope she mopped that wine off her leg."

"Aw, shucks," I said. "I should've done it for her right then. You know she probably smells like a doggone still."

Hiram's African was a liaison person between Ghanaian businessmen and Americans. Since Hiram's been the city representative, whose job is to get more business into Philadelphia, he's been deluged by all these Africans, and when he suggested they get one person to represent them, they found Kofi Rockemore. How he ended up at the wedding, I'm still not certain, but sure enough he had maneuvered Arneatha into a corner, and they were having a little tête-à-tête.

"I should've invited Bill Williams so you'd have some company," I said to Tam.

"Bill Williams is for display purposes; he is not to be used at home."

"What are you talkin' about? We've been out together; he's very easy to be with. What I like is he never forgets where he came from, but you can still take him anywhere."

"Williams is a show horse, Rozzie. *Know what I mean?*"

She was making fun of him. "Well, God knows he's for show, and you know I don't usually do too much looking."

"Don't get your knickers in a twist, Roz. The man is a Ken doll. You ever talk to a Ken doll? No. They have very little to say. That's because they are made of plastic. *Know what I mean?*" She tapped her head.

"I think y'all just haven't found your way to communicate yet. Oh, well, then, I'll have to get my entertainment from Neesie."

I shouldn't have been so nosy, but when everyone had their plates and was sitting down, I did actually sashay over to see how she was making out with the African. He offered me his chair—his manners are just exquisite—and then got one for himself. Most women friends would give you the eye at this point, but Arneatha just made her half-smile.

"Did you wash that champagne off your leg?"

"You just couldn't wait, could you?"

"I never thought of introducing you," I said. "But I forgot you like that ethnic groove. All I can say is I hope this one wears deodorant."

She started to get huffy. "Maybe our combined aroma will cancel each other out, Roz."

"I'm sorry," I said. "I have to say these things."

Then Kofi came back.

"I've heard Africans are very spiritual," I said.

I thought Arneatha would die. But *she's* the one goes around wearing the African fabrics and talking about the spiritual component of textile weaving and pottery and mask-making and all that stuff.

"I would be loath to call one people more spiritual than another," he said. "But there is something in what you say. Not genetically, but culturally."

I laughed and nodded yes. "That's just it. You know what I'm trying to say."

Not jungle bunnies, either, is what I thought, but I wouldn't breathe a word like that. Arneatha would sure enough have my hide.

"I've been in politics all my life, Mr. Rockemore, and I've found that if I don't ask a lot of stupid questions, I miss out on a lot of very interesting answers."

I always say that.

"Africans wake up thinking about God and go to bed thinking about God. Europeans and Americans are driven crazy by it. Even our black brothers. In the fifties Richard Wright visited Africa and said he wanted them to start waking up thinking about how to get their trains to run on time."

"Richard Wright said that?" I asked. "Why would he?"

"Because he wanted them to be able to compete on an equal footing with Europe. He wanted them to become a continent that Europe could no longer exploit."

"But of all people," Arneatha said, "Wright knew the price you pay for godlessness in a culture: terrible, terrible neurosis."

Kofi lifted his eyebrows and shrugged. "Yes, he knew. Of course. It is a dilemma, isn't it? But look what a price they were paying under the existing circumstances: colonialism and the mess that followed. I suppose that's what he must have been thinking."

"See," I said—I couldn't help making the point—"I'm glad I asked. I've got a thousand questions about Africa, and you just feel so ignorant asking."

Maybe not a thousand. Maybe like two. For one thing I wanted to know why rich Ghanaians had those coffins made in the shapes of cars and butterflies and airplanes, and for another I wanted to know about clitorectomy.

"So exactly what brought you to America?" I asked.

"Exactly? Interesting. I came to attend Wharton, of course, but there are business schools in Britain. What exactly brought me was that I wanted to see the country that had produced Emily Dickinson, whom my father adored."

Arneatha could not have been more surprised. Perked her right up, thank the Lord. I looked at her like: See there.

"You read poetry, then," she said.

"I? Not particularly, no. But my father used to quote Dickinson poems regularly and one in particular. He said it took him years to come to an understanding of it. I had to see a country that could produce Emily Dickinson, Coca-Cola, Otis Redding, and Mickey Mouse, too."

"Which poem?" Arneatha asked.

"You want me to recite it now?"

"If you remember it."

> "Nature and God—I neither knew
> Yet both so well knew me
> They startled, like Executors
> Of my Identity."

Arneatha ate it up. I never did see all the fuss about Emily Dickinson. He could tell. He moved on to another topic just as nice.

"I was telling your friend," he said, "that she must come visit. You must come, too. All the black Americans arrive, and they go to the castles, and they go to the dungeons, and they cry and cry for the ancestors. Very cathartic. They love it. You must come." He laughed.

"Aren't you going to Uganda for the diocese?" I asked.

"I don't know," Arneatha said, pursing her lips at me. "Nothing's definite."

"Oh," Kofi said. "The reverend has been holding out on me. Thank you, Mrs. Prettyman. You've been very informative."

"Glad to be of help," I said. And I had to keep from laughing out loud, because I knew that she didn't want to go, and this African was going to work her over about it.

"You don't want to go?" he asked her. "I can't believe it."

No, she didn't want to go. She didn't want to travel or do missionary work or preach anymore. Didn't date. Since Larry had died seven years before, Arneatha had stopped a whole bunch of things. At first she called it a crisis of faith, and we all waited for her to get over it along with her grief, but it's like we're still waiting. I thought an African trip might get her out from behind her darned headmistress's desk. So, after I dropped that little old bomb, I excused myself to go give Tamara a hand with the cake.

Like I said, the cake was gorgeous. Everybody took pictures of it, and we stood the bride and groom in front of it with the little bridesmaid and Junior and the spoiled rotten ring bearer making faces, and they took pictures with us, the mothers, and Hiram and the James Brown boyfriend, who kept saying to me, "Now the children is married, what that make us?" To which I finally replied: "New friends."

They cut the cake, and then, all at once, Crystal smashed her handful of cake right into Bryant's face. I was so shocked, I just screamed.

"See that! See that! What did I tell you?" Crystal's mother shouted. I swear she's got a voice like a sheep. Loud and flat. She kept it up. "She how she is? See? Don't nobody believe me. Everybody say: 'Why you badmouth the girl? She's sweet-natured.' Now you see what I been goin' through."

Crystal threw the flowers over her shoulder, hiked the dress way up to her thighs, and lit out for the front door. My daughter Nicki had the nerve to catch the bouquet and squeal. Bryant took a minute to get some cake out of his eye, and lit out after her. It was raw outside. They didn't care. Some of the young people ran out after them. So much for what was left of the evening. So, I didn't care. I tipped over to the door and when Nicki and the stupid boyfriend ran by, I reached out and snatched the bouquet out of her hand. I hate playing house.

Then I went to join Tamara at the window. We could see when he caught her. She yelled bloody murder and fell and he dropped down on top of her. The other kids caught up to them, and I heard them shouting: "Lick it off, lick it, lick it, lick it off."

"Well," Tam said, stepping back from the window. "Fightin' and fuckin'. That'd be one prediction."

"Maybe I should just go out and stop this foolishness," I said.

Audrey had come up behind us. "Guess it's too late to have it annulled."

"Here's one way to think of it," Tam said. "Earlier today I asked Arneatha how she could do this thing in good conscience and she said to me, 'Do you know how many young men I have *buried?*' "

"Oh, well, damn," Audrey said. "If that's the choice: do you want him out on the ground humping the heifer in their wedding clothes or you want 'im dead? If that's the choice . . ."

"Shhhhh," I said. I could hear the rolling undertones of Arneatha's voice in the next room, but I couldn't believe my ears. "She's giving him her phone number."

"Who?"

"Neesie. The African."

From the next room, we could barely make out the sounds of Arneatha's and Kofi's voices. All of us threw on big surprise faces, mugging, trying to laugh without making any noise. Arneatha! The seven-year widow, wrapped up in her work, life devoted to a bunch of snot-nosed kids.

"Wore her down with culture talk," Audrey said. It was the first time she'd smiled all night.

I remember thinking at that moment how big and musical Kofi's voice was, and how it kind of matched with Arneatha's. And slow, too. They both use three words when one would do, and they like to roll each and every word around in those deep voices. He said something about going to New York, and then he said: "I've never dated a priest before."

Then—I couldn't believe it—Arneatha laughed and said: "You know priests do everything other people do."

My mouth was hanging open. Tamara snorted, and I thought we would give it away.

Then he said, real suave, "Oh, I certainly hope so."

Audrey made a kissy face, but we couldn't hear any more because the kids were back and cranking the music. Bryant came in doing cartwheels and landed right in front of his mother. He picked her up around the waist and swung her around. Audrey looked stunned.

"It's gonna be all right," he said to her, just like he used to when he was little. "Everything's gonna be fine now." Then he ran back to the vestibule and we lost sight of him.

I remembered an earlier conversation and turned to Tam: "Are you really losing your job?"

She tripped her tongue. "Don't worry about it. Go see whether Hiram's sucked all the money out of the new john."

"Shut up," I said.

"Make me."

I grabbed a black-and-red wool-blend shawl Tam bought me in New York and slipped out the front. The gas in my gut felt like a knife, and I was hoping to get a little relief. But just eight paces to the west of the door I saw where one of the boys had puked and fallen face-first into his own mess. Three guys came right behind me carrying newspapers and a garbage bag, a bucket of water and a rag.

"We're gettin' him out of here right now, Mrs. Prettyman."

"Just don't let my husband get a whiff of this."

"Can we take him upstairs?"

"Back bedroom," I said. "The little one with the white walls and blue trim. Not the all-white one in the middle, hear me?"

Talk about gas. That upset me so much, it got worse rather than better. So I kind of lurched around the back of the house and found Hiram and Phillips sitting on the patio, smoking cigars, with a bottle of champagne on the table between them.

"Hey, baby doll, come here," Hiram said.

Something big was happening. After twenty years, you sense it. I picked up the matches on the table and lit two of the glass-and-copper lanterns on stakes by the patio.

"Now I can see you," I said.

Then I sat on the arm of Hiram's chair. It was my black wrought-iron set, so heavy you can barely move it. Other stuff is more comfortable, but I don't care. I love wrought iron. It's classic.

Hiram put his arm around my waist. He wanted Phillips to see us this way. That's why I lit the candles. People get all hyped about what candidates say on TV. Mostly it doesn't matter what they say. What really matters is how you look. People get a feeling according to how you appear to them. They keep that image in their heads, and it stays connected to that feeling in their hearts. And when they pull the curtain in the booth, believe me, that's what they're voting on. If they don't get a feeling, they stay the heck home.

Hiram is the "family candidate." Every donor and every potential donor has to see him that way. He has to be the family man they wish they were, or think they are, or wish their fathers were. Even rich white men have to see him like this to some extent. And that is no small feat to pull off. 'Cause mostly, the only black man a white man will look up to is an athlete or a soldier. Basically, if they think the man can kick their behinds. I remembered that it was Hiram's toast about family that broke Phillips up.

He'd given five hundred once before, which wasn't bad, but it wasn't the thousand-dollar limit. Also, he had a law firm that could make a corporate contribution, and he had a wife, and he could make a contribution in her name. But then, he was really a Republican. I wondered whether he was one of those people who give money to both sides, just in case, or whether he had given to Hiram because we were neighbors, and it never hurts to grease the wheels. The suspense was killing me.

The kids had the music cranked loud. That was OK, too. The bigger the party, the more it showed that Hiram had the kids and their energy under his roof and under his control, so to speak. I took Hiram's hand in my lap and smiled.

"Listen, honey," he said over the music. "You know that Latimore Dixon's recent operation was for cancer?"

I hated Dixon, but the cancer made me feel sorry for him.

"He said he'd see the term through, but Phillips here tells me that he can barely keep going—"

"He's how old now?"

"Got to be eighty."

"Him and Thurmond," Phillips said. "You gotta admire the guy's stamina."

"Yep," Hiram said. "He's tough, all right."

I didn't say anything. We had hoped Dixon could hold on. The election wasn't until November, eight months off. If the governor appointed somebody now, he'd have that much of an advantage over the challenger. And the governor, Phillips's friend, would no doubt appoint a Republican to replace Dixon the Democrat. It only made sense.

"How would you feel about switching parties?" Hiram asked me.

I wasn't sure he meant what it sounded like.

"To Republican."

It was a real shocker. The kids were playing a rap and shouting: *"Ain't nobody's business!"*

"What do you think, Roz? Hiram tells me he can't make a move without you," Phillips said.

Hiram sat back and smoked. By this time I had gas so bad I was ready to grab those little cigar scissors Phillips kept twirling in his fingers and cut off my own foundation garments.

"You know what?" I said. "We've been saying for years that the Democrats have come to take black people for granted. Although I've got to tell you in all honesty I myself never thought seriously about changing. Phew. This *is* a lot to take in."

Hiram shook his head, and Phillips grinned. "This is American political compromise, isn't it? The way it should work, I think, anyhow. Pluralism, after too long a wait. Democracy at its best, and I mean that from the bottom of my heart.

"You know, Dixon's district is a funny district with half white, half black voters. He told the governor, told Lou directly, that the reason he was soldiering on was because he didn't want the black voters to lose one of their few reps. He said, and he's right, that if Lou made a typical white suburban appointment, the black candidates would be at a double disadvantage come November."

"So the governor—"

"Threw the question open. Called his closest advisors. I don't mind telling you there are about four or five of us he consults on things like this."

"And they said ask Hiram?" I did not want to get myself disappointed. He could still be blowing hot air.

"They said to find someone who can do the job, knows the voters, knows the issues, can win in November, and will be true to the constituency that Dixon has cared about, and has every reason, frankly, to be protective of.

"I'd be lying if I didn't say outright that we think Hiram is just about the only man on the scene who can do all this—and bring new money in from moderates who haven't been excited enough to get off the bench, and bring in new voters, black and white, to join the coalition the party is pulling together from all walks of life, so to speak."

"My Lord."

"It's good, isn't it? Elegant and simple. And Dixon likes it," Hiram said.

"If he knows it's going to be you, he'll be willing to step down," Phillips said.

"Did you guys tell him you wanted Hiram in as Republican?"

"I'm not sure, Rozzie. I wasn't in on those talks specifically."

"Phillips says I could expect to raise a hundred thousand in corporate donations, honey, and that much again in individuals, and that once that happened the soft money would be behind me. Which we've been saying all along doesn't happen worth a damn in the Democratic party. The soft money really does . . . well, it moves by you so fast, and they don't tell you like they should. So you don't know: this is what I can depend on to have backing me up. It's a problem."

"He can raise some money now," I said. "Friend of ours said it was like a holdup on the subway: they come in with their money and they leave with nothing but the clothes on their backs."

"Republican moderates, so to speak," Phillips said to me, as if

I needed more convincing, "are very eager for somebody like your husband. Very eager, Roz. We need more people who are fiscally responsible, but have a progressive social agenda, rock-solid family and personal credentials, and a strong record of achievement. The campaign experience and your time in the state legislature qualify you for sure, but, Hiram, what you've done to bring business to Philadelphia as our city rep—well, I think anybody could run on that. Do you have numbers?"

"I do. I'll have to make them more detailed. I have a young guy who could do that for me."

"Right, and make them more descriptive, too, which is what we need. So people know what it is they're hearing. Make it easy for them to get the message. Listen, Hiram, Roz, don't mention anything just yet. What do you say we go around for a few weeks, talk to some people confidentially? Do our own feasibility study. You like what you hear, you can go from there."

"Fair enough," Hiram said.

"But I'm almost sure that in two weeks you'll have good-faith offers over fifty or seventy-five thousand. That's before you even announce. And I'm being—"

"Conservative." They both said it at once and laughed.

The moon was high. It was almost full, blue-white and cold-looking. I shivered.

The song finished up with the rapper's voice, a young girl with that hard New York sound, saying that only God could judge us all.

Phillips poked the air with his cigar. "Now, I never heard *that* in a rap before."

"Politics," Hiram said, patting me on the hip as if to reassure me that he was with me, he hadn't blasted off in a rocket ship to the moon. I took hold of his hand to try to keep him from knocking out of me the biggest, most explosive fart that Phillips had ever heard. "It's always something new."

3

Hiram switched from Democrat to Republican, and everybody carried on as if the sky was falling. It was a mess. Arneatha got very upset, and being Arneatha, she came to the house to talk to him face to face. It was such a mild March that I planted some of the pansies from the wedding in our window boxes in the city. Last year after surgery I promised myself that from then on I wouldn't just think about this kind of thing, I'd actually do it. Neesie loves flowers, too, so I potted some for her to put on the window ledge outside her office at school. I set up coffee and Kahlua in the living room and watched the *Oprah* I'd taped while I waited fifteen or twenty minutes. Neesie is almost never late.

She was distracted when she arrived, so needless to say she didn't notice the flowers, except to trip over them in the vestibule and kick dirt all over the floor.

"Oh, Lord," she said, and kind of jammed them back up against the wall.

"They're for you," I told her.

"Thanks, sweetie."

She was nervous. "He'll be right down," I said. I handed her a cup of coffee. Arneatha hates confrontation, but she'll walk herself through it if she feels she has to.

"Tell me about Kofi Rockemore," I said.

I expected that they might have talked on the phone or gone to the movies. Instead she told me that they'd been to the opera, a performance of a Senegalese dance company, and a screening of Louis Massiah's new Du Bois documentary.

"Kofi? He's lovely," she said. She flung her arm out and hit my brass floor lamp. It rocked but didn't tip over. "Sorry."

"Lovely . . . He convinced you to go to Africa yet?"

"Yes."

I was shocked. Last I heard she couldn't possibly go—couldn't leave the school, couldn't walk away from the church's community policing project in its formative stage.

"You know what? I think that God is sending you to the motherland to preach to those people."

She pulled a crooked smile and shook her head. "They don't need me to preach to them. Is Hiram coming down, or do I have to behave badly now to get his attention?"

"They keep him hung up on the phone. He'll be down. Listen, *we* need you to preach."

"Rozzie, you've got an agenda for me, I know. But it's not *my* agenda for me."

"How could you say *my* agenda? Neesie, you were called; that's what you told us."

"God, I'm exhausted. I'm exhausted, Roz. What do you want? We all remember each other's early ambitions. It's the gift and the curse of long friendships. I remember when Hiram—"

"—was going to make it to Congress," I said.

"—wouldn't make deals."

"He always made deals, Arneatha," I said. I didn't mean to flick my wrist at her, but I did. "I'll tell you what *I'll* never, ever forget is when we were about twenty-five, you preached about after the crucifixion, when Jesus comes to the disciples in the upper room. I was there, and while you were preaching, I could feel His presence, Neesie. I've told you this: I felt Him come and sit beside me. I'll be a witness to that till the day I die. I love your little school, but anybody who can do what you did needs to preach, and you need to travel, and you need to be about the business of moving up and stop letting white men make all the decisions goin' up the ladder in that church."

Arneatha spread her arms out on the couch and lay her head back, and I thought that maybe she had gone back to the sermon I'd mentioned. After a long time, and with her eyes closed, she said: "When you talk like this, I feel like an aging actress whom people keep wanting to look as she did in her first films. I'm not that girl anymore, Roz. I could no more preach that sermon now than I could fly."

She sat up and leaned her hands on both knees. She was wearing black wool pants, a black shirt, her white collar, and a black-and-white herringbone jacket. Right before my eyes she did seem older. It was like I hadn't really been looking for fifteen years.

"But," she said, "I do do an excellent job of building and running an elementary school, which could be of some use to the Ugandan diocese. So that is the expertise I will offer them.

"Now, I'm going to give Hiram another five minutes, sweetie, and then I gotta go."

"Oh, you gonna stand me up, are you?" said Hiram, coming down the steps.

"Great timing as usual, Hi," Arneatha said, standing.

She handed him one of his cigars out of the humidor on the coffee table and, kissing me as she went by, took him outside to talk. It was raw and damp.

"Go ahead and use the greenhouse," I said. I don't allow cigars in the house, but the greenhouse is an exception. It's really a little breakfast nook off the kitchen, but I've filled the windows with so many plants, it's got a hothouse feel now.

"Thanks, anyway."

The door slammed.

I don't mind. The two of them have been doing business around that church and her school for years. And she has done things for him—benedictions, blessings, lending the church for functions. It was just that she was so distracted this time. So, I went to my study upstairs and opened the window a crack, just enough to let in the smell of his cigar and their voices. I didn't figure it was wrong, since they both tell me just about everything anyway.

I missed the first sentences, but I was shocked to hear Hiram using his business voice, very cool: "So you're going to start disinviting me to meetings at church you used to beg me to attend? What's up when you come back? Community policing. You're starting it with the big MOVE remembrance, right? Don't I remember workin' with you on that? You plan to cut me out of the credit now that I'm ready to run for office? You think I'm a fool or an idiot? Which one?"

She answered very calmly: "And, the truth is, I don't want you to do the fund-raising we talked about. It's too much."

"Look," he said. "I'll get you the money anonymously. A big gift shows up, and brings in two dollars for every dollar, at least. You can't argue with that."

"You have somebody in mind, don't you? Tell me and we'll contact him ourselves and use your name."

"Oh, come on, Neesie. That's so ridiculous, I know you're not serious. We've been here before. Remember when you were in that bind with thieves breaking into the church and somebody who will remain nameless got a little baksheesh going in your district, and you were so offended? 'Member that big fight we had? This isn't the first time purity meets pragmatism and doesn't like the way it smells. I understand. The world needs both, though."

"OK. Forget it. Let's just give each other some breathing room. Let each other alone," she said.

The sharper her tone became, the more conciliatory Hiram grew. I've seen him do this. He is very good, very persistent.

"I can't let you alone. Saint A's is not just a political base, it's our church home. You're stuck with me.

"Of course, it could be I won't even find a donor. Or when I do, you still have the option of refusing. How's that? I'm trying to see what the hell the real problem is here."

"Lemme go get my coffee," she said. "You want yours?"

"Sure," he said, "and put some of that stuff in it."

I heard the door slam, and then she came back out.

"Being dishonest always puts you at a disadvantage," she said.

"You're right. I don't want your money."

"You don't want my *dirty* money. What about other money? You took Phillips's donations before. Are you gonna turn them down now? Educate me. Explain this to me, because I don't get it."

"I didn't like the speech you made at the chamber of commerce when you announced you were gonna run, Hi."

"Well, then, why the fuck didn't you call up and say, 'I didn't like the chamber of commerce speech, Hi,' and forget the histrionics?"

" 'Cause I mean the histrionics."

I smelled one of those French cigarettes she sometimes smokes when she has a drink. She's funny that way. Makes Audrey furious how Neesie can smoke two cigarettes one night and not pick one up again for six months.

"We've got to get business back into the city, Neese," Hiram said after a long pause. "And there's a shortage of investment money in this country. You of all people should know that."

"No, I don't know that. There is no shortage of investment money. That's a smokescreen. Investment money grew in the eighties like rich folk can't even believe themselves. What there is a shortage of is good-paying jobs. That's the shortage, Hiram, and you know it."

He sucked his teeth. "Do you know how many speeches I give in a month, Arneatha?" he asked her. "Do you have any idea how many jobs those speeches help create?

"And lookahere, Neese. I intend to get myself into a seat where nobody can take it back once I get in, sayin', 'Hey, we'll redistrict this nigger 'cause nobody but his own'll vote for him, so that's his ass.' Not gonna happen. Not this little black duck."

"You're using us, Hiram."

"So what. You used me to get the deputy commissioner to go to your community policing meeting in June. Everybody uses everybody."

"What's your point, Hiram?"

"I'm still the same man."

"I don't know who you are anymore."

His tone changed. He nearly growled. I've seen him do that, too. "What's this about? Just what the fuck is this whole thing about, Neese?"

There was a long pause. I heard a match strike, and I figured without even having to see that it was Hiram relighting his cigar.

"I think you know what this is about, Hiram."

"I don't know shit if you don't tell me. I do not have telepathy, and I am not a mind reader. You want me to know something, tell me."

"I saw something last week I never thought I'd see, Hiram."

"And that's it? You 'saw something' and twenty years of friendship is shot? Jesus, Arneatha, what the hell could you have seen? What we do helps thousands of people. Will you please come down off the mountain and get your eye back on the damn prize?"

"I'm talking about my girlfriend."

"I'm talking about your girlfriend, too. She loves that church, and she worked like a dog to help you build that little school. So what? Is this a threat? I tell you what. You don't like what you saw, next time don't look."

She said something in a voice as low and rolling as a lullaby. I couldn't get the words.

"Let's get in out of this weather," Hiram said.

I hurried to beat them to the living room. As they came in Hiram said to her, "You ought to know, Arneatha, Democrats don't have any respect for black people. None at all. They been getting the milk since FDR, and they're not even thinking about buyin' the cow at this late date. Why should they?"

"Don't lecture me, Hiram."

"Giving 'em's easier than taking 'em, isn't it?"

"Don't argue," I said. "Please, not you two. Don't fight."

She left, and we went to bed, and I lay awake a long time staring at the ceiling. What did she see? was all I could think about. And, as I had done for years, I made myself not think about it. Inside my head was like a broken record, saying, I-saw-something-don't-look. And that's all. I didn't run any scenarios. I didn't do any recriminations. Just the words going up and down to the sound of his breath.

4

Latimore Dixon resigned from Congress in a teary press conference on a Monday morning from his Baptist church in south
Philadelphia—the place where he first announced nearly sixteen
years before. Few people attended. We decided that I would go
as a courtesy and to check out who was there, give our respects,
and cover our bases. Dixon and his wife cried buckets. His skin
looked gray, and despite all the money he stole over the years,
now, in his final public performance, he was wearing a toupee
that he might as well have scrubbed the floor with. Look like
after all these years he could've afforded a decent rug. Made me
wonder how we'd end up.

Meanwhile Hiram met with the governor and his assistants in
Harrisburg. I hired a car-and-driver and arrived just in time for
the governor's announcement that Hiram would fill Dixon's seat
until the next election. Then he was sworn into office. It went
on the midday and evening news, backed up by a nice sound bite
from the head of the Black Caucus talking about Hiram's record
and how pleased they were, no matter his affiliation. "The governor appoints the man, not the party."

We've used that quote on every black radio station since.

After a flurry of attention, good for the most part, Hiram put
five suits and a couple sets of sweat clothes in the car and moved
to an empty faculty apartment our friends told us about on the

Howard University campus. It was convenient, affordable, and great PR. He came home some weekends, and some weekends I went there. I hate to travel, but I did it. Couple times I showed up unannounced, too. But he didn't have time to do anything but work. He had the seat and a round of freshman midterm appointments—meeting people, mostly. Making friends and alliances. But at the same time we were looking toward the November election.

Even with Brook Phillips's pledges and his help, we still had plenty of money to raise. It is the worst part of this business, and it might as well be a marathon. Or one of those triathalons they run on TV, where the athletes start out so gorgeous and so strong, and by the time they get to the finish line the crap is running all down their legs and they can't even help themselves anymore. Raising money'll kill you.

One Democrat hopeful, this *awful* white woman, a former state prosecutor, decided to start running Hiram down the day he went to D.C. about the flowering pears that he fought to get planted in our district when he was state senator. He ordered four hundred of them. Turns out that particular hybrid grows just so big, and then the wood gets too fragile to bear its own weight. They were bred for their flowers, not their wood. Every time there's a good rainstorm—not even wind, just the weight of the water on the leaves—ten or twelve will split right down the middle. So she tried to use the trees to say he was an incompetent legislator and that she and some concerned citizens were going to start a monitoring committee to watch how he voted. We knew what that was about. White botanists come up with the hybrid; white horticulturists recommend them; but the black man in the chain who bucks white city bureaucrats to get something green in the doggone ground—he's incompetent.

Hiram went right back at her. He went on the black morning radio talk show and said, "They're gonna monitor me? Great! They'll save me the trouble of having to publicize my record."

He avoided playing hardball with her, because the paisanos and the Poles and the Irish will kill any black man who attacks a

white woman. Word on our streets was that while he was planting trees, she was planting black men in jail. We got almost a
thousand voters to switch parties on that issue alone.

And then there were my shooting lessons. I hadn't had so
much fun with anything since Tamara's mother, who raises dogs,
took me to dog training school back when the kids were little.
This was, in a way, the same kind of thing. Basically, it gave me
something to do to get my mind off everything, and time to
myself, pure and simple. The other thing about firing lessons—
and dog training, come to think of it—is that everybody there is
focused on one thing. It's like its own self-contained universe,
and I'd go there and shoot and, for half an hour or an hour,
forget about the whole world.

The cancer counselor and everybody keeps talking about em-
bracing illness and accepting vulnerability, but I'm here to say,
hey, I've seen vulnerable, and I've been vulnerable, and I much
prefer the alternative. Shooting made me feel safer, I guess. Not
that I wanted to shoot anybody; I just wanted to know how. Big
difference.

And then, because I already had Aisha Crane, this aggressive
young black reporter built like a pack of cigarettes—I mean,
short, flat and wide—on my tail and on my trail, I eventually let
her come along. Once she was in like Flint she stopped talking—
just clammed up and started taking notes. Sometimes it felt like
she was a vampire, sucking the life out of me to put in her story.
Weird.

Eventually, though, I kind of forgot about Aisha—if you can
forget about a five-foot bulldog sitting in the corner carrying a
tape recorder.

It went like that for a few weeks, and I got friendly with my
instructor and the regulars—mostly because I was pretty good,
and they hadn't expected that out of a woman—a woman, you
know, who keeps herself up and doesn't come on real strong.
And when they found out who I was, they were completely
amazed. They took good care of me.

It's almost all men there, and you can tell: the whole place feels like men, smells like men. They lounge around and talk trash. And shoot.

Reynaldo, my instructor, is one of those real beefy men. He's got great big hands like half a ham, and he carries his own automatic shoved into the back of his pants, in the small of his back, right in the indentation, with big old love handles on either side. In the morning he works as a nonteaching assistant at one of the school district's disciplinary all-male high schools. The kids call them bam-bam schools, because, I gather, they sort of bang on those hardheaded boys when necessary. In the afternoons and evenings Reynaldo works the firing range. He tells stories about his school, and no matter what the story's about, it always ends with him saying the same thing: "So I tell him that I'm gonna stick my foot so far up his ass that he's gonna be tasting leather for the next three years."

They've all got mouths like that, but I don't mind a bit, because I know he cares about those kids. And I'll tell you something else: if he doesn't do it to them, somebody else will down the line, and it won't be a bit funny.

Fact is, I felt safe in that stinky old firing range. So this one day, he asks me why I never bring my own gun to practice with. And I told him I didn't own one, which I didn't, and he was shocked.

"I never sold you one like the one you always practice on?" he asked me.

"Nope," I said. "I've never bought a gun from you."

Well, what did I say that for? Him and Dallas—that's the black cop who comes and practices there all the time—they started in on me about owning my own gun. But I did not want to continue the conversation in front of the reporter—they'd forgotten about her, see, but I hadn't—so I motioned to them and sort of cut my eyes over to Aisha.

When she left, they started up again. Back and forth. They couldn't believe that Hiram didn't have a firearm in the house. They had one argument after another. Someone in my position should know that there was a time when black people couldn't buy guns. They wouldn't let us, just like in South Africa. Now we can buy them, Reynaldo said, and half of us is scared to have them.

I asked Dallas wasn't it true that for every gun owner who shoots an intruder, there are four who freeze up and the robber takes the gun away and shoots them with it, or else the owners' kids get to playing with it and some child shoots his friend? And what about every Christmas when some boy in the service comes home on leave to surprise his parents and his father shoots him coming in the door? While I'm talking Dallas just shakes his head slowly. None of that would happen, he said, if people were trained to use a gun correctly, like I'm being trained.

Now, like I said, there's an atmosphere in the firing range. Almost all of the people in there are men, and the times when I go, they're mostly black men. They knew I was Hiram's wife, so they were respectful and all, but still, they look out for you. And they were just nuts on the subject of me having this gun at home, especially considering Hiram's high profile and how often he's away from home. We have security systems on both houses, but, as Dallas said, he's answered a lot of calls where something happened between the time the police were notified and the time he got there.

So, I bought the gun.

I continued to practice with it, and Aisha came every so often. She took a few notes and shot a couple rolls of film.

When Hiram made his first speech on the floor of the House, that's when she got the *Philadelphia Inquirer* magazine to run the piece she'd been writing about me. They ran a black-and-white shot they'd used before of Hiram and me sitting together on the love seat in the library alcove of the living room, and a color one of me at the firing range. I'm wearing the ear protectors and the goggles and I'm aiming the way Reynaldo taught me, one hand under the other.

Time picked up the photo and ran it along with a story about the new breed of black conservatives—although we're not conservative the way they mean it.

When the story broke in *Time* I was flying high with the phones ringing and people calling. Hiram was flying, too. Somehow, it seemed to people that he had to be pretty secure to let his wife share the spotlight. We never would have dreamt how much mileage he got out of it.

I mean, we were on the upbeat. But, like I said, things can change in an instant. And mine came when I got home one night from a meeting with about forty Hmong women crammed into somebody's living room. Maybe five of them spoke English, and thirty-five did not want any trouble from some outsider. I distinctly heard the *N* word twice. Tam had this old Dick Gregory album where he said they put all the immigrants in a room and teach them to say *nigger-nigger-nigger-nigger* before they let them become citizens. I swear. So, I'm muttering all this to Nicki as I come in and turn on my little radio in the greenhouse study nook behind the kitchen and make myself a cup of tea.

Then I collapsed in the chair. I was worn out. Beyond worn out, so I asked Nicki would she please go upstairs for me and get my slippers. Here I was, dog-tired, and she's standing there, sixteen years old, healthy as a horse, with them stupid knots all over her head, and she starts whining. So I ask her: what is wrong?

"What could be so wrong with you that you cannot go upstairs for your mother who has been out busting her butt? Just what could be wrong?"

And I go on, like I do, no biggie, until I realize that she's not talking back: no excuses, no sass, no nothing. And then she just breaks into tears.

She didn't have to say a word. I knew.

5

Boom, in the face. But I cannot say it came as a total surprise. In the back of my mind, I had half expected something like this.

Strictly speaking, our kids did not have what you would call a normal childhood. In some ways they were privileged, but none of us got much of Hiram or privacy.

That's the price of the ticket, though. I always tell them, because they need to know. Working people want money; rich people want everybody to love them; busy people want free time; people on the bottom want to get out from under. But nobody gets on the ride for free. I do not want my children to grow up fools. One way or another, you pay for everything. I want them to have heard it here first.

But it's not easy, and it's not always pretty. Nicki never stops throwing in my face that every time we had a really important public event, I took her into the bathroom and beat the devil out of her. Well, it's true. I never had to hit Junior or Bryant more than once.

But Nicki—every time she knew we had something important to do, look like she was determined to start down the completely wrong road. By the time we got to where we were going, I had to tighten her up. This was no mystery. You'd think she'd've learned. Hard head makes soft behind, and I'm sorry, but by the time that child got herself worked up all crazy, a few cracks on the butt was about the only way that I could get through to her.

When she got older, we paid good money for a therapist, because half the time she's depressed like my mother was, and the therapist gives her the idea that she gets bladder infections now because I beat her in the bathroom when she was small.

So what I want to ask the therapist is: if we messed Nicki up so bad, how come Hiram Junior and Bryant didn't have any problems? A lot of political kids, I know, are overwhelmed by their fathers. Dad is in the papers; they see his pictures; everybody wants to know about their fathers and not about themselves. And boys in general tend to take this life harder.

A lot of things you can say about Hiram, but you can't fault him on the kids. He said that his daddy disappeared—just like mine—and he intended to be a real father. I mean, he'd drive from Harrisburg on occasion, arrive at midnight, wake up at five; I'd hustle to get the boys dressed, and then he'd take them back to Harrisburg and carry the two of them through the whole day. Junior loved it. He liked the attention, and it never turned his head. Bryant was always more serious, but he had a good time, too. They still talk about those trips—couldn't have been more than ten or twelve in all.

Hiram tried to take Nicki to Harrisburg when her time came, but couldn't. She'd tear the place up. When she was two or three and he won the state house reelection, I'd campaigned so much the last week my back went out, so we watched on TV. She ran up and hit the screen, that's how mad she was that Hiram wasn't home. We had a gorgeous poster one time of the five of us; she tore it off the wall. And yet she's the one who would brag on him at school. She's the one who begged to ride in the limousine when we went out to a function.

Maybe I should've beat her *before* we left home. My grandmother did that before we went to church, like drinking ginger tea to ward off a cold. Now, my grandmother could tear you up. First she'd say: "I'ma talk to you this once. Next time you get a whuppin'."

Next time come, I mean the slightest pretext, Grandma'd say: "Now I's *really* mad at you."

She'd get you in the bath, on the road in front of your friends, out back behind church; she'd get you with the electric cord or the hairbrush or the broom handle. I have a mark on my thigh to this day where I ran under the house and she poked till she broke that broom in half.

And I really didn't need much whipping. I was the kind of child, when the kid next door got beat, I'd be good for a week. Plus with my mama gone North. Look at me hard and I'd start crying. But she beat me good anyway. Truth was that she'd just go off. Start to beating somebody, look like she went crazy. It was awful. Like she was a whole 'nother person. But she never left us. My grandfather died, and my uncles left, one by one, to find work in the city, and she stayed right there and kept a roof over our heads and bread in our mouths. Got to give her that.

So, now Nicki was pregnant. Go figure. Good schools, music lessons, Twigs (which I always liked better than Jack and Jill), ballet classes at Philadanco, summer camps in the mountains, tennis lessons—I mean the works—and she's knocked up like anybody else. Only thing to do was deal with it. I'd call my gynecologist in the morning. I told her I would.

Then the second shoe dropped. She wanted to keep it. More tears. She and Andre could not destroy their child, and hadn't Daddy and I always been against abortion, and how come I was all for Bryant and Crystal getting married, and Andre was just about Bryant's age, and I wouldn't support my own daughter?

"Look at me," I said.

I know better than to trade word for word with a teenager, but I told her: Bryant was not under my control, and Crystal couldn't do any better. Really, for where Crystal started, this was the best option for her. But not for Nicki. Then, because it seemed important for her to know some things, I tried, honestly, to talk to her. She did that staring-out-the-window thing. How she was going to raise a child and couldn't even look me in the eye, I don't even know.

I told her how Hiram and I started out over the bar, about the Black mafioso who invested in the business and then was shot dead two weeks later. I told her what it means to build even the smallest of fortunes and the responsibility of being one of the nation's leading families, which is who we'd set out to be, and who, with God's help, we could become.

"Well," she says, to ice the cake, "how can you be sure that something like this won't get out?"

Lord knows, I do not take well to being threatened, and when she dropped that particular bomb, I just went off. I stood up, and I banged my fist on the end table and I broke every nail on my hand, literally every nail except my thumb, and knocked over the table. It's a little Queen Anne end table with green leather inlay. Not heavy, but it made a terrible crash. Then I stamped my foot so hard my heel hurt for the next two days.

"You didn't have sense to keep your legs closed. And when you opened them, you didn't have the sense to use birth control. And then when you got pregnant, you didn't have sense to call Deborah Kirshner and say, 'Mom's gone to you for years, and I've been with you since my first period, and I've got this problem,' and get your no-good little nigger to scare up the money. That's what he should've done. Or if he didn't have the sense to get the money, you could have gone to your Aunt Tam and said, 'Aunt Tam, I got a problem.' And that would have been it. That's a lot of different options.

"Instead, you decide to plop this thing in my lap and come cryin' about Bryant and his pregnant heifer and then you have the nerve to threaten me. I'm still fighting this cancer. Do you know that? See all this upset you caused? This stuff goes right to my cells."

She was scared, but not too scared to try one more tack.

"Could we talk to Daddy?" she asked.

I stepped toward her, and she had the nerve to flinch.

"No," I said. *"We* may not talk to Daddy. In fact, I'ma make you a deal. If *we* talk to Daddy, I promise I'll drop everything—campaign or no campaign—and I'll spend the next year of my life getting you straight. Now, if you want me on you like white on rice for the next year, you go talk to your daddy."

That night I heard her banging around downstairs. I padded back and forth in my room. I keep a little radio everywhere I tend to be: got one in the bathroom, up high so I don't electrocute myself, got one in the bedroom, one in my study, one down in the kitchen and in the breakfast nook. I keep on a little music, low, all the time. Well, I had one station on in the bathroom, and a different one in the bedroom. I took a bath to some plain rhythm and blues, and I went in the bedroom and filed my nails to some easy listening, and I went down to the basement and did yoga exercises to a gospel tape I had in down there. When I got into bed I tossed and turned to the sound of the classical station for an hour until it hit me how to proceed. I'd call in Andre and give him a chance to get off the hook. I was almost sure he'd jump at it. Five minutes later I was sleeping like a baby.

Nicki stayed home from school, sick as a dog, like she'd been for weeks but trying to hide it. She stayed up in her room. Miss Pidgeon came to clean that day, and found some reason every hour to be up in that room giving her tea and watching TV with her to keep her company. I went about my business and my phone calls and my errands without so much as a word to her. I made them turn off the TV, and asked Miss Pidge to please leave her alone and let her "rest." I wanted to let last night stand. I wanted her to think. And sweat.

By four o'clock I was finished with my work for the day, really, but I went down to Delancey Antiques to look at a set of three gold-leaf and ivory-finished Florentine nesting tables that I'd seen the other day driving by. They were gorgeous. He had one small cobalt-blue bowl on top of them and a gardenia floating in it, and I bought the whole shebang and carried them right out to the car.

"I want the gardenia, too," I said, "or it's no deal."

"Here, take the gardenia. Here, I'll give you two."

I bought a rotisserie chicken for dinner and woke Nicki, because she'd fallen asleep, and told her to eat quickly; Andre was coming in half an hour. Truth to tell, I think she was still groggy when he came. I was like that with Junior. After three-thirty or four in the afternoon, forget it.

Andre arrived wearing his sweats. He smelled like the gym, but he did have the decency to apologize for his clothes and take off that stupid bandanna they all wear now. He'd had to leave practice a little early, he said, and came right here in order to be on time.

Nicki grinned at him like a darned fool. He'd arrived on time, and she was so proud. It was all I could do not to shake her. Hurt me to my heart. With all her daddy has done, with all he is, how could it take so little to please her?

I asked him to sit down, and I let them wait a moment before I began. Hiram does that sometimes, partly to collect his thoughts, partly to give people time to get worried. I began the conversation with Hiram's name, since I know that Andre is afraid of him, saying that he was out of town, but that he would be here with us if he could. Then I told the essence of Nicki's and my conversation, and I assured him that although Mr. Prettyman and I understood their initial desire to go ahead and have the baby and start a family, we hoped that they would wait. Especially with Andre's college career and his sports and his prospects for the future—I emphasized those. I told him that we had decided for me to talk to the two of them as adults instead of calling in his parents, and I hoped we were doing right.

He nodded instantaneously. I've heard bad things about his father's temper. In fact, when Andre realized that I was finished talking and that I was offering him a no-pain-no-blame way out, the boy was so relieved, his whole body said: "At ease."

I knew he'd go along. But after what Nicki told me about how he wanted her to keep the baby, I certainly had expected a struggle from him. Or at least a show of one. But I got nothing. Zip. Like he was ready to pack girlfriend off to the clinic on the next trolley car.

Nicki said that they needed to talk about this alone. And his answer was: nope, no need to drag things out, and good thing she told me, and not everything was meant to be, and all like that.

To tell the truth, he was *so* glad to get out of it, I lost what little respect I had for him. And like all these kids who've had everything handed to them from day one, the money didn't even enter his mind. Or if it did, he didn't say. Before this one, she had another boyfriend named Ray, who was in their school on scholarship. He was brash and arrogant, and Hiram didn't care for him, but I liked Ray. He wore these wraparound sunglasses day or night, rain or shine. The kids called him Ray-Ban. He would have known to ask whether he could help pay to get this thing taken care of.

Andre saw that I caught his drift. He turned to Nicki, then, and held his dreadlocks out of his face with one hand and cupped her chin in the other hand. He told her that this would bring them even closer together, and that they really did need more time together, just the two of them, to get to know each other better before they started a family. Stuff like that. Now that his personal butt was off the firing line, he laid it on thick. Then he said that he wanted to know when her appointment was. He wanted "to be there for her." I hate that, like a doggone Kodak special moment.

"What about the money?" I asked.

Andre looked from one of us to the other.

"If we have to foot the bill, we will, of course, because Nicki is our daughter," I said. "But we are not the ones in trouble, and Nicki didn't get that way by herself."

Nicki curled her mouth up in a sneer so bad my whole palm itched to smack her face. I can't tell you how sick I was of the two of them.

"I will pay for it, of course," Andre said. "But I don't have it right now. How much does something like this cost?"

"Something like this," I said, "costs five hundred dollars. That's at a private doctor's. Unless you're going to take her down to some clinic and go through the right-to-life picket lines and get her picture in the paper when someone recognizes her, and then sit next to every child on Medicaid for three hours until it's your turn. That experience only sets you back two and a quarter."

Nicki started sniffling again. I watched Andre's face for signs of . . . something; I don't know what would have satisfied me at that point, but I didn't see it. All I could see was how he'd look twenty years from now when he'd cut off those dreads and got a bank job and married some biracial bimbo from Gladwyne. I'd meet him at a fund-raiser. He'd have that same look of deep concern on his face as he asked me for news of Nicki—and he'd be just as insincere. I wondered how my daughter could have allowed herself to be snowed like this.

"We're a political family, Andre. Politicians know how to face facts."

"Politicians use people," Nicki said.

"What did you say?" I asked her.

Then she mumbled under her breath. "Nothing."

"Could I reimburse you?" he asked. "In installments?"

I didn't say anything. I just cocked my head to one side, like: I'm listening.

He offered fifty dollars a month for five months.

"Half, that is, you're offering."

"Yeah. That's what you said, wasn't it? 'Cause, I could just go on and, um, pay more, like until I'm in college, and just, well, until it's paid off. I could do that."

He appealed to Nicki. She was paralyzed by this time. He never had wanted to keep this baby. I could see it now. It had been her all along.

"You can do half," I said. "Unless you decide you really

want to contribute a larger share. If so, in that case, we'll accept it."

Andre turned back to Nicki and asked when she'd like to get this done.

She shrugged. She'd been waiting for Mr. Lover-Lover to defend this crazy idea that they'd have their little love child together and live happily ever after on a wad of Monopoly money. Once he bailed out, I think she was stumped. She was frowning and looking at the floor.

"You OK?" I asked.

She leaned toward Andre with that blank face. "Yeah," she said.

I told them that I'd made an appointment with my doctor tomorrow afternoon. They both groaned. The next day Andre played in the private school basketball league semifinal. Before Andre could say whether or not he'd skip the game, Nicki let him off the hook. He promised to come after. I suggested he wait until the next day, seeing as how they'd both be tired, and Nicki was likely to be feeling poorly. Nicki turned on me with a—I can't call it anything else—snarl.

"You always get everything your way," she hollered. "So at least we could see each other."

"OK. All right."

"And you haggled over the money—"

"Yep."

"—like some old Jew."

Now I jumped up. "Lemme tell you something, Missy. An old Jew is gonna get your black behind out of trouble tomorrow. So, remember that—the same Jew that got out of her bed sixteen years ago and brought you into this world, and you better be glad of it.

"Andre, this is still my house, and I'm afraid you'll have to leave it now."

I was through. I went into the kitchen, turned the radio on to country and western, and opened the fridge. Then I closed the door. I hate getting fat.

I went in the breakfast room behind the kitchen, and I sat in my favorite chair, and I put my feet up, and I sipped some port and closed my eyes and thought of the beach. Just like the stress management woman said. I let the waves roll in and out, and pictured myself at the water's edge. Like "Wade in the Water." I did that until I calmed down. Then I opened my eyes and poured myself half a glass more.

I dialed the twenty-four-hour number on the *Bloomingdale's by Mail* catalog and ordered their gold damask fleur-de-lis bedroom collection to go with the new Florentine tables. I'd had the page open to that set for a week and a half, but because of the new expense of Hiram's and my travel back and forth to D.C., I'd been holding back. What for? I asked myself. I was tired of our old floral bedroom. Darned flowers were about to run me out.

An old Jew? I thought. A turtle perched up on a fence post doesn't get there by himself, and she didn't come up with that on her own. Andre was a bad influence all kinds of ways. I remembered a book he gave her that was supposed to show how the Jews were behind the slave trade. The authors were anonymous. I maintain that that should have told her all she needed to know right there, and made her give the book back to him.

I heard Nicki and Andre kiss good night at the door. Before this happened, they used to step outside, but I suppose now she figured no need to pretend.

When the door clicked closed I called her in.

"Your appointment is for two in the afternoon," I said. "You can stay in the bed till noon for all I care, but at one o'clock, I want you washed and dressed and in the living room ready to go, do you understand?"

She grunted through her teeth. My relaxation dropped down to the soles of my feet and fell right off the end of the recliner. I felt like those cats you see on cartoons when their hair stands up in peaks and their backs arch up.

"And listen here: the next time you say Jew, something good

better follow it out of your mouth. And if we are ever, *ever* campaigning—"

She rolled her eyes as if to say she didn't need any instruction on what to say in public. "Can I go to bed now? I'm tired."

"I bet you are," I said. "But just you know that if Jesse Jackson could make a slip of the tongue, so could you."

"Jesse Jackson is stuck in the seventies."

"Yeah, well, he ain't knocked up, is he? He was born out of wedlock, and you notice he didn't repeat the same mistake."

Then I took my pressure pill, left a message on Hiram's answer call, and went to bed. I didn't mention Nicki's trouble. I figured I'd see Hiram on the weekend. By then the thing would be done, and I could just let him know what had happened. After, when it was taken care of.

In Kirshner's office I stood on Nicki's left folding the clothes she'd dumped on the chair. We'd had a few words about the clothes. She came down in some funky jeans and these red high-heeled sneakers that cost seventy-five dollars, and she thought were such a great sale at forty-five. I told her to go back up and put on a blue print baby-doll dress we bought her, because on the way home she'd want something loose, and some loafers. She chose a skirt and long sweater instead, which was OK, and some of those shoes that look like combat boots.

"Okeydoke," Kirshner said, after she had gotten Nicki draped and prepped and into the stirrups. "Can you schooch down a little further? Right to the edge. That's the way." I turned around and tried to hold Nicki's hand. She pulled it back.

Kirshner patted her other arm and sat down on the little stool at the bottom of the examining table. "We all make mistakes," she said. I could hear the click of the light going on.

"I hope this isn't another one," Nicki said.

I didn't say anything. My thing was: just get it done. The less said, the better.

But I mean Kirshner is good. She's been at this for a long time, and she knows what she's doing.

"You know what?" she said. With her head down and through the drape, Kirshner's voice sounded as if it were coming from the clouds. "I think you'll find in years to come that you've done the right thing.

"Now you'll feel the speculum. It'll be cool, I'm afraid. OK. The next thing you'll feel is the clamp. I'm simply going to clamp the tip of the uterus. Okeydoke?"

"Uh-huh," Nicki said. She was scared.

"Now, this next part will pinch. I'm going to numb the uterus with a needle. It'll be a prick, and it's no fun, that's for sure. But after that, you won't feel much of anything."

Nicki jerked. It's a terrible feeling, that needle. It is cold and sharp and mean. There's nothing like it. Cramps and all are bad, but they're natural. When this thing clamps on to you, you know good and well that it's like nothing else that's ever been up there.

I had mine done in 1974, the year I turned nineteen, the year I married Hiram, and the first year you could legally walk into this clinic and have one of these things done in Pennsylvania. The timing of it was the worst. I was almost sure Hiram was going to ask me to marry him, but he hadn't yet. And I knew Hiram. If he'd thought I was trying to catch him with a baby, he'd've bolted. And who could blame him? That's just the way we thought back then, and, for all the so-called progress in women's rights, it's still the way people think. You have to. So, I got rid of it.

I went to this clinic thirty miles outside the city—the suburbs had them earlier than the city did, of course—which meant walking from my house to the bus, transferring to the King of Prussia express bus, and walking about half a mile from the mall up to the clinic. Took me two hours to get there. They gave you Valium then, too, but I was so upset, it barely took the edge off.

When that needle hit me, the tears started coming, and they just came and came. Just like Nicki. I didn't even make a sound. Just a little stream of water ran down to my ears.

They turned on the machine, and it made a high-pitched hum, tinny, like a tiny, little vacuum cleaner, the most awful thing you can imagine. They put this great, big old pad on me, and sat me in a room for half an hour and fed me some chicken bouillon. And when I could walk around, in another twenty minutes or so, I put on my clothes and left.

Took me another two hours to get home, and by the time I did, I had bled through two pads, and a lady on the bus gave me a John Wanamaker shopping bag to carry behind me on the street. My mother was in bed when I got in, so I sneaked up to my room. All I could do was put that shopping bag underneath me and lie down on the bed. I couldn't even wash my own behind. That's how finished I was. I said to God: "God, don't let this be for nothing." And I laid there and cried myself to sleep.

Next week Hiram asked me to marry him. I'd spent up all my wedding dress money at the clinic, and I couldn't tell anybody, but Tamara went to her mother and got her wedding dress. Her mother was a well-to-do Jamaican, or what they call well-to-do, comfortable enough to have had a lace dress with a train. We married at St. Augustine's, because Arneatha and her dad went there and knew the priest, and he said, Come on. They made us tea and cake in the parish hall and that was it. No money, but it was a beautiful wedding.

I hadn't thought about any of that for years. I do not dwell on the past. In fact, I try to put the past behind me and keep it there. Then I watched those tears make that same track from the corners of Nicki's eyes down to her ears, and I almost cried right along with her. Except that somebody had to keep it together.

Kirshner must've known, because she kept up a line of patter, which is very unlike her. She told Nicki she was lucky, that her womb wasn't tipped back like mine is, that her cervix was so beautiful she wanted to take a picture of it and put it up on the wall, that she'd moved to these new offices partly because her old ones were so cold, and weren't these warm and sunny?

While Kirshner talked, I found myself wondering what Arneatha had seen. It was clearer than ever that I could not just leave Nicki and trail around D.C. with Hiram and guard his doggone body. It's not like none of this hadn't occurred to me before. It's just that I had too much pride to stoop to figuring out how to try to keep control of my husband. Better just to see no evil. Like a damn monkey.

On the way home, Nicki sat in the front seat with her head back, her eyes closed, and tears rolling down. Then, to top it all off, Andre didn't show. He called her. I'll give him that; he did call. But his father had him on punishment for screwing up at school, and the father was there at the basketball game, saying that Andre had to go directly home with him after his shower. It was a school night, and he was not allowed to visit.

On punishment! They were children, for God's sake.

Nicki'd been holding together for that visit, and when it didn't happen, she just fell to pieces. I sent her to bed to cry herself to sleep.

Then I went to my bedroom and did the same thing. Almost Easter, I thought, and I couldn't bring myself to say a prayer.

It is stilling a heartbeat, like they say. I know that.

6

It was the Thursday around Easter. I had attended a board meeting of the Philadelphia Black Business Council, and then stopped by the accountant's to pick up checks, dropped them off at the bar, checked on the leak in the back storeroom, and called four roofers to come give us estimates, hoping that one of them wouldn't be a crook.

On Friday I had to go out to the Pond House and get it ready for the dinner party we'd planned to bring together Hiram's new staff, aim them toward the November campaign, and slide our old manager off to a dignified retirement. He had been with us since the beginning, and he was a warhorse, but he wasn't all the way on board with the change in party, and he was not the man Hiram would want to take to Washington with him as a chief of staff. For that job we had Romeo Ng in mind.

We were trying to decide who would make up the group, and how to mold them into a real, winning team. Junior had his act together. I had no more time to mess around with Nicki.

She'd been laid up in the bed for twenty-four hours. I figured that was enough, and I wanted her bony little behind back in school Friday morning. Spring break was coming, and I had hatched a plan to send her down to make a long-overdue visit to my grandmother. I was going to ask Junior to go with her. I hadn't decided whether or not to tell him why, although Junior could be trusted to keep his mouth shut. Before the break, however, I wanted her back in school, out of my hair, and out of that doggone bed feeling sorry for herself.

I sat down at my desk in my little study at the rear of the house and started making phone calls.

Nothing went right, though.

Grandma said she didn't feel up to having the children come visit, even though I told her they weren't children anymore, and that Junior'd be able to help her outside and Nicki could cook and clean for her. She said the place she was living was too small for overnight guests, but when I offered to put the kids up at the outside of town, she said she didn't want them staying with strangers. We send her three or four hundred dollars a month, and I asked her whether or not it was enough. She said she had plenty of money, but she was sorry we hadn't sent the kids when she was young enough to take care of them and enjoy them.

There's a foggy, burning feeling I get sometimes in my head, but it also feels like it's all around me, like I felt once when I was supposed to carry some money to my grandmother when I went home in the summertime, and I lost it. I knew the minute I stepped off the bus, the minute my foot hit the pavement that I'd left it in the bus station in North Carolina where we'd stopped and I went to pee. A tunnel vision closed in on me all of a sudden, like a dark cloud on either side of my eyes, and I stood there confused, trying to figure some way to go back in time to that nasty old stall where I'd left the money. I never get the feeling as bad now that I'm grown, but I do get it a little bit, and it knocks me for a loop.

I felt that way when I got off the phone with Grandma, and without even putting down the receiver, I called Arneatha at her school. When she came on she seemed distant. I found myself trying to mend fences and going about it all wrong.

"You know, Neesie," I blurted out, "it's just naïve to think the two parties are so different."

"What parties?"

"Democratic and Republican. Besides, what the Republicans

need, and what Hiram has, is a very sound, very restrained economic policy with some moderation in social policy. That's where most black people are anyway, really."

"Is this what you called for, sugarpie?"

She talks like that. It was good to hear her sounding like herself again.

"Listen to me, Neese," I said. "We need you. We need the school, we need the church. We can't break up. Everybody breaks up these days, and it's terrible. That's how white folk keep us down. We start from behind, and then tear our own selves down worse.

"Besides," I said, "it's all big business. No matter how much we think we're changing the world, business is running it now. It's money and government on one side and the people who work on the other. That's all it is. I swear. Don't leave Hi over this."

"Nobody's leaving Hiram. What's wrong, Rozzie? What's wrong with you? You're talking a mile a minute."

I didn't go into the abortion business, but I did tell her about Nicki getting out of hand and about Grandma. Neesie reminded me that Grandma is an old woman all alone—husband dead, daughter dead, two sons who barely speak to her, no grandchildren closer than six hundred miles. Neesie also said something that I forget and don't want to be reminded of: Grandma doesn't really know my children. I felt like I'd lost something.

"When's her birthday?" Arneatha asked me.

"Next month."

"Go down and see her for a weekend. Take 'er somewhere."

"When your grandmother was alive, you took her to Montreal, didn't you?"

"Now, that's a great city for older folks. Very civilized. Gentle."

"I can't do stuff like that. I can't just drop everything. I got a family to take care of."

I knew that was a low blow, and I knew she wouldn't come

back at me. Like something in her wouldn't quite engage. Some things she'd be very firm about, but some she'd just let ride. What I wanted to say to her was: We know why I don't spend time with my grandma—she's a pain, and I'm too selfish—but you love family so much, why don't you remarry? You love kids, why don't you adopt? If there was ever a single parent they'd go for, it'd be a priest headmistress who's beloved by the whole doggone community, for God's sake.

"Just an idea, sweetie," Neesie said. "Gotta hang up. I have a hundred loose ends to tie up before I take off tomorrow."

"Oh, my God." I just started screaming. "Oh, my God. You're going to Uganda, aren't you? When? When is it?" I had totally forgotten.

"Yeah, tomorrow," she said. "Tamara's driving down to see me off. My plane leaves at four. Wanna come?"

How I would get from the airport to the Pond House in time for dinner at six I didn't know. But I felt bad. She never asks for anything for herself. "You two have it all arranged. I don't want to horn in."

"Horn in? Oh, Rozzie. Bring Audrey. Please come. I'd like all of us together before I go. I don't know why. I'm only going a month. But—"

The school secretary came in and said something. I heard a child crying in the background.

"You've got to go?" I asked.

"Yes, Lord. Did I tell you Tamara was not granted tenure?"

"No."

"Well, now you know. See you tomorrow."

The distant tone was back in her voice. Something occurred to me. "Are you scared of going on this trip?"

"Some," she said. "Mostly, I'm just rushed. Sorry."

Before I could forget I rang Audrey. She wasn't home, so I left a message with her mother and one at her job and hoped for the best. I called to let Hiram know that he should make sure to come to dinner on time tomorrow, because I'd have to be late.

Then it was time to deal with Nicki.

. . .

"You and your mess," I told her, "are crowding out the sun. Neesie's going to Africa tomorrow and I almost forgot, shucking around with you."

She made a sound like an apology, but I couldn't hear much because her whole head was under the covers. All I could see was fuzz.

Three or four days' worth of clothes lay on the floor, in a pile, right where she'd stepped out of them. My grandmother's sister used to talk about how the girl in the house where she cleaned would step out of her panties and leave them there on the floor for my aunt to pick up. For her, those drawers represented everything that was nasty about white folks. I threw the clothes on top of the hamper. Andre still had not called back.

"In a day or two, Miss Nicole," I said, "you're going to go through that pile and take the laundry downstairs to be washed and the other things out to the dry cleaner. But first, you're gonna get out of that bed and have a shower and put on some new sheets and get ready for school tomorrow. Life goes on, honey. Up."

I pulled off the cover, and Nicki whimpered. See, this is what threw me. As fighty as she can be, all she was doing again was crying. So, I sat on the side of the bed and told her just exactly what I'd told myself the night before. I did not choose to tell her about my experience. I didn't feel like justifying my life to her, and I didn't want to give her another stick to beat me with, now or in the future. But I did say that she was young, and she'd have babies later. I told her they're not really babies yet, and what I really like to think is that they just go back to God and wait to be born another time.

She looked at me like I was the biggest ninny in the world. She wasn't crying about the baby, she said. She was crying about Andre. For a while there, he, too, had wanted the baby and wanted her. Now, because *I* had forced her to have the abortion, because *I* had stepped in and bullied them and dominated everything, she was going to lose him.

"You got yourself knocked up, but *I'm* the problem?"

Might as well have pushed a button. I went right over the edge.

"Get up. Get *up* and stop being a fool for a preppie nigger who's so glad he's outta the soup he don't know what to do."

I grabbed at her nightshirt, this great big old thing with Tweety Pie on it. She's bigger than me, so I just clutched onto the nightshirt and pulled her out of the bed and rolled her onto the floor.

Well, didn't she give me back word for word? Talking about how Andre wanted to take her to the doctor himself, but *I* couldn't wait till after the semifinals. Talking about he's gonna pay us back every dime, even though it's only half his responsibility. Talking about how he's the first one ever took her seriously.

I grabbed the shoe off my foot and went to smacking her wherever I could find some haunch. I was crazy. I'll admit it. "Get up," I screamed, "before I hurt you!"

She did get up.

"Now, you and me, we're gonna make a whole new start. Get dressed, and I'll take you to the hairdresser, the young one. Perm or braids. Your choice, but all them raggedy naps are goin'."

I got to the door. She had dragged herself to her vanity, and was looking into the mirror. Her hair never did dread all the way. It was puffy from the scalp to about an inch or two off her head and then these little two-inch twists stuck off like teats off a nanny goat. I was sick of them and sick of her.

"I'm not goin' to that hairdresser."

"Yes, you are."

"I'll go back to Miss Mary for a perm."

"How come?"

" 'Cause."

"Don't ' 'cause' me. I thought you like the new one."

She shrugged.

It seemed like each choice I tried to offer her, each time I tried to let her have some say, she used it to go tit for tat with me. "You can't give me a better answer, you go to what's-her-name and too bad for it."

"Her name is Duchess and she's fucking Daddy."

It was like she had reached over and punched me. The wind flew out, and I'm standing there, my one hand on the doorknob, the other still holding the shoe, sucking for air. I felt like I was going to puke. I heard myself groan, and I saw the shoe in my hand fly over and hit her vanity. Then I reached down and grabbed the other one and threw it, too.

"Gimme my shoes," I said. "Pick up my damn shoes and give 'em to me.

"Before my mother left South Carolina," I said to her while she got the shoes and made these stupid little jerks toward me, "she and my aunt and uncles would be out back of my grandmother's little shack slugging it out. You know what? That's my first memory, my very first memory: them knockin' over the barbecue drum Granddad had rigged up and the coals comin' down on my arm."

She knew the scar; it's a big keloid the size of a dollar bill going from my arm over to my chest right about where they went in for the tumor.

"They didn't have nothin', didn't want nothin'. I decided a long time ago, and I mean it, that I am not going to live my life crawling around in the dirt, and neither you nor anybody else is going to drag me down into it.

"How you could let that filthy word come out of your mouth in the same breath with your father's name, I don't know. He has worked day and night for us, and we reap the benefits."

She was standing an arm's length in front of me, looking at the floor.

"Give me my damn shoes!"

She put her arm out, like she was afraid to get too close.

"I can't reach 'em," I said, and she stepped closer. I would not stretch out my arm.

"You let a filthy lie escape your lips."

"She bragged about it in front of me."

"That doesn't make it true."

"But we don't know what he does."

"We don't know. That's the first point right there. And we don't know because he don't rub our noses in it. Now, you heard one thing, and you got your feelings hurt, and you are trying to hurt me, too. Well, too bad. You just keep all that hurt to yourself."

Nicki stared at the floor. She still had her pout on, but I could see her shock. Where do they get the idea that nobody knows anything but them?

"Gimme my shoes."

"You think she was lying?"

"Now you want to make excuses for him? Make up your mind. All I hear you talking about is growing up. Well, welcome to it. Children eat the chitterlings, grown-ups scrub the crap. Stinks, don't it?"

"How could you live like that?"

"Like what? I live beautiful."

I stood with my hands crossed over my chest. She had finally shut up. She handed me the shoes, and I turned for the door.

"So," I said, "you don't want to go to that little hairdresser whore, fine. Don't go. Your Aunt Tamara's coming down tomorrow to see Aunt Neesie off on her trip to Africa. Call her and see if she'll take you back to New York and get those knots cut off. You do something. I've got my own work."

I went back to my sitting room to my list of phone calls and errands. My eyes felt so dry and scratchy I took my contacts out for a while and put on my glasses. Usually I can wear contacts twenty hours a day. Miss Mary gave me an appointment for myself. I called another roofer, a young guy I remembered just starting out, to go see about the bar. I called our caterers to give them the final count for the next night's dinner. Then I went to the pistol range.

Practice went great. I loved it, pulling that trigger, feeling the recoil—*bam!*—back through my elbow and shoulder. *Bwam*. Not thinking about anything else but that white outline of the man on black paper, looking, when I close the right eye and focus, like it's right in front of my face. See the spot; hit the mark. Can't miss. Adjust my hand up a hair. *Bwam*. Perfect. I hear my own gun's little pops over the other guns, mostly automatics. Men like those best 'cause they're fast. But I like the revolver. I like to place each shot one at a time. Make each one count. I hate waste.

I load the bullets into the chamber, one by one, thinking of how, over the years, men have sat down with each other playing Russian roulette. I think about it every time I load: one bullet, two bullets, three, four, five. The inner circle on my paper figure is almost shot through, so I go to the circle on the head. *Pop. Pop.* There's so much smoke in my chamber. It's like sweet black metal gas that curls up at the back of my tongue.

When I stepped out of the range, Bryant and Junior were waiting outside the door clapping. Junior had gone to get Bryant and take him out to play some basketball. Then Hiram was taking them out to dinner.

"What's the occasion?"

"I got into my second choice of law school," said Junior.

Well, I hollered and jumped and acted the fool. I didn't care. I screamed like those girls on the radio when they say "Power 99 is my favorite station. Now give me the key to my new Boyz II Men Toyota Land Cruiser!" God, it was good, especially since I've felt like Junior has been edging me out of his life, pushing me away, always politely, with that big old grin, but like I just wasn't part of the picture anymore.

To his credit, Bryant could not have been happier for Junior. He never begrudged him a thing. In the spirit of happy-happy, I said that I was going to see Audrey soon, and that I'd tell her I saw him. Bryant shrugged.

"You know she'd do anything for you," I said.

He kind of pursed his lips and set his jaw. Then they kissed me and took off, big, beautiful, and strong. There's nothing like having sons.

I thought maybe I'd fire off a few more rounds, but the hour had passed, and somebody else was in my stall, so I put my revolver into its case, and then into the leather shoulder bag, and went home.

Audrey's mother got the message wrong, so Audrey came driving up almost at bedtime, huffing and puffing like somebody was chasing her. My first thought was: Oh, Lord, Audrey wants somebody to cry on, and my shoulder is full up." And it ended up being me that needed the help. Audrey said she sensed it, and it's true, she does sense things. Drunk or sober, always did.

"So, Hiram's not back yet? Let's go somewhere and have a bite to eat."

"Nah," I said. I told her about Nicki and Junior, but not the hairdresser. "It's just about all the excitement I could take."

"Then you need what I need: a night off. Besides, if I have to go back in that house with my mother, I'ma slit my wrists. Let's go to Warmdaddy's. I know one of the musicians."

Well, my ears pricked up at the name of the new blues place on the Delaware River everybody was talking about. Hiram and I hadn't had time to go.

"Only thing is, we have to take my brother's car. The driver's side window won't close, and I'm afraid to leave it on the street with his tools in it. My neighbor lets me put it in that garage he built around the corner, but he won't be home till midnight."

It's always complicated with Audrey. I didn't even argue, although I knew the ride would be awful. And it was. The Nova smelled like fumes inside, and, of course, Audrey was smoking like a maniac, which it seems she does twice as much since she stopped drinking, so I kept my window open, too, so we wouldn't die of asphyxiation in there.

Audrey laughed at me the whole way. Everything felt out of whack, so I just tried to go with it. I did ask several times whether or not it would bother her to go to a place like this with drinking everywhere. She said she'd be fine fine fine. She didn't want to be one of those fanatics who hide out, scared of booze, don't go nowhere, don't do nothing, just stay home so a drink doesn't jump down their throats. Made sense to me. So, I asked would it be all right if I had a taste. She said wouldn't bother her a bit. Fine.

I mentioned that Junior and Bryant had stopped by the shooting range, and I told her about Junior's acceptance to law school. She congratulated me and said she had to remember to get him a card. I knew she wouldn't remember to get him a card, but the thought counts for something. I'd tell him she sent her best.

"I think he's gonna go and not defer."

" 'Cause you all talked to him?"

" 'Cause of the new girlfriend. Bryant told on him. You know it's serious when they hold off tellin' you about it. 'Least, that's how Junior is. But I think Miss Brandy likes his legal aspirations."

"That her name?"

"Oh, no, no. Bryant says she looks like Brandy, the singer. Her name's Elizabeth. Jack-and-Jill Negroes from Connecticut. Father's with a big trading firm."

"You know you love it."

"Did I say I didn't? But I'ma be cool."

"What else did Bryant say?"

"You should call him." I hesitated before I said more. But I figured she should know. I told her that he had been very hurt by her refusal to buy him the mountain bike he wanted a couple years before when he went to Temple.

"I didn't have the money."

"But you were the one offered him the bike in the first place."

"Roz, how the fuck did I know he was going to want some five-hundred-dollar damn piece of machinery? I thought he wanted a regular bike."

"You need that kind of thing to ride up to north Philly and back every day, Audrey. Why would you begrudge him? He needs the wide tires; he needs the gears. If you'd have just talked with him he would have settled for a three-hundred-dollar one. Plus, you know you could ask us for the money anyway. You know that."

"What else didn't I do?"

"The zoo." I didn't want to say more.

"I figured that."

That's all she said until we got to the place. The valet came running up to the curb to park the car. He opened my door, and when I went to step out the shoulder bag like to pull me out with it. I had forgotten to stow away the revolver, which was packed in its case and lying at the bottom of the bag. Audrey was embarrassed by the car and kept snapping at me to hurry it up so that the valet could drive it the heck away—although I say, what's the point of driving it if you're going to let it dominate the whole doggone evening? I took my wallet out of the bag and put it under my arm. Then I took out my lipstick and a comb, put them in my pockets, and tried to fold the shoulder bag in half, over the case, and shove it under the seat. She's humphing and sighing the whole time. But her brother had that space all junked up with tools. Behind the seat was a big old pile of cobblestones looked like he'd stolen from some construction site.

"Can you pull open the trunk lock, please?" I asked the valet.

Audrey sucked her teeth. "It doesn't work, OK?" She just about hissed it in my ear, flounced around the car, reached over the valet, shoving a face full of bosoms into his nose, grabbed the key out of the ignition, and then opened the trunk. The other valets were cracking up, and so was I. A line of cars was forming behind us. I found a corner way in the back of the trunk behind a closed-up case of something and some Sakrete, and then I was ready. By now she was huffing and puffing so bad that I got devilish.

"You sure you want to go in now, or you want to call that nice young man back and tell him we'll just drive around the block and pick up some men?"

"You do that," she said, handing the boy the keys and stomping toward the door.

I loved the place right off the bat: the red and blue lights and the music and the TVs along the wall showing blues videos and the smell of the food and drinks and cigarettes. And crowded. A nice-looking young man in a turtleneck and jacket met us at the door. He recognized me, called me by name, and talked into his walkie-talkie until he found us a table up near the front.

"I'm just going to have a little appetizer and some seltzer, or maybe a Diet Coke to keep me awake," I told him, and he came back with a sampler the owner sent over, including some crab cakes. That gave me a taste for catfish.

So, we ate dinner, too. The food was beautiful, plenty of spice like I like it. I should've just had dinner without the appetizer business, but we ate them both. And even that wouldn't have been so bad if I hadn't eaten all the stuff that went with it—the candied sweets and greens and coleslaw, the cornbread squares and biscuits. We ate till we were stuffed.

And the men they had playing tore up the music. We stayed two sets. By the second set, the singer was getting downright nasty, talking about how this uncle used to baby-sit her, and then she got bigger, and he told her: "Come on over here, Chicken, 'cause you got something over there between your legs worrying the hell out of me."

People were dressed up, some of them; some dressed down. A few folks came over and spoke to me. I saw a lot I knew, but nobody really major-major. So I relaxed and drank a wine cooler and looked at the people and the singer in her sequins and the men in the band wearing their black suits and red cummerbunds. The guitar player's hands were horny as a farmer's feet. He kept looking over at me, and when he'd look away Audrey would hit me in the arm—like I wanted them rough old cob hands rubbing on me.

When they took a break, Audrey asked me for my lipstick. I told her it was a little too light for her, but she put it on anyway and went over to see the keyboard player, who she knew. While she was talking to him, I took it into my head to change up to a cocktail I once drank called a Singapore Sling. Sweet like I like, and almost no whiskey taste. That's how it gets you in a sling.

So, Audrey talked on some more, and next thing I know, she's sitting down on the piano stool next to this man with a cross between a Jheri Kurl and a conk, and she's playing some old low-down, four-handed boogie-woogie with him. I don't know what it was, but they banged and bumped and grinded and he sang. It was really good. It's a shame she only plays a few funeral parlors now, because you can tell that this is the stuff she loves.

So, she sat up on that little stage, and they did the do for a while, and she's grinning and laughing to beat the band. I had me another Singapore Sling. Everything's beautiful; everything's nice. Then she came back to our table talking about how she hates the MFer's guts, and back in the day he screwed her out of this and screwed her out of that, and she's hissing in my ear, and the waitress came by and I wave my hand in the air, and she slung another Sling from Singapore at me, and I didn't have no better sense than to pour it on down.

By the time we left, it was all I could do to hold out my credit card and sign my name. And here's Audrey, sober as a judge, driving me home.

I do remember saying, "Well, this is a switch," and her laughing.

And didn't I have just enough liquor in me to tell her to drive across the tracks for a minute, and over to where that skinny-behind hairdresser 'ho lives up over her shop? And didn't them Singapore Slings tell me to make Audrey drive around the block again? And didn't I reach into the backseat and almost throw out my whole, entire back pulling up one of those cobblestones, and hold it in my lap?

"You just slow down at that little red Mercury," I told her. The vanity plate said DUCHESS.

The minute I chucked that cobblestone, the glass just shattered. *Crash!* Sound was so loud, I swore the cops were going to swoop down out of the sky and arrest us. Soon as I threw it, I screamed. I went rigid with fear. Audrey, on the other hand, took off. All I heard after the crash was her laughing, and that noisy old Chevy grinding through the gears. Audrey drove that sucker. All across south Philadelphia. Clutch pedal, gas, brake, gas, brake, clutch. I don't know how we got home. I closed my eyes and everything went swirly. I opened them, and Audrey was flying me through the streets so fast I couldn't stand it.

At one point she started laughing like a maniac, saying this rhyme her mother used to say when they couldn't find something in their crazy house—which was pretty often.

> *"St. Anthia, St. Anthia, come around.*
> *Something's been lost and cannot be found."*

"Whatcha lose?" I asked.

"Nothin' at all," she said. "I got nothin' to lose."

Finally, we arrived home—alive. She came in with me and put me to bed.

I told her how good she played at the place. She turned her head away.

"That wasn't shit, Roz," she said.

Just like that. Sounded so cold and sad. I tried to say something but, let's face it, I was a mess. Then I felt bad about what I'd done, and how I dragged her into it, and I apologized. Audrey laughed that hard kind of bark she does.

"You just decided to go out and get blind. You're entitled. I would too if I could. Besides, what else would I have done?

Gone in my bedroom and put on some of that Frank Sinatra suicide music and sit in the dark?"

Audrey kissed me, right on the mouth like she always does. She tasted like cigarettes and Coco Chanel. "Go to sleep."

"Check on Nicki before you go, please."

"Don't worry about her," Audrey said. "She's got you twisted around her finger."

She left, and I dreamt some terrible dreams.

It wasn't until the next morning I remembered I'd forgotten the revolver in my shoulder bag in her brother's car.

7

Audrey drove up to Coatesville the next morning to return the car to her brother. His name is Walter, but we always called him Buddha on account of his big belly and the fact that he is easygoing. Nothing ever bothered him, which set him way apart in that family. I rang up there and left a message on the machine for Audrey to call me before she left. One thing I did not need was my little practice revolver roaming around the Delaware Valley like a lost dog.

It should only have taken Audrey forty-five minutes to get to Coatesville, but she's scared of highway driving, and the back roads wind around so bad you can spend an hour and a half to make a lousy forty miles. So I went ahead to pick up the PRETTY-MAN IN THE HOUSE T-shirts—royal blue on white, Hiram's campaign colors—for presents. When I got back I checked my answering service and called them back. I talked to one of Audrey's know-nothing nephews. He had no idea whether or not she'd gotten my message.

"Is she there?"

Buddha's four boys are just as big and round as him and his wife. They don't speak to you. They grunt.

"Well, do me this favor. You put the phone down and go check. Find out for sure. Ask your mother. Ask your father. And then come back and let me know. It's important."

He came back no sooner than five or six minutes later, I swear. Buddha had just driven her to the train. I started to ask whether they had a phone in the car, but then I caught myself.

I was still off my rhythm. So I tried to get back to basics.

I'll tell anybody who wants to know that the only true cure for cellulite is deep massage. Ten minutes a day. An expensive masseuse up in New York taught me that years ago. She cured me of mine, and I've been massaging myself ever since. Hard. Almost till it hurts. The idea is to get blood circulating in and around the globbed-up fat cells and wash them away, I think. You have to be regular, though. A measure of my upset is that I had forgotten to massage all week. So I gave myself a twenty-minute treatment. My thighs were *burning*, but that's how it works.

I stepped back from the problem, took some deep breaths, and went down to my room in the basement to do my exercise. I forgot that Miss Pidgeon was coming to work. She let herself in like usual, came downstairs, and stood there watching me. When I looked up, I liked to die from the start.

"Whatchoo want for lunch?" she asked. "I see salad stuff in here. I guess you'll be wantin' that."

"Nothin'," I said. I reminded her that I had to get her out to West Chester to clean for the dinner party and help the caterers.

"Nicki needs a meal when she gets home."

"She picks."

"While you gettin' ready to go, I'll fix her up a plate. No harm in that, is there?"

"Well, don't put any bacon on it. You know she won't touch it if you put on pork."

She started up the stairs, mumbling: "White people got them thinkin' they can live forever."

"I heard that," I said.

"You like any numbers?" she asked.

"I'll tell you my girlfriend's flight number if I can remember."

I rang Audrey again from the car on my way to West Chester.

I had Miss Pidge rolling each blue-and-white shirt and tying it with a red ribbon. Audrey wasn't home. Her mother answered the phone, which is always a pain in the neck, not so much because she had to put her finger over her throat hole to speak— that, too—but mostly because she doesn't hear very well and won't admit it, and she doesn't half-listen to what she *can* hear. I asked if she would please hang up and let me leave a message for Audrey on voice mail, but Mrs. Ransome wanted to know why I would talk to a machine when she was right there.

"I'm in the car, and I wanted to leave a long message, please," I said. I had to tell her to get me the doggone gun.

"Well, I ain't got nothing but time. You know that. And you in the car, right?"

She was watching a soap opera.

"OK," I said. "You got your pencil ready?"

"Pencil's . . . kitchen . . . You hang on."

A commercial came on for cold medicine. The commercials were louder than the original program. It sounded like a whole Broadway show singing in my ear.

Mrs. Ransome wheezed loudly into the phone. In my mind's eye I could see her putting her finger to her throat, but I couldn't catch more than every other word.

"I'm sorry," I said. "What did you say?"

"What?"

"I want you to get a pencil."

"What are you saying?"

"I said I wanted to give you some numbers," I shouted.

"If you yell into the phone, your voice just gets all blurry. Now say it again."

I repeated myself.

"Don't she have your number?"

"I'm on the cell phone."

"Long as y'all been friends, seem like she'd have your number."

"OK, Mrs. Ransome." I gave up. I thought to ask her for Audrey's brother's Coatesville address, but I didn't want to get into a long discussion and didn't want to tell her my business. I wasn't going to drive up there by myself anyway. "Please tell her to call me when she gets in."

"Now, did I need a pencil for that? I swear you all would run me into the ground if I let you."

"You could've saved your money on that one," said Miss Pidge.

Neesie and Tam told Audrey not to move back in with her mother so soon after giving up drinking. But I agree with Audrey. What was she going to do? Tamara can talk, because she's never taken care of anybody but herself. Arneatha neither, quiet as it's kept. I know she's dedicated her life to service, but that is not the same as having some little juniebug to nurse every couple hours or some old person ask you eight times a week how come Donnelly started a business directory when they already got the regular phone books. Audrey's sisters and brothers won't do for the mother, and somebody had to. That's all there is to it. But it had to be a tough row to hoe. Of course, Audrey doesn't pay rent. But she does pay the mother's doctor bills. Always a trade-off.

In West Chester, my caterers were just pulling up to the back door. Miss Pidge knew the drill and so do they. After we ran over the checklist, I was able to jump in the car and hightail it back into town for lunch with the wives of two black investment bankers who were just opening a new Philadelphia office for their D.C. firm. Neither woman was older than thirty. I promised to get them on some boards. They treated me real polite, like I was their auntie.

Then I rushed home to meet Audrey. At the door, I asked whether or not she had brought back the gun. Nope, she hadn't. Had Buddha given her the message? Nope, he never gives messages. I shouldn't have left one.

"I've gotta get the gun, Audrey."

"Shit," she said. "Why didn't you tell me last night?"

" 'Cause I didn't want the valet parking people to hear me. Then we got inside and I forgot."

"It'll be all right with my brother," she said. "He keeps the car in his garage and doesn't even drive it except to do his odd jobs on the weekend. And my sister-in-law doesn't drive, period."

"She doesn't drive? Up in that one-horse town? How's she get around?"

"She doesn't. That's just how he likes it."

"Well, I'll take you up there tomorrow."

"Just calm down, Roz. It's locked up, and I'll get it next week. Get Buddha all hyped up about a gun in his car and he and Mimi'll freak. I'm going up next week anyway. I'll get it then."

On the drive to the airport Audrey described every deadly disease in Africa. When she got to the Ebola virus I couldn't listen any more. I was already nervous. Just scared for Arneatha to go. I don't know where all this came from—I've never been psychic—except that Arneatha had been strange recently, and distant, and because I knew that she didn't tell me everything. She'd been fasting and meditating. I'd asked her how meditation was different from prayer, and she hadn't answered beyond saying she was emptying herself to receive the gift of the trip and pay strict attention. Then I'd asked point-blank: "You pray?"

"I meditate at this point."

She's a priest. What kind of answer was that for a priest? I guess I was scared that God might be fixing to teach her a hard lesson.

At the airport's international terminal Tamara had already spread a table with a blue-and-white picnic cloth, a pot of bright yellow daffodils, and tulip glasses and sparkling cider. I have been discovering over time that colors cheer me and help me throw off morbid thoughts. My mother was morbid. It is something I really try to keep a lookout for.

"I swear," I said to Tamara. "You need to get married."

"Yeah, that's what I need, all right," she said.

Arneatha had had a haircut. It was close to a fade on the back and sides. And since she'd been going out with Kofi, she'd begun wearing makeup again. The white collar set off her face. When he was alive her husband used to say: Arneatha is a handsome woman. She still is. Not pretty—not with those thick facial features or them great big hands and size ten-and-a-half feet she's always falling over—but Arneatha can be handsome.

"You look gorgeous," I said to her.

She rushed up from the table to greet us. "This is all your fault," she said to me. "This trip and all. You sicced Kofi on me, and he convinced me, really. I wasn't going to go."

When I handed her a little present she smacked her open palm against her chest: "For *me?*" It was a gesture Nicki used to do when she was small and someone brought her a gift. Girlfriend had no qualms, like grown-ups do, letting the world know how much she liked to receive gifts.

We laughed, remembering, while Arneatha opened the red paper and ribbon so carefully it'd drive you crazy.

"Oh, tear it," I said. "For God's sake."

She raised her eyebrows—typical—and continued meticulously running her fingers underneath each piece of tape. Inside were bottles of nail polish: dragon red; a clear undercoat; a shiny, no-chip top coat; and the dry-quick coating.

"For your toenails," I said. "When you get there and you're wearing sandals. You always compliment my feet."

She grinned. "Thanks, sweetie." Then she folded them back into their wrapping.

"And here's from me," Audrey said. She handed her three small bottles of Dettol disinfectant.

"Oh, Christ, my mother used to use that on everything," Tamara said. "And now Nurse Irons brings it to the airport."

"Hand washing prevents illness," Audrey said. Stone serious like a public-service announcement. She was on a mission with that disinfectant and did not intend to be distracted.

"But Audrey, you are paranoid," Tamara said. "If Mum knew you'd take this Dettol thing to heart, I don't think she would have gotten into it. Really, this whole scene would distress her."

Audrey didn't laugh. "You keep one in your pocketbook."

"Oh, Lord, you know she's gonna drop and break 'em." I didn't mean to say it out loud.

"I got plastic," Audrey said.

"Jesus," Tam said.

"Thanks, sweetie." Arneatha packed our things into her carry-on bag with great care. "How's Bryant and Crystal?"

"Fine. He's working like a dog. Gettin' *A*'s and *B*'s at Temple, holdin' down a night job over at UPS. She's big as a house and still has two months to go. We're sending him a little money every now and then. It's supposed to be for a dinner out or the movies, but they bank every nickel that's not glued to the floor."

Audrey watched Arneatha shove the bottles into the corners of her bag. "I didn't bother to bring any condoms 'cause I guess if anybody can be trusted not to fuck over there it's you."

"Oh, Lord." Arneatha had to laugh herself.

"Kofi's not even gettin' any yet, is he?" asked Tamara.

Arneatha pursed her lips. "Now you've gone too far."

"He's not. I know he's not."

The attendants began boarding the plane. Arneatha picked up her bag.

"Wait till the line goes down," I said.

"La Roz is the one who worries. She's the one who used to read people's diaries," said Tam.

"You were *dying* for somebody to read them. You left them at everybody's house. Sex, sex, sex. We couldn't miss 'em."

"Yeah, well, I don't keep diaries anymore."

Arneatha looked at me strangely, then turned to Tamara and said, "Good."

Neesie didn't notice that her sleeve had knocked my glass. Luckily I had my hand holding down the stem. "Now she writes books," I said.

"Damn book seems likely to have fewer readers than the diaries."

"You should leave copies of the book over people's houses," I suggested.

"Or publish 'em yourself," Audrey said. "Ask Hiram to help you. He loves to back new businesses."

"You all get wackier with age," Tamara said. "One wants me to self-publish the biography of a black drag queen, and the other is worried that Neesie's going native."

Arneatha turned to me and smiled. "Are you?"

Tamara had read my mind. Or else it was all over my face. Since they were boarding the plane there was no time to beat around the bush. So I blurted it out: "Think about it. Do you know anybody who hooked up with an African and had it go well?"

"Rozzie, honey, what are you talking about?"

"I'll tell you what I'm talking about. I'm talking about that woman—you gave me the book, Neesie, when I was sick—and her parents died, and she fell in love with the Nigerian. Remember?"

"Marita Golden," Tamara said.

"I didn't read it," said Audrey.

"I'll lend it to you. You gotta read it," I said. "Anyway, remember how she goes to Africa, and they have a son, and he won't let her do anything, and she threatens to leave and he says: 'You will never take my son out of Africa'?"

"Rozzie," Arneatha said. "I'm just seeing Kofi. No husbands, sugarpie, no babies."

"It's not too late, you know."

"Well, make up your damn mind," said Audrey.

Arneatha got up and made ready to go. Only a few people were still in line.

"Bring me something back," Audrey said.

"What would you like?"

"I don't know," she said. "When you see something that looks like me, bring it. Just a little something. You know me."

Arneatha looked at each of us in turn. "Half the time, anymore, I don't know what I know."

We embraced as if it were the last time. Then she turned, kicking up the rubber-backed carpeting on the ramp, stopped, made people back up so she could put it right again, and walked down the ramp. It was a funny good-bye.

"I gave her money to buy me material," Tam said to Audrey, "and jewelry. You can have some of mine."

"No, you know what?" Audrey said, fumbling in her pocketbook. Then she called Arneatha: "Wait."

She held up a twenty-dollar bill. "Take this and get something for Bryant's baby. Anything."

"Pay me when I get back," Arneatha said over her shoulder.

The attendant took her ticket. We stood and waved until she ducked into the walkway to the plane and was out of sight. I wrote down the flight number to give to Miss Pidge.

"The baby's going to be a girl," Audrey said. "You know what the yella heifer's gonna name her?" We turned back toward the table. "Brianna Lakeesha LaClaire. Why do that to the child? I mean, what is *wrong* with her?"

"It does have a certain rhythmic panache," Tamara joked.

"Oh, shut up," said Audrey.

I suddenly wished I had told Arneatha about Nicki. I wished we were young again and had our lives and our dreams in front of us, perfect—like the fields the night they're plowed, before they're planted—not too-plump like I looked in Bryant's wedding pictures, with lines going from my nose to my mouth, practically down around my chin. I wished that Larry was still alive, and that he and Arneatha could take their walks at six in the morning holding hands. I wished that Audrey hadn't drunk away her twenties and thirties, and that Tamara hadn't jumped from one academic department to another until she ended up after so many fits and starts with no tenure and only a half-finished book. I wanted my children to be babies again so I could smell them; I wanted them singing Christmas carols in the choir and riding with me on the train to New York to see the window at Saks; I wanted to come home after our first inaugural ball and sit in the car in the rain listening to Ray Charles singing "America the Beautiful."

I wanted Hiram to look at me like he used to when I weighed a hundred and six and he would put his hands on either side of my head and run his fingers through my hair and breathe in the scent of me. He'd make me take off my clothes and stand me up on the vanity chair so that my face was even with his, and all this the minute he got in the house, before he even took off his jacket. I wanted to hear his breath catch in his throat again. I wanted him to groan as he ran his lips over my breasts and my belly. I wanted to hear him say, "Girl, you're so young and so sweet, they're gonna come arrest me. Gimme quick 'fore they take me away." I wanted to hear his belt buckle clink as his pants hit the floor and he sat on the side of the bed and pulled me down to sit on top of him, facing him.

"Spread those luscious thighs," he'd say.

I wanted to hear him call them that again, luscious, and watch his mouth make an O when he came and looked almost as if he were going to cry. Then I wanted us to talk about the day, just like that, with him still inside me, and then wash up and eat dinner.

My life was more than half over already, I thought. Cancer or no cancer. We'd used up more than half our lives. Hiram would never look that way at me again. Junior wouldn't go to another prom sporting those great big tall girls he liked with the eye-level boobs, as we used to call them; I'd missed Bryant riding down the steps of the art museum on his mountain bike we bought him, because I'd been too scared to look, and it wouldn't happen again; Nicki would never break out in another such delighted grin—not even if I bought her the whole wide world—and say, with that happy anticipation: "For *me?*"

I wished that I'd put my foot down with Hiram a long time ago. Why hadn't I? Why hadn't I done it? It was like I'd been so busy bracing for the recoil, I didn't take proper aim. Why hadn't I grown into the kind of woman a man wouldn't cheat on—

wouldn't dare—and the kind of mother who only had to look hard at her children to get them to mind? I never thought of myself as somebody who was letting life pass me by, but I was. I'd become an anxious little woman getting plump as a damn chicken, a woman who maybe had new cancer cells just waiting to grow again or maybe not, with a cheating husband, a natural and an adopted son who kept me at arm's length, a miserable daughter, and girlfriends who felt strange to me, like I didn't know them.

I was late for our dinner at the Pond House.

"I gotta go," I said.

Tamara told Audrey she'd give her a ride into town, since she was picking up Nicki at our house anyway. Then Tamara held me tight for a moment.

"The heck with City College," I said. "You weren't happy there anyway."

"I'm not worried about the college," she said. "I'll teach at a junior college and have a great time. You know I don't care. It's my book."

She linked arms with Audrey and me and walked us back to "our" table, which we began to pack up.

"I've submitted it three times, and each time the editor sends it off to readers, who write comments and suggest revisions. Each time I've gone back and done the revisions and sent back the new manuscript. The whole process has taken two years, and I just got it that this son of a bitch is dickin' me around.

"Like what's wrong with me? Why didn't I get it?"

"Fuck 'im," Audrey said. "I keep telling you, you should publish it yourself. You didn't get tenure. What've you got to lose?"

Tamara stopped folding the cloth. She squinted at Audrey and then threw back her head and laughed so loud and long that people around us turned to stare.

In her parents' Jamaican accent she said: " 'Ow many times I tol' you to get a business? Stop workin' for the academic boss-man.' "

"The Celestine Prophecy was self-published, you know," I said. "Now, see, that was a great book, and nobody recognized it until he sold it on his own. And then the New York publisher picked it up after that."

Tam rolled her eyes at the book, but she went stone silent as she stuffed the picnic things into a backpack and flung it over her shoulder. Then, my nonchalant, ironic, sophisticated girlfriend, the one I thought I knew so well, took our hands and danced a little jig around and between us.

"This, girlfriends, is a very funny moment. It's like Arneatha said: we don't know what we know. What'd you say, Audrey? What do I have to lose?"

"Yeah, that's what I said, and I don't think I'd've said it if I'd known you'd start going off like this."

"Dependence," she said. "Dependence is what I have to lose. Goddamn tenure track made me a punk. The allure of security. Jesus. I could be independent now."

As far as I could see, she'd had no little crumbcrushers to take care of, plenty cash, good jobs, a cute little car, and a rent-controlled apartment in New York for fifteen years, so I had to ask: "Well, if you haven't been independent all this time, Tam, just what have you been?"

"A sham," she said. "A horse's ass. A drag queen in the military dreaming of pink boas and a pair of big, strong arms to hold me."

8

Over dinner Romeo Ng announced that he had talked to a lobbyist from the National Rifle Association who wanted to make a donation to Hiram's campaign. Romeo says the donation could be up to the five-thousand-dollar limit, enough to be of help, but the point is that when they give like that to Hiram, the Republican National Party starts noticing that he's pulling his weight and starts thinking that he should benefit, in generic sorts of ways, from their big old soft money. In addition, the NRA's stamp of approval got Hiram on the map with their big contributors. Rome had already worked with Brooke Phillips to bundle no fewer than fifty to-the-limit individual contributors at a thousand a pop. Plus some of them had companies that could give the corporate limit, plus some had enough to give in the names of their wives and adult children. Very few minorities get onto that payroll, and believe me, it's a deep pocket.

"We all know," Rome said, "that the threshold for Congress has to do with how much money you can raise. Well, it looks like we're about to darken that doorstep."

For the first time I can remember, Romeo Ng laughed. I mean, opened his mouth and showed his teeth, punched his arms in the air. Everybody laughed and screamed with him. This was a sure enough pep rally. Just for us. 'Cause we've got to get psyched up first before we can go out and raise hell with the rest of the world.

Then he said: "And the person who really got this rolling so fast—we all know Hiram's the man, and we know we got a winner, and we know the money would have come in eventually—but we owe this jump start to *Mrs*. Prettyman."

Next thing I know, here comes Junior with his glass raised and a little jewelry box in his other hand. Some sixth-grade teacher of his had had the nerve to tell me one time that he thought Junior was getting a Napoleonic complex, and I said I hoped he would: where would Napoleon have been if he'd been happy being a short nobody?

Then, in college, it seemed like Junior coasted. He partied and had fun, took four and a half years to graduate, earning a B-minus average and talking about coming back home to work in Hiram's campaign. It was the hardest thing in the world for me to tell him, but I did, when I was in the hospital: "Your father is no meal ticket, and God bless the child."

Like I said, it was the hardest thing. And I'd like nothing more than to have him keep on hanging around here for the next twenty years. But then, he'd wake up one day and say: "Why did you do this to me? Why didn't you help me be a man?"

He was still in his own apartment, working at a law firm downtown. He'd been accepted first at Penn State's and then the University of Delaware's law school, but he hadn't said anything more about it. Neither had I. Neither had Hiram.

"Y'all better keep an eye out for my moms," he said. "She grew up down South. She listens to that crazy country music. She's done the wife-and-two-kids thing; she does the business. When I was a boy and Daddy got sick running for state senate, this lady went out and gave his speeches for him. I remember. We kids had it memorized 'cause she repeated it like a hundred and ninety-nine times in the car on the way.

"She has faced down the big *C*. And now, as you know from the popular press, she is armed and dangerous. Ladies and gentlemen, I'm going to Howard University law school just so I can keep up."

I hollered. "Howard! Howard! When'd you hear from Howard?"

Junior hugged me—"Last week," he said, grinning—and then he showed me what he had in the box. He'd ordered it from some place in Texas, and the new staff had chipped in to buy it. They were sitting around the table with their blue-and-white T-shirts pulled on over their clothes, watching me lift the piece of jewelry out of the box. I screamed. It was a tiny silver gun-and-holster brooch, funniest darned thing I'd ever seen.

"This is from me and Bryant and Crystal and Nicki and the new staff," he said. It was his way, I saw, of helping to educate them. A lot of time they think the wife is just in the way. Junior was making them know that I was to be figured into the mix. It was a little gift.

Of course, while I'm laughing, I'm thinking about that doggone Chevy Nova up in Coatesville. If Audrey didn't get it, I'd have to brave that Negro Dogpatch myself.

I wondered whether they'd come up with this before or after the NRA money. That's not cynical; it's just curious. I also wondered whether Romeo had approached the NRA person or been approached, as he said. Aides are a funny breed. You want them to be ambitious and aggressive—some of them are practically pit bulls—but you don't want them to turn on you; that's the trick. They have to know your strengths and weaknesses, but they've got to keep admiring or needing or, best of all, loving the candidate and putting his needs first.

I watched Romeo's face. Junior could have been his rival, but Rome had been too smart for that. He'd let the candidate's son be the son, and now, Junior'd be out of his hair at crunch time. Very savvy. Who knew? He might even work with Junior sometime, too. I liked an aide who could keep his ego under control. Now his face told nothing. He laughed and clapped along with the rest of us.

Finally our old campaign manager declared that he would

help Hiram in any way he could as a consultant and old friend, but that he'd step down and make way for new blood to head the new campaign.

"Ng—what the hell's your name?"

"Rome. Just call me Rome, sir."

"Yeah, well, Rome here knows Washington and he knows this new age. I'm old-style. Don't want to be—what they say?—all in the Kool-Aid and don't know the flavor."

"All in the diaper and don't know dookie." Romeo grinned.

"Shut up signifying," our manager said, " 'fore I have to kick your nigger-nese behind."

It was more validation that this was a man who could not go national.

"Amerasian is the word you're looking for, sir," Rome said. He grinned, but the look in his eyes probably shot four times more arthritis into Dewey's tired old body.

"Well, I need you both," Hiram said. "I need you all."

Hiram had been having heart-to-hearts. I could see that. The feeling in the room as they ate their dinner showed it. Hiram never forgets the time with staff. People talk about his charisma, and he has that, for sure. But they don't see when he takes these people aside: smart people, driven, compulsive, aggressive people, but people who, for some reason, don't like to be out front. Hiram makes them loyal. He makes them love him, and they stick. And when necessary, he knows how to punish. You got to do both. That's why our old manager stuck all those years, and a host of others in all sorts of positions. This dinner was the beginning of the campaign for us. Hiram had done his homework; I'd done mine. We were in good shape.

The thing was, though, that I didn't feel like it. I didn't feel like anything. For the first time in our lives, it was like I just wasn't hungry anymore.

We spent the night at the Pond House, and I soaked in the tub a long time. When I came out, Hiram was lying on the bed in his shorts. There's a fireplace in the bedroom that we almost never use. He'd lit a small fire in it.

" 'Member when I used to drive home from Harrisburg from the statehouse," he said, "and you used to say the only thing I ever came in with was bad news and a hard-on?

"Well, twenty years later, we got good news. This staff is *it;* Rome's been working the moderate Republicans, and they're happy as pigs in shit to find a black candidate who is not rabid conservative and looks doable; and you and this Annie Oakley thing is crazy, definitely crazy, honey, and it's working. Come here."

He patted the bed next to him. I know that motion. I was dressed in my bathrobe and a bra, which I wear to bed now, and panties.

We hadn't done much of anything, except for a couple of times, since the cancer. This was a big deal for us to have the night to ourselves. He'd put some effort into clearing out the staffers. Usually, they would've stayed late and made plans.

So, what was the deal? Tell the truth, I think, my stock had gone up. I've always known, like my grandmother, who sold eggs and cream and took in laundry, that my husband values me partly for how much I can enrich our household. Nothing wrong with that. That's the way a marriage is. Let's get down to it: I was attracted by his potential for success, and he knew I had more ambition and energy than many people show in a lifetime. We've both lived up to our end of the bargain.

But then, over these years, with the children and the work, though, I sort of let myself get beat down, too. You don't mean to, but you do. The cancer made me look at that.

He got up and turned off the light, and came to me where I was standing in the middle of the floor. He started to rub me through the robe. He did it exactly like the masseur showed us in the workshop about sex after cancer. It didn't feel like him, because for twenty years, that's not how he started. I just stood straight as a soldier.

"You still love me?" he asked.

I thought I'd pushed Nicki's hairdresser comment out of my mind, but I hadn't. "What else do you want me to do for you?"

"You're so busy out shootin' and getting publicity, maybe you got better things to do."

I still didn't say anything. The massage felt good now. I hadn't wanted sex before. The cancer does things to you.

"You still love me?" he asked again.

I did. I do. I knew I did. Call me a fool. I love him so much I didn't dare think about it. Doggoned if I'd say it, though.

"You're not doing right by me," I said. "I was sitting in that bathtub, and I didn't even care, Hiram. I didn't care whether you won or lost. I was sitting in there, and I didn't care if you got fifty-two cents in the campaign fund.

"I could stay home and do my yoga exercises at this point, Hiram. Nobody would blame me. You are doing me dirty, Hi, and I can't take it anymore. I won't."

"I'ma do right now."

"What did you say?"

"I said, 'I'ma do right by you, Roz.' " He looked me straight in the eye, serious as a heart attack. "If I don't have you, what do I have?"

I had never heard him talk like this. He hadn't said such a thing to me before, ever. I sucked my teeth. He kept rubbing me—not sexy rubbing, just nice.

"You changed this year," he said. "I'm changing. This cancer thing affected me, too. I can feel, Roz: you're fed up. I know you been mad at me. I know I've got to change, but you've shut me out."

I had. I very nicely pulled the door to. No hard feelings. I let him get away with his dirt all this time; I brought it on myself. I'd keep on like nothing had happened. That part of the marriage, I told myself, was over.

Hiram spread his hands and leaned over and massaged my lower back, and then all the way down my legs. He got on his knees and rubbed my thighs, front and back. He opened my bathrobe and put his head on my belly.

I held his head—so smooth now that it's shaved, so hard and smooth against my stomach—and it all came back. It just flashed in front of me: the first time we ever did it, and I thought I would die because he was so strong and I knew he'd be a big man, bigger than anybody I'd ever met, and he was begging for me, calling my name, asking me to hold him tight and don't let go; I remembered the first time he won in the state legislature, and the people just cheered and clapped and hugged one another, and I'd never seen anything like it, and Milo Miles, the black limousine owner, sent us a car, and Hiram had my whole dress open in the backseat, and when we got to the hotel, I wrapped my mink around me and nobody knew but us. Nobody knew. I loved it. I swear that was the night I got pregnant with Nicki.

He slipped off my drawers. We didn't even have the little radio on. Nothing but the fire crackling and the sound of me getting wet. I held his head down there by my belly.

"I'm fat now," I said.

"It's good, baby," he said. "It's all good." Then he laughed real quiet like he used to when we were first in love, and he would get up on his elbow to look at my body in the orange glow of the streetlight in the apartment over the bar. He'd laugh like he was filling himself full of me, how I belonged to him. After all these years, that was still a private laugh. There wasn't much we'd been able to keep to ourselves. When you live a public life, you use everything you have—every idea, every movement, every smile. When he smiles at us now, it looks like the man on the TV. But this laugh was fresh, just like he had had it in a box for twenty years and never shared it with anyone but me. That's what I like to think, anyway; that's how it sounded to me.

"You love me?"

I wouldn't say it.

"This all mine?" That's what he'd say years before, rubbing his hands up and down the length of me, pausing to finger the crotch hair that I dyed to match the Dusky Sahara on my head until I got juicy. I don't dye it down there anymore, 'cause there isn't enough left to bother with.

So what did some stupid twenty-five-year-old hairdresser have I didn't have, or any of them, for that matter? What? More fur. Probably suck anything he wanted. That's probably what he got from them was blow jobs. Nasty old blow jobs. Well, they could have it. For twenty years I never sucked nothing, and I didn't intend to start now.

"All mine," he said.

"I never could say 'all mine,' " I said. So what if it sounded bitter? I was hurt, was the truth. I'd been hurt for years.

"I am too old," I told him, "and I've worked too damn hard just to take any old thing you hand out and lap it up like a hound dog, Hiram. Why should I?

"When do I get to say 'all mine'?" I heard my voice start to crack. I was on the verge of crying for the second time in a week. "I won't get to say it till you so damn old you can't do me dirty no more."

"Now," he said, "you say it now." He pulled me down to my knees. I was facing him, both of us on our knees.

"Don't play me, Hiram."

"Say it now, you want it. You're a different woman, Roz, from the girl I married, who didn't care what I did so long as I came home afterward. You say you want it, now you got it."

"What about before?"

"That's before. You want to change what's already gone?"

He was rubbing up and down my waist and back now. I was moving with him. It felt like he unhitched my bra in the back, but I didn't pay it any mind. It had been so long, and my body had been closed up and full of sickness. I was a prison where the inmates took over and tore sinks out of the walls. Then they pumped in chemicals and the rioters died, but I couldn't get out for a breath of air.

Now the craziness had died down. My body wasn't the same,

but it was working again. I wouldn't get out of prison, but it was minimum security. I wanted to believe that we could zap the cancer out of our marriage, too, and then go on and recover.

"Why couldn't I have it before?"

"You never cared, Roz. You never asked. You never insisted."

"You a lie."

"Make me true," he said. "Make me. Hold me here. Don't let me go nowhere, and I won't let you go neither. You don't want to go, do you? You do care."

I could feel myself swaying there on my knees, and his hands holding my waist loosely as if I was a ballet dancer. We was real, real close. Every time I rocked, I felt him hard, bumping against me.

I let go holding up the bra.

"You've given up enough," he said. "Come on. Time for me to give up something, too."

I knew that because of the new campaign he was only prudent to stop running around—but he didn't have to come back to me like this and make me this offering.

I accepted, hoping that I wouldn't seem too grateful. Hiram never wanted anybody who wanted him too much. I didn't intend to lose what new ground I had gained.

When he lay me down on the bed and came into me, it was the old Hiram and the new one, and I was the old Roz and the new Roz, too plump, with one good breast and a smaller one with a gash. And having him back, all for me, felt so good I dug my heels down into the bed and ran my hands over his smooth head and his smooth haunches and his shoulders and the muscles in his arms holding him up over me, and I knew him so well, it was like plowing easy through a well-turned, well-watered field, only better.

People can change. I have to believe that.

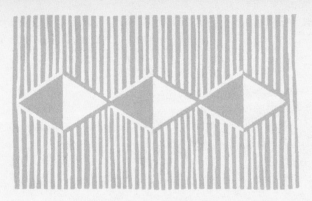

T A M A R A

9

"Listen," I heard myself say, "you don't have to make any vows to me. Why don't we just take time off for good behavior, like medieval monks? I'll say Hail Marys."

He made a terse laugh. Then seriously he said: "You know I'll never have anything like this again. Couldn't possibly. You know that."

"Why not leave it open? OK. *You* can't leave it open. I got that. I'll leave it open. You don't have to."

"It's been so good. Don't do this now."

"You're the one doing it. What am I doing? You're on top, just like you like it. *Bend Over.* My book title continues to collect irony."

It had been our running joke for fifteen years. What does this politician want? Or the dean? The law firm that donated a thousand dollars to the campaign and thirty thousand to the Democratic National Party? We'd remind each other whenever we had difficulty or when one or the other was locked in some sort of struggle, me in the academy, him in politics. We say in faux British accents, thick-tongued, very Oxbridge: "A cry rises up from the multitude. The purest expression of the common man. Bend over and let me fuck you."

We'd laugh and laugh.

I should not have referred to it in this conversation. I should not have betrayed the high-gloss cynicism, the nig and supernig, as we called it, nature of our relationship. Above the rules. No strings. For fifteen years we'd had an understanding.

Except that I had let myself misunderstand.

Some critical part of my brain curled up on the windowsill, catlike, leisurely, merciless, wondering when it had happened. The rest of me dropped down on one knee, hands clasped in front of my face like an R&B singer from the seventies, not too proud to beg.

"Christ, Tamara," he said, "I would have wagered money that you of all women wouldn't start this shit."

"Well, so you can be wrong, too. That's a comfort."

"Don't get pissy."

"You gonna miss this stuff here, old man," I said sweetly.

He'd freaked out about turning fifty. The head-shaving business, which he billed as an act of solidarity with Roz after her surgery, was actually something he'd been toying with to fix the receding hairline problem. Roz knew it, too. But she's the ultimate team player. Which is how we've gone undetected for so long. The old-man comment was another low blow, as it were. I could hear my mother's voice saying: 'ave a *little* pride, at least.

"Gotta run," he said.

I searched my mind for a witty rejoiner. "Go fuck yourself," I said.

Nicki came into the room. I hung up the phone before her father's baritone leapt out from the receiver.

"You and your wild and crazy love life," she said, shaking her head. I assumed she'd been listening.

Wild and crazy. I still had some of the sex-enhancing drug I ordered from Italy and that we'd used a few months before for a three-hour session so dreamy and intense that we felt the orgasms coming a long, long way off, like watching a Midwestern thunderhead floating in, big and black and full of sparks. It was like that inside our skins. Jesus. I get hot just remembering.

How could he just put an end to it?

Had anyone told me twenty years ago, or even ten or five, that

I'd be begging some married nigger not to leave me, I'd have laughed in his face. But Hiram was closing the longest-running and most satisfying chapter of my adult love life. For fifteen years he was an exciting lover, an experienced and intelligent friend, a challenging debating partner. During some years over that span, when I lived with other men, for instance—I did three such stints—or when he ran for Pennsylvania state senate, or the year Roz gave birth to Nicki, we might have spent no more than two or three weekends together. A few years, when Roz and the kids went to the shore for the summer, we rented a studio apartment in a garage in Camden and indulged in long, late-night sexfests. I can summon up his taste in an instant, and everything else, too: the long, smooth slope of his hamstring, the smell of his hair and crotch, the feel of his lips and his teeth and his tongue. I can call up precisely the excitement and fear, I suppose it was, when I said that I wondered what it would feel like to be the man, and he reached for the Vaseline, rubbed a glob of it on my third finger, tucked his knees under his chest, and told me to stick it in.

"Try it," he said.

I went slow until he started to relax, and then I reached underneath and worked both ends. It was exciting doing that to him. Every now and then I bent down and kissed him. His breathing was ragged. My greed to control him took me by surprise as much as his submission. I took my time jacking him off. I watched him. I studied his desire and worked it up.

At any moment of the day or night, I can still hear his voice in his throat when he came, almost against his will. I can feel the pressure on my finger and in my hand.

"You liked it, didn't you?" I asked him.

"Shut up," he said.

That was when I was twenty-nine. My body was magic with him. Although he came into me like any other man, I felt self-contained with him, self-replenishing, fantastic.

"I want you to do me every way there is," I said. He did. We did.

And yet, our affair conformed to every circumstance of our lives. I loved Roz and the kids, and so did he. We both understood that. But because the relationship had endured with such adroitness and adaptability, somewhere along the line I guess I came to assume that no strings meant no end, as if we had the love equivalent of wildflowers that grow by the side of the road no matter what.

Enter the landscaper: Rozzie. A place for everything, everything in its place. High noon and high time to get Hiram and his dick back inside the corral. Whatever she'd said or done had made enough of an impression that instead of "Let's get more discreet," he was saying, "Let's get it over with."

Secretly I applauded her. As I said, I was working on a lot of levels with this.

"Was that your boyfriend?" Nicki asked.

"I wouldn't use that word."

"The Black Narcissus?"

"No. The Black Narcissus lives in Philly and is not a serious relationship."

"This was a serious relationship?"

"Guess not. Ultimately." It was a stupid thing to say.

"You should call my mom. She loves when you tell her about your life. She says it's like living a fantasy."

"Maybe later," I said. "So, what do you want to do this weekend, Nicki?" I asked.

She was studying me.

"Let's see," she said. "My mom just made me have an abortion, and she's not speaking to me. I just broke up with my boyfriend, so naturally he's not speaking to me. My brother just got into law school, so he can't do anything but party for the next five months. And Dad's running for office again, and he can only talk to people who have a thousand dollars to put toward the campaign, so he's not speaking to me. So I don't know."

"You got girlfriends?"

"Like you all were girlfriends? Nope. Not like that."

"So what do you want to do?"

"I want to escape."

"Me, too. What's your escape look like? Or is this it, coming to New York?"

"Sort of."

I poked out my bottom lip thoughtfully. What would be a good getaway? I wondered, having decided impulsively that Nicki's desire to escape was exactly the right diversion for the moment. I thought of places I knew within two or three hours' drive of New York: the Poconos, the Berkshires, the New Jersey shore. Hiram and I had used all of them.

"We could take the Metroliner to D.C.," I said. "Or the shuttle to Boston." Spending money had to be part of the deal. Then, afterward, I could look back with amusement and a touch of remorse. It'd be almost as good as going down to the river and rolling naked in the mud on the banks, smearing my body with dirt and stumbling mute through the streets.

"Orlando," she said.

"Perfect. You want my yellow bikini or the white one-piece?"

"Can I wear your blue Speedo?"

"No. Only I wear my blue Speedo."

We took a late flight and changed in Atlanta. Because of a recent crash the el cheapo airline was offering discount prices. On the plane Nicki listened to LL Cool J rapping about licking vanilla ice cream off his girlfriend's thighs. In another song, he assured a girl he admired from a distance that what he felt for her was not a crush, but true love. Her boyfriend smoked too many butts, while he, Cool J, was working out each day thinking of what he was going to do to her. Nicki had me listen to that one.

I thought about Billy Williams, the Black Narcissus with the ultimate 1950s name. He had told me that he thought about me when he worked out alone in his gym in the early morning or at night, after he closed. I'd repeated the line to my girlfriends because it sounded so lame, so testosterone and vinegar. I'd wanted him to be a little less obvious. God knows I enjoy fitness and I love the look and feel of men's bodies, but his was too-too, as we used to say, as was his desire.

LL Cool J also told the girl he admired that although her boyfriend gave her chump change to have her hair done, he and she could go to a whole new level.

"God help the sister who can't scrape together enough money to get her own hair done," I said, handing back Nicki's Walkman.

She rolled her eyes and eased the earphones over her own feathery new do. She rapped quietly to herself while I prepared a lecture on black women sculptors and their use of texture. Hair had something to do with it, but I couldn't quite figure out how to work it in.

I fingered my own dreads. Hiram didn't like them. They'd come in quite nicely on top. Now, I was sorry that I had kept the back short.

By the time we caught the shuttle to our hotel, it was past midnight. We put on our bathing suits, bought tuna sandwiches, corn chips, soda and wildly overpriced shorts of sparkling apple cider from the twenty-four-hour café. Then we headed for the pool.

A fiftyish white couple sat in the Jacuzzi petting and kissing with big, open mouths.

"Eeeew," Nicki said as we headed for the other side of the patio. "That is so nasty. They should go inside, where nobody has to look at them."

I thought to give her a mini-lecture on the difference between looking sexy and feeling sexually fulfilled, but decided against it. We sat on our lounge chairs in the moonlight, ate our picnic dinner, and giggled. The weekend would set me back a thousand dollars, I figured. It was perfect. In a couple months I'd be out of a job.

"I walk on the wild side," I said, mimicking one of Arneatha's many silly sayings from Disney movies she's watched a hundred times with her kids. "I laugh in the face of danger. Ha, ha, ha."

Nicki asked me whether or not I'd ever been pregnant.

"No. Never have."

"Everything smelled different."

I sniffed. The air was warm and humid. It smelled like earth and chlorine. I could hear the woman in the Jacuzzi moaning.

"I am not getting in there," Nicki said.

It occurred to me that she shouldn't swim at all. "I think there are too many germs in the pool for you. You're still too vulnerable to infection. I think that's the case."

"The doctor gave me a piece of paper with all that stuff on it, but I left it home. I think you're right. I forgot.

"What's funny is how you're yourself, then all of a sudden you're pregnant, and everything's different, and now I'm myself again, except I'm not, really. And I'll never be the same."

I stood up and slipped on my thongs. "Listen to me: I'm spending a thousand dollars for an escape," I said. "You and I have had this same conversation three or four times since we got on the plane. Look. I'ma do you like my mother did."

I tore a corner from a napkin, fished a pen out of my pocketbook, and wrote Andre's name on it along with the word *pregnancy*. I showed her the paper and nodded until she nodded back. Then I rolled the paper up tight like a joint and stuffed it into her empty soda can. I indicated the trashcan. She followed my lead, got up, and threw the can away.

I dove into the water and did six or seven laps. A globby, greasy depression was starting to congeal in the corner of my consciousness. I sliced my arms through the cold water, as if activity would break it up. I surfaced next to her.

"Have you ever loved someone who didn't love you back?" she said to me.

"No," I said. "They all loved me, loved me madly: my art collector, my buppie corporate man, my medical doctor who smuggled body parts—what would make you think that they didn't love me with undying passion like LL Cool J?"

"I'm serious." She was whining.

"Well, I'm not. I'm not going to wallow in my self-pity, and I don't intend to listen to you wallow in yours. Got that? Now, where are we going tomorrow?"

"Magic Kingdom," she said.

"Done." I felt agreeably tired. "Let's hit the rack."

We were at the gates when they opened, ready to elbow all the little kids and people in wheelchairs out of the way to get to the good rides first.

Frontierland was done in pioneer kitsch. Inside Splash Mountain, Brer Fox and Brer Bear tried to capture Brer Rabbit. We floated on a make-believe river in hollow plastic logs. Animated birds and woodland creatures flapped their mouths and moved their heads herky-jerky at us as we glided by. It was the sound of high-pitched darky laughter floating through the centuries of wishful Southern literature right through Joel Chandler Harris and Uncle Remus to *Song of the South*.

We turned a corner and saw Brer Bear strung up in Brer Fox's rope, going up and down, up and down as Brer Fox tried to untangle him while berating him for tripping his trap. Possum young'uns hung upside down singing; frogs croaked. It was happy, happy, happy down there underneath the ground in Splash Mountain, and the bear's big brown feet, caught in the noose on either side of his shoulders, and his big brown ass, displayed for us, went up and down some more. It was like a mock lynching. All in fun.

Finally they caught Brer Rabbit, who was desperately asking not to be thrown in the briar patch, and the vultures overhead croaked sinister warnings about Brer Rabbit's laughing place, and the African tale came back to me, all at once: Mmotia, the fairy whom no man can see, slapping the gum baby in her crying place and getting stuck, images on top of one another, like a totem, instead of in a line, like cartoons.

As if in answer to my mind, the ride pulled us up to the top of a rise and plunged us down five stories, the PR says, into a splash of water.

We screamed.

Then our plastic log floated around a dark corner to a veritable nigger heaven of happy chickens, singing singing singing— what else?—"Zip-A-Dee Doo-Dah," a song so stupid and sunny it could only have been created by the backwash of white Christian hierarchy.

By the time the college boy in the cowboy hat pulled back the lap bar and told us where to exit, I was dazed.

The park takes photos of each and every roller coaster car that goes down the big splash, and then offers you a print. We bought one for ten and a half dollars, and I stood in the sun staring at it while Nicki stopped in the bathroom.

The idea came to me to blow up the photo to poster size, stand it against the back of a large cage, crawl in in front of it, and sit still on a pallet of hay like a cross between the Venus Hottentot and Kafka's hunger artist. I'd grow too thin and weak to stand. Then they could make *me* into a Disney character, a set of dancing bones under a jolly mop of tailored dreadlocks, doing a jig to a bluesy danse macabre, sticking out a big, high, black, round butt.

Hiram and I used to slow dance naked, and I loved to feel him getting hard. Must've been the bones that brought it to mind.

It was difficult to imagine that the whole thing was dead, a relationship longer lasting and more rewarding than most marriages. Dry bones. My mum's friends used to come to our kitchen and sit on our secondhand chairs with feet like run-over shoes and talk about the men the world had dealt them, like cards. It would be years before I would learn about my father's shadow family in Jamaica, a young woman with a limp and his other baby, my little half-brother Pete.

Nicki appeared and asked me what I was thinking about, but it was too bizarre. I joked about renting space to build a virtual reality Nat Turner attraction where an animatronic slave owner in his nightshirt runs through the shadows, pursued by Nat and friends with their blades drawn. Then the lights go off, the audience hears a gasp and a gurgle and feels a spray of warm blood in their faces before the lights flicker on to reveal the slave owner's wife hunched over a fence post, her neck slit.

Like that was less bizarre.

"Deep," Nicki said.

"Went too far for you, huh?" She'd been with me at first.

"Yeah," she said.

"What pushed you over the line, the blood?"

"Yeah, for real, the blood. Come on," she said, pulling my arm, "let's get back in line before the whole Weird Lake band gets in front of us."

I looked around. Twenty youngsters wearing shirts that said WEIR LAKE MARCHING BAND were scrambling up an incline toward the ride.

We waited the half hour, inching forward in tandem with sunburned redhead newlyweds from Wisconsin. Why, we wondered aloud, had they come this far when the Disneyland in L.A. was closer?

"This one is the real thing," they said. And besides, who could tell when they'd ever have such an opportunity again? A man wearing Mickey ears turned around and explained that's why he'd brought his two-year-old, also wearing Mickey ears, grinning and laughing as if he was having the time of his life.

"I didn't have the heart to leave the little guy," said the man.

"But he'll never remember it," I said.

"I don't know," the man said. "I think with something like this," he motioned at the park with a big heavenward sweep of both arms, "some part of it's got to stay inside you somewhere."

We rode through the singing and the lynching and the vultures and the happy, happy resurrection or amalgamation or whatever the fuck was going on and then hurtled ourselves onto the next ride, one story after another swirled into the goofy Disney melting pot with a Cuisinart in the middle that ground all human experience and culture into a pink-and-green cultural puke.

Crazy. The whole day was crazy like that. Lines and rides. Up and down, careening through a synthetic starry night in a tiny rocket ship, chugging around the park on a choo-choo train. In the haunted house a small child begged to be let out, and her parents slammed her into the rolling divan that whisked us into the darkness: *"C'mon!"*

We exited into brazen sunlight, hearts pumping like crazy to find more rides, more assurance that good would triumph over evil, that God was in his heaven and all was right with the world. Phew.

In the evening we ended up on the porch of a restaurant called the Crystal Palace, waiting for our late dinner reservation, watching, with thousands upon thousands of others, the parade of floats, blazing with strings of colored lights just inches apart. The music from every Disney movie swelled out of speakers, which must have been placed everywhere, because wherever we turned, we were wrapped in lush stereo sound.

"At the World's Fair in London in the mid-eighteen hundreds," I said, "there was an exhibit called the Crystal Palace. People said that when the Industrial Revolution made people materially comfortable, everyone would become so happy and live such wonderful lives that we'd all live in crystal palaces, with no need to hide for shame."

Nicki looked at me blankly.

We copped a space on the porch. Along the perimeter grew thick gardenia bushes nearly three feet high. The heavy smell of the blossoms made the air thick and sweet to breathe.

I was too tired to resist anymore. The floats and the people dressed in green sequins and the characters from childhood and dreams kept coming: Mickey, Donald, Goofy, the Little Mermaid, Aladdin, Lady and the Tramp, Peter Pan and Tink, Beauty and the Beast, each with his or her own song, the orphans, the outcasts, the separated ones, the apostates struggling alone before reunification with the one true spouse, the one true people, finding safety and home and love, forever.

No American could be immune. It was the final moment in

the reeducation camp that we'd been undergoing all our lives. Dumbo floated by and all I wanted to do was flap my ears and fly with him. Exhausted, eyes heavy, Nicki begged me to take her back to the hotel room. She didn't even want to wait for dinner. We waded into the crowd, but it was impossible. The fireworks had begun.

We gave up and went back to the Crystal Palace to watch. Colors burst against the night sky, to the left of Cinderella's palace, just like on TV and on the posters: delicate greens and pinks in circles and oblongs, then pinpricks of purple and white. At the end, after a pause, the Disney music was replaced by "America the Beautiful." Fireworks exploded in red, white, and blue, as big and loud and gaudy as those some small cities display on the Fourth of July. The music was just right: dramatic—OK, melodramatic—but fast-paced and rhythmic withal. God shed his grace on us, and the orgy of emotion ended, and I'm not ashamed to say it, I was so riled up, I was ready to run out and shoot the first fucking foreigner I could find.

Instead, thank God, the round-cheeked college girl in mob-cap and full-length frock called our name, and we were led into the air-conditioning, out of the noise and heat and crowd. Nicki ate macaroni and cheese from the kids' buffet, and I picked through a heartland paella. Winnie the Pooh and Eeyore stopped by our table. I drank three glasses of iced tea, Nicki drank soda, and we regained our composure. The trance was broken. We walked slowly through the crowds toward the ferryboat back to the parking lot. Crickets chirped in the pond next to us from a foot-deep bed of bloodred impatiens.

"You think they're real?" a man next to us asked.

"Hah!" I laughed.

Nicki shushed me.

The next morning I rang my father, who lives in Miami part of the year and in Jamaica the rest of the year. It's the same arrangement he used to have in Philadelphia. He lives with his new wife, who used to be his Jamaica woman, and their son, Peter.

"I'm talking to you on a Mickey Mouse lamp-and-phone thing from a hotel room in Orlando," I said. "I'm here with my goddaughter. Just for twenty-four hours."

"You coming down here?"

"No. I'm telling you: we came Friday night and we go back this morning."

"Go back later."

"I can't. I've gotta get this child back to her parents, Daddy."

He sucked his teeth. "Who's that? Hiram the Pretty Man and that little blond wife, your girlfriend?"

"Yeah."

"He's a big man now, isn't he?"

"Yep. How's Peter?" I asked.

"Oh, Jesus. I'm too old to have more children. Peter's fine. He wants to get up every morning at the crack of fuckin' dawn and run on the beach together."

"You love it," I said.

"I do. You know what I love most?"

"What?"

"The fact that I can still keep up."

"What about Selena?"

"I keep up with her, too."

"How's she doing?"

"Fine. She's working. You should come down. Rent a car and drive on down. We got room; we'll feed you, take care of you. Peter loves you, you know."

"Not this time."

"Forget it, then," he said with typical sarcasm. "Go back to making Disney and them rich. They need your money bad."

He asked what I was going to do now that I'd have to leave City College. I heard myself telling him that I might move back to Philadelphia to live because it was cheaper. I said it all quite sensibly despite the fact that the idea had just occurred to me.

"You going to move back with your mother?"

"Oh, Jesus, Daddy, no."

"Why not? She's lonely, you know, since your brother died."

"Mummy's impossible to live with now. Really. She's got it like a fucking museum in there."

"Always was a tidy woman."

His laughter was kinder than mine. He never had to help keep our house astonishingly clean. He never had to put up with her rage in the months while he was gone.

"It's just that I hate to see her miserable, you know. That's all."

"Yeah, well. Just because you did her wrong doesn't mean I have to make her happy, you know."

He laughed again.

We said good-bye and I replaced the receiver in Mickey Mouse's gloved hand. Then, leaving Nicki to sun on the balcony, I went downstairs for a workout in the new Nautilus room. We had just enough time to shower and dress and catch the shuttle to the airport.

On the plane home I convinced myself of the wisdom of moving back to Philadelphia. Besides, now that I would not be seeing Hiram, there was no need to stay in New York. I no longer needed anonymity or a full salary. I did not need to attend department meetings or go to parties at the homes of people I disliked or defend my syllabi against attack from visiting alumni. More than that I could drop the cotton sack of excuses I'd been dragging around these fifteen years to explain why it was I'd jumped from art to art history to cultural criticism to African-American studies. I'm not an academic. I'm not a scholar. Not in my heart of hearts.

And whereas I've been good in the classroom—even brilliant, occasionally—I don't want ongoing relationships with all these young people. I am bored by their ideas and their emotional struggles. The American bourgeoisie and its young are very demanding.

What delicious relief to contemplate escaping to my cheap

little hometown city. Maybe I'd go to the foreign car garage near Broad Street and flirt with Bill Williams and his vet friends while they restored the Karmann Ghia. My life was acting out a new politics of space, I realized, that gave me freedoms I had forgotten.

10

My mum was not charmed when I told her about Orlando. She
said that if I played the part of an impulsive spendthrift, I'd end
up living in a trailer park like my father.

"You know he'll never retire. She is going to work him till he
drops. Serves him right.

"So, I suppose you went and took your goddaughter to visit
him and the gimpy whore."

"Not this time. I wanted to get home."

"What for?"

"I'm packing. I'm moving back to Philadelphia for a while."

My mother brightened. "I'm so relieved. You can't imagine.
Come to the Odunde festival with me. I'm minding a table for
my friend Lila, who sells books in the gallery."

"Why?"

"Why what?"

"Why are you minding Lila's table?"

"Because she's had a stroke, and we're trying to keep her
business going for her until she gets back on her feet. My friends
are starting to fall apart. It's good you're coming home. Spend
some time with us before we're all gone."

"How're the dogs?"

My mother has raised toy poodles for years. She likes the

brown ones because they're her color, and because they're less popular, and therefore less inbred than the white. She paints their toenails red and gold.

"The dogs? I don't know. I think this'll be my last year for shows. I can't take all the hauling and lugging. . . .

"Hey, what the hell is wrong with your friends the politicians? *Rozzie, little Rozzie,* is in the paper aiming a gun, and Hiram's become a stinking Republican. Next time you talk to him, tell him I can no longer support him now that he's allied himself with that party. Tell him. Who's doing this, him or Roz?"

"Both."

"Jamaica same way. People like your father helped it happen."

My parents had been socialists in their youth. Mum came from a relatively well-off family, Daddy from poverty. They met at political meetings, married, produced my brother, then sailed to America to get rich. You can't get either of them to come clean, but I think their unspoken assumption involved the Robin Hood theory of immigration: Suck off some of the cream and then, twenty years later, bring it back home to enrich the island's economy.

"Hiram's going where the power is."

"Well," she said, "someone who cares for him should tell him that there's no return from *that* country. You have a very special relationship with him, I suspect. You should tell him. Or Arneatha: surely she can see what he's doing."

"I think they've had a bit of a falling out over this already."

"So he can't hear her. All the more reason you should talk to him, darling.

"Oh," she added, veering, as she did, from one subject to another, "and before you come, will you do me a favor and send me down your book?"

"About Eugenia?"

"God, no. The guide to black books and culture you made up

for your students. I'd like to copy it for the women minding Lila's store. Half the time people ask for things, and they don't know what they're talking about."

"I want to publish this other book."

"So you publish that one and give this to me. This one is no problem. It's already done, right?"

"How were you a socialist, Mum? You like selling better than anything in the world."

"I'm a West Indian. I can't help it. Besides, I was born with six fingers. The Africans say that means you'll be good in business."

"I was born with six fingers, too. Audrey suggested self-publishing."

"That's what I'm trying to tell you. *Send it down.* Send it overnight mail. I always liked Audrey the best out of your friends."

"Why?"

"I don't know. She was good with the dogs. I tried to teach Roz, but she was too . . . stiff or something."

I sent my mother my students' study pack, which had grown over the years to a book-length collection of digests: of folklore, mythology, thumbnail sketches of books, poems, autobiographies, essays, black newspapers, and black arts movements. It contained every bit of background that I wanted them to have. At the end was a bibliography and a section where they were to write down family stories and folklore, jump-rope jingles, hand claps. *The Norton Anthology of African-American Literature* made my little guide redundant for college students, certainly, but it might still be of help to people like my mother and her girlfriends minding the book stall.

Then, in the weeks between the end of term and the beginning of June, when I was to move, I packed up my apartment, stacked the boxes by the door, opened my book about Eugene/Eugenia, and began to re-read it. Because no one had ever been arrested for beating Eugene to death, let alone prosecuted, it could not be the so-called academic murder mystery I'd been calling it for years. There had been a murder, but it remained a mystery, all setup and no payoff. I didn't know what to do with this book that I loved, but had failed to do right by.

After a week of this funny, monastic life, I lay in bed one warm night with the windows open. I'd worked until three o'clock in the morning reorganizing chunks of material, shuffling them like cards, coming up with new ideas and rejecting them every few hours. The book lay on the floor of my bedroom in the corner, in its box. I lay in mine.

I felt horny, bored, alone.

Then the phone rang. It was Arneatha calling from the Episcopal diocese office in Uganda.

"Were you awake? I thought you might be."

"Yes."

"I have been ill," she said.

"Oh, my God, Arneatha," I said. "What do you have?"

"Something like dysentery. Not cholera, but similar. I'm much better now. Listen, are you alone?"

"Yes."

"I saw you and Hiram in New York a couple months ago, Tamara. I went up for a meeting, and it ended early, and I tried to call you and something was wrong with your phone line, so I thought I'd stop by. It was raining, and I was walking from the subway.

"I saw Hiram get out of a cab and zip into the building. I called, but he didn't hear me. I was at the other end of the block. When I got to the building a woman let me in, I guess because of the rain, and also I was wearing my collar.

"Anyway, I had to take the stairs up to your floor because somebody was holding the elevator. He was already inside, and I heard you, the two of you, making love, just there, or close enough to the door, at least, for me to hear. I was shocked, Tamara. I was stunned. I stood there for a minute telling myself it couldn't be, but I know his voice, of course."

"Why didn't you say anything all this time, Neese?"

"I should have. I didn't know what to say. I didn't know what to do . . . at all. But I should have said that."

"We called it off."

"Oh?"

The transatlantic connection echoed and lagged. We were stepping on each other's words. When no one spoke, the line ponged at the sound of our breath. I could hear her trying to decide whether or not to believe me.

"Yes. Really. The congressional appointment changes everything."

"I still don't know what to say," she said.

"Have you talked to Hiram?"

"Yep."

"Roz?"

"No."

"It wasn't something new, Neese. We'd had a thing on and off for years."

She didn't say anything. The judgmental and expensive silence felt oppressive. "How could I do this to Roz?" I asked. "That's what you're thinking?"

"Sure. Other things, too, but that. It's so hostile. It's so mean."

"It's over. In fifteen years we'll shake our heads and grunt about it. Come on, Neese. I do exactly what I feel like without thinking, and you think about everything so much you don't do anything—bad, that is."

"You think," she said. "You think all the time. You knew what this could do to us."

Us hadn't really occurred to me. "Well, you know. I've always liked my freedom, is all."

"It's hard to be free."

When we hung up I squeezed my eyes shut like I used to when I was a kid and Daddy went back to Jamaica, and I didn't want to cry.

A vision of Eugenia came to me then, as if to distract me from crying and bring me back out of sorrow into something else.

My affair with Hiram began after my two-week visit to Eugenia and my brother Joe in San Francisco convinced me to stop fantasizing about Hiram and try to get him into bed. Joe hadn't come out at home. I'd never seen him with his friends. At twenty-five I'd been in school all my life, and never with people like these gay men. My own sexuality drove me nuts, but I didn't do much with it except date and screw, all conventional, straight-up stuff. For a while when I was sixteen, I'd had a crush on Audrey and made an awkward but delicious pass at her. She was soft and open, not shocked at all, a little drunk, matter-of-fact, with pinky-brown nipples and a purplish clit that she offered up good-naturedly in the shower. It was a friendly dalliance we kept up on the odd occasion, as it were, before she was married. Then she had her baby. Then they broke up. I thought we might take up where we'd left off, but her little drunks were becoming big drunks, and her anger at men became anger at sex. It's much easier to be Audrey's girlfriend than her lover, which may be true of me, too.

I fantasized constantly and masturbated like crazy, but it never occurred to me to find a lover whose libido matched my own, the hormonal equivalent of the woman in *The Godfather* with the giant vagina who finds the guy with the giant dick, and when they hook up the two of them are satisfied for the first time ever. It never occurred to me to take those disparate lessons and apply them to my own life.

Joe and Eugene and their friends made a world for themselves where sex was not hidden away, but evident, like the imprint of their penises in the fronts of their jeans. Big, hard, obvious. They kissed one another on the mouth, they rubbed one another's backs and shoulders in affection, and touched crotches and behinds in naughty insinuation. The sexuality that I'd fought so hard to keep underground—or at least underground enough to function—they enjoyed out in the open.

I returned from San Francisco bored with art history and my dissertation on twentieth-century bronze sculpture and went about seducing Hiram.

It didn't take much, of course. We'd been hot for each other as long as I could remember. Hiram plays his life with the brilliant aggressiveness of a chess master, but also the care. He took the risk of sex with me, but it was a calculated risk. He told me that Roz would always remain first in his life, and I told him so would my freedom. Our affair was supposed to stay secondary, even tertiary. Neither of us expected it to go on, like a little marriage on the side.

Hiram and I used to lie in this bed joking about politicians he knew who got into trouble over their sexual dalliances, men who had not managed to find partners as enthusiastic and simpatico as we were. Another man who mistook his dick for a brain, we'd say, and laugh.

So how was it that I ended up a forty-year-old woman who mistook her orgasm for a life? I began by *wanting* freedom. How had I lost it?

Arneatha always talks about the power of intent. I'd intended to stay free. But what had happened? Seduction is tricky. By definition.

Eugene in drag was a girly-girl parody when I first met him, a black Marilyn, all hair and eyes, breathy voice, padded hips, and plumped and padded breasts. I'd written about him as seducer, martyr, guide: the queen with the heart of gold; the vamp who taught me to vamp; the gal who'll stick his tongue up your husband's ass if you're too fastidious to do it yourself; the guy who's not afraid to be a gal, his/her own opposite; a friendly envoy from the world beyond, like a character in one of the recent queens-on-the-road movies helping us all to discover the little bit of faggot within. Clichés.

I didn't know what to do with his religious conversion at the funeral of a friend who died of AIDS or his sudden conviction that performance art was a trap, and that he was being engaged by the gatekeepers of the art world to parody himself. He'd become, he said, a modern version of Lerone Bennett's Negro Exhibit. He whomped up a one-person show about the life of Mahalia Jackson and revealed an amazingly Mahalia-like voice. He even did the play at St. A's when he came through Philadelphia. It had their mouths hanging open in the choir loft.

"But no church will truly embrace me," he said. "Pun intended."

He wouldn't stop loving sex and loving men.

"Queens know what niggers know, and black queens know it best of all," Eugene told me when I called him for an interview, years after my brother's death. "Swallow it," he'd said. "You've got to take it all in."

A month later they beat Eugenia to death outside a club in his hometown of Chicago.

Now he and my brother were gone, and I'd become, despite my pretentions to freewheeling sexual adventure, somebody's mistress.

"Swallow it down."

I thought of Piaf, the French sparrow, and the song she sings about a mistress making her man comfortable when he comes in. The song's lyrical self-abasement always made me vaguely queasy. Twat song, it sounded like. Crotch music. The punkinanny polka. I could say such things because I paid my own rent and received year-end statements of my TIAA-CREF pension fund.

I asked myself whether or not I wanted tenure. I did not. Was I lying to myself? No. Then why had I pursued it? What did I intend?

I asked myself questions out of habit, because that's what I've done for twenty years instead of taking my pulse.

I turned on the light, got out of bed, and lifted the manuscript from its box. I felt wooden, a reverse Pinocchio, a real-life boy turned to a puppet by the hearth. I kept thinking in order not to fall apart into a pile of splinters. I hated the book for its compromise. I hated Hiram and myself. Arneatha, too.

Once, when I was bitching and moaning about some dean or

other, Hiram asked me what I would really like to do with my life. I'd been mildly miffed. It was a point of pride with me that I was living the life I wanted. But later, after we made love, he asked again, and I told him that I wanted to bake elaborate cakes, have sex, live in a city, and write about it. He laughed, and I laughed, too, and ten more years passed.

The book was shit. Eugene deserved better.

When June came I moved to a small third-floor apartment back in south Philadelphia where I had to walk through the hallways of the first- and second-floor tenants to get to my place.

"Evening, Ms. Hendricks. How you doing?"

"Evening, Tamara. I can't complain. God is good."

Colored Community, capital C's, and everybody in your business, no privacy whatsoever. Had to masturbate standing up or else the person downstairs would hear you. I remembered why I'd felt so cooped up twenty years earlier, so desperate to leave.

Ah, Philadelphia, where the nineteenth century was just last week, where tiny houses on back streets hadn't gotten indoor plumbing until after the Second World War, and people in north Philly held good-bye parties for friends moving to Germantown, two miles and forty thousand dollars a year away. In the summertime black men wearing red bandannas drove slowly through the streets in ancient pickups loaded with New Jersey fruit and vegetables, just as the old guy with the horse-drawn cart did in our childhood in the sixties, singing "Red, ripe cherries! Watermelons!" And an eighty-year-old man on a bicycle delivered newspapers all year round—just as he did when we were girls.

My God, I'd returned to the provinces. The hallway of my new house, like the hallways in Stendhal's tenements, smelled like stewed cabbage, and the neighbors watched my every move with detached and not altogether friendly amusement.

Someone stole the battery out of my Karmann Ghia, and everyone in the house had a theory, which they talked about for hours, even when I was not there. I took the old car to Big Ben's Foreign Car Garage, where Bill Williams's friend in the wheelchair fitted it with a lock and chain under the hood and trunk.

"Glad to be home?"

I was in Roz's vestibule, in the south Philadelphia house they kept just eight blocks from my new apartment in order to maintain a residence among their constituents. *Oprah* was on in the background as if Roz kept a continuous loop of all her shows on the VCR. I had stopped by to return a pair of diamond earrings Nicki had put in my jewelry case for safekeeping, and then forgot, when we went to Orlando. I'd offered to send the earrings by Fed Ex, but Roz asked me to hold them, because they were special diamonds that she and Hiram had purchased—well, everything Roz purchases is special.

The Orlando trip seemed to have been a lifetime ago. I felt awkward with Roz. During the years Hiram and I slept together, I'd felt no discomfort in her presence and no guilt. I hoped that eventually I'd feel that way again, someday when our affair felt as far from me as, say, the Disney World trip, but that hadn't happened yet.

I was making excuses and backing out of the vestibule when Rozzie pulled me by the arm and whispered in my ear. Her perfume was sweet and heavy. Her mouth smelled of Juicy Fruit gum, which I know she chewed when her sour stomach gave her sour breath.

"Listen," she said. "Tell me whatcha think. I left my pistol in the trunk of that car Audrey borrows from Buddha—don't ask me how—last month, and it is driving me crazy to have it there."

"Why don't you get it? You know between Audrey and Buddha, it could take a long time to get back to you."

"Well, that's what I know, and every time I try to get her to go with me, something else comes up."

"Go yourself."

"I'm not going' up with those crazy country Negroes by myself. They got dog packs loose in the hills, and nothing's marked. You go the wrong place, those fools come out and shoot you. Remember that time the man shot at Audrey's car?"

"You want company?"

"Well, see, now I can't go, because Buddha and Mimi have loaded up that old RV and gone to some lake they go to. Must be really cheap."

"Where's the car?"

"Audrey said he locked it in his garage with the other two or three that don't half work. He locks up every summer, she says."

"So don't worry about it." We were still whispering.

Hiram opened the front door in a rush. He banged into me and then her. His tall frame overwhelmed us in the narrow entryway. The outside air still clung to his skin.

"You smell like the street," my mother used to say to us when we came in from playing. That's how he smelled, and as familiar as my own childhood.

Forced into a narrow line by the architecture of the house, Hiram and Roz and I moved single file through the narrow entry to the living room.

"Glad to be home?" Hiram asked me, just as Roz had asked.

He kissed her lightly on the mouth as I had seen him kiss her five hundred times. I stared at his lips and her face, the planes of light on their cheeks and noses. I used to get up on the kitchen counter and squat so that he could get a faceful at eye level. His mustache would be going every which way. Now we stood around like Lucy and Desi and Ethel.

Hiram flashed the friendliest of old-friend smiles and pecked me on the cheek. "Rozzie told me you hired Bryant and his friends to come up in a U-Haul and move you. How was it?"

I laughed. " 'How was it?' you ask."

"Yeah," he said. "How was it?"

"Fine."

"Good," he said. "How's your new place?"

"Affordable."

This time Hiram laughed and ducked into the kitchen.

"Look," Roz called in to him, "I got vegetables cut up in some of those Ziploc bags, and there's fruit in the bowl, and some bread up above, and ham and cheese in the meat drawer."

Hiram emerged carrying a box of Triscuits, a hunk of lunch meat, and a bottle of imported nonalcoholic beer that I introduced him to since he's been trying this last year to keep off weight.

"I'll be upstairs making phone calls," he said to Roz. Then to me he said, "Pop your head in before you leave, will you?"

Roz insisted on showing me her new clothes and shoes. We spent forty minutes in the middle room on the second floor, which she had turned into a walk-in closet and vanity. She told me about the new bargain stores that had opened downtown where you could get surprising finds. And she wanted me to come to Hangers, her favorite discount designer shop on Rittenhouse Square.

"We can walk up there and help me work down some of these hips. I am so glad you're home," she said. "But listen, can't we just drive to Coatesville and see if one of the sons can't open the garage for me? I'd feel better."

"Oh, Roz, let it alone. If you go up there and get the sons worked up, they're likely to do nothing for you, and then get curious later. Suppose we leave, and two weeks from now, they're breaking off the lock to see what the fuss was about. Then you'd have a problem."

She folded her arms and pursed her lips.

"I just worry about things. I can't help it."

When I told her I'd have to go, she reminded me that Hiram wanted a word with me.

"What's he doing up there?" I asked.

"Fund-raising calls. Rome must've given him fifty new names."

I waved my hand at Roz.

"Just tell him I said good-bye."

"He asked you to pop in, Tam. You know Hiram don't say anything he doesn't mean."

"He's not the Lord God, Rozzie."

"You're the only one of our friends who hasn't just, like, jumped down our throats for changing parties. That means a lot to both of us," she said.

I climbed the little steep staircase to his office on the third floor. I felt like I'd done nothing since I got to Philadelphia but mount flight after flight of narrow steps, all with brown deck paint and white risers. Roz went downstairs, past Nicki's room, where the door was closed and the music playing.

I stood in the hallway while Hiram finished a phone conversation.

"Absolutely," he said. "Well, I'll tell you the truth. If it's for education for kids in the city, I'm going to vote for it. I know that's not what you want to hear, but better you hear it now than later. . . . Right. . . . Well, I tell you, I know something about those kids you're talking about, and it's either pay now or pay later. . . . I just want us to be straight from the beginning. . . . Sure. I can see where you're coming from. And thanks. Thanks very much. . . . Right. We'll talk again."

Then I opened the door. He looked up at me. I had myself battened down now. "Doesn't sound like you're going to get much from him."

"Son of a bitch builds prisons. What does he care whether kids graduate high school?"

"Really? Is that what he really does?"

"Yep. There are a lot of decent people in the Republican party," Hiram said, "but that wasn't one of them."

"What do you want?"

"I want to know were you talking to Nicki?" he asked.

"Why would you ask me that? I do have my own admittedly twisted code of ethics. And talking to the kid is definitely out."

"She's been at me since you guys got back from Orlando."

"Saying what?"

"General questions. Nothing specific."

"No, I wouldn't say anything to her. You know that." I felt weary. And weary, too, of Hiram.

"Yeah." He said it without conviction. He was a candidate again. Everything proceeded from that one fact.

"Why'd you move back?" he asked.

"It's cheap."

I walked out of the house with a sense of dread. For a few moments I stood on the stoop trying to determine whether or not to go back inside and tell Roz, just Roz, about Hiram and me, and to tell her that it was over. It would have been a relief, but I wasn't sure what else it might do. I was on new ground.

Back in my building, I had the standard conversation—"Evening." "Good evening." "How you doin'?" "Fine, thanks. How 'bout you?" "Oh, can't complain."

Just as I got to my door, I heard Mr. Hendricks, the first-floor tenant, calling my name. "You got a package down here," he said. "I had it leaned up against the steps where I thought you'd see it, but you walked right by."

I went downstairs and took the box from him.

"My wife and I, we said, 'Put it there, no way she can miss it,' but you did." He chuckled to himself and chattered on.

"Your mother stopped in. Very nice-looking lady. Very, oh . . . very well-spoken and all."

She'd probably swept through with Madame Walker and her still slightly British accent and her air of impatience and blown them all away.

"Carrying a little dog under her arm, too," he said. "Funniest thing. I guess she doesn't live around here, huh?"

"No." I didn't tell him that she would have gone to most any lengths to keep from having to exchange her apartment house in Bryn Mawr for a cabbage-scented south Philadelphia walk-up.

I took the box up to my apartment and opened it. It was a small white loose-leaf binder with a black, gold, and red design made from long, thin, Dahomey-style masks making a frame around the words *I SHOULD KNOW THAT!* and underneath *Classic*

Black Art, Literature and Culture done in simple lettering. Inside were dividers with category names such as Africa, the Caribbean, U.S.A., Latin America. The pages were punched with three holes to fit. It looked almost exactly like the recipe book Mum's church had published the year before. The note she'd stuffed in the box explained that she thought we could make money in the future by selling new pages as I saw fit to include them. Why just sell them to her friends? she wrote. Why not sell them to everybody who came to the bookstall?

It was perfect: black cultural self-improvement, as earnest as fifties housewives studying the *Better Homes and Gardens* cookbook for table settings and appetizers. My mother the immigrant had picked up the essential American desire to better oneself and married it to the new black consciousness and so-called pride. Some of it was pride, surely, some compensation, some bravado, some bald chauvinism and curiosity and enjoyment. No doubt well-intentioned men in dashikis would give us solemn lectures at Odunde about our laudable Afrocentricity, although the most Afrocentric thing about it all was probably my mother's business sense.

I reminded myself to keep a computer list of all buyers so they could be compiled into a mailing list for later subject issues—if the silly damn books made any money. Truth was, though, that I already wanted to do a blues section and a section on the Middle Passage, and an inexpensive but attractive pack of empty pages where we'd encourage people to write down their own stories and jingles. I wrote down one that my great-grandmother used to say:

> *Down to the market, sticky fish*
> *If you want some, bring your dish.*
> *One for a nickel, two for a dime,*
> *Johnny got a haircut just like mine.*

Then I paired it with one the girls outside the stoop were saying, that very moment, as they jumped double Dutch and simultaneously played a game of guessing the color–number of fake hair braided into their natural plaits. "I'll bet you Dionne wear a number four. Her hair lighter than you think. Stop turnin' all 'flicted. Jump:

> "Big Mac, Fillet of Fish,
> Quarter-Pounder, french fries,
> Ice-cold milkshake,
> foot-foot-foot-foot
> Hop-hop-hop-hop
> Walk-walk-walk-walk
> Criss-criss-criss-criss."

Fish sold at the market and at Micky D's spoke to each other from opposite ends of the twentieth century, and I was going to try to sell laminated cards about it, next to cards about Richard Wright, voodoo, Xhosa, Gustavus Vassa, Marcus Garvey, Lena Horne, and "Amos 'n Andy." It was a low-brow, bourgeois, ridiculous thing to attempt, and utterly American. No wonder nobody would give me tenure. They saw that fold-out card table and vending cart underneath my briefcase.

> Criminal-minded, you been blinded
> Looking for shoes like mine, can't find it.
> Mine's cost more; yours cost less;
> Mine's Foot Locker and yours Payless.

I should have pulled out years ago, before I gave them a chance to deny me. So I could have said I quit before they could say you're fired. So I could have said: "Good-bye now. Kiss my black ass."

It loses its punch after the fact.

I found myself sighing, taking more notes and sighing again.

After I ate dinner, but before I convinced myself to go for a run through the mean streets, the telephone rang. It was Jasmine from Old City Nautilus and Spa letting me know that Billy Williams wanted to welcome me back to Philadelphia with a special six-month complimentary membership.

"Thanks, Jasmine," I said. "Please tell him I accept with pleasure."

11

Arneatha was due back on the first Saturday in June, but her plane out of Entebbe made her miss her connecting flights from Nairobi to London, and from London to Philly. She called Roz from London and left a message saying that it was important that her father come to the airport, and would Roz see to it because he wasn't home when she called and didn't have an answering service. Audrey and I couldn't make it. Audrey had to work a double shift—she pulled doubles constantly now, although what she did with the money none of us could tell—and I'd promised my mother I'd work Lila's bookstall with her at Odunde.

At eight-thirty, or half eight, as my mother still says, we drove to Lila's house. Mum had instructions to open the garage door with a key she'd been given, and then drive away the minivan that was parked in the garage and loaded with inventory. We transferred our needments to the minivan's front seat—the other seats had been removed to make room for books—and parked my car in the garage.

Mum had brought Madame Walker, of course; a shallow tub for her to lie in, in about an inch of water, in case the weather got too hot, and her airplane carrying crate in case of a crush; biscuits for Madame; nail polish; spring water; folding rockers; a six-by-nine red-and-black fake Persian rug; and a cellular phone.

As we drove off, Mum wondered aloud what she'd forgotten,

and came up with a short list fast. I kept driving. I did not intend to stop at her house for a pocket knife or binoculars or her own contemporary novels to sell from a secondhand bushel basket or a box of fifty bookmarks she'd bought the year before from the Christmas bazaar at Arneatha's school. She wanted to sell those bookmarks.

Mum made faces and poofed the hair on top of Madame's head with her fingers. "I meant to send them out with my cards last year, but the puppies were born the twelfth of December, and I couldn't send out one card. What am I ever going to do with them?"

"Give 'em to Lila."

"Look, I'm already giving her my labor."

"Give 'em as a promotion with *I Should Know That!*"

"Maybe I'll hold on to them for this Christmas."

An officious little policewoman would not let us drive onto South Street to unload. My mother saw other vendors' cars beyond the barricade and argued. How were we supposed to unload books? she wanted to know.

"These are heavy books here. Not everyone is selling T-shirts and stinking snake oil," she yelled.

Bill Williams, the Black Narcissus himself, came up behind her and waved at us. He was still wearing his long, black hair in a ponytail. In addition, he'd taken up the current fashion of sporting a two-day stubble, another of my least favorite male styles, although he pulled it off better than most.

The policewoman was not immune to his charms. After they chatted amiably, she pulled back the barricade.

"You got half an hour," she said to us.

"They're worse than the men," my mother muttered.

"I guess she's just bein', like, super-careful, know what I mean?" Bill said.

I hadn't seen Bill Williams in the glorious, sculpted flesh since he'd given me the free membership to his gym. I worked out first thing in the morning, and he came in in the afternoon and stayed until closing. Unless one of us radically altered our schedule, we would not meet. We didn't meet. But every day he left me notes scrawled in big, open hand-writing on pink telephone message paper, always the same breezy and shallow cheerfulness as if life were a new ab ma-chine: "Have a great workout!" "Try the Skywalker, you'll love it!" "We can't keep meeting like this!"

Through the glass window he'd installed at the back of the gym, I saw the space painted in yellow where he parked his motorcycle. I half expected that eventually he would show up one morning with some task at the gym as an excuse. He never did.

My mother insisted we roll out the rug under the table before we set up the portable shelves and the books. As soon as it was laid, Madame Walker jumped on it from the driver's seat, scram-bling to keep her polished paws off the asphalt. Bill threw his head back and laughed.

"So, Mrs. Burke, I see you're, like, seriously into this little dog you got here."

"She raises them," I said.

"Oh, wow. All I got is fish. I bet fish don't do nothin' for you."

"I love fish," my mother said. "They're beautiful, except I can't raise them. We had a tank for Tam, and the thing turned like a pond. The what-you-call—algae—took over and the water evaporated, and the goldfish was swimmin' around in four inches of green-black water, and all you could see now and then, like every two or three weeks, was the flick of a gold fin, and then . . . not'ing."

He laughed again, that heartfelt belly laugh, and I liked him better for it. Mom giggled like a girl.

"So, you gonna help us unload or what?"

"Wha' you say, cut the small talk? I gotcha. I hear you. I'm a businessman. Time is money, ain't that right?"

He helped me unload the book cartons in our allotted half

hour, telling my mother what she should have done with her tank. Philadelphia water is too alkaline, he said, which promotes algae growth. If she started a new tank, she should get drops to make it more acid. And a filter. And no goldfish: too dirty. We finished, him keeping up a steady riff on the damn fish tank, and parted company.

Then I drove eight blocks to park in front of my building, where Mr. and Mrs. Hendricks were already seated in their folding chairs to watch the festival preparations from a distance. They quizzed me on the minivan, then vowed to protect it.

"Got a Club? Good. You go ahead and put the Club on and lock the doors and leave it," Mr. Hendricks told me. "I'll set right here and watch it all day. Got my tea, got my cigarettes, got my chair, got my cut buddy here—" Mrs. Hendricks laughed. "Don't you worry about a thing."

He wanted to know what was in it, and how long I'd be. He checked to see that I had indeed locked the doors as I said, and then told me I should get back to Odunde before the vendors from New York took all the best stalls. I told him I had a stall, and my mother was holding it. He said that that didn't matter, because the West Indians would push her out.

"And cuff or cut you, one or the other, if you say anything to 'em."

"My mother's a West Indian herself."

"Well, you put your foot in it now," said Mrs. Hendricks.

"Oh, excuse me, doll, I forgot. Don't matter anyway," he said. "The rough ones, they don't care. They'll knock over their own mothers. Jamaicans, especially. She not Jamaican, is she?"

Mrs. Hendricks elbowed him.

"I don't mean to give no offense, honey. She know that. You know that, don't you? I'm just telling you what I seen. This my experience. These ain't no tales outta school.

"Here," he said, " 'fore you go, lemme hold the keys in case I need to move it for some reason. You never know."

I could not keep these people out of my business. I handed him the keys, knowing he'd pop his head in for a little look-see in an hour, and that later we'd have to have a discussion about the various features of the Dodge Caravan and the Plymouth Voyager, and the SE and the LE and the Grand and whatever other models exist in the known universe.

By the time I got back to South Street, Mum and Bill had charmed each other senseless. Bill had brought us a Little Play-mate full of ice and a large *kinte*-cloth umbrella stuck in a bucket of sand. Mum had convinced him to buy a beaded bracelet from the woman next to her and a copy of *I Should Know That!*

"I'm looking forward to this," he said.

I smiled and shrugged. On Twenty-third Street the New York food vendors had lit fires under eight five-gallon woks. The smell of frying onions drifted down to us.

"Tell her, Mrs. Burke. I can read. She'll believe it if you tell her."

My mother laughed; he threw me a kiss and went back down the street to his stall. I could just see the portable backdrop to which one Spandex-wearing assistant was attaching photos, blown up to poster size, of people working out at his gym. Jasmine was piling carrots and oranges into huge baskets behind a juicer.

"Well," said Mum, fanning herself with her hand. "What else you could possibly want, I don't know. He rode down to Wash-ington, he told me, for Memorial Day. He went to Edison, you know."

Thomas A. Edison High School has the distinction of having lost more graduates in the Vietnam War than any other high school in America.

"I wonder why he didn't go to Vietnam?" I was slightly non-plussed to realize how little I knew about Bill. We had had only five dates in as many years—not even dates, really, since Roz had set him up as my escort to Hiram's political events. No doubt, I'd been so busy doing an imitation of life as the nonadulterous girlfriend that I'd almost completely ignored the big guy in the tux next to me. Mostly I'd noticed that he didn't talk much, and when he did, he used a glib patois of jock talk and happy-face clichés. Who thought to talk about war and peace to a muscle-bound mook with a ponytail?

"He got a football scholarship to Grambling and tore up his knees," said Mum. "He's had twelve operations on them over the years."

"You just found out everything there was to know, didn't you? So now he feels guilty that all his buddies died and he didn't."

"He says he went to the dedication of the memorial and that he's gone every Memorial Day since. Interesting man. He's really quite cautious with women, I gather. More than meets the eye." She laughed at her own joke.

"I don't know, Mum. It's too predictable. Besides, I'm taking some time off. Without going into sordid details, let's say this is a period of reflection and celibacy for me."

"Oh, well, Tamara Burke, it's a little late for *that,* isn't it? I mean, whatever's left, no need to start saving it up now."

"Mummy, I do not live in a man-centered universe."

"Sure you do. We all do."

A local black entertainment show host instructed her cameraman to take shots of the women cooking collard greens over open flames, and a man turning Flintstone-size racks of ribs on an oil-drum barbecue. When she walked by, she picked up our reader's copy of *I Should Know That!* and thumbed through it.

"You don't remember me, do you?"

"You look familiar." It wasn't quite a lie. I thought I remembered her mix-and-match figure—saddlebag hips and puffy legs underneath a tiny torso, a funny body built on purpose to sit behind a TV anchor desk. I'd been watching as she sashayed up and down the street, waiting to be recognized. Green contact lenses gave her eyes the look of the living dead, hard and flat.

"I remember *you*," she said.

I couldn't be bothered to play games. I didn't answer.

"I went to Girls' High with you. You were a couple years ahead of me. This is your book, isn't it?"

She was signifying that she was still in her thirties.

"Yes."

"Well, I could use something like this to have as an easy reference at the studio. Do you have an agent? Could you have your PR people send one over?"

I was about to say something rude, when Mum piped up. "I'm the PR. I'm the mother. And since you're an old friend, and you're in the media, here, you take a copy. Just take it with you. Read it in the car."

Mummy handed her a book, and she walked away.

"She may have you on her show," my mother said. "This is the thing I've got to do. I've got to get a list of people like her and make up an announcement and send them out. Hand me that pad."

Mum found a Yellow Pages and worked on her publicity list, and I sold thirty books by noon. It was hot, and organizers were reading the opening ceremony. Yoruba elders and priests were ushered to the front of the parade. Many were dressed in white. One woman wore bright yellow, the color of Oshun, the guiding spirit, a man told me, of the river. And because Oshun loves sweets, four men carried a litter heaped with fruits, cakes, and honey to throw as an offering into the Schuylkill River, where, in the seventeenth century, Africans were brought in boats to be sold at the South Street auction. The stiltwalkers did not come that year, and the children were disappointed. But the organizers were happy to see two dozen Latinos take their place in the parade behind the Yoruba elders, carrying a SANTERIA banner.

The drums began, and we walked and danced the seven blocks to the bridge, where the priestess in yellow said words I could not understand, and then, at a signal, the sweets went into the water. A woman handed me an orange so that I'd have something to throw, too.

A man sitting on the wall of the bridge told those of us standing below him that the city made arrangements to drag the river a ways downstream to collect the fruit for the zoo. I found myself staring at him to see whether he seemed credible. Odunde brings out fascinating people. Afrocentric autodidacts, history buffs, kooks. You had to listen carefully to figure out who was who.

"You don't believe me, do you?" he asked. "Lot of things about Odunde people don't know."

He said that he and his buddies had been coming since the early days when no more than a few dozen people made the trek to the river. "Now it's about makin' a buck," he said, watching the fruit bob on the brown surface of the water. "After this ceremony here, we go home now."

I met up with a woman from my street in the crowd walking back. She told me that there was a big commotion at my building. I peeled off and jogged home. A crowd of people had gathered on the sidewalk and the steps. I heard choked cries from the open first-floor window.

"What happened?" I asked.

"Their grandson in L.A. was shot last night. Robbed 'im and shot 'im and left 'im in the street."

"Toussaint?" I asked.

"The one in Los Angeles."

Toussaint had wanted to act. An eight-by-ten glossy of him sat on the mantel. *To Pop-pop and Mom-mom,* it said, *with love and thanks for all your support. It's all going to pay off! I swear! Love, T.*

He had matinee looks. He'd worked as an extra a few times, and recently had scored a part with lines. The Hendrickses had shown me the postcard with two inane lines of dialogue written on it, underlined twice.

From what I could gather, neighbors had broken up the couple. The women had Mrs. Hendricks lying down in the back bedroom; the men had Mr. Hendricks in the parlor. I milled on the sidewalk until I could no longer stand the comments: "It's always the good ones who are taken from us"; "We're doing the white man's work for him by killing each other"; "None of these people deserve this"; "Keep this up, we won't have *no* men left at all."

I found our second-floor neighbor, an arthritic single woman in early retirement, and told her that I was going back to the stall, where I'd left my mother.

"Let 'em know I was by, will you?" I said. "I'll be home later tonight if they need anything."

I had gone about two blocks when a boy came running after me, calling my name. "Mr. Hendricks say here's your keys, and he say thanks for comin' round."

"Thanks. Tell him I'll check in with them tonight, before I go up, to see if they need anything."

A stupid phrase that I found myself repeating.

Half a block from our stall, I stopped to look at some packs of five pen-and-ink print cards. The one on top was of an old person's hand clasping a child's, sentimental but drawn with close attention to proportion. I bought a pack of cards so I'd have something in which to put a piece of money to give to them that evening.

"Where have you *been?*" Mum asked.

"Don't ask," I said. "I stopped by the house. My neighbors just found out that their grandson in California was shot."

"It's everywhere," she said. "You can't get away from it. Where can you go? For years I threatened to hightail it back to Jamaica, but they got it there now, too. Crack and *Baywatch.*"

Except for perfunctory conversation with customers, we didn't talk much. By midafternoon we grew weary and hot, exhausted by the parade of people and the interactions. Mum poured an inch of water into the shallow pan she'd brought for Madame Walker, slid the pan into the airline crate, and laid the grateful dog in the makeshift bath, where she could get relief from the humans and the heat rising off the asphalt.

"Now," Mum said, "I'd appreciate your filling my pan and

putting me into my crate, too. What? Left it home? Well, pass me the damn ice water if that's all you got."

Then, out of the crowd, Roz appeared on Bill Williams's arm, and behind them, carrying a baby, Audrey, still in her nurse's uniform. Bill pointed toward us, and Roz waved and tried to shout over the hum of the crowd and the reggae band. I couldn't hear her. She gestured toward the child. Audrey held the baby aloft and grinned.

"Whose baby is that?" Mum asked.

I shrugged.

Bill saluted me, as if he were handing them off, turned around, and plunged back into the human river flowing back toward his table.

"And why would they drag 'im out in this crush?" Mum asked.

As if in answer, Roz said, when she got to within eight feet of us: "Jesus, girl, if I'da known there'd be a million people out here, I would've stayed home."

"I told her," Audrey said.

"All I wanted to do was show you this baby."

"Whose baby is it? And why do I have to see it?" I've never been gaga over infants and children. And what was Audrey doing home from work?

"I thought you had a double shift."

"Fuck it." Audrey mouthed the words behind my mother's back.

"She came to the airport with me and Mr. Frank to pick up Arneatha," Roz said. "And this here little baby came off the plane with her. Can you believe that?"

I looked at Audrey for an explanation. Roz could keep us there guessing all day.

"Neesie says that somebody, some woman, pushed up against her at the airport in Uganda," Audrey said, "and pressed the baby, all swaddled in blankets, into her belly."

"Neese said she put her hands up in a kind of reflex," Roz said, "like you would grab at something so it won't fall—"

"And the minute she did, the woman just looked right into her eyes and darted away through the crowd."

"Oh, my God!" my mother said. "Oh, my God. And this is the baby!" She reached for the child. "And why do you have 'im out here in the 'ot sun and the crowd?"

"Good question, Mrs. Burke. 'Cause I'm a fool. 'Cause Arneatha told me to take him for a walk, and stroll him around Odunde, and I, who've raised three children and ought to know better, I listened to her. She was wearing her collar, Mrs. Burke. That's my only excuse for following like a sheep. But look at him," Roz said. "He's gorgeous. Just gorgeous. Great big old eyes. Kissy little mouth."

Audrey handed him to my mother over the table.

"She should've had children, Arneatha should," my mother said, taking the baby. "You women wait so late—well, you two didn't," she said, indicating Roz and Audrey.

"Where the hell is Arneatha?" I asked.

"Passed out at my house," said Roz. "You know the planes were impossible. Well, *we* knew that. But, then, with the baby, she couldn't hardly sleep once she got on, even."

"Didn't the baby need papers or something?" I asked. In an age of metal detectors and visas, it seemed incredible that a tiny human being could pass unrecorded from one continent to another.

"Apparently not," Roz said. "Neesie tells us that if they're younger than one, they don't need a passport or anything."

"Is he well?"

"Far as you can tell without blood tests," Audrey said. "You know what Rozzie did? She drove right from the airport to Ardmore, where this doctor lives, and then she knocks on the door, and makes the woman get up from her breakfast table and check the baby out."

Roz flicked her wrist dismissively. "All Hiram's done for that family, she better get up."

"How old is he?" I asked.

"Look like four to five months to me," my mother said.

"That's what I thought, too," said Audrey. "Doctor said he may be a little older, but just small."

"He is alert, though." Mum was already a partisan. "Very alert. Not slow or sluggish."

"This is going to change Neesie's life," I said. She had begun to rise through the church's hierarchy. She was head of the deanery—the *Very* Rev. Then there was her fledgling love life with Kofi, which could probably be nice if she stopped keeping her sexuality chained in the dungeon.

Roz rubbed her thumb against the bottom of the baby's bare foot. "Makes you want to do it again, doesn't it?" she asked wistfully.

"No," said Audrey. "Although when my case comes through, I'll have enough money to have all the children come over and hire a baby-sitter to watch them for me like this family I used to work for."

"Oh, very grand," said Mum. "That's the way to do it."

I rolled my eyes. She's been suing the city for years.

A trim, sixtyish man in a crocheted skullcap picked up our reader's copy of *I Should Know That!* Mum balanced the baby with one arm and pushed a stack of fresh copies toward him.

"That's for you to look through," she said, "but if you want to buy a copy, you take one of these. See? The pages are in plastic, so they'll stay clean till when you get home."

"I saw a woman up there reading one," he motioned toward the east with his chin, "and she said it was good, so I asked her where she got it. How much you want for it?"

"Fifteen dollars," Mum said.

"I was hoping it'd be more like five or ten."

"Now, you know," Mummy said, "that you spend fifteen dollars on the lottery in a month."

He made his mouth into a line and looked at her. Then he looked at us. He pulled his lips in and slowly pushed them out again. "Why she gotta say that?" he asked.

We smiled. The baby began to wail.

"My daughter wrote that book."

"Uh-oh. The daughter wrote it. Well, I guess I'm lucky it's not twenty-five dollars, then."

"It's wonderful. You already spent fifteen dollars here today on some of that barbecue over there."

"How you know?"

"I saw you."

"All these thousands of people, how you see me eatin' barbecue?"

" 'Cause I watched you pickin' out which ribs you wanted him to give you."

Our customer looked flattered that she'd noticed. He started to say something else, but Mum talked over him.

"And what do you get when you finish with that stuff? Huh? Greasy mouf and belly aching."

The South African woman in the stall next to us laughed and nodded her head. "Hey, fellow," she said, "buy this book, man, so when you go home you have something worthwhile to show for your day. Don't go home with—what she say?—greasy mouth and belly aching."

"Oh, Lord," the man shouted, "they're ganging up on me."

The baby cried loudly.

"Now you scared the baby."

"He's fine as long as you're walking," Audrey said. My mother had been standing still during the exchange. "That's how we got started over this way."

My mother began to walk back and forth, three steps each way behind our table. A busty woman in her thirties wearing a leopard-skin blouse and black shorts picked up one copy of *Blacks in the Bible,* three *Color Purples,* two collections of J. California Cooper short stories, one hardbound *Beloved,* some Ezra Jack Keats kids' books, two *Black Boys,* and three *Waiting to Exhales.*

"Nothin' like reading," she said.

I agreed with her and made change. Audrey had gotten down on all fours to play with Madame Walker through the door of her crate.

"You know," she called up to my mother, "if this was any other poodle, she'd be a nervous wreck."

"Yeah," said Mum. "Madame's always been unflappable."

"Whatcha got down there, a dog?" the woman said.

"Uh-huh," I answered.

She bent down under the table with Audrey. I heard Audrey convincing her that she ought to buy a copy of my book and telling her about my mother's dogs.

"I can't get over Arneatha coming home with a *baby,*" Roz said. "Can you imagine, somebody just handing her a baby like that? It's unbelievable."

"But Arneatha's the one," Audrey called from under the table. "If there's a whole airport full of people, who else would you choose?"

"Plus, I take it she was wearing her collar," said Roz.

I offered the customer one of Mum's used shopping bags, a pink one with a black parasol and glove silhouette from Blum's, a store that closed here in Philadelphia more than twenty years ago. Instead, the woman put her books into a big new red, black, and green leather shoulder bag and again bent down next to Audrey.

"Oh, I love these little dogs," she called up from under the table. "Is the dog for sale, too?"

"No, dear, not that one," Mummy said, "but I raise them, if you're interested." She turned to our reluctant customer.

"Look at this young woman, bought a dozen and a half books, and you're still debating that one. Don't buy it. Don't. I'm particular about who reads it, and I'm starting to take a dislike to your book-buying habits."

"Guess I'ma have to buy this damn book," he said dryly.

"No. You stand right there and commit the whole darn thing to memory."

They were flirting. Mum handed the baby back to Roz. When he began to cry, Roz rocked him energetically, just like she used to rock Junior and Nicki. I hadn't seen her make that movement in years. Suddenly I could feel the years drop away and pile up again all at once. Roz was becoming a grandmother and Arneatha a mother; Audrey was sober; I was truly single for the first time in years.

"How much that little dog cost? Two or three hundred dollars?" The woman crawled out from under the table and stood up.

My mother raised her eyebrow. The gentleman opened his wallet and began to finger through his bills. Mum turned from him—he'd be there a while longer, either because he hated to part with his money, or from his banter with my mother, and we didn't know which yet—and toward the woman. That she knew and was not appalled at the ballpark price for a pedigree was a good sign.

"Yes, more like three hundred, but that includes papers and shots and everything. I'd take her out of the crate for you to hold," Mum said, "but I've got her laying in water to try to keep 'er cool in all this heat."

The woman asked: "You carry her around in a basket when you go out? She rides in the car, no problem?"

"Oh, sure," Mum said. "I take her everywhere with me. Restaurants. Stores. I take her food shopping. Ask my daughter."

I nodded.

"Oh, she's Old Faithful. Whatever you train a dog to do, she'll do."

"You give me your card," the woman said decisively, "and I'ma call you. Last year this time I got divorced. I started this little book group, and I'm going to church again, and I'm walking in the morning. . . . Here, pass me that pen. I'm gonna write my name and number for you, too."

Roz and Audrey and I turned to look at her. She was proud of herself and it sounded as if she had good reason to be.

"You just got yourself together," Roz said appreciatively.

Having waited to break into the female self-congratulation

exchange, our gentleman customer pulled out the oldest-looking twenty-dollar bill we'd seen all day. "I can't get a word in edge-wise."

Later we figured it must have been at precisely that minute that two impatient young women half a block away—cousins or friends, according to different accounts—tried to push through the crowd with crying babies in strollers. Someone ran over someone. Someone pushed, got shoved, pushed back.

"Watch where you goin'."

"No, you don't step on my son's motherfucking stroller."

That's what people nearby say they heard. That's what they told reporters, and what, in censored form, appeared in the newspapers.

All we heard was a pop.

Pop.

It's funny how the gun sounded: small, faraway, too close, unreal.

Pop-pop-pop.

The sound threw panic into individual bodies and the crowd. We fell down, onto and into each other: the busty divorcée, the gentleman customer with his twenty-dollar bill in his hand, Roz holding the baby, Audrey, Mummy, me, the African woman at the next table.

"Oh, my God."

"Jesus."

The dog's crate turned over. Madame Walker scratched and whimpered. The water spilled out and onto the ground, wetting our knees and feet and the fake Persian rug.

We crouched down and leaned in against the building. The crowd pressed against us. I stuck out my elbows to keep my mother from being crushed. Roz turned to squeeze under me, too, so that both our bodies would shield the baby. I understood what she was doing and made room. My mother pointed to the dog, and Audrey tipped the crate right-side up. I could feel the vendor from the next table trembling against my arm. For a long, quiet time nothing happened. We wondered whether it was over, or whether someone else would pull out another gun and answer the first reports or start a new fracas.

Then men ran by, hands full of radio supplies: a boom box, packs of unopened audiotapes. Had they shot a gun in order to steal, or had they been so ready to exploit any situation that they looted the moment the gun popped?

"You all right?" the South African vendor asked Mum. "Baby all right?"

"Fine," Mum said.

"Shit," said the woman who wanted to buy a dog. "Always gotta ruin something."

Still holding his twenty dollars, our gentleman customer replied: "Ain't it the truth? Try to have somethin' nice, and niggers gotta fuck it up."

People passed information along in certain tones. No one was hurt. Someone had been killed, a couple people. It had only been firecrackers, a stunt, and shame on the kids for doing it in a crowd. All wrong, it turned out.

Audrey put her arms around both of us. She was shaking. Mum gave her a glass of ice water and made her sit down. Mum clucked about this and that, but none of us spoke until Roz said: "Those weren't any firecrackers."

We heard ambulances and cop cars. As it happened, two people were injured, but no one died.

Audrey's shoulders went up and down as she gulped mouthfuls of air. I was standing behind her. My mother had been keeping her from smoking a cigarette, saying her body needed air, but then she gave in. Audrey lit up, closed her eyes, and her head lay back against my hip.

Roz shifted under the weight of the baby, so I held him for her. He fussed, but did not cry outright. On top of his head, where his skull had not yet grown together, his skin sank in. I watched his pulse beat right there in the top of his crown.

"What'd it do, just trigger something, Audrey?" Roz asked, kneeling in front of her.

Eyes closed, Audrey nodded.

I promised myself to remember to slip the card under the Hendrickses' door whenever I got home.

Bill Williams came to within hailing distance. "All right?"

Mum and I waved back to him, and he nodded.

Fragile. Everything felt so fragile.

12

From what I can piece together, Arneatha thought Roz already knew about me when she told her on the night of Odunde. I heard soon after. I gather that Roz was congratulating herself because she'd shifted the balance of power in her marriage, and that Arneatha went one better by congratulating her on keeping the focus on her marriage and not on me. Something like that. Neesie has a big mouth, but then, you can't blame her, really. Duplicity isn't her strong suit.

Rozzie went berserk. But, of course. Arneatha was reluctant to give details, but she allowed as there was screaming and crying, plus knocked-around furniture: the works. Histrionics, Hiram would say. Bet brotherman-candidate got some sho nuff histrionics his own self. Arneatha said that Roz claimed to be glad her gun was locked in Coatesville, because she'd be tempted to use it if it were right in her file drawer. Why do people always hide guns in file drawers?

I had a few hours' suppressed panic recalling the gun that they keep at the bar and her recent well-publicized relationship with firearms. I kept telling myself that Rozzie would not drive to the bar, get a gun in sight of every alkie on Christian Street, and then come around the corner and shoot me dead. Or blind—I saw myself opening the door downstairs and her manicured index finger pulling the trigger and splattering my face onto the striped green wallpaper. Or lame? And who has said the word *lame* seriously since the Salk vaccine?

I hadn't expected it to be this bad. In fact, after going undetected for so many years, I really thought we'd get away undetected.

Nope. Not this time, not this adulterous affair, not this little black fuck.

"Omigod! The bitch slept with her girlfriend's husband!"

Although I knew that such a view of things could exist, from the moral center of the universe, I'd never, shall we say, fleshed it out. The affair had seemed, for all those years, to have nothing to do with Roz. I figured we'd do what we did, and, because of respect for Roz's delicate feelings, we'd leave her out of it.

I hadn't expected the fear, really. The evening Arneatha called and told me, I stayed up half the night just emptying my bowels. Clichés do fit the crises of our lives: this business—just knowing she knew—did indeed scare the shit out of me. My stomach fluttered. I couldn't eat. I couldn't sleep.

Then came another nasty surprise: remorse. I recollected the pleasures of the preceding years in the quiet of my apartment—if not in tranquillity, per se—and I saw clearly that I could have gotten those pleasures elsewhere. Farther from home, because with my brother dead and my father running as fast as he could to keep up with his new progeny in Florida, my old girlfriends felt like home now.

I also felt foolish, found out, discovered, hunger artist and Hottentot again, starved down to nothing but neediness and buttocks, all displayed to the crowd.

Luckily Bill called to distract me. He had enjoyed the book, he said, and he'd like to read more.

"I don't have any more like that," I said.

"What's the book your mother said you were working on?"

"It is a biography of a gay performance artist who often did part of his act in drag."

"Whoa!"

"Yeah."

"Always full of surprises. Come to the gym at closing time. I'll give you your own personal workout."

"Not tonight."

"Tomorrow."

"OK."

"Will you bring some of the book?"

"Nah."

"You still think I can't read, don't you? I had a whole year without football at college. Literacy was the only option. Bring Chapter One. Or don't you work that way? Maybe true intellectuals never start at the beginning and write through to the end. Too quotidian."

"Stop showing off. I'll see what I have ready."

"Great. Man, I thought I'd have to pull out some more vocabulary. I'll see you tomorrow night at nine. We'll work out and go somewhere for a bite."

The moment I hung up, my mind went back to my newfound shame. To distract myself, I opened my manuscript mess to a chapter titled "The First Date," based on Eugenia's hysterical bit about dressing for a man he's only met once before. It was Eugene/Eugenia at his best, ironic, sardonic, visual. He'd transform himself from a slight, thirtyish man in an Italian-cut suit and loafers to a hip-hop brother in low-slung, knee-length shorts to a diva in off-the-shoulder burgundy chiffon to a smart-aleck homegirl in cut-off Daisy Duke jeans and vest.

"Who does he want? is not the question," Eugene says to the audience, throwing clothes over the screen. Everything comes over the screen, including bits from outfits he never puts on: the blue boa, the garter and stockings, studded jeans, leather chaps. He would pull the same clothes on and off the screen and mutter: "Too *ob*-vious. No whimsy. No sense of humor. No dignity. Hopeless."

At one point, to the music of *Swan Lake,* four little black girls wearing white tutus and tiny wings tippy-toe onstage. They appear lost, vulnerable, perfect tiny brown bodies against the white tutus and the lush but formal music. From behind them as they recess left, Eugene comes out from his screen. His body moves sleek and strong in a plain white leotard, neither particularly masculine nor feminine, but androgynous. He dances around the little girls, herds them together, sees them safely across the stage. Because there are no words in this part of the performance, only movement and music, and because the audience identifies with the girls, we are grateful for Eugene's sudden appearance as dancer/father/uncle/sprite. After he shepherds them safely off-stage he dances back in, in big, high leaps, holding something—a tutu, which he discards downstage before he goes back behind the screen to change into the next outfit.

"As I was saying," he continues once the music stops, "pleasing him is not the point. Discovery is the point. Exploration is the point.

"I say you should always go all the way on the first date, if for no other reason than to decide whether to waste your time on the second."

Then he reappears in the gray Italian suit. "Keep 'em guessing," he says, stepping into the spotlight and circle of the tutu.

My mother rang. "Well," she said without preamble, "you really fouled the nest."

"They called you?"

"I called thinking I'd find you there to ask you to run me back to Lila's, and all hell had broken loose over there—because of you. How many friends do you think you get in a lifetime?"

"You know who I blame? I blame your father. This is what he did. Like bein' faithful to your wife and children was too bourgeois for a towering intellect like himself. So, running to the gimpy whore showed unparalleled imagination.

"Like father, like daughter.

"I have been very unlucky in the children department. Just when I got used to the idea of Joe being a faggot, 'e died. And now you with this. I'm not going to get used to it, you hear? What is it? What is it you want anyway?"

She banged down the receiver. I dropped my phone back onto its cradle.

I've wanted to be the man. Ever since I could remember, so long that I'd forgotten it until my mother pulled her victimhood out of her throat like a magician's chain of colored scarves. I've wanted to be the one who came and went, not the one who sat by the window waiting, whining, pining, bitching. I don't wanna be the bitch. Screw the rules and the need. I wanted to live beyond them both, in a heightened state of pleasure and awareness.

It was, for certain, sophomoric bravado. Why hadn't I out-grown it sooner? That and my lust for Hiram. For what it had done for me, I could have moved on after eight months, and now our record would be almost clean again, like a parolee's or a former smoker's lung.

I hadn't wanted to hurt Roz so badly or cut the others to the quick. I suppose I just hadn't wanted to need them. I still didn't want to. I wanted to want them, but none of that mattered now. I'd been pushed out of the space module into nothingness. My arms and legs were pumping pathetically, pointlessly.

I was in the rowboat, cut adrift and bobbing on the ocean waves.

I was out of control and alone.

That night, not having eaten meat that week, I took pack-ets from the freezer and began to make country pâté; then I found old bits of vegetable and started a stock; then some marmalade from old oranges and lemons in the back of the salad drawer. It felt essential to cook it all, every shriveled cit-rus and knuckle of ginger; every frozen turkey butt. I was preparing a feast, noting to myself how skillfully I was making use of every scrap.

I made black-eyed peas and rice; Russian tea cookies rolled in powdered sugar; *doro wat,* the Ethiopian chicken concoction that required fourteen spices, some toasted and crushed in the mortar and pestle. I ran out of paprika and went to the twenty-four-hour Pathmark for more and bought seventy-five dollars' worth of supplies: sugar, onions, canned tomatoes, crystallized ginger, gelatin, flour, butter, garlic, cooking wine—red, white, sherry—capers, pecans, vanilla, veal, heavy cream, pistachios. When I got home at two, I started in again. This time I made ginger muffins, tomato aspic, and salmon mousse. I finished the country pâté. I cooked until dawn, took a nap till about eleven, and then headed to the Italian market to buy coffee, Parmesan, roasted peppers, black olives, and dried figs. The walk and the market felt good. They pulled my mind back to the present—the taste of this olive, the look of this pigeon nestled under an eave, the sound of this particular vendor hawking her fish—and out of my manic night of obsessive preparation . . . for nothing. I figured I'd stop on the way home and order a freezer if I passed an appliance store.

While I was in the spice shop buying French roast, the store owner next door went into the room behind his shop and came out with a BB gun to shoot a rat. Rats at the Italian market, where spoiled produce sits in mountains in the street, are big and aggressive. Few, however, come out in broad daylight. This one did. It stood by the curb, slow, insolent, dazed, we speculated, from somebody's load of poison bait, picking through the leavings in the gutter. The man shot at the rat several times. We all came out of shops to watch. He hit. The rat jumped into the air with a whine and ran toward the corner. The man shot again. This time he missed. When the creature reached Christian Street it threw itself down the sewer. A barrage of BB's *ping*ed off the iron grate.

"He probably got a whole kingdom down there," somebody said.

"Like the phantom of the fuckin' opera."

"Well, he'll need some kind of mask, because I shot the side of his fuckin' face off."

They laughed, and I paid my money and walked home. I walked past the projects, where Roz and I had fought a big ten-year-old girl with pee stains down her leg for Roz's bike the summer of our sixth-grade year. I crossed the blue-stone side-walk and street design of the new arts boulevard past a failed Muslim-inspired vegetarian restaurant that had opened only on weekends and the old First Baptist Church, where a historical marker told the story of how in the 1800s two members raised money to buy their minister out of slavery by selling themselves into slavery.

Our bodies, ourselves. Those people knew it, I thought. My own body kept working, exhausted and jittery, hyperalert, but missing beats. I noticed the roses that were just blooming, but I stumbled over cracks in the sidewalk. I was halfway up Roz's block before I knew it, and I didn't want to turn tail and run. I hesitated. Then she came to the door and looked up the street.

My bowels flopped inside me, and my temples went hot. I forced myself to walk toward her. I convinced myself that this meeting, at least, would be all right. She wouldn't make a scene on her street. These were Hiram's oldest and most loyal support-ers. She wouldn't want them to know. She wouldn't want any-one to know. I felt like I was taking a free fall. I gulped the air. Maybe she herself wouldn't want to know more than she had to. She'd been content simply to change the rules of engagement with Hiram and keep going; maybe she'd be willing, after an understandable period of anger, to do the same with us.

She looked dear to me suddenly, with her tight black slacks and the big belt meant to emphasize the waist above her belly, the azalea-pink shell and matching cardigan over her shoulders. Her hair was just long enough for a short bob. It gleamed in the afternoon sun. She watched me from behind cat's-eye sunglasses. If not for the maple-colored skin, she'd look like a matron from Greenwich, Connecticut, lost on Christian Street. The street seemed noisier and dirtier once she stepped out of her doorway. I tried to collect myself. I looked at her and then away until I drew closer. She did not take off her glasses.

I stood at the bottom of the steps with my pack full of food on my back. Children on bicycles whizzed past me, shouting at one another. Roz looked down at me and did not speak. I could not think what to say.

She turned, reached behind the door, and pulled out Bloomingdale's shopping bags, three of them, one inside the other for strength. One bag was lined with the red-and-black wool shawl I bought her years before in Canada. I could see the fringe falling over the side. She half-dropped, half-threw the bags down the steps at me. Inside were the crumbled remains of a ceramic statue I'd done of her during my last year of college in a studio art class where we made life masks of people we knew, then filled the life masks with clay. I'd done Roz because her bones were so good: an open forehead, rounded cheekbones, a strong nose and chin. She'd have had to smash the head with a hammer to have broken it up like this. Also in the bag were the remnants of every meaningful or costly gift I'd ever given her, equally defaced: a pair of jade earrings like some I bought for myself and she'd admired; a tiny ruby ring; a poem I wrote about us in high school that she framed; the white lace teddy I gave her for her bridal shower— all torn, hammered, shredded, cut. The one thing not disfigured was a white leatherbound Bible I'd given the kids at their confirmation.

Why I reached into that bag, I'll never know, but, of course, there were pieces of glass—including an antique gold-gilt mirror I gave her for her fortieth birthday—and I cut my hand. Still, I picked up the Bible and handed it toward her.

"I was a good friend to you," she said. "I loved you."

"This was for the kids, Roz." Through it all I was conscious of my low moral standing. I understood that she was the wronged one, that I'd betrayed her. I was willing to take her punishment. But I'd given the Bible to the kids, not to her. I found myself wishing Nicki could go on not knowing.

Then she did it. She drew back her head and spat. I saw it coming. I remembered that she used to do it when we'd get into fights. *Can't get it on, get a fair one goin'*. I remember her doing it when we finally got free and knocked the poor pissy girl from the projects off Roz's bike. Before we rode away she spat on the girl, and I saw the wad on the child's cheek, clear around the edges, viscous and white in the middle like a filmy old eye. I'd felt sorry for the girl, who'd been degraded enough. All this came to me in the long millisecond between her rearing back her head and my feeling it on my forehead, right at the hairline.

It felt hot and wet and heavy. Disgusting. I was sickened the minute it touched my skin. Revolted to know it was on me. Appalled to feel it trickle down toward my ear and eyebrow. My stomach heaved.

I bent over immediately, and with my hand, which was now quite bloody, I searched in my backpack for a tissue. Since I had none, I tore a piece of white paper from the coffee bag from the Spice Corner and wiped off the bulk of the spit. The skin on my forehead felt filthy. I looked down. My hand was cut in two places. One gash went across the palm from the index finger to the pinky in a cutlass-shaped sweep.

"Oh, shit," I said.

Roz did not take off her glasses. Nothing in her face or her body moved except her lips. "That's what you get," she said. She stepped back into the entryway, and hoisted out another Bloomingdale's triple-shopping-bag parcel onto the step.

"Listen," I told her. "You get that one, that one time. That's it, Rozzie."

The blood was pumping through me so strong I could have leapt up the stoop and thrown her across her living room. We stared at each other for I didn't know how long. I wanted her to know that was the last public humiliation I would take from her. She knew damn well, in that arena, she had more to lose than I did.

She slammed the door. I told myself that I should leave the fucking bags on her steps, but part of me—sentimental, or thrifty, or both—as she must have known, could not. I couldn't bear to leave it all. I'd save the Bible (no matter my thoughts about it as an intellectually crippling document) because I gave it to Nicki, after all, when she was twelve and confirmed, and I, the godmother, looked on. I'd try to piece together the poem and the letters and cards and see what I'd want to keep for myself, a record that I, too, enriched in this relationship, and not only destroyed.

The kids on bikes slowed to watch the spectacle. My hand dripped blood onto the steps. My nose was running, and later I saw that where I'd wiped it with the back of my hand, I'd left a shiny stripe of blood across my cheek. I picked up the bags and avoided their eyes.

"You all right?"

"What happened to her?"

"What she do?"

"It's OK," I said. "Go on. Shoo."

"What happened to you?"

The bags were heavy. By the time I got to my apartment my fingers were cramped, and my back and neck and forearms were stiff.

I heard Mrs. Hendricks when I got to my floor, but I closed my door anyway, hoping to avoid conversation.

"Ms. Burke! Ms. Burke!" Mrs. Hendricks yelled up the staircase.

I tried to ignore her, but she kept at it. I wiped my face with a tea towel and opened the door. "Yes?"

"Here, come here, sweetheart. I can't get up the stairs. I didn't mean to bother you; I just wanted you to see how beautiful this card is. We got it framed."

I came downstairs. The gold distracted the eye and the mat was too narrow.

"It's beautiful," I lied.

She smiled proudly. Then she handed me a preprinted thank-you card from the family, which she'd signed and dated.

"I also thought you would want to read this," she said.

It was a three-paragraph obituary from the funeral in L.A., terrible prose. Toussaint Hendricks was a "caring and sensitive individual," it said, who "attended schools in the Philadelphia Public School System and graduated from The School for the Creative and Performing Arts in 1994." He left Philadelphia for

Los Angeles the same year and "had been working ever since toward his 'Big Break.' "

It was the "Big Break" that pushed me over the edge. I felt the tears slipping down my cheeks.

"I knew you'd appreciate that beautiful writing. That's why I saved it for you," Mrs. Hendricks said approvingly.

13

In half an hour, I composed myself enough to call Bill on the telephone and postpone our date. We waited a week, during which I worked and treated myself to museum day trips. At the Afro-American Museum I took in an exhibit of black sculptors that included a 1937 bronze by Meta Warrick Fuller depicting a nude boy kneeling over a skull in the ground. At first glance, I dismissed it as derivative: alas, poor LeRoy. But it wouldn't be ignored. Alive and mysterious, "Talking Skull" managed, as the best bronzes do, to combine size and weight with perfect detail. The boy's toes looked as if at any moment he might wiggle them. The skull, half sunk in the mud, must surely rise up, I thought, when the museum closes and talk to the busts.

The smoothness and depth and richness of bronze suited our cultural vision—and our skins. But it was so expensive and took so many people to accomplish. I imagined Meta Fuller, in the 1930s, sculpting her plaster model, then making a negative mold of it, coating the inside mold with wax and filling the center with sand or ash. Then I thought of the foundry where the metal workers would melt down the copper and tin and pour it in the mold, a stream of metal so hot it glows, so hot it drains the air of red and orange and yellow and takes it down with it, melting the wax and coating the mold with every appearance of life.

It made me want to see the cold-work bronzes of the ancient

people of Benin. So on Friday, a week after the Roz incident, I treated myself to a day trip to the Met in New York. I ate lunch with a former colleague, who told me all the gossip, including the quiet reinstatement of the student I'd nailed for plagiarism.

"I've been to see the Benin bronzes," I said.

She said she wished she, too, could go look at them again, but she'd promised to write an introduction to a book we both agreed we'd wished had been written by someone with a sharper mind.

"But it does the job," she sighed.

I took my tuned-up Karmann Ghia out of its fifty-dollar-a-day garage berth and drove back to Philadelphia to make my date with Bill Williams. The Benin bronze alloy doesn't cast as well as its Greco-Roman counterpart. It's softer. But once out of the mold, it works better cold. The Africans carved all over their bronzes: jewelry, scarification, pubic hair. It let them layer the image; the initial work, when it came out of the mold, was still up for revision. The whole process was more forgiving. That, no doubt, was what I'd gone there to remember.

In Philadelphia I parked my car in front of my house, grabbed my gym bag from the backseat, and walked into town to the gym. It was hot and muggy. I knew that I needed the exercise after sitting behind the wheel all that time, but if it hadn't been for this date, I'm sure I would have gone inside, turned on the air-conditioning, and laid supine in my scented lair. The place still smelled of spices from the Night of Food a week ago. My carpets and upholstery smelled like the tent of some minor North African potentate—full of garlic, coriander, and fenugreek. It had been hard to sleep in there all week. Staying out was a relief.

When I arrived at the gym, the sun had just set. Downtown felt like evening, that funny mix of workaholics just getting home and residents strolling to restaurants, bars, video stores, coffee and ice cream shops. I stopped on Locust Street to look in at the Charles Searles paintings and sculptures at Sande Webster's gallery. The colors were simple and bright, the designs sharp and exquisite. By the time I reached the fitness center I felt preternaturally calm and attentive, even though I knew perfectly well that the Roz encounter had changed everything.

The familiar gym was welcoming. Maybe because of that, Bill felt easier to be with than he had before.

"Hey, there you are," Bill said. "Did you get my message?"

"No, I came straight from New York. What was it? Did you call it off? Am I supposed to go home? Was I supposed to bring dinner?"

"You're funny," he said. "I wanted to know if you like Peking duck, because I ordered some from Joe's. I hope you do, because I called them already. But, hey, if you don't, we can do something else."

"That's fine," I said.

I sat on a stationary bike and began pedaling to warm up. He mounted the next bike and watched me with what felt like practiced attention. The arranged dates we'd had over the years had always been big public affairs, not on my territory per se, but at my friends' request and because of them. Now we were on Bill's turf. I felt the difference.

"OK," he said. "You got you a disturbance in your energy. OK. All right. I'm going to give you—" Bill vaulted over the bike and stood under a white banner with THE HEART ATTACK printed in foot-high letters.

I'd seen the banner, but never paid it any mind.

"You are too corny. Don't people get offended by that thing?"

"See what you say at the end of the next forty-five minutes. Right now, I am your personal trainer, know what I mean?"

"Isn't this a bit of a busman's holiday for you?"

"Hey, I love it. I love what I do. Don't you love what you do?"

I could tell that my unresponsiveness activated that easygoing jock manner that always made me suspicious of the depths be-low rather than intrigued by them. True to his word, Bill took me through the machines, urging me on to another three reps, or readjusting the height of my seat to avoid strain. After every three machines, he'd bring me to the mats in the center of the room to show me stretches that would urge warm muscles toward greater flexibility. At first I felt weak and embarrassed by it.

"Don't worry about it; just push," he said. He was standing next to me, talking into my ear. "Lemme see."

I was working a butt machine, lying on my back, knees to my chest, pushing a bar that rested at the back of my knees until my legs stretched out straight. I hated that machine. It was awkward and pulled at my lower back.

"Hold up," he said. He adjusted the bar and the seat.

"They told me to put them there," I said, trying hard not to whine defensively.

"You're all leg," he said. "They set it to your height without really taking that into account. Where you had it was a strain. Try it now."

I pushed down with my legs and felt all the muscles in my thighs and butt move together. The weight felt lighter.

"Now do it slow," he said. "Till it burns."

It really was a bit of a cheesy scenario, except that everything he said made sense and held true: isolate the muscle; feel it; keep your shoulders down; pull in your elbows; don't forget to breathe, hard as you can, harder; exhale and push from the big muscles in your upper arm; the forearms will fail faster; tuck in your pelvis; keep your chest up; don't collapse in on yourself; it makes it harder for your lungs to fill up.

He said nothing—not one instruction—I hadn't heard fifty times before. But he said each one exactly when I needed it to keep going.

"I'm surprised you took up workouts," he said.

"I've been doing it for years."

"Right. It's still surprising. Most intellectuals don't bother."

"When I was in my mid-twenties we were all reading French intellectuals, you would call them, and talking about opening up to experience all life. You think with your brain, so I exercised my brain. You experience the world through your senses and your body, so I began to exercise my body."

"Experience everything, eh?"

"Yep. That was the idea."

"I see."

I finished the workout. I felt limp, spent, flat, yet buoyed by a simple, utterly biochemical sense of well-being.

He put me to a five-minute cooldown on the bike. The sweat ran freely, so I sat on a towel. For the first time in weeks, and maybe much longer, my mind went quiet. The timer on the bicycle beeped, and I lay my forehead on my hands.

"There, now," he said. "Feel better?"

I nodded. "Thank you."

"My pleasure."

"No, really."

"Yes, really. My pleasure," he said. "I love doing this."

I took a shower—by myself, no funny stuff. When I came out, he was waiting for me by the door, holding two helmets.

I put on my helmet and got onto the bike behind him. The cycle itself was huge. My part of the seat was braced by a wide metal seat back to which crisscrossing shoulder straps had been attached. He told me that he'd rigged the seat for Big Ben, the double amputee veteran who hung out at the garage and worked out his powerful upper body at the gym.

We dropped down the ramp to the Schuylkill Expressway. I held tight to his waist, flattened myself along his back, and felt the air and the spring of the machine over the road and my own flushed good health and fatigue. We stopped in Chinatown to pick up the Peking duck for two, then zipped to the four-pronged expressway and local road intersection near the foot of the Ben Franklin Bridge, a feat of modern engineering in an abandoned, eighteenth-century section of town that has resulted in a traffic pattern so complex that no tourist and few natives ever negotiate it successfully, and zipped back onto the expressway. Bill left the expressway a few miles past the city line and drove over a bridge back into the city limits to Manayunk, a partly gentrified section of town perched on the north bank of the Schuylkill. He drove through narrow, European-looking streets hugging the hills and up a cobblestone lane to a tiny mansarded house and garage with a string of tiny white twinkle lights wrapped around the lone tree in the front yard.

Bill parked the cycle in the garage, next to a car such as I've seen only in old World War II movies. It was a shiny white sports car with a black top. The handles were small buttons with a metal thumb hold on one side and a keyhole in the center.

"This thing is marvelous. What is it?"

"You like sports cars, don't you?"

I love sports cars, from convertible sixties T-birds with fins to Porsches and Fiats to MGs to the completely uninspired but small and basically do-the-job Mazda Miatas. But I'd never seen this car. I walked to the front, where the hood sloped gently to a close, round bumper. In the center was a flat hood ornament in the triangular shape of the face of a foxlike animal.

Bill crossed his arms and regarded the car with accustomed pride. I walked to the back to read the make: GTE Puma.

"It's a kit car," he said. "They were made for a while in the seventies out of Brazil."

"A what car?"

"A kit car. You build it."

"You built this from a kit?"

He laughed. "Mostly. Me and Big Ben. I bought the kit from some white guy in the eighties. It took us like almost a year, really. Aw, man, you should've seen us trying to get this thing together. Some of the stuff didn't work like it was supposed to. We made parts, we welded things together—"

"You ever drive it?"

"Yeah. Take you for a drive later if you like."

Indoors was conventional and cheerful, like top-of-the-line Ikea, all going together as if he'd make one big purchase every five or ten years and not bother with anything but maintenance in the meanwhile.

The pine floor in the entryway was varnished with a gymnasium finish. Small parlors to the left and right were carpeted wall-to-wall standard in beige. Pieces of white pine and white lacquer furniture sat here and there: adequate and cheery and basic. The obligatory oversize fish tank gurgled away against the wall in a dining room that he obviously never used.

Bill took my helmet and hung it next to his on hooks on the wall. He looped his keys over another hook and slipped off his cowboy boots and stood them in what was obviously an accustomed spot under the table that held his mail. He bent down and motioned for me to pick up my foot. I did, and he slipped off one shoe and then the other. Barefoot, he padded into the living room, where he motioned me to follow. He turned on Brazilian music, less humdrum than the usual fare, and took a bottle of clear rice liquor out of the cabinet below the CD player. We toasted, drank our shots, poured tea, and ate in companionable silence. It was a relief to eat something other than leftovers from my cooking jag.

"This is fun," he said. "I don't usually have company."

"Don't usually have company," I said. "I bet. Do you go out?"

"Last trip I took was down to D.C. Big Ben and I went for the dedication of the memorial. Looked like ten thousand vets on motorcycles. The place was crawlin' with these fifty-year-old guys in jeans and bandannas."

"That all have ponytails, too."

"Nope. Only me. 'Sides, this ain't a ponytail. This here is what you called 'pulled back.' "

"Excuse me."

"You didn't know." He became serious again. "I've gone to

the monument here in Philly, too, except it's been defaced four times, which is enough to make you sick."

"My mother told me that, with your coming from Edison, the war means a lot to you."

"My best friends all went to Nam, and most of 'em didn't come back, you know what I mean? Ben came home in a wheelchair, and the rest of 'em was on drugs."

"You didn't go—"

"Unh-uh."

The music stopped. On the long wall, French windows opened onto a cement patio. Through the screens I could hear crickets and the first cicadas. A few frogs croaked in the shrubs. Fireflies rose up from the grass.

Bill loaded up the CD with new music and came back and sat next to me. Some group I didn't know was playing with guitars and recorders—too much, too lush, but what the hell, so was he. When he leaned his head back against the couch and closed his eyes, I looked him over at my leisure with lustful appreciation. I kissed his mouth, very lightly.

"I've been wantin' summa you for a long time," he said.

Oh, Christ, I thought, remembering the cowboy boots and imagining him notching his belt. Here comes the shit.

I got ready. Too good to be true must be, right? After that one old boyfriend got into the illicit body parts business, I have been ready for anything. I once went out with a man who asked me to roll up his hair for him. I looked at Bill's black ponytail suspiciously. When I went to bed with a civil servant I met at the opera, he began whispering violent nothings into my ear: "I want to suck your tits and bite off your nipple." Shit like that. I knew a man who went out to Nevada and came back extolling the virtues of sheep. Who knew? Then something occurred to me. Ben. The hair, the earrings, the occasional cologne.

"Are you bi? Is that it?"

Bill laughed so hard he coughed.

"Go ahead, choke. You *should* choke. You have a size twenty-two teddy upstairs you want me to put on you. Or you want a dog involved. Or a zucchini. No vegetables. No gerbils. No, no, *no* preowned sexual aids. I want 'em sealed in plastic. Dildos and Halloween candy. *Must be wrapped.*"

I decided to joke, because I was having too good a time to ruin it, and because even if I didn't want to go with him into his particular sexual backwater or lagoon or whirlpool or who the hell knew what kind of waterworks, I had not enjoyed his company as much as I could have, I realized, looking back over our occasional five-year dating relationship, and it would be nice not to burn all my bridges at once.

"That's how you wanna be? 'Cause I haven't even mentioned the woman took me home on date number two and had her kid calling me Daddy. Or the woman who stopped by the gym after the first date asking for fifty dollars to do something with—I can't even remember. Or the one wanted me to go beat somebody up for her. Tell you they have jobs, and they don't. Tell you they ain't got children, and they do. Women'll tell you anything just to hook you in."

He had a whole riff like I did, and we laughed about it.

He began to caress the nape of my neck, lightly, with two fingers. He grew serious again and silent.

"A lot of women think if we're not talking, there's something wrong," he said.

"Where do you get this 'lot of women' shit? What 'lot of women' have you been with all your life?"

"Bimbos. I told you. Bimbos. I work out. I ride a cycle. You won't believe this, but many intelligent women think I'm shallow."

Then, because he was not forthcoming, and because he'd grown serious again, I thought of HIV. I asked if he'd tested positive. You have to ask. Then you have to decide who's lying.

"No, thank God. But I am wary. I'm wary of everything. For a while they thought I might have prostate cancer. They did a lot of tests. It was not cancer, and I'm fine now, but it makes you think. Makes you say like, Suppose I couldn't. Would I be with this person? I don't know if you ever had that kind of experience."

"My friend Roz had cancer."

It popped out of my mouth before I knew I'd said it. Bill turned and kissed me.

"See, not everybody would think that way. A lotta women would only be thinking like, Damn, is something wrong with his johnski? But you understand. I'm talking about life and death."

Just saying Roz's name brought me down.

"How is she?" he asked. He kissed me again. It was confusing.

"What're we doing? Hots or meaningful discussion?"

He sucked my bottom lip thoughtfully. "She in remission?"

"I think so. She doesn't give out clear medical information."

"Some people don't. Like the way some athletes don't want to talk about their game."

"That's silly."

He shrugged. "It is if you say it is. Put your head on the couch. I wanna see your neck."

I laid my head back. I was so tired I thought I might doze.

"You got a nice neck." He moved his mouth from my jaw to my collarbone, but slowly, so as not to set up a superficial tickle.

"That's all?"

"That's all I got to, so far."

"So," I said, "you had your brush with mortality when?"

"Not quite a year ago."

"Not quite a year ago, and now you're a changed man."

"Yep, that's my story. 'Cause, hey, they put that green hat on you and say good night and put you on the table, and nothing in the world matters like it did before. So, like I say, everybody got a story. That's mine.

"The other thing is, once you start thinkin' along those lines, you don't want to be bothered with bimbos. At least I don't."

He raised both eyebrows in a matter-of-fact interrogative gesture. "I want a grown woman."

"For what?"

"For this." He kissed me again, and we were losing our veneer of banter and cool. "And to travel with, go to Brazil. You wanna go to Brazil?"

"Sure." I laughed in my throat. "You got a thing for Brazil."

"Yeah, I do."

"You had a woman since your prostate scare?"

"No."

"Good."

"You up for it?" he said, mouth on mine, hands everywhere, having hiked my blouse up to my armpits.

I whispered very gently: *"Up* for it?"

We laughed and rolled on the floor. He pulled me on top of him. I took the elastic out of his hair.

"You're different this time," he said.

"From when?"

"From before, when you used to come down from New York."

"Could be," I said. "You never tried."

He laid his head back on the carpet.

"I thought . . . I dunno, the intellectual thing made me figure you were just a snob."

"Just a snob?"

He ran his hands along the outside of my body, from the thighs to the shoulders, slowly. He was getting to know my body.

"You cook?"

"I cook."

"Anything. I eat anything."

"Believe me, baby. *I cook.*"

He made a satisfied humph and continued to rub. I was almost afraid to touch him. His body is so extraordinarily strong and articulated, I was afraid to behave like a pig, like a teenaged boy with his first set of big bazooms.

"Touch me," he said, pulling my hand to his crotch and then rubbing it up and down his chest. I helped him slip off his sweatshirt and ran my mouth along the line of his chest. His nipples were hard and almost black against his red-brown skin, and the muscles shivered and rippled underneath. It was like stepping into a porno movie right before it gets so stupid it turns you off.

I put my head down in his crotch and rubbed my face against his hard-on. He pulled my drawers down, ran his hands over my clit, and I came like an alley cat. He kept going, and I came again, and he came in his pants. He swore to himself and lay back. I moved my face to his belly.

"It's been too long," he said. "I'm not always like this."

"Well, I was just as bad." I made to get up.

"Don't pull away," he said.

And I answered, "Don't hold me," and he kissed me and let me go. In a slant of light from the street, I poured us a couple more shots of rice liquor. We sat silently and drank.

"Wanna come to Brazil with me?"

"Brazil with you?"

"I'll pay basics. You bring shopping money."

Then he said again, seriously, "Come on. I'm forty-eight years old. I want to take you to Brazil and show you the Mardi Gras. We'll be great together."

"That's silly," I said. "What's with these decisions for intimacy? Out of nowhere you start with Brazil. Now you've decided we'll be great together. That is really ridiculous."

"No, it's not."

"You don't even know me."

I'd been pacing back and forth between the coffee table and him. The thought of being a nice little couple made me feel desperate.

"Besides," I said, "if you knew me, you wouldn't want me."

"Come 'ere." Bill put out his hand in the dark. He caught my wrist and pulled me to him. He stood, picked me up, and carried me—I've never been carried; I'm too tall—upstairs to his bedroom. He pulled down the sheets, laid me in the bed, opened the window, and turned on the ceiling fan. The CDs had stopped playing. I heard the crickets chirring, chirring, looking for love, trying to get something juicy, like the rest of us.

He went to the bathroom and came back crinkling plastic. I assumed he was opening the wrapper to a condom. He put it on the night table and went to the bottom of the bed and began rubbing my feet with oil from a small bottle he'd also brought from the bathroom.

By the orange-gold slants of the streetlights I watched his hands on my feet.

"You had a woman in Brazil, didn't you?"

He didn't answer for a long time.

"Yeah, I did."

"And something happened to her."

"Yeah."

I flipped myself around so that we were face to face. "She didn't die?"

"Nope."

"What?"

"She got married."

I don't know why, but I suspected that she must've been black like me, with long legs and high cheekbones. I figured she was younger, and that she grew tired of living in a pumpkin shell and waiting for his arrival once or twice a year. Or maybe after the prostate scare he didn't go down, or didn't get down when he went. Who knew?

He put on the condom and crawled onto the bed next to me with his feet to the headboard, then covered me with his body, so heavy I could hardly breathe, except that he held himself up a little in his elbows, and slipped into me.

The whole scene felt pathetic: my lover had dumped me, my girlfriend had spat on me, and I was in bed with the aging athlete, whose twenty-five-year-old love goddess had dumped him. Two losers. Like Audrey's mother loves to say: "See how the mighty have fallen."

I began to cry.

He pulled out. "Damn, baby, I never expected you to be a crier."

"Nobody does."

I told him about Hiram and Roz.

"I don't want to do this as a booby prize," I said.

"*Booby* prize?" He jiggled one breast and laughed at his own joke. "I still say, like, it could be great together. I'm goin' with my absolute gut on this, you know what I mean?"

"No, I don't."

"Sure you do. Look. You like a little room; I like a little room. We could be together and still give each other space, know what I mean?"

"I know what you mean. You're incapable of commitment and I'm incapable of intimacy." He was getting hard. "And that turns you on? This is fucked up."

He took my hand and encouraged me to fondle him again. So, OK, I did, and found myself becoming hot, too. He had a good smell. A man's smell is important. I liked his.

"Way I figure it," he said, catching his breath, "is I don't want no wife and babies, you don't want no husband and babies. Right? And we both understand about, you know, livin' an active life and all. Livin' in your body. I don't know where some people be livin'."

I stopped rubbing and scootching against said body long enough to give a flip answer.

"I have been living the life of the mind. I hope to continue to do so."

He sprang to his knees, put my hands to my sides, and ran his fingertips from my shoulders to my feet, then back again, but harder, then down, stopping to pinch my nipples, twist a finger in my navel, slip one in and out of my vagina, and grab handfuls of cheek.

He whispered into my ear: "I think you live the life of the body, too, know what I mean?"

He pulled me up onto my knees to face him and rolled my face back and forth between his palms.

"Come on, come on," he said. "I know where you live. You live right here."

He slipped two fingers inside me, and I went down on him again.

We made love hard and greedy and rough. We told each other that we'd never had such partners before. And damned if it wasn't the truth.

After we were sated with sex we lay in bed talking for hours. More confession followed, including my secret wish to get my nipple pierced and his instant lusty response. He admitted a long-standing envy of Hiram, which partially explained his boardlike behavior at one after another of Hiram's political fetes.

At dawn, he suggested we go to a diner. Before we left the bed, Bill rolled to the side and propped himself on one elbow. "The friend who had the cancer—Roz," he said. "What if she saw us here now, five years after she tried to matchmake us?"

"She'd say something Southern, some Calvinist bon mot like 'Oh, how the wicked do prosper.'"

It's become one of our standard jokes.

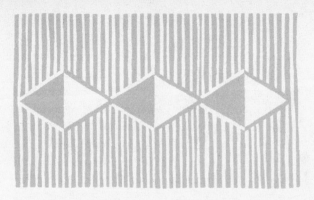

A R N E A T H A

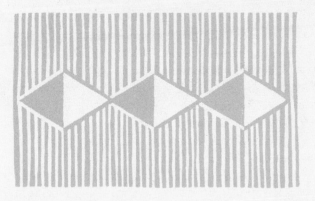

14

Father Bigombe greeted me under a bright white Ugandan sun that made his fertile green valley almost too vivid to bear. He seemed at once relieved and disappointed when I told him that I did not preach. When he introduced me in church on Sunday morning, I said simply that it was my birthday, and that I was grateful to have lived to see this day and to worship among them.

Father Bigombe talked about our connection with one another as "living members of the body of Christ." He told the people that I was here to share what I'd learned about building church schools, and that in this way the body of Christ provided for its members. The Christians in Mityana were a finger on one hand and the Christians in Pennsylvania were a finger on the other; through suffering we experience the humanness of Jesus, and through faithful service to one another, we experience his love. As he spoke about our interdependence he held his hands above his head and pantomimed an animal puppet show to keep the children amused.

There were lots of children. Most women gave birth to at least six or eight and some men had two wives. Then there were the AIDS orphans, some with AIDS themselves, who were raised by grandparents, aged and tired at forty from relentless childbirth and farming—"every day we must dig" was how the people described their lives. The deluge of parentless children strained the resources of villages, towns, and cities in a country no more than two generations removed from the chaos of Amin's rule. Anemic women bore one child after another; six-year-olds carried three-gallon water jugs a mile uphill; men with AIDS lugged loads of pineapples along the road to market. I was glad for a chance to see them at rest.

At the end of the sermon, the congregation began singing. I recognized the words, but not the tune. As they sang teenagers came dancing up the aisle, jumping high on one foot and then the other. The priest stood, not dancing, but swaying and smiling. He motioned for me to join him, but it felt like intrusion, so I held back. The kids jumped higher and higher, not losing but gaining energy as they danced. The staid African worshipers kept time with their heads and bodies, including three thin women with matching almond eyes and broad cheekbones whose shaved heads indicated that their mother had recently died.

After church, the parishioners gave me a basket woven from the ivory-colored sisal plant, filled with green bananas, pineapples, and a sack of local coffee beans, the best, they said, grown on the highest hillsides. When I asked the rector about having it sent to the States, he suggested that if I wanted it to get there, I should take it with me.

I presented the church with several books for the children, a sewing machine, pounds of sterile gauze and antibiotic ointment, along with bags of Gummy Bears and Gummy Worms, which made them laugh.

Because I wanted to see the countryside, Mrs. Bigombe volunteered to walk me along a four-mile detour through the bush and the next village while the rest of the family went straight home. Her husband indulged her, and she instructed her eldest daughter to finish the dinner preparations she'd begun.

"So," she said, once we were alone, "your birthday."

"Forty years old," I said.

"No! You cannot be. But then, Americans look young. We never believe how old they say they are."

"You thought it was just white Americans?"

She snorted, and we giggled like girls.

"Well," I said, "most of us don't do back-breaking labor now. And the women have fewer children."

Mrs. Bigombe nodded knowingly. She herself was pregnant with their fifth child, and she had lost two. I knew she was thirty-two, but she looked at least as old as I did, and we both knew it.

"And then there's also the fact, you know," I said, "that we don't grow up. It's almost an article of faith."

She laughed, which gave me the courage to ask why, in a country so pressed, and with so many mouths to feed, so few people practiced birth control, even when it was clear that the family had enough hands to work the land.

"Well," she said in a light voice, "God gave you these children to give birth to them, so why are you stopping it?"

She pointed out a field where during Amin's reign, when citizens could no longer depend on police to protect them, a vigilante group had killed a stranger in town suspected of robbery. "Right there they killed him," she said. "They buried him somewhere nearby. So this is a field of blood, right here, underneath the *matoki* trees. Those who saw said nothing, because everyone's life had become so unbearable."

I thought of our community policing project at home, the delicate balance between authority and fascism, community power and lynching. I'd walked with the town watch and cop watch groups. We'd stood on corners in mute witness as police pulled men out of cars and as young men passed drugs and money. Each group hated for us to see what they did. We hated to see.

It took us two hours to walk home. When we arrived I was hungry and thirsty. We ate maize pudding wrapped in palm leaves, steamed and served with ground nut sauce—the only protein I'd had since I'd arrived, and the last meal I ate for some time.

I came down with a fever that night and dysentery in the morning. I couldn't shake it, so Father and Mrs. Bigombe took me to an infirmary affiliated with the diocese. The round-faced young British doctor claimed to have ministered to Michael Jackson's entourage on the aborted African tour and chatted me up as if I were not a patient but a fellow expatriate. He told me that when he'd arrived in the Sudan a couple years before, he'd seen children brought in with diarrhea so bad that they lay on makeshift tables with holes in the center and a bucket underneath. The mothers sang a haunting lullaby: "Eat the belly of the house/Eat into it/Whet your appetite." The children fell unconscious and died within hours.

I lay in bed for ten days, afraid to close my eyes but not strong enough to keep them open. I thought I might die there in that infirmary, and the aloneness was excruciating. Like old people, I summoned my own past to keep me company, particularly the cold, sunny winter days in Manhattan at the divinity school when Larry and I were falling in love, and the camaraderie of the late nights when we'd study the Bible and theology in groups until somebody got punchy enough to pull out the stupid seminary jokes:

> *Saint Peter goes down to the earth to see what's happening, and brings souvenirs back to Heaven to show the saints.*
>
> *"This is a beret from France," he says; "you wear it on your head. This is a kilt from Scotland. Wrap it around yourself like this. And this is a bologna from Italy."*
>
> *Mary claps her hands: "I know that one," she says. "That's the Holy Ghost."*

Or:

Question: Why don't Baptists make love standing up?

Answer: Because it looks too much like dancing.

When I dozed, I entered a violent, black-and-white nightmare in a bleak, futuristic wilderness, loveless and desolate. Heads of people I loved appeared, close up, while someone shouted questions at them in Kiswahili and Luganda. Because they couldn't understand and didn't answer they were shot, execution-style, in the back of their heads. *Pop*—and Kofi would jerk and fall over, or Daddy. Or little Cara at school, or Maia, my secretary, or Audrey.

Then they'd appear alive again, whole and unharmed, standing in the Communion circle at St. A's. I'd hold out the chalice for them to drink. Palm trees grew out of the floor. In the wine was the poison that the Ugandans use to kill monkeys.

In a week I awoke at dawn drenched in sweat, stinking, and weak with gratitude to be alive and in my right mind. A young Episcopal nun held my arms to help me up to the bucket. A woman sitting on a stool turned her back to give me privacy. At the base of her spine bulged a huge abscess dripping pus and surrounded by flies. My young nun explained that the government tells people to bring their own needles to medical workers, and that some nurses take the needles right from people's hands, fill them with medicine, and administer the shot. Then the puncture area becomes infected.

"I'm sorry," I said helplessly.

She looked at me like we look at white people at home when they rail against one of a thousand indignities we've learned to hurdle. "What can you do?"

When I recovered, I rang Tamara, because I did not want to hold the secret any longer. Tam sounded vulnerable and thoughtful when I called, late at night, her time. I was relieved to hear that

she and Hiram were through, but still I felt a sense of dread about
our future together. I went through the rest of my official duties
subdued, as if I were waiting for something. At night I wrote
postcards home:

*Amazing place. Have been ill. Much better now and can finish the
job, thank God. Love, Neese.*

What else could I say?

My bowels continued to rule me. I still could not travel far
without stopping to go to the bathroom. We drove to rural
schoolhouses, and while the priests and lay teachers and children
waited for me, I squatted in toilets and outhouses and holes in
the ground. I was sore and embarrassed and exhausted. Clumsy
as always. I'd slip and have to catch myself. Then I washed and
rewashed my hands with disinfectant, a tiny drop going whitish
from the half cup of water I poured into a small blue-and-white
china bowl that I was likely as not to spill before stuffing it back
into my bag. I held the bowl at the small of my back and ground
my teeth together as I let the burning disinfectant water trickle
down to rinse my bottom, too.

The schoolmistresses all knew and were excited about programs that I told my host priest the Pennsylvania diocese was
considering but had not yet funded. One woman asked me
point-blank how many of her students I could accommodate in
our international summer camp, and when I told her that that
program might not get off the ground for two or three years, she
crossed her arms, reared back on her heels, and narrowed her
eyes as if to see through my impostor's mask.

"Then why have you come?" she asked. "To tell me how to
start a school? I already have done, as you see, out of dirt. They
squat on rocks for chairs, and they write their letters in the dirt
with sticks, and work their sums in the dirt. The parish sends me
old books from England with pictures of white children and
snow on the ground. Look at these. I am to have the children
recite the stories:

" 'The little match girl lit one of the matches to keep herself

warm. Inside the houses she could see the wealthy people making merry for Christmas.'

"It is like a parable, isn't it? Wry British humor."

My intestines curdled inside me. My garrulous host priest had
gone with the older children to inspect the green vegetables they
grew according to their nutrition chart. But, the woman said,
because the foods were not part of the traditional diet, the families didn't eat them, but took them to the market in town—
where the foreigners would buy them—to earn money toward
their children's school fees.

Children inside recited their times tables. The teacher and I
stood alone on the porch listening. She taught these children
because she loved them. But despite her love and fierceness, they
would drop out at ten, and go to dig and dig. They would stay
poor and drink bad water and work themselves to death by
thirty-five or forty years old. That would be true for the major-
ity—even if we managed to arrange scholarships for one or two
or four to attend boarding schools or international summer
camps in Ghana or even college in Europe or the U.S.

"I'll send you benches and a blackboard," I said. "Personally.
I'll see to it."

"Take these," she said, handing me a bag filled with church
literature picturing the standard Da Vinci–inspired Jesus. "Thank
you for your concern."

At another school, the priest held vespers at the end of the day
and finished up with a foot-washing ceremony. At dinner I ate a
bowl of rice and broth from boiled ground nuts that his wife
made especially for me, and I drank a tea that soothed the twist-
ing at the bottom of my belly. After dinner she and I talked
about using older children to write down the stories of younger
ones, and then letting the little ones illustrate their own stories
and read them back. Four of the younger children were
Rwandan refugees who had been smuggled across the border by
one of their parishioners, a man who had since died of AIDS.

"And these children he brought have no language almost,"

she said. "They speak bits—of Tutsi, Hutu, English. We've spread them among different families. It is very hard for mothers and fathers to take food from the mouths of their own children and give it to their new ones. But the children work hard for their keep. Very hard. They can see the burden they have put on these people, and they try to make up for it the best they can. We took two boys ourselves. Brothers. They have come a long way in a short time."

"Do they talk at all about what they've seen?"

"No. Our children found a dead woman out on the road. First thing in the morning. She must have been sick and coming to the infirmary and died, just died, on the way. Our children screamed and screamed. You could hear them from there," she motioned toward the horizon, "as far away as you can see, but these other boys—by the time we got to them, they had kicked the body into the bush, hidden it, in other words, and walked away. They said nothing. It took us an hour to find the body and days to figure out what had happened. When we told them that what they had done was wicked, they apologized, but when you looked in their eyes, they did not even look like children."

We spread mats behind their two-room house on a leveled and swept dirt patio that overlooked a river valley. It had rained that morning, and the children had gone down the hill to look for the white ants to eat. My hostess stayed home so that we could paint each other's toenails with the dragon-red polish that Roz had sent with me. On the other side of the valley was a coffee plantation. I'd never been in a more beautiful place. Glorious birdsong and insect and frog croaking echoed in the valley.

"It's a good thing your parishioner brought them back here."

"Umm," she said. "Why do you put on three applications?"

"So it will stay on. The friend who sent this does her toes in gold and has the pedicurist stick a tiny rhinestone on her big toenail."

"What does the rhinestone look like?"

"Like a diamond."

"Oh!" She stood, walked into the house gingerly, toes held

off the ground, and returned with a tiny basket of buttons. She settled back on the mat, took the top, like a gnome's cap, off the basket, and extracted a broken pearlized button surrounded by rhinestone sockets, all but three empty. With the back of an earring she worked a rhinestone loose. Roz had included a tiny tube of Super Glue for repairs, and I used it to cement the stone to her nail. Then I polished over and around it with acrylic top coat, and handed her the tiny bottles.

"You must thank your friend," she said, admiring her feet.

Then, very soon, it was over. I *felt* less innocent and more sober, more entitled to membership in the global fraternity of black peoples, and yet separated from them by material privilege and American power. Kofi and I had talked about these things, and I'd understood them in my head. Now I'd lived in the belly of the house. In the Entebbe airport breezeway I leaned against the wall, and prayed that the flight would not be too terribly late.

It was.

15

Four hours late. Everyone was exhausted, and, despite walls open to the breeze, the air was close and warm. Women sat on blankets on the floor feeding their children sips of tea from dented mineral water bottles. Men roamed the place, carrying toddlers who would not be still, and collecting intelligence about the status of our flight.

An old man wearing a navy blue jacket over embroidered white robes and flanked by two huge young bodyguards appeared at the entrance to the breezeway and approached the tarmac. His appearance created a commotion. People bunched together to get a look at him and his entourage, all headed, the word was, for a small private jet on the tarmac.

As we nearby passengers followed the progress of the entourage, a smallish woman with hair cut short like mine and an ample wrap thrown over her shoulders pushed her way next to me. She frowned and looked me in the eye as if examining me, and I smiled. In a moment, when the line formed, and people crowded in toward the gate, she turned and pushed against me hard in the crush.

The moment I lifted my hands to my belly, I knew she'd given me her baby. Clumsy, I thought to myself. Don't drop it. Careful. Oh, God.

He was tightly swaddled. Tiny infants don't need passports. I thought that, the instant I felt the pressure.

She ran back up the breezeway toward the entrance. People stopped to look at her, but with only moderate interest.

"Wait."

It's true that my first response was to reject him, reject change, reject the blessing.

"You want her?" Seeing that my arms were full with the baby, a man near me made a move as if to run after the woman. He hadn't seen the exchange.

"No, thank you. It's all right."

The rich man's entourage having passed, we were ushered through security to the tarmac. The baby was silent, eyes open. Did he sense the danger, I wondered, and keep quiet? Did he sense nothing, and feel no need to cry?

Only ticketed passengers were to pass the security gate, but families pushed through to stay with loved ones a few moments longer, and no one stopped them. We placed our carry-on bags on the conveyor belt, and a man looked at the screen occasionally and talked to us all.

A flight attendant checked the tickets we'd bought in Kampala. God help you if something was wrong, because there were no ticket counters in the Entebbe airport.

"You have separate papers for the baby?"

"No, the American embassy told me it was OK." Like the Grinch, I thought up a lie and thought it up quick.

"Yes, it is OK, but some Americans get papers prepared for every member of the family."

"Silly, isn't it?"

"Reverend, you wouldn't believe it. I've seen white Americans travel *with their dogs*. In little crates. Under their arms!"

The baby whimpered.

"Here," he said. He stapled my ticket stub and motioned toward the plane. "You go ahead and get settled."

Still in shock, leery of being called back, I hurried across the hot asphalt, up the metal steps, and into the plane. I felt as if I were holding my breath the whole way to Nairobi and through the larger, more modern airport there.

During our layover I bought a glass bottle, a tin of premixed baby formula, and a small pack of disposable diapers for ten dollars.

Then we boarded the plane. Next to me a chatty Gambian man sat reading *Jet* magazine. He was delighted to have a black American with whom to discuss the articles—and the ads. We went through hair-care products, insurance, cigarettes, beer, booze, and finally skin bleach. I did not want to talk; I looked at the baby and barely answered him, so he kept up the conversation by himself.

"Women in Gambia started that skin-bleaching foolishness in the seventies, and I'll tell you what we did. Say she was on the bus. You know the stuff is so expensive they could only afford to put it on their faces and hands. Well, a fellow would sit next to her and—*crack*—smack her hand, which was resting on her own knee. And when she screamed he would say: 'Oh! Madame, excuse me! I thought some cheeky fellow had put his hand on you!' "

After an hour, the seat belt sign went out, and I excused myself immediately to take the baby into the bathroom, where I could examine him at leisure.

What I'll never forget about that moment is his smell. That I'll remember till the day I die. I put his tiny fingers to my mouth to kiss them, and they smelled of his mother—strong where he must have dug in to hold on while she nursed him for the last time. It felt like holding a lover who smelled of another woman's sex.

The thought was crazy, and I knew it was crazy, but I convinced myself that everyone would notice, that the smell would give us away and he'd be taken from me. In the blue fluorescent light I ran my hands over his tiny body. He was medium brown, long and thin, but not obviously malnourished, with a wide forehead, small, far-apart, shiny black eyes, and pointed pinky-brown lips. I wondered whether he might not be a Tutsi refugee from Rwanda. I rubbed my hands over his limbs as we do to detect illness and restore bodies to wholeness in healing ceremonies. I'd never known such a visceral feeling of possession. If I'd had to lick the scent off him, I would have.

Instead I disinfected the basin with my ever-present Dettol, filled it with warm, soapy water, and washed him down. The trunk of his body fit in my hand. He cooed and fretted and bobbed his head to look at me with those shiny black eyes. I brought my face close to his so that he could see me better. He focused and watched me. I dried him with paper towels, sat on the closed lid of the toilet, and diapered him in my lap. Then I struggled and shimmied myself out of my silk camisole. I wanted that next to his skin before I wrapped him in his swaddling clothes again and held the smooth skin of his cheek next to my face.

He turned his head and tried to suck my cheek. I wished for full, fat breasts like I'd seen nursing mothers pull discreetly out of their blouses. But I had none. My own barrenness lay right in the midst of my sudden and awkward quasi-motherhood, hard and impenetrable as a stone. I couldn't help believing that his mother must have smelled it on me, as she must have been able to smell the years of spiritual preparation, and the weeks of illness that had worn away layers of pride as surely as flesh.

The flight went on for what seemed like days. I knew about nursery school-age children, but a tiny infant seemed infinitely more difficult to care for—and more boring. Thinking he might be cold in the air-conditioned compartment, I asked the flight attendant for a blanket. She took a new one out of a plastic wrapper, and warmed the formula. I felt gladder than I could ever have believed.

After three hours, he grew tired but couldn't fall asleep. Only walking would comfort him, so from Africa to Europe by air, we walked up and down the aisles until I felt I would fall. Once when I did stumble an elderly Ugandan woman crooked her finger at me. She was one of a handful of people who'd come from Entebbe. When I leaned over she told me that she had seen what had happened and was keeping watch to make sure I would not abandon him. She advised me to make up a song for him reassuring him that I would stay with him. I resented her help and her knowledge, thanked her, and kept walking.

As we descended into Heathrow, the baby screamed so badly that I rushed to get us off the plane and forgot my open tin of formula, back in the flight attendant's fridge. We had half a day's layover. So I dragged from shop to shop at Heathrow in search of more. I found a six-pack of tiny zip-top cans and heated one in a sinkful of hot water in the bathroom while I changed his diaper. Then I fed him, drank some tepid airport-kiosk tea that smelled like yesterday's butter, and took the Tube to the first stop that looked green. There, we walked to a public park and sat on the bench in blessed sunshine and a warm June breeze. A young man sat on a bench near us and turned on a boom box to a station playing reggae rap.

Then, with characteristic infant contrariness, the baby fell asleep. I put one ankle on the other knee to make my lap into a square, and then cradled him there while I lay my head back to rest. I could hear the DJ on the radio. He was broadcasting from a van in Brixton, laughing at the police, who had failed to catch him the day before.

I dozed until the baby awakened with his staccato *aa-aa-aa*. The young man was smoking a joint. He smiled at us like old pals. Over the reggae I sang in a big, bosomy contralto, like the voice in which my mother used to sing her made-up songs for me. The trick, of course, is to create a seamless improv, to come up with the lyric without missing a beat or a rhyme. I sang to the melody of "Climb Every Mountain": "Stop cryin', baby/Stop cryin', dear/I won't ever leave you/Not another tear . . .

"Shall I call you Kintu? Huh? Too much name for a little guy?"

Kintu was the name of the first regional king of Buganda, in the south of Uganda. I'd heard of a political party called Bana ba Kintu, "Sons of Kintu"; and I knew that Kintu'd been a powerful symbol of autonomy soon after the British left. I liked Kin as a nickname. He was my kin now. My son. I'd also name him Francis after my father.

"Do you like Kintu? Kintu F. Thomas? Frankie for play? Kinny for fun? Pooh-Bear for short?"

The radio played a reggae rap remix—"Mister Lover-Lover-Mister Lover-Lover" over the old Marvin Gaye "Sure Do Love to Ball." I sang more made-up lyrics—"Change every diaper/ Dry every pee/Wipe away the poopie/Your poop don't stink to me."

Suddenly full to brimming with delight, I grinned. The baby watched my bright, shiny smile and grinned back. At that moment I felt my mother's presence: she was in my cells, in the bones around my eyes, in the mirror, in Baby Kintu's funny, turned-back lips. She floated in with the Marvin Gaye music from the speakers of the boom box.

"Watch, baby," I said in my mother's deep voice. "This is how you laugh."

I threw my head back in a big stagey guffaw and tears sprang to my eyes. I missed Mom so sharply that I could have sworn she'd died only last week. How could she be gone?

I stopped laughing and blessed Kintu, crossing my hands over his tiny body. The young man on the bench stopped in midgroove to stare. He soon got up and moved on.

An hour after I began my sojourn through the aisles of the 747 from London to Philadelphia, I started singing any song that came into my mind. The baby dropped off to sleep. I sat down, wedged my knee against the seat in front of me to make a nest for him, and let myself doze. I dreamt I was in Roz's Pond House, sitting on the floor in front of the fire, laughing and laughing at a silly joke that Cherokee Jones, the priest at St. A's, is fond of telling: "We had a membership drive the other day, and we drove off twenty-five members."

I slept through the meal, and when I woke they apologized because they'd run out. So I drank Pepsis, ate peanuts, watched the movie without earphones, and did simple breath meditation. As compensation for my missed meal the flight attendant brought me a car seat in which to strap the baby. I unlocked the grid of my knees, lifted Kintu into the chair, and, with the attendant's help, strapped the car seat into the empty seat next to me.

Then I stretched my cramped legs and dozed: a nervous, skittish sleep shot through with fear for my new baby and myself.

16

Daddy and Roz and Audrey were waiting for us when we came through customs. At the sight of the baby in my arms their mouths made silent O's. I was so tired that I dumped the carry-on suitcases, still unzipped from customs, on the floor in front of Daddy, handed Kintu to Roz, gave Audrey the shopping bag of baby things I picked up on the trip, and collapsed onto the nearest bench. My friends and my father stood around me. Roz probed Kintu's wraps, shook her head, and grunted softly.

"Whose baby is this?" Daddy asked.

"Jesus Christ," Audrey said, "what happened to you?"

Daddy frowned in recognition. "He's not ours, is he?"

I nodded. Daddy shook his head.

"You are skin and bone," Roz said. "Just skin and bone carrying a baby. Uncle Frankie, can't we get her a cart?"

Still shaking his head, my father flagged one of the men driving carts for the handicapped, loaded us on, and whisked us to baggage claim. Audrey and Roz took care of the baby, and Dad waited for the bags. I called Kofi and told him about Kintu.

"So now we know why you had to go. Are you going to name him Emmanuel?"

"No." Unaccountably, my feelings were hurt. "Kintu."

"It's a good name," he said. "I've missed you, you know. You've probably been too busy to notice."

"It's been an extraordinary month."

I had missed him, too, but I was too pouty to say so. We arranged for him to come to the house for a short visit that night.

"You can see the baby," I said.

"I want to see you."

Daddy had carried the bags to the curb outside and gone to fetch the car. I could see Audrey and Roz motioning to me through the windows that his car was approaching. I hung up the phone and stepped gratefully out of the airport into the air. Daddy loaded us all into his cream-colored Lincoln town car, opened the windows, and reclined the front passenger seat. I fell asleep before we were out of the short-term parking lot. When I awoke, we were at Toys "R" Us.

"What are we doing?" I asked.

"Well, meat don't beat no steel, so if you're gonna keep this baby, I guess we need a car seat," my father said.

"What's his name?" Audrey wanted to know. "Or is he gonna be Baby Africa like the MOVE people?"

"Unh-uh," Roz said. "You know what happened to them."

"Or Baby Surprise?"

"Or, like your mother's mother used to say, 'Zip-What-Is-It?'" said Daddy.

"Zip," Audrey said. "Call 'im Zip."

"You all like all them crazy nicknames. Don't call the boy no Zip."

As we shopped for a car seat I told them the name I'd picked as well as the story of how he'd come to me. But I was tired, and I was not telling it well.

"Just walked up to you?" Roz kept saying incredulously. "Look at this Perego. I saw a woman with this kind. You take the car seat out and snap it like this to make a stroller."

"How much is it?" my father asked.

"A hundred dollars," I said. "My Lord, can that be right?"

"I wouldn't buy that one yet," said Audrey.

"The earlier you get this, the more use you'll get out of it," Roz said. "Babies grow out of things so fast."

Rozzie was in her element. "They didn't make paper diapers half this good when Nicki was little. And look at this: a window shade with suction cups for the car. I sure could have used that."

I remembered how much Roz loved children's things—looking at them, talking about them, shopping for them, comparing and buying them—and how easily I'd been bored by it all when her children were young and I was in college and seminary. Now, having just once bumped along a plane aisle with a fat bundle of diapers, I could appreciate the convenience of extra-thin ones. Already I was primed to pay attention to the pink or blue color coding.

"What's the difference?"

Amused by my ignorance, Audrey answered, "The boys' have more padding in the front, girls' in the back."

"I don't care how much this car seat thing costs," Rozzie said. "You have got to have it. Come on, I'll go in with you."

"No, Roz," Dad said. "This'll be on me. Old Granddaddy's got to start 'im off with something."

"The woman who bumped against you," said Audrey. "What'd she look like? Sick?"

"I can't remember. Her hair was thin. Maybe she . . . felt ill."

Audrey scrutinized Kintu, who was staring, dazed by the bright lights. "Get 'im checked out before you get too attached, Neese."

Roz made a characteristic chopping motion with her arm, as if to stop misfortune at the door. "Audrey, don't even start. We are not going to think that way. Look at this beautiful baby. In fact, I know just what we're gonna do. We're gonna drive out to the doctor's house right now."

"What doctor? It's Sunday."

"The pediatrician." She took out her cellular phone. I've

always been irritated by how Roz will take over a situation, but I was tired, and I knew that she'd be likely to think of absolutely necessary steps in the baby's care that I would miss. Standing next to the strollers and car seats, she arranged for us to drive directly to a suburb twenty minutes away to the house of a pediatrician who owed Hiram some favor.

"There," she said, sounding satisfied. "This little man is going to be fine. We'll be dancing at his wedding, too."

Audrey rolled her eyes. "Hope he waits awhile."

"Who's giving the baby shower?" Roz asked.

"For who, Bryant's yellow heifer?" Audrey sniffed. "How the hell do I know?"

"I was getting out my baby things for them," Roz said, sounding torn, "but now with little Tu-Tu—"

"Kintu Francis," I said. "Give 'em to them, Roz. They need the help. Kintu'll have more than he needs. Worse come to worse, we'll do like I do when I forget my raincoat. I'll grab something from the thrift shop at church."

"Oh, no. Promise me you won't," Roz said.

"You know she will, Roz," Audrey said.

"But if I give my things to you, see," Roz said, ignoring Audrey, "I know you'll take care of them."

"Oh, Lord, don't give 'em to me. I can't take the weight." We laughed, but I was serious. I didn't want Roz quizzing me down five years from now about the whereabouts of some blue-and-white snowsuit with matching hat and mittens.

"You know what I have?" Roz said. "I have a baby tux, size eighteen months. Gorgeous. It's all downstairs in the basement. I kept it in boxes according to size, and I have a list of contents in each box."

"That's some sick shit, Roz," Audrey said.

"Uh-huh."

We checked out, spending more than three hundred dollars, and drove to Ardmore.

The pediatrician told me that the baby would need blood tests, one now, and another one at fourteen months to determine if he was HIV positive. And they'd want to check for other diseases: TB and polio in particular. I was to call in the morning and tell her appointment secretary to make a space during her special infant hour, from ten to eleven. Otherwise, she said, he looked great.

From there we went to Roz's house, because Roz was eager to take care of Kintu and me, and because I couldn't face going home to care for him alone. I needed sleep.

"You come over," she said, "and we'll watch him till you catch up."

"And I had the nerve to think I'd be in church today," I said.

I remembered to tell them that he liked to be walked. "Try out the new stroller."

"I'm not going out into the middle of Odunde Sunday with a little-bitty baby just off the boat. You can't get a stroller up the sidewalk."

"Oh, for heaven's sake, Roz, he's been in airplanes for hours. He needs the air and he loves to be walked. Use the kangaroo carrier."

"Your old baby isn't any different from everybody else's," Roz said quickly. "There is nothing special about a baby's liking to be walked. All babies like to be walked."

"Go to sleep, Neesie," Audrey said. "We'll get Kunta Kinte here out for a walk."

"Don't call him that, Audrey, please. I was afraid people would do that to his name."

"Oh, go the hell to sleep, Neese. Let the old grandmas take care of things."

Feeling peevish, I lay on the bottom bunk in what used to be Bryant's and Junior's room—and fell asleep in an instant.

Four or five hours later I awoke with woozy jitters. For a moment I thought I was ill again and back in Mityana. Then I remembered that I was on Christian Street in Philadelphia.

Audrey was gone. Junior and Bryant and some of their old

friends had congregated outside. They were drinking beers out of a trash can filled with ice, laughing and talking with passersby, who were offering them three dollars a can.

"We could've made some money."

"License cost two hundred and fifty dollars."

"Fuck that."

"We could still make some money. Hot and thirsty as these niggers is, we could make us some Kool-Aid and sell it for a dollar a glass."

"What about the license?"

"What they gonna do? Arrest me? I say I'm giving somebody somethin' to drink. Now, who's to say different?"

"Sell 'em some water for fifty cents."

"Suck a ice cube for a quarter."

Hiram had left for a conference of black lawmakers in Washington. Nicole offered me a glass of iced tea and took two tall glasses into the breakfast room. I followed her sleepily. She indicated Roz's comfy corner chair and footrest, put my tea on the side table, and pulled up a chair to sit facing me.

The house looked less perfect than usual. There was already a used teacup next to mine on the table; the trash can had tissues in it; some of the leaves on the umbrella plant next to me showed a fine covering of dust.

"Miss Pidgeon still working for you guys?"

"Unh-uh. She hit the lotto and quit."

"You're kidding."

"Nope. She's moving to Florida."

I laughed so hard I cried. I laid my head back on the chair. My eyes were so dry the tears burned. So I kept my eyes closed.

"And Audrey was so *mad.*"

"I bet she was."

Nicki asked if I would tell her something.

"I don't know, sweetie. Tell you what?"

We were close when she was small, but in her teens she'd pulled away. Now she felt older to me than I remembered. She was sadder, more direct.

"How you four became friends. And what Mom was like when you met her."

"Why?"

She shrugged.

"Rozzie was on a mission. You know they say, 'Get a life'? Well, your mother was on a mission to get one. And *my* mother was on a mission to give her, as she used to say, half an hour of childhood before her period came on.

" 'Oh, honey,' Mom used to say, 'don't frown 'cause your mother is depressed. Some parents and children just ain't suited.' Then Mama would tell Roz about her own parents, who were total and complete hermits. Black hill folk. Stayed up in their cabin alone and spoke ten words all weekend long.

"The catch was that my mother was *intensely* social. For her, life in a house with two phlegmatic people and a hunting dog was prison.

"Well, she said, when Monday came around, and she saw that yellow school bus hanging sideways off the hillside, headin' toward their stop, she'd just start to squirm. And *her* mother, my Grandma Vine, would say, real gruff: 'Stand still, girl. Them white people ain't nothin' to us.'

"So Mama didn't say a word. And she'd get on the bus, and sit down real nice and wave good-bye to her mother, and the minute the bus pulled off, honey, she'd jump up and run around to all her little friends and hug 'em and kiss 'em. And the bus driver would holler back: 'I want the little colored girl to sit down!'

"My mother would tell that story and have your mother in stitches. *Your* grandmother, if she were living today, would probably benefit enormously from some of the medicines they have now to correct chemical imbalances that cause depression. I believe she was very depressed for a long time. She wasn't easy for your mother to deal with.

"But then Ms. Marlowe swept into our lives. She was a cinnamon-colored woman, bangs cut straight like Cleopatra. She wore brilliant colors and sandalwood perfume and myrrh beads that she'd pass around the classroom so we could smell. She was a French teacher, pressed into duty as a long-term sub. We called her Madame. She taught us French and English and art. For math and science we learned stories. I still remember them: 'Go home, *mes amis,*' she'd say. 'Sit in your tubs. But observe how your bodies—yes, yes, yes, I said *bodies,* Mr. Jackson, *bodies!*—observe, please, how your bodies displace water, which is what Archimedes noticed and how he detected the presence of silver in the king's so-called solid gold crown. *Comprenez?*'

"If it hadn't been for her, who knows? When your mother brought in those mothball cookies that nobody would eat, and went out and dumped them and started to cry until she made herself throw up, maybe we might have laughed at her. Maybe we would have beat her up."

"You wouldn't have beat her up."

"No. But Audrey would have. Tam might. And I was certainly capable of standing back and taking comfort in knowing it wasn't me. Don't look so appalled."

I stood carefully, so as not to knock over Roz's side table, and hugged Nicki. She didn't say anything. Nor did she pull away.

"So, now that I've told you all your mom's business, where is she?"

Nicki pointed me toward the basement.

The basement was Rozzie's world. She'd had the builders lay white tile on the floor and install walk-in closets. In the south-facing powder room window at the front of the house she asked for glass shelves to display blue-and-green bottles that turned the square of sunlight into shimmering slants of turquoise. On one wall a big-screen TV broadcast a nature documentary. Most Philadelphia basements feel like caves. Roz let you pop down the rabbit hole into another dimension, cool and white and blue.

"Close the door behind you," Roz called, "and come look at this."

She held up a tiny blue suit and soft leather black wingtips not much bigger than my thumb. Kintu was gurgling happily in a baby swing. In front of his face dangled a bright mobile in primary colors. Every time he batted successfully, it made a tinkling noise, and he shrieked with delight.

"This baby is *so good,*" Roz said. "Although I should never have listened to you about going to that crazy doggone Odunde."

"What happened?"

"Some fool shot off a gun."

"Oh, Roz, don't say it. For years they've been having this thing with no trouble at all. Jesus, and you had the baby out there."

"I knew I shouldn't take a baby into that crowd," she said accusingly. "We came back, I was shaking, the baby was wired, and all Audrey could say was she needed a drink."

"Where is Audrey now?"

"Gone back to work, thank God. She took the time off and didn't get permission first. No wonder she can't keep a job. You know, there's nothing you can do with Audrey. You can talk till you're blue in the face, and it don't even matter. It must have to do with being an alcoholic, I swear."

"At the airport she told me that she and Hiram are working with two drug counselors to start a rehab afterwork program at St. A's. Is that for real or just preliminary? I feel like I've been away longer than a month."

Roz pursed her lips and shrugged. "I think the thing is, they got an angel, and they don't want to let him get away.

"But she's like off and running. Left a message on the machine at two in the morning talking about they could have an eight hundred number: 1-800-R-U-DRUNK. Now, you know . . ."

I didn't know what I thought about Audrey and a rehab, or a rehab and St. A.'s. I didn't know the counselors putting the program together. I wondered if Cherokee Jones had begun talking to vestry about it, tentatively, so that they'd feel involved and would support it if it happened, but wouldn't feel too cheated if it didn't.

I grinned at Kintu, and he opened his mouth in a toothless smile.

"Where'd that come from?" I asked, motioning to the swing.

"I told you when we got back, the child was wired. I came down here to find something to help him out. Then I saw all these boxes, so I decided to stay down here where it's cool and go shopping in the basement."

"Please save it for Bryant and Crystal," I said.

On the couch behind Kintu were piles of undershirts, cloth diapers and rubber panties, nightgowns, and one-piece snap-up suits. More than one baby could ever use. I felt anchored to the ground just looking at it all.

"Not the good stuff," Roz said. "In three months it'll look like rags. She came over here earlier, big as two houses and whining and complaining so bad I sent her home."

"Didn't I hear Bryant outside?"

"He came back. She's so pregnant and evil, I guess even old Bryant needs a break every now and then." She held up a tiny red paisley bow tie and matching hankie the size of a cocktail napkin. "See this? Do I want her taking this to the Laundromat? Throwing it in with some overalls? No. Now, you wanna know what's really cute?" She pulled a second set from behind her back. "We got Bryant and Junior these at the same time. Hiram had some just like 'em."

I remembered when Hiram had begun wearing bow ties, in the seventies. He worked as an assistant to the city's budget director in the day, and then came home, ate dinner with Roz, took a nap, and worked in the bar from nine until closing. Roz worked the bar during the day, setting up, ordering food and beer and liquor, bartending in the afternoons. Until she died Hiram's mother worked the late afternoon and early evening. Her brother, Hiram's uncle, the retired policeman, sat on the stool at the back of the bar by the pool table while the women worked. He carried a gun in a shoulder holster and worked for free beer.

Roz's mother, on the other hand, never came near the bar. Mrs. Purnell told Rozzie that she and her church friends, the saints, were praying for her. Before she died she took to calling to suggest that they sell the bar and open up a fried fish store.

We would gather at the apartment some Fridays. It was like playing house. Tam and I were freshmen at Penn, and Audrey was working as a nurse's aide and taking nursing courses at Roxborough. We sat drinking iced tea—Tam and Audrey poured vodka into theirs—until, at five forty-five, Roz would stand abruptly and say, "Lord, what am I going to fix Hiram for dinner?"

"Oh, oh, oh," Tam teased, half joking, half irritated, it seemed, by Roz's new self-importance. "Ma hubband, he hongry."

And we'd laughed in disbelief that one of us actually had a husband—not a boy our age, but a grown man, charismatic and ambitious, with a clip full of money in his pocket and a thrilling capacity to lead.

Audrey always told Roz to do what her mother had done when dinner wasn't prepared, which was to fry onions and green peppers in the pan to make the house smell like dinner.

"Then, after he come home, and y'all finish drinkin' and fightin', you burst into tears and say: 'I can't cook now. You ruin everything.' Then you get some white bread and plop some mayonnaise on it, and smear some of those onions and peppers on it and give it to the kids to eat, and if they don't like it, tell 'em to put some potato chips on it and make a potato chip sandwich."

"But we don't have any kids," Roz said, laughing. What could go wrong with her big, beautiful husband and her clean little apartment and their business and their love and their life?

"Good," said Audrey, "then after you finish fightin', you and him can eat it straight out the pan. Don't even have to share. Hey, more for you."

When Hiram came home, we crowded around him. He seemed to accept our presence as naturally as if we'd been family. Tam and I were only eighteen, Audrey nineteen. We tiptoed on stocking feet across the linoleum to greet him. Then we watched with sudden, breath-catching lust as he bent low to kiss Roz in the kitchen, their mouths open, his long fingers raking through the dull sheen of her new antique-brass hair. We heard the wet touch of their lips and tongues.

We had to make friends with Hiram through our desire. It wasn't easy. It occurred to me that part of the reason I hadn't noticed anything between Hiram and Tam may have been that early on I was busy, without knowing it, fending off my own attraction. The maleness emanated from Hiram like heat. This new man in our lives was not father or brother or uncle, not boyfriend, but a permanent and powerful presence.

My husband, Larry, had a tendency to act goofy around my girlfriends. He complained that the ambient estrogen gave him the bends. Hiram spread his arms wide, inviting us to his home and his table. I even remember wishing Larry were more like him.

Rozzie squinted at me. "What are you thinking about?"

"Thinking about when you lived over the bar. And now here we are, twenty years later, the two of you—because it is the two of you—running for Congress."

"You know Hiram and I have not always had the best marriage," Roz said. Her mouth was set in a grim curve. "I've looked the other way for a long time, Arneatha, and that's no good. Then, about a month ago, I got all crazy thinking about it. I don't particularly like women, anyhow, except for you three, my real girlfriends, and that's the truth. I don't trust women."

I wanted to grab the baby and run out of the basement. Without realizing it, I looked toward the steps—in slow motion, because of the jet lag. Rozzie looked, too, to see if anyone was coming. She was packing the baby things from the sofa into an empty U-Haul box lined with a clean white trash bag. She set her mouth in that stark little smile again.

"When I was in the hospital and I dreamt about those snakes—'member I thought they meant death, and you said they could mean resurrection? Could mean wisdom? See, you say this stuff, and you don't think I'm listening. But I *am* listening."

"I think I said that resurrection can mean that being willing to die makes you free to live. Because you asked me about death," I said.

"Right, well, they put me under the knife and I didn't die. And they zapped me full of radiation, and now they say the cancer's in remission, but a young black doctor told me that he doesn't like radiation, because when the cancer comes back it's crazier, like the radiation makes it worse.

"So, after that, I started thinking about what you said. And I told Hiram that things have to change. I told him he had to treat me right. Be a do-right man to me, not just everybody else on the planet. I mean that."

"And what did he say?"

"Said OK."

"That's it?"

"I am no fool, as I keep having to tell people in this house. I know he's running for Congress, and that's half the reason I can say this now and get some doggone results. I know that, but still, he said OK, and you know Hiram. If he didn't want to be bothered, he just would've told me, 'Well, baby, you done put up with it this far, better figure out some way to stick your head back in the sand, 'cause this here is Papa's business.' "

"And what about her?" I asked, incredulous.

"What about her? I spent a whole month worrying about her. I didn't marry *her*. *She* didn't stand up next to me on the altar and promise to cleave only to me, forsaking all others. He did. Forget her."

"You still love him?"

"Yes, I do."

"And Tamara, too?"

The moment the name left my lips, I wished to God I could take it back.

"What's this have to do with Tamara?" Roz's back was to me, and I saw the start in her spine.

I could not think what to say. The secret, I realized in sudden, awful hindsight, had been all mine to keep. I felt the pressure of it retroactively. Fear flopped in my belly like a fish in the bottom of a boat. "Nothing," I lied.

"Tam?" She turned and screamed the name. *"Tamara!* What about Tamara?"

I shook my head. She'd frightened the baby. "Shhh."

"You said Tamara! *And my husband!*" After the shouting, she was silent for a moment. Then she said quietly, "Since when? How long did you know?"

"Oh, Jesus, Roz, it's nothing. There's nothing to know. I don't know anything." My mind searched the evidence and came up with flaws. Just because it sounded like them from behind a door didn't mean it had to be them. I hadn't actually seen them in the act.

Roz ran past me to the bathroom. She slammed and locked the door. I heard her crying. She choked, and then threw up. The powder room was so close I could hear everything.

I wanted to go to her and hold her. Instead I picked up the baby, who also had begun to cry, opened his fingers, and lay his warm palm on my cheek. I felt as if I'd been part of a conspiracy.

The young people thundered over our heads to the basement door.

Bryant called down first. "What's with Auntie Roz?"

"Nothing. It's all right."

"Mom OK?" It was Junior.

I went halfway up the steps with Kintu to meet them. "I spilled something on her. She's in the bathroom to soak. Lemme go back and help her. You guys go on up."

They left and I closed the door.

"How long? Long as she's been Nicki's godmother? Just since she moved back? Since when? God*damn*it!" she screamed from behind the door. I heard her throwing and breaking bottles. "Goddamn her!"

Then she shouted a sound like *aah* again and again. Finally, the wailing ended and she simply sobbed. The baby cried, too, now, big sobs just like her. I stood on the outside of the door. Much as I hated it, I couldn't help remembering standing outside Tam's door and hearing Hiram groan differently.

"Fuck her!"

"Oh, come on, Rozzie. Stop it. Don't talk like that."

"Why not? Maybe that what he likes."

I called Kofi and told him that he could not come see me as we'd planned. We talked only for a moment. He said again that he'd missed me.

"If you can come later, or if you want me to come get you and the baby, call me back. I'll be up."

I beeped Hiram at his conference in Washington. When he rang back, I told him what had happened. "Oh, shit. We were really doing great, you know that? So," he asked, "do you want me to come back early? Does she?"

"I don't think so."

"OK. Tell her it's finished. Been finished. Period. I'm glad you're there. Reassure her."

"If I hadn't been here, she wouldn't have known."

"Better from you than a stranger," he said. Then he went back to his conference.

That night, seeing her mother's disturbance, Nicki cooked dinner. She fried chicken, Roz's favorite, and made up plates with macaroni salad and glasses of sweet iced tea. Roz thanked and hugged her, then brought the tray into her bedroom and closed the door. I'd just fed Kintu. Roz picked him up from his infant seat, took him to her bed, and propped him next to her.

"You're going to be sitting up in no time," she said to him.

Then she turned to me. "He hasn't spit up once since he's been here. Pass me a drumstick."

She pulled off the meat and gristle and gave Kintu the bone. He grabbed and sucked vigorously. Roz dropped the meat onto the tray and licked her fingers. That was her dinner. The two of them stared at the big-screen television while I ate and fell asleep again right in my chair. When I awoke, Kintu was sleeping in his bassinet, and Rozzie was sitting in her same position on the bed watching an old cowboy movie.

"See," she said. "It's just like the Indians. White people broke promise after promise, and they kept trusting."

She clicked the remote until she came to a Fred Astaire musical. "I like this one," she said. "You go on back to sleep. I just need to sit here and enjoy my movies. I'll be all right. I'm feeling better."

I tried to shake off the muzzy feeling in my head. "Turn it off, Rozzie," I said. "You don't need more TV, you need prayer. Come on, I'll pray with you."

I turned off the TV and got on my knees at the side of the bed.

"Oh, so you prayin' now. I thought you didn't do anything but meditate."

"Do you meditate?" I asked her.

"No."

"So, we'll pray."

I don't generally pray on my knees, but I know that Roz does. She slid down next to me, as if grateful to have something to do.

"Lord God, be with us. Be with your servant, Rozalind. Remind her that you promised never to leave us alone, even in our times of greatest need. Dear Lord, Roz has forgiveness in her. Let her know that in time, she will be blessed to forgive. Help her know that in time, fresh wounds will heal, and that in you all things are possible. Let her feel, through her disappointment and hurt, the complete and perfect love that you have shown through your son, our savior Jesus Christ. We ask this, we pray, in his name. Amen."

Roz grabbed me around the neck and held me tight. We were on our knees by the bed. She whispered into my ear: "You're the only one who hasn't hurt me. You know that? I hate him for doing this to me, Neese, and I hate her. I can taste it, like, at the back of my tongue."

"The forgiveness will come, Roz. It'll come one day like rain. I'm telling you. It'll be such a relief."

She humphed. "You know what? Now I know why my gun is in Buddha's old car, locked up in his garage. Now I know why. God is protecting me from myself. 'Cause if I'da had it, and if she'da been here, I could've shot her dead. That's how I felt this afternoon."

"How 'bout now?"

"I could do it now. I swear to God I could."

We turned and sat on the floor with our backs resting against the bed. I didn't know what to say.

"This is just how crimes of passion happen," she said. "I told Reynaldo."

"Who's Reynaldo?"

"My shooting instructor. Would you come visit me and pray with me in jail?" She was joking now. That was a good sign.

"What? If you shot Tamara in cold blood, would I come visit you in jail? I don't know, sweetie. Probably."

"But not for sure . . ."

"Oh, come on. It's a grotesque hypothetical."

She sucked her teeth. "Maybe. But that's why everybody in jail comes out a Muslim. Muslims go to folk in jail. The people I know who can turn the other cheek are rare as hen's teeth. 'Member when Audrey became a Muslim?" she asked. "Wore that black thing over her face."

"I think Audrey was looking for discipline."

"Discipline? Get out. I think she was looking for a man wearing a suit and tie. That's what I think. With a job."

"I think Audrey was looking for discipline."

"Nobody's *lookin'* for discipline except you, Neesie. She did it for the costume. Makes your eyes look sexy." She hid the bottom half of her face with her hand."

We snorted and sniggered. "That, too, no doubt."

Hiram cut his conference short and returned home just after daybreak. When Kintu and I came downstairs, he and Roz were drinking coffee in their breakfast nook. They appeared as they always did: composed and in control. Nicki came down, poured herself a glass of juice, and sat at the table. No longer the aggrieved teen I'd seen in recent months, she appeared to have flipped a switch inside herself and decided to join in the family portrait. I felt in the way. I busied myself making Kintu's bottle with one hand while I held him with the other.

"This Rehab After Work thing is pulling together a whole lot faster than we thought," Hiram called to me. "I was telling Roz that Romeo's been in touch with a very wealthy brother whose boy got sober in one of those programs. The family feels that the recovery program really gave them back their son. He's since died of AIDS, and the father's looking to do something significant as a memorial."

"Originally they're from right around the corner, Neese," Roz pitched in. It was her public good-news voice. "And their son went to meetings at St. A.'s. Isn't that something? How's the baby? He and I hung out last night watching TV until Hiram came in. He took that three forty-five train from Washington so he could be here and we could have breakfast together this morning. Wasn't that nice?"

"Yeah," I said. I couldn't help believing that they liked the excitement of it, or the challenge. When my dad arrived, I was relieved to leave their household and return to my own affairs.

17

June was a blur. I was up nights with Kintu, and pushing through the days to keep up my work at St. A's and write my report on Uganda for the diocese. Because of the baby, I no longer walked with the town or cop watch, but I became the natural contact for Rehab After Work. Suddenly Audrey and I were working together. The church wanted to set up an oversight committee.

Audrey and the counselors balked. They'd studied other programs and were trying to write their own, and raise money to hire experts to tailor the outline to St. A's community. They wanted more time to put the program together before they presented it. The church members worried that the rehab people, funded by outsiders, would not be accountable to the congregation, or as Ed, an ad hoc vestry member plagued by manic and inevitably homeless episodes, said: "We don't want the tail wagging the whole damn church."

Ed sleeps on my enclosed porch sometimes, when his sister, a harried mother of four children, can't take him anymore. I offered to let him stay in my house while I was gone, but he himself cautioned me against it, saying that he was afraid of leaving something on and burning the house down. Then he laughed. I thanked him for the warning.

Ed's dog is Special Ed. I don't know who gave him that name.

They eat and work at the church. Special Ed lies in the corner surveying the humans. Ed keeps the garden beautifully, although I'm told he once dug a five-by-five-foot hole outside the baptistery, saying we needed a proper pool.

He was adamant that the rehab people had to report to the church. After one meeting at the church, Ed stopped me on the steps to say that although Audrey was my friend, he'd been sober for thirteen years, and he could see that she was not yet on the AA beam. He told me to keep an eye on her.

"What do you mean, 'not on the AA beam'?"

"Just what I said." We were interrupted by a woman who came asking for money for carfare, because her five-year-old was in Temple's hospital, admitted the night before, she said, after being penetrated anally by an uncle who'd used a rubber-tipped dildo. I've been hustled for money outside and inside church a thousand times, but the terrible shame of the story, the details, and the dead look behind her eyes brought tears to mine.

"Wish I did have a dollar," Ed said, "so I could *not* give it to your ass. Get out of here saying things like that on your own child—if you even have a child."

She turned to face him with that blank expression and then looked back at me. "I could take a token," she said.

"No, my dear," I said. "But if you're hungry, we're serving dinner now, and you're welcome to it. And if you're in need of prayer, we can go in now and pray together."

"No, I ain't in need of prayer," she said. "That's the last damn thing I need, somebody praying and all. What they servin' today?"

"It's a soup kitchen," Ed said. "They servin' soup."

"I had crab there once, left over from a restaurant," she said, smiling wistfully, and, for a moment, you could see the little girl she must have been. "Still fresh, though. I never did forget that dinner they served us that day."

Something occurred to me. "You like fish?"

"Yeah, I loves me some fish. Fresh fish now. Gotta be fresh.

Otherwise smell like you know what, and I don't want nunna *that.*"

Ed rolled his eyes.

"Listen," I said, "my dad's gone fishing today. He's gonna bring home some fish from down New Jersey. Why don't I put one aside for you?"

"You'd do that for me?" Her face opened up into a surprised smile. One front tooth had broken off halfway and never been fixed.

"Sure."

"Fried?"

"Sure. You stop by tomorrow, I'll have it in the fridge. You ask for me."

"What's your name?"

"Reverend Neese."

"No. That's my name! Neesie. What's it for, Denise?"

"No, Arneatha."

"Oh." She looked suddenly angry, as if everything had been going swell until I came up with the wrong name and wrecked it. "All right, then, I see you tomorrow. What time you get in?"

"Generally about eight, eight–thirty. I'm either here or over at the school there, in the office."

"Well, all right, Reverend Neesie. I'll see you tomorrow."

Ed's lips were pursed tight. "She ain't even comin'," he said.

Daddy came to my door in his fishing clothes, holding the ice bucket.

"How was it?" I asked.

"Beautiful. Ocean was beautiful. Sky was clear. Fish jumped outta the water. Said: 'Take me home to Neesie's frying pan.' You got grits?"

"Did I know you were going fishing? Of course I have grits."

Dad had already cleaned the catch and put it on ice. I took

two good-size fish from the chest and packed the rest in freezer bags. Kintu kicked and cooed in his baby chair on the counter while Dad told him how big and strong he was. Then, while I fried the fish and cooked a pot of grits to go with it, Daddy went upstairs to shower. Remembering Neesie, I took a fish from the freezer and dipped it, too, in egg yolk and bread crumbs.

Dad and I ate together as usual. Every few bites he put his finger into the grits and held the finger to Kintu's mouth. The baby sucked with greedy pleasure. Everything was the same, and everything was changed.

"This is nice," he said, "having a little grandson. Wouldn't yor mother love this?"

"She would."

"You know, I used to wonder what it would do to you, losing her right when a girl really needs a woman."

"I don't know."

What I didn't say was that her death, and Dad's and my recovery from it, had everything to do with my calling to the priesthood. We went back to church because my grandmother suggested it to Daddy.

That first Sunday Daddy relaxed at Communion as if he were falling backward into a pool, or into the open arms of the Lord God. Tears ran down his worn-leather cheeks and he licked his lips and shook his head, powerless to stop them. Yet he smiled.

The Communion table shone like a circle of light then, and we were suffused by it. This was the vision I had at that moment. The light made everything clearer: the hands of the worshipers, our mouths and hair and eyes—with their Christian sense of unworthiness and gratitude, with their love and faith, dishonesty and fear. I wanted to *be* glass, colored and intricately wrought, like the rose window at the top of the high rear wall, to stand in the center of the church with nothing to do but wait for the light to shine through me and break into gemstone colors of the spectrum.

After Communion that day we returned to our seats and I heard the words of the prayer from my childhood: "Eternal God, heavenly Father, you have graciously accepted us as living members of your son, our savior, Jesus Christ. . . ." I closed my eyes and let myself become a member for the first time. The light passed through me and left me empty and clear. When I opened my eyes the world poured in with sudden and sensual intensity: the bodies and winey breath of a hundred people around me, starched white linen on the table, red carnations and vestments like tongues of fire; a final fugue on the organ, spiraling its violent demand for redemption. Batter my heart.

The Communion table was my call to clerical life. I did not hear a call so much as I saw the light. Around that table, for those few minutes, full as I was with light and life and love, I did not miss my mother. Not that I forgot; not that I saw her flitting around the celestial choir. At the moment I stood at the table, I accepted that she was dead, and the bleeding, ragged wound was staunched.

Leery of putting a baby so newly separated from his home and family into day care, I took Kintu to school with me. What a time. In my office, he would study shadows on the wall and suck his fist. When he wouldn't I carried him in the pouch; swung him in the wind-up swing; gave him to sixth-graders to carry up and down the steps—one of his favorite rides—and lay him down to nap in the blue-and-white-striped bassinet the music teacher had kept since her eighteen-year-old son's infancy and given to me solemnly, like a sacrament.

Each activity of the day took on double scheduling: Thursday's second lunch meeting of sports faculty meant not only figuring out what to do with the fifty neighborhood kids who showed up every day wanting in, but also changing Kintu just before, and did I have time to warm his bottle so he'd be quiet during the meeting? After I changed him, and he fell asleep in the swing while I made two phone calls to the diocese, what then? He'd been fretful all day. Could I transfer him to the carry-all without waking him, to take him with me to the cafeteria? How bad was the precedent to let Cara and the other older girls stay in my office and watch him as they'd been begging to do? How much time would we lose if I sent a message for the teachers to bring their lunches to my office to meet there, and how many times could I do that without creating resentment among people whose own children were not with them but in day care?

Kofi appeared in the evenings after his daily swim. I'd already noticed that he had mild facial tics; they were most noticeable on the few days he did not get to swim.

He brought presents: Thai food, Afro-pop and jazz CDs; a rubber duck for Kintu's bath; a pewter cup. He brought me a book of short stories by Márquez and talked about the magic and grotesqueness and community of my neighborhood. When I told him that I like opera, he borrowed a videotape of *Tannhäuser* from the public library. We sat up late one night glorifying in the music and clucking over its love goddess and pilgrims.

> But mortal, alas, have I remained . . .
> A god can endure unceasing joy . . .
> I long for pain as well as pleasure.
> O Queen! Goddess! Set me free!

"Christianity aboveground and pagan lust beneath," he said. "No wonder my poor father went South."

I learned that one summer in his early adolescence Kofi's father, Herbert, had accompanied his own father on a business trip to Ghana. Herbert Rockemore completed college and seminary with never a mention of Africa. As a young minister he applied for missionary duty and was sent back to the place he had secretly fallen in love with.

"My father had all the makings of a typical colonial missionary. I know it. But then two things happened to him. The first was my mother. The second was independence.

"Father was fond of a Martin Buber story about a rabbi whose son goes every day to the woods to pray. The rabbi tells the son that God is the same everywhere, so he need not leave the village to go pray in the forest. The son answers: 'I know that God is the same everywhere, but *I* am not.'

"It is how my father tried to explain his living in Africa, a situation about which he felt rather self-conscious, I believe, especially after independence."

Kofi worked for fifteen years as an oil company engineer, but tired of engineering and enrolled in the Wharton Graduate School of Business. The job as liaison between Ghanaian and U.S. business interests came along before he finished.

On Saturday mornings we drove out of the city to Valley Forge, where George Washington camped his cold and tired troops in the winter of 1777–78. It is now a national park of rolling green hills and hardwood forests watered by a winding creek that empties into the Schuylkill River. Along the crest of one gentle slope, beech trees stand against the wide-open sky. We took long rambles and then walked through the creek to cool our feet. We'd squat to let Kintu watch the light play in the stream. When his hand touched the cold water, he'd squeal with fright, and then reach to touch it again. At the bottom of our favorite hill, Kofi would put on the baby pouch, and we'd plow up a path mown through the hay and look down into the valley. By the time we reached the top, we'd be shining with sweat. Then we'd spread a blanket in the shade for Kintu and sit on logs where the woods met the field and eat picnics of bread and cold chicken and fruit, iced tea and chocolate.

Kofi insisted we go to the country because I'd been closeted at church each evening preparing for a districtwide community-policing rally, to be held at St. A's on the fifth of July, the day when black Americans in the nineteenth century celebrated American freedom and protested their lack of it. The rally would culminate six months of organizing neighborhood town watches, civic associations, block groups, and other churches. The commissioner was scheduled to attend, along with the captain of our police district and the officers who'd been walking our neighborhood beat as an experiment. The neighbors loved it; the officers spoke repeatedly about the benefits to their job of developing relationships with law-abiding people, and it showed: crime on their beat was way down.

To be effective these public rallies had to be well orchestrated. Politicians and officials had to see that large numbers of poor and working-class people could get it together to meet, pool their money, sign petitions, and stage consistent, disciplined demonstrations of united action—boycotts, voter registration, volunteer work—before they'd take them seriously. The people *themselves* had to see the group's organization and its power to force politicos to act before they could believe in it, too.

I could not stop my mind from running over the details. When Kofi asked me whether or not I was happy, I told him, truthfully, what I was thinking. Then I added: "I am very happy to be here with you. And I am happy, after that illness so far from home, to be alive. My gratitude these days feels very basic. Like the old folks say, 'I'm glad to wake up in my right mind this morning.'"

It came out sounding more formal than I meant, like an opening session to the morning prayer group.

"You still mistrust happiness, don't you?" he teased.

Sitting on top of our favorite hill, finishing the last iced tea from the thermos, we felt full and flushed and aroused. The flat faces of wild roses at the edge of the meadows gave up their sweet smell to the sunshiney air. My body felt stronger than it had since the dysentery and alert to Kofi's every move. He drank down his last swallow of tea and sucked his lips in, first one, then the other to enjoy the final drops. I enjoyed his relish.

Kintu had fallen asleep and was letting out tiny snores. I turned him onto his stomach. He drew his legs up under him. Kofi reached over and ran his finger along Kintu's toes, even and plump where they peeked out from under his diapered bottom.

"My parents were dear people," he said, "but deeply suspicious of happiness. Which is why, of course, I feel so at home in America."

"And with me? Should I take this personally?"

"No, no." He laughed. The tic in his eyelid jumped to a steady beat. He took off his glasses and rubbed his eye. Without the glasses, one eye tended to wander. "Don't take it personally. This is my own long-standing conflict with Puritanism."

"As in H. L. Mencken's definition of a Puritan as a person who is afraid that someone somewhere might be having fun?"

"Yes, you have it exactly."

"Did you have fun as a boy?"

"You mean, am I indulging in mythmaking? A return to childhood paradise? An *African* childhood paradise into the bargain? No, darling. God, no."

I'd never been with a man who could say the word *darling* naturally, but he did. The accent helped.

"I can't see you as a boy."

"Which is fortunate for me. I was the missionary's son, brown, not black, which was OK much of the time, but not always, and I had the most awful time figuring out how to keep my damn face under control. As you see . . .

"But beyond that—happiness was the subject; see, you've switched, but I'm on to your kind—it was made very clear that only so much unalloyed happiness was permissible. Religious joy, yes, but not the sheer delight of this world. Although—or perhaps because—my father was a deeply sensual man, the sort who trembled at the sight of a glorious sunset or the slap of a wave against the sand."

"Or poetry."

"Or poetry. Quite. Or my mother. I was too young to get it, but after dinner sometimes, he'd come to where she was washing up outside and run his finger along the line of her cheek, and he'd look transported. I can understand that now. I can understand how he'd want to try to keep desire from taking off like a chariot and running his life."

He lay the back of his hand along the side of my face and traced the plane of my jaw in a way that made me aware of my own skin, and how it might feel to him.

"So," I said, "you've come all the way to the U.S. to find a black woman priest who takes herself too seriously so that you can make her be happy."

He kissed me, a few times quickly, as if for our mouths to find the best situation, the most nerve endings, the place where the curve and puffy flesh hit the hard outer edge and the inner softness just right. He pulled his head back and looked into my eyes.

"All right? I'm told that with American women one should ask repeatedly."

I surprised myself by laughing and kissing him back. I was giddy.

"All right," he said, "if that's how it is, I'll kiss you again. Here—" He brushed his open mouth slowly against mine.

I laughed all the more. We lay on our sides on our blanket for a quarter of an hour, kissing, touching each other's face, fanning mosquitoes off ourselves and the baby.

Happy was his goal? I hadn't been so happy in years. I told him so as we stood to leave.

"So, I'll come home with you tonight?" He pulled me to stand in front of him, and, with the baby between us, embraced me in the darkening green twilight. "And we can make each other very happy indeed."

Fireflies began to rise up from the ground in blinking gold spirals. It was later than I thought.

"Oh, dear." Believe it or not, I'd resisted thinking about sex with Kofi. Until now, of course, it would have been premature. "Not tonight, certainly."

He watched my indecision and my desire. "But sometime."

"I don't know."

He made a clicking sound at the back of his throat and slung the backpack with our picnic things onto his shoulder.

We started our walk down the hillside. I'd not seen the need to say that I'd been celibate since Larry's death, but now it occurred to me that, in this day and age, he might assume that I hadn't been.

"I have to think," I said.

He made an impatient face.

"Oh, Kofi, I am a priest." Something troubling occurred to me. "Is this about your father?"

"No, no darling," he said. "This is about us."

"But you knew I was a priest when you started coming around."

"Yes. Sorry. I thought you might be willing to be a woman to me, too. As you are to your friends, and your schoolchildren. What was I thinking?"

I was stung. On the ride home he interviewed me with polite interest about the next day's meeting, but when he dropped Kintu and me at my house, we parted coolly.

Tam rang on the phone that night. She was full of good news. A fortyish black guy in Atlanta who'd made a ton of money from car dealerships and fancied himself a patron of the arts had agreed to publish her study guide, as we'd come to call it, for an advance of ten thousand dollars. In addition, she and her mother were buying out Lila's bookstand and changing the name to Tomorrow's Books. It was a play on her name, although no one pronounced her name that way except her parents.

"Clever," I said.

Hearing the chill in my voice, she questioned me a few more times to make sure that I did actually like the name.

"Roz knows," I said.

She sighed. For a long while we said nothing.

"There's nothing I can do about it now, Neese."

"I don't know what you should do. I don't understand what you thought you were doing. I don't understand the friendship you say you have for her in the light of this, although I'm trying to understand, because I think *we've* been friends, haven't we?"

"Stop it. I didn't sleep with Larry."

"Well, there's a terrible thought," I said.

"Speaking of men, how's your African?"

"Fine," I said. "He's a marvelous man, and I'm enjoying his

company enormously." I did not ask her about Bill Williams. I didn't want to know. I didn't want to trade sex stories with Tamara.

"A lot of big words. Did you do it or not? If not, why not? If so, how was it?"

There was still a hint of Caribbean lilt in her voice, just a tad, like you can hear sometimes in Sidney Poitier's early films, enough so that cab drivers will ask her where she's from. I was angry with her. All these years we'd held together, and she'd busted us up. She'd made our group a lie.

"No. Because we're not married."

"Right," she said, sounding caught off guard. "You're not married. He's not married. What's the problem?"

"That's the problem, Tam. We're not married to each other. We have a lovely friendship, and I live as a clergy in a community. I tell young people to live by the rules, so I figure I should, too. And even if we start interpreting things quite loosely, I should still think hard before I do something that might get out and make me less effective doing my work. Perhaps you've noticed how sex with people you're not married to has unintended consequences. It really does, you know. It affects other people."

She was silent for a few beats. Then she said, "You know, you seem so normal, and I've known you so long that sometimes I forget that inside your head it's not the nineteen-nineties yet."

That night, for the first time in weeks, after I rocked Kintu, I could not fall asleep. I went downstairs, put a sleeping bag and a plastic bottle of water on the porch for Ed and a bowl of water for Special Ed, and locked the inside door.

Upstairs, I opened the Márquez book Kofi gave me to a story about a Brazilian widow who leaves her children and grandchildren in the months after World War II to go to Rome to meet the pope. From the ocean liner she sees a dead man floating in the bay. At the only hotel with its own dining room, a row of Englishmen with identical pink knees recline on chairs in the foyer. On account of the men she chooses a different hotel—actually, just another floor in a large elevator building. When she goes out for dinner, she refuses to touch a local dish made from songbirds, the only poultry left after the war, and buys a cup of coffee for a panhandling priest with onion breath who tells her that "Centuries ago the Italians learned that there is only one life, and they try to live it the best they can. This has made them calculating and talkative, but it has also cured them of cruelty."

When the widow returns to the hotel building, the English are being carried out on stretchers. They are all dead from eating oyster soup in August in the hotel's private dining room. They should have known not to eat oysters in August.

I closed the book. Funny to say about the country that houses the Vatican that the people have learned there is only one life. It *would* seem to make sense that such knowledge would make people calculating rather than cruel, but you certainly couldn't say it about Italians after World War II.

Of whom could it be said? Black militants in the 1960s had claimed the opposite: that African-Americans' staunch faith in the hereafter made them too willing to accept cruelty in this life. For these militants there could be no liberation theology, no justice ministry. These were old arguments that I'd set aside years ago. No doubt, I told myself, you are clawing at Christianity because you want to take a lover.

I still felt married to Larry; that was part of my trouble. Although he had died, I had not, in my mind, become single again. Just as I'd never think of changing my last name back to my maiden name, I'd never changed my marital status back. I'd accepted that he was gone, but not that I, therefore, was single again.

Ed knocked on the door to the enclosed porch before he and Special Ed stepped in. He called hello several times, but I did not answer because I did not want to talk. After a few minutes of bumping around and drinking water, they settled on the pallet in the corner and bedded down for the night.

I lay back on the couch, dozed, and dreamt that I went down a long stone stairwell, past underground dwellings in sedimentary layers. In a rock cave, like the Hollywood-epic version of early Christian catacombs, were three large rooms lit by lanterns. I saw them all at once, as if the rooms were cut open for my viewing, like the ant farm in our fifth-grade science class.

In the room closest to the steps were Philadelphia politicians crowding around a conference table and interrupting themselves to talk on telephones. Hiram was in there, shouting into his phone. In the middle room were the apartments of a medieval pope; in the farthest room stood my bed, ornately carved in the shape of a sleigh and covered in red velvet bedclothes with heavy gold-and-black tassels. Sometimes the bed was empty; sometimes Kofi and I were in it, making love. The dream went on a long time, and so did the lovemaking, but I could not abandon myself to it, because I was afraid that the pope would hear us.

When I answered the ringing telephone I was sleepy and confused.

"I'm sorry to wake you, darling," he said. "But I want to apologize for this afternoon, and the foolishness about my Puritans and happiness. And my parents. You have integrity, and I love you for it. The fact that I find it inconvenient is no reason to, uh, go at you. That's unfair."

"Can you come over now?"

"Now? Are you quite sure?"

"Yes. Come to the back door. Ed and the dog are on the front porch."

"Ed and the dog?"

"Just come to the back. Walk quietly. The dog is hard of hearing."

I poured brandy into two juice glasses, placed them on a small wooden tray, and waited by the back door. I remembered a small blue votive candle I kept in the fridge for emergencies, put it on the tray, and dropped a box of kitchen matches into the pocket of my bathrobe. Then, since I could think of nothing else to do, and because I did not want his knock to alarm Special Ed, or Special Ed's barking to wake the baby, I went back to my post at the back door.

After Larry died, I took to standing by that door to watch the sunrise and the birds. I fed them. Sparrows appeared first on the top of my back fence; then a pair of mourning doves, crooning sadly as if they missed Larry as badly as I did; and then house finches, small brown grosbeaks with a touch of red on their sleek little heads, along their breasts, and under their tails. Last year they disappeared as mysteriously as they'd come. I was angry that they took with them their color and their cheerful, melodic song, as if color and song were mine to enjoy. My seeds, my yard, my birds, my joy.

Then Kofi knocked. I opened the door and he kissed me with that light touch, lips full, warm, just enough for me to recognize the new contour. I tilted the tray; the candle and the glasses slid, a splash of brandy spilled, and we fumbled to grab the glasses, bumping things, bumping each other.

Special Ed let out his early warning bark, a low *whoo-whoo-whoo*. We shushed each other and closed and locked the door. Kofi laughed quietly, that deep voice tiptoeing around in his chest. I was close enough to feel the vibrations.

"Give it to me," he whispered. "You know you're hopeless carrying more than one chalice at a time."

Then he caught my hand and sucked the brandy off my fingers. I hadn't expected him to do such a thing. I'd been expecting married sex again: late at night, familiar, sleepy, perhaps, with shorthand touches.

"Come up," I said, surprised at the seduction in my own voice. A little abashed.

He had permission now, so his one free hand touched the small of my back as we went upstairs, and his fingers brushed lightly the curve of my behind, just so I could feel my own movement under his palm. At the top of the steps, I turned to kiss him again. I did not hide my excitement as I'd been doing for weeks, although I was still embarrassed by it.

We made love in my bedroom. His hair and the crevices of his body were still damp from his shower. I was shy, tentative. It had been so long. He was different from Larry, and we had to use condoms, because you just do these days, and I couldn't have felt more awkward. Hot excitement turned to anxiety. I got myself wound up three times in the silk pajamas that had never before been out of the box; one elbow hit him in the chest getting free. I kept my legs closed like a girl, and when he nudged them open with his knee, my foot flew to where his glasses were perched on the night table and knocked them clattering to the floor.

"My Lord," I said when we finished, "I guess you wonder what I was making all the fuss about."

He said we'd do better. Then he dozed, and I lay looking at the ceiling, listening for the baby's light snore over his. When he woke we sat up, lit the candle, recovered his glasses, and drank the brandy that we'd forgotten in our haste.

"You haven't had enough, have you?" When I mumbled a denial, he clicked his tongue and began unbuttoning the pajama top that I'd put back on.

"No, no," he said, "you've only just begun. Let's see if we can do something about that."

Luxurious: that's the word that the Jacobeans used to describe women who married twice, or otherwise gave evidence of sexual desire. With Kofi my body became luxurious. I felt beautiful. He rubbed his hands up and down my torso for his pleasure and mine. He told me to turn over, and I found myself on all fours, arching my back like a cat.

My marriage had been loving and warm and as delightful as teatime. This new, older, sexier sex shocked me. I forgot the internal ledger that calculated how much was enough. He'd massaged me for five or ten minutes; now it was his turn. As if I'd finally found the delayed promise of adolescent hots, this sex made me greedy: *Gimme, gimme, take me, gimme some more, do it hard, get it good, put it deep. Don't hold back your jellyroll.* Afterward, I felt amazement. I was sated, but only temporarily. Some wild woman inside sat with her legs wide open and her eyes at half-mast belting out her theme song: "I said more, baby. Gimme some *more.*"

Incredible. He kissed the corners of my mouth. I found myself remembering the way Hiram and Tam had sounded behind that closed door in her New York apartment.

"Why did you hold back?"

"I don't know," I said.

"You hesitate, you know that? You wouldn't go to Africa at first. Why? And why won't you preach?"

"Fear, no doubt. It's always fear."

"But you have everything you need. What? What are you afraid of?"

"I don't know."

Love with Kofi opened a flood of other feelings. New vanities took me completely by surprise. For the first time in years I'd begun wearing eyeliner again. I bought a twelve-dollar tube of lipstick called "Mulberry Crush" that a woman at Wanamaker's cosmetic counter said brought out my blue undertones.

Sex was new again, and so were sudden stabs of jealousy that his former lovers were no doubt prettier and more exciting, with smaller bones and delicate feet, not clumsy with their clothes and hands. I was particularly bedeviled by thoughts that his former white girlfriends in England may have been more attractive to him than black ones, than me. I thought I'd done with such insecurities in twelfth grade. I was as shocked by these worries as I was to see myself traipse into bed wearing a gold necklace and anklet a Senegalese woman convinced me to buy four years ago at Odunde.

Within two weeks we began to talk about marriage. I had carefully thought through every decision I'd made in the past twenty years. Now, I was planning to marry a man I'd known for four months, and I was ecstatic. We are not, I reminded myself, who we think we are. This season of change felt like an unfolding, although it could, I knew, be an aberration.

On Pentecost, the body of a little boy was found in a Dumpster near church. We held a memorial vigil for him at school and then at church. Audrey came, anxious and agitated. She had called me three times the night before saying she couldn't sleep for thinking of the little boy, and that she had seen the family, seen the very child in the soup kitchen. He liked sugar, so the women in the kitchen would give him two sweet rolls. She'd seen his uncle take one of his rolls and was convinced he'd killed the boy.

The next day I sat fuming in church as his cousins and play-mates marched up to the altar, at the grandmother's insistence, to lay red carnations in front of a photo of him. Along with arrest and jail, these funerals served as rites of passage in a community where adulthood held almost no promise at all. "If only he'd of lived," said one of the young speakers, "he could of done anything he wanted."

The boy's mother slid off the pew onto the floor and had to be carried out. The grandmother shouted the child's nickname: *Butter—Butter—Butter.* Through her teeth Audrey said that she couldn't "hold up much longer."

I drove her home after the service.

"You know," I said, "if you're sad, there's nothing wrong with crying."

Audrey looked away from me out the window. "I have to hold it together," she said. " 'Cause if I start crying, Neesie, I swear, I'ma just roll up in a ball somewhere and dissolve. It's all I can do to put one damn foot in front of the other."

Living with her mother was part of the problem. But now that her mother was sick again, she couldn't leave. Maybe, she said, she shouldn't have taken on the rehab. I suggested she leave the rehab organizing to the counselors, but she wouldn't. All her life she wanted to do something big—well, not *big,* she corrected herself, but worthwhile—and each time an opportunity came along, she'd blown it or drunk it away. Hiram was trying to get enough from the donor to pay her a small salary so that she could quit her job and prepare for the rehab full time. She'd try to hold out for that. Or maybe, if he couldn't, she'd try to get a foundation to underwrite her.

"They got money they don't know what to do with," she said.

"Have you ever looked at those grant proposals?"

She sucked her teeth.

In addition, Audrey said, she'd seen her mother's father on the bus. He'd sold his gold teeth to raise money for a ring for his new girlfriend, and then the girlfriend had left him.

"He was coming out of Mass at seven-thirty in the morning. I know what he's doing. He goes to Mass to keep him from going crazy till the bars open. That's one sorry ass," she said. "No wonder my mother's such a nut case."

"What kind of dentist would take out gold teeth and give him money for them?"

"Who says it gotta be a dentist? George put 'em in an envelope and sent them to a lab. They advertise in magazines. Then they send you a check. He told me, 'I wouldn't want to send my teeth away in the mail, but, hey, twenty dollars is twenty dollars, right?' Sorry ass."

We rode a few blocks in silence. I tried to keep the reluctance out of my voice when I told her that she could come stay with me for a while if she needed to.

"Thanks," she said. "You don't know, at this point, how much it means to me, I'm telling you, just to have the option. Tamara offered, too, but Roz told me about her and Hiram—I know, I know, and you told her not to bother me with it, and she told me not to tell you I knew, but if everybody knows, well, what's the damn point in nobody telling, right?

"Anyway, let's see who else I can rope into living with Mom."

"Or maybe we can find a nice place for her."

Audrey shrugged. "I work in those places, remember? And evil as Mom is, they'll treat her like shit. She's a pain in the ass. I promise you, within three weeks, somebody will've stolen her little chump change and knocked her upside her head. Ain't nobody want to be bothered with my mother. Or she'll be dead as that little boy in the Dumpster. The final fuckin' solution."

I was overcome with sadness that afternoon. The sadness did not lift over the next week as we made final preparations for the community-policing meeting. When Kofi held me, I felt the precariousness of life that my recent sensual pleasure and joy had blotted out. At first I'd been afraid to love him. Now I was afraid of losing him.

18

Our rector, Cherokee Jones, preached about our biblical call to justice. He told a story from a black ministers' conference he'd attended the week before. It's one of the many stories about a foundling, in this case, an eagle brought up in a henhouse. When the farmer shows a visitor how high the eagle can soar, the visitor warns that the bird will fly away some day.

" 'Nope,' says the farmer. 'Lookahere.'

"And he takes out the feed and starts callin' like we used to do down in West Virginia: 'Here, chickee, chickee, chickee.'

"And, lo and behold, the eagle dropped down out of the sky and sidled up like the rest of the chickens."

The congregation laughed loud and long in recognition.

"We are not chickens," he said. "The unchanging love and power of the God I serve tells me that we are not chickens."

Hiram and Roz and Hiram Jr. and Nicki were there, and I heard Hiram's "Amen" ring out from behind me. We clergy, the vestry, congregation, school, and staff were pumped up about the meeting and the politicos coming, and the commissioner's attempts to take back our neighborhood's beat cops, who were there for the service: an Irish Catholic man and a black Baptist woman. They'd promised to come to the afternoon meeting, but we were moved to see them in church.

"We are realists, and we're willing to compromise," Cherokee said, "but we are also a people of God, and we have learned to expect miracles."

Women served coffee and a light dinner following the service. The school's drama club had joined the after-school and summer youth groups to produce a skit about safety for the afternoon meeting. Every skit they came up with involved a cap gun. The drama coach successfully lobbied the vestry to allow the kids to shoot the gun in their skit, but now that the day was here, church people were getting cold feet. Several came to me right after the service to complain, but I had neither time nor patience to rehash the debate. Besides, the kids had worked hard; I would not undercut them.

While they rushed into the sanctuary to practice, I checked on our other arrangements. The weather was fine, so the children played outside in the school courtyard. As we'd planned, ten high school students positioned around the yard passed out balls and sidewalk chalk and acted as crowd control.

Rozzie, looking indeed, as Tamara says, like a country singer in one of her favorite pink peplum suits and matching slingbacks, had held Kintu during the service. I took him back after church so that she could mingle and I could change him before the afternoon meeting. I went to the Sunday school room where I'd stored our diaper bag and locked away the stroller. Hiram followed me and closed the door.

"Listen," he said without preamble, "I got ahold of the police commissioner last night, and the cops-walking-the-beat thing, the experiment, is over. That's it."

"But I talked to his office on Friday—"

"And they were still thinking about it. He told me. But he got the numbers Friday afternoon, and he thinks it's too expensive to implement citywide. And if they can't do it citywide, how're they going to justify doing it down here across the tracks in south Philly?

"Plus, between you and me, Neese, the man does not want some cop gunned down on foot on the street. The cops' union doesn't like it."

"But the officers love the beat, Hiram. They love it. They came this morning for service—did you see 'em?"

"He wants to do mini-stations."

I knocked the baby's soiled diaper off the table. "Oh, hell, Hiram."

Mini-stations were bunkers. Nothing about them promoted the kinds of relationships our beat cops had developed—with old people, families, store owners, kids, single mothers, men going to and coming from work, men out of work.

"That's what it's gonna be. I'm here to keep you and Kee from ruining your meeting by trying to get something out of the deputy that he's not authorized to give. And I know 'im. He's a vindictive son of a bitch. You humiliate him today, and you won't *get* a mini-station. He'd rather give it to some neighborhood in the northeast anyway.

He squinched his eyes at me as if to figure out how to get through to me. "Way I understand it is, in these public forums you gotta show some success, right? Don't want a thousand people there, and you ask for something, and he says no. Then whachagot? You got a thousand disillusioned people talkin' 'bout 'I knew they couldn't do shit.' And it'll be years before any of 'em'll try political action again.

"So, I'm telling you what you *can* get. Your own mini-station right here. Cop on duty twenty-four seven."

"Thanks." I didn't say, because I assumed Hiram already knew, that Cherokee would call the commissioner at home just before the meeting to double check what we'd agreed on.

"But I got an even better idea while I was talking to him, and here it is. Listen up: he could set up the station right back there in that curacy building behind the courtyard. Think about this: the police renovate the building with *department money*. Are you listening to me? *They* do all the sewers and structural and electrical work; *they* bring the building up to code; and then *you* keep ownership, of course, so if things ever change, the place is up to snuff and functional, plus you keep the lease on the top two floors. Maybe for the Rehab After Work to put their offices.

Couple studio apartments for your sexton, a junior clergy, the seminary students you have visit sometimes."

He raised an eyebrow and looked at me.

"Think about it for a minute," he said. "You can get the cop in the station to come to all your meetings and meet people just like they're doing now. . . . Talk to Kee."

I pursed my lips. "You talk to Kee."

"No. I'd rather it come from you."

Cara, the sixth-grader who'd become my shadow, rushed in with two cousins. She was wearing a powder-blue shell with a matching short-sleeve cardigan—I was sure Roz had given it to the thrift shop—and a pair of white pants that her grandmother had bought for her birthday a month before and that she'd worn every Sunday since. She'd come to ask me for the five dollars I'd promised her as a reward for reading five books in one week. They were Babysitter's Club books and mysteries; she'd ignored *Sounder,* and *Roll of Thunder, Hear My Cry,* and the C. S. Lewis I'd suggested, but she had read her quota, completed the questions listed at the back, and scored 80 percent. She'd earned her five bucks. Now she wanted to collect so she could sport her cousins to junk food.

Cara's cousins exclaimed when they spotted Kintu's stroller in the corner.

"Whoa. Looka this. This da *bomb.* Could we take 'im to the store?"

"You should see this thing. It turns into a car seat and everything," Cara said, with shared ownership in her voice.

As her younger cousins began to pull at the handle as if it were a large transformer toy, Cara pushed their hands away and carefully flipped the release to unlock the car seat from the stroller. She showed it around like a model from the home shopping channel, and then carefully reattached it.

I said sure. Their trip would give me two minutes to think and ten minutes to talk to Kee. "But I want you to be your most observant and careful, Cara, y'hear?"

She grinned at me and, with her tongue, flapped her eye-tooth, which had been loose for weeks. "You know I will."

When I got to Cherokee, he was on the phone with the commissioner and motioned for me to sit down. I wrote on a piece of paper: *Hiram says do not agree to mini-station unless he promises to use curacy and renovate on his budget. Do we have to settle yet?*

Cherokee read the note and rocked his head back and forth between his shoulders. His eyes said: I don't know.

He'd worked so hard for this: he'd stood outside check-cashing places, on subway corners, and at the front doors of super-markets to get people to sign petitions and join town watch groups. He'd brought in grassroots organizers from other cities to train us to gather up people's anger and passion and give them outlets for it. Like church-based activist groups in Brooklyn, Baltimore, and San Antonio, we'd started with small, winnable projects: getting a local store to exterminate and provide fresher meats; forcing the Department of Licenses and Inspections to clean and seal abandoned houses where drug dealers and addicts congregated. Kee's eyes looked tired, and the black cowlick be-hind his bald spot stuck up toward the ceiling.

"It's too soon for compromise, Commissioner. Around here we are still waiting for a miracle." He made a pro forma laughter sound and hung up the phone. "That man's the big-gest two-face I ever knew. Makes the mayor look like a model of integrity.

"What are we gonna do?"

Just then Cara's cousin came running in.

"Some boys came up an' start messin' with us, and took Cara's money an' ran away. Cara ran after 'em."

"Where's the baby?"

"He awright. He's with my sister."

"Come on," I said, taking hold of her arm, "show me."

"You want me to come with you?" Cherokee asked.

I shook my head. The meeting would begin in twenty minutes. With me gone, he already had more to do than one person could handle. "I'll be right back."

"What's your name, dear?" I asked the girl. At the back of my head my mind began a list of errors for this situation. Not learning the cousins' names may not have been the first mistake, but it was the first to go on the list.

"Shakeeya," she said.

"What grade are you in?"

"Fif'."

I quickened my pace.

"I can't walk that fast," she complained.

I kept hold of her arm. "Then you'll have to run."

When we turned the corner, I saw Cara at the end of the block. Her cardigan hung off one shoulder. Shakeeya shouted at her as we approached.

"Where's Taiyeesha?"

Cara shrugged. She crossed her arms over her chest and scowled like a mask. This is how she'd looked every afternoon that first year at St. A's, when she was brought to my office straight from her third or fourth scrape of the day.

"Where is she?" Shakeeya screamed.

"She went back to Granma's house."

"Way down Tasker Homes?"

I let go of Shakeeya's arm. She took off running to join her sister. I was so afraid for Kintu, so angry to be greeted by Cara's old mask of self-pity and rage, so mad that I let her take my baby, the hand I had taken off Shakeeya's arm began to shake.

"Quick, where's the baby?" I looked up and down the street, expecting to see my bright white stroller with the navy blue and white polka-dot ruffles standing somewhere in sight.

She shrugged again. "Ahn't know."

I don't know. I couldn't take it in. My mind flailed around for answers. "Did you leave 'im at the store with Mr. Kim?"

"I never got to the store. These boys came an' took my money."

"Did you leave 'im with Taiyeesha?"

"Unh-uh. 'Cause one of the boys hit my cousin, too."

"Where were you when this happened?" I asked.

I had her by the back of the sweater, walking toward the store. I was trying to trace her steps, to keep thinking, to keep panic at bay until I could come upon the information that would take me to the block where I would turn the corner and see the stroller, bright and clean, in the middle of a group of gawking kids; or next to a disapproving old woman who'd been watching out the window and would chastise her for leaving and me for entrusting the baby to her; or a Moorish Temple family, the father and son wearing red fezzes with black tassels and the mother and daughter in red turbans, debating what to do with the child; or two tall, thin black men with leathery faces, Amtrak maintenance men a year or so from retirement, hangin' in there, as they'd say if asked, wearing black suits with red flowers in their lapels and white gloves, on their way to usher at First African Baptist.

"Help me," I said over and over. Each image was hope.

Cara had been talking, but I hadn't heard her. I knew she was telling me the long version of the episode, and I knew that at least part of it was a lie. She never told her part. She'd never say that she knew these boys, or laughed at them when they walked by, or that she was waving her five-dollar bill at someone leaning out a second-story window so that they saw it and decided to have some fun and get some money, too. She'd never say that she'd forgotten all about the baby and took off after them, leaving her two younger cousins alone with an infant they did not know.

We were around the back of the church now, by the abandoned curacy. Cara rolled her shoulders to get my grip off her cardigan. Still enraged, she was ready to fight me, too. Then she muttered, "Get off," and something inside me exploded.

I found myself dragging her the few feet behind the curacy, off the street where it was deadly still. The sun streamed down on us at a sharp angle from between the high stone walls. It was as if we were at the bottom of a deep, wide pen.

I felt a terrible savagery rise up in me. In my whole life I had never wanted to hurt anyone before. I wanted to hurt Cara now.

"If anything happens to him, I swear to you before God, I don't know what I will do to you; do you hear me?

"I am too crazy right now. You understand? *I want that baby*. I don't care about anything else: not *you*, not this collar, not jail, not God or the devil."

I picked her up off the ground a few inches and rammed her against the wall for emphasis. At seventy pounds, she felt light in my arms. I could have done it ten more times. I used to wonder how slave owners could beat men and women until their arms were too tired. Now I know.

"Do you understand?"

Cara understood. Of course she did. She'd known violence and the threat of violence. Before she came to St. A's it was what she'd known best. The grown-ups in her world had been terrorists. Sometimes they were kind, and it had given her enough hope to make her craven and resentful by turns. Did she understand me? Her eyes said that she understood me perfectly. She knew that underneath it all, I was like the rest. She understood that Kintu was mine and she wasn't. She understood the clear message of her own fear. I hated myself for my rage. I hated Cara for cowering. And I hated that neither of us could help ourselves.

"Now show me where you left him."

With a teary face and my hand clamped around her arm, she hustled up the block to the corner and pointed. The corner was empty. On the muggy Sunday afternoon few people stirred outside. Something told me to listen. I put my finger to my mouth. Cara stopped sniveling. Kintu cried out his staccato yell from a nearby alley.

Life and death in the power of the tongue. I mumbled Mark's words to myself like a mantra—I, who had been mute so long; I, who had stopped bothering to argue with my faith, and shelved it, like something cracked that can neither be used nor discarded. Cry out, little man, I thought. It is life or death now. *Cry*.

We followed the sound. Dogs growled and barked at us as we ran through the alley. They were mean dogs; people kept them for protection. One threw himself against a rotting wooden fence that looked as if it would give way with every thrust. Cara screamed and begged to be left on the sidewalk. She'd been attacked by a dog once; I'd seen the scars on her arm. Still I dragged her with me. She'd helped the crisis happen. She would help resolve it.

The alley opened to where an abandoned project rose up like a monument: blind, boarded-up windows stared over our heads. The ground around, smelling of human urine and feces, was worn as smooth as Soweto. In the middle of the lot, in plain sight, an orange plastic supermarket basket perched atop a gray milk carton. Kintu lay inside the basket.

I ran, grabbed Kintu up and inspected his face. He was hot and flushed from the sun. Sweat plastered his fluffy hair to his forehead. The bright red-and-blue playsuit that Roz had ordered overnight delivery from L. L. Bean was untouched. The hand-made blue-and-white quilt that Tam had brought back from the Senegalese tailor in Brooklyn was tucked under him. Only the stroller had been stolen. The thief must have scared or seduced or distracted or bribed Cara's cousin away for just long enough to take it, then left the baby out in the open for his mother—me—to find.

I fell to my knees because my legs would no longer hold me, moaned out loud with gratitude and relief, and rubbed Kintu's fat cheek against mine.

On the way back to the church Cara and I passed a Dumpster at the bottom of a construction chute.

"That's where they found that little boy," Cara said. "They say his uncle did it. I don't think so."

Kofi was waiting on the steps when we returned. The meeting had just begun ten minutes before. He asked me what happened, and I briefly told him. He inspected Kintu, just as I had. Then he held me. I was still shaking.

"I'll go in and leave a message for your reverend, and then I'll take you home. OK?"

He went inside, and I put my arm around Cara's shoulder. I held her to me, and she relaxed her body into mine. I could not apologize. I'd gone too far for sorry.

"You going in?" I asked.

She nodded, as if to ask what else was there to do. "But I'm hungry," she said.

"Go in the kitchen and see what Mrs. Johnson has left," I said.

"Mrs. Johnson, she mean," she said. "Will you go with me?"

"No," I said. "But tell her I sent you and I'm asking her, please, to fix you a plate, please. Try to say it nice."

She left. Kofi returned with Cherokee, who was able to slip out while the Pentecostal minister gave her summary of our work so far.

Kee patted me as if I were a girl. "Kofi says he's taking you home. You go ahead. Don't worry about this afternoon. Everything here is under control."

But it wasn't, and I couldn't. I listened in my head to the appalling summary of events I had just given Kofi. After what had just happened, how could I go home and draw the blinds, hoping to escape the scourge rather than fight it?

With the two of them on either side, and Kintu safe, I felt stronger. I pulled my notes out of my pocket and shook them.

"Well, then, go," said Kofi, "before you miss your place on the program."

Inside the kids were well into their play, a strict morality tale, as all their plays tended to be, about a boy who drops out of high school, works minimum wage jobs, and then, bit by bit, begins to sell drugs. The community policeman notices, befriends the young man, fails to save him from the street, but wins over his younger brother.

I'd seen rehearsals, and I knew what came next. Alone, the kid brother practices foul shots that miss. The beat cop shows him to shoot with his elbows tucked in for more power. He shoots two out of three when we hear the commotion off to the side and the older brother runs onto the court followed by a dealer and a sidekick. As the elder brother reaches into his waistband, the cop pushes the younger one, who screams his brother's name, to the ground. The caps go off, the dealer runs up the aisle, and the older brother lies dead. The younger brother crumples next to his adored sibling as the cop runs after the killers. In an epilogue, the younger brother appears, obviously grown up, wearing a suit jacket and carrying a trench coat.

"That beat cop couldn't save my brother that day, but his being there did help save me."

The music came up again, and the cast danced into the center altar rapping over it:

> Cops who walk the beat
> Can take the heat
> They show they care
> By being there
> They don't talk the talk
> They walk the walk
> They don't talk the talk
> They walk the walk.

I waited for the applause to subside and stood to speak about our officers. I named them and thanked them for their work and their time among us. I told the people how one officer said that in a squad car tension was followed by short bursts of reacting to violence, but that on the beat, he *created nonviolence* through relationships with people. He had power, as the kids' play showed, over and above the power of his gun and badge. And it was, I said, because he was walking the walk:

"In our own lifetimes, Martin King taught us how to walk

down injustice. But we're beginning to forget the lesson. Now that the day has become a national holiday, everybody talks about the dream, the dream, the dream, and McDonald's puts it on commercials and the airlines superimpose his face on a cloud and float him away. They use our martyr to make a buck. In order to use him, though, we have to tame him, declaw him, take out his teeth. We forget how hard-won nonviolence is, how hard-hitting and hard-nosed. We make the civil rights movement look easy. We make it look inevitable. He was a warrior who taught us to fight for freedom, and we've made him look like a midwife who stood next to history and let justice slide out naturally. They've made our warrior into a dreamer, and we forget the blood that was spilled before, during, and after. We forget his blood, spilled for us. But you know what else? We forget the work.

"Before the dream came the work. In 1956, after his house was bombed at the beginning of the Montgomery bus boycott, Martin King took out a gun permit."

A rustle of surprise went through the thousand people crowded into the sanctuary. I'd stopped shaking. I felt buoyed up, full, strong, myself and not myself. I heard my own voice at a slight delay and spoke my thoughts before I quite knew them.

"Imagine the work it took for him to quiet his fear and his anger. We've learned about his sexual exploits. Imagine the work to try to control his own personal demons and do the task God had assigned to him.

" 'My God is so big: that's what we teach the children in kindergarten. They sing that little song and march around the auditorium. But we adults are afraid. We don't want the revelation. Could be scary. We don't want the work. It's hard work. Don't feel like it. We want to put it on the altar and leave it there, say God is good, and walk away, unchallenged, unchanged.

"But that's why Jesus overturned the money tables in the temple; that's why, as Luke reports, he told his disciples to sell their clothes and buy a sword; it's why he reveals himself to John, with a voice like the sound of waters and a two-edged sword in his mouth: he's telling us to fight for justice.

"We have got to harness within ourselves and among ourselves—in our communities—not just God's goodness, but his sublime and hideous power. If we want justice we need to stop beating the resistance out of our own children, and teach them whom to resist.

"If we wanted justice and if we believed that God is big enough and bad enough to make it happen, it would change the very cell structure in our bodies. God help our enemies if we believed as David believed when he gathered the stones, the five smooth stones from the riverbed.

"God help us when the master says, 'Come forth,' and he comes, stinking from the grave, wrapped in the burial cloth, but alive, alive-o.

"God help us if we pray, 'Lord, help us walk the walk,' 'cause he has the power to say, 'Rise up. Rise up, O Jerusalem, and do my mighty bidding.'

"Say it with me, those of you who know the Psalm:

" 'The Lord is my light and my salvation; whom shall I fear? / The Lord is the strength of my life; of whom shall I be afraid?' "

My own cells did change as I spoke, and it was nothing like I'd hoped for or imagined. I put my arms into the air as if to accept the gift, and instead of grace, grief shot into me like fire, like hammer shattering rock.

I sat down amid the echoes of amens, arms clasped around my own shoulders as if to hold myself together, stunned.

I shook my head at Cherokee. He indicated words he had written in his program: *And who shall stand when he appeareth?* He motioned to the pianist to play our congregation's favorite song. It was a simple spiritual:

> *Thank you, Lord.*
> *Thank you, Lord.*

Thank you, Lord.
I just want to thank you, Lord.

Been so good.
Been so good.
Been so good.
I just want to thank you, Lord.

Been my friend.
Been my friend.
Been my friend.
I just want to thank you, Lord.

As we were singing, Roosevelt Scott from the Wednesday morning prayer group came down the center aisle dancing. Once a member of Alvin Ailey in New York, he now taught at a local dance school and took care of his lover, who was dying of AIDS. Over Christmas, Rosie had had his own first AIDS-related infection. He'd lost ten pounds and was all sinew and skin: tall, silent, golden, and not robust, but taut.

Now as I watched Rosie's spontaneous dance of life and death, I felt the underground pressure, pushing, heaving. There are springs like that under streets throughout Philadelphia. There's one behind the church. All of a sudden the street heaves and falls in.

Rosie finished and the church rose up, glad for an excuse to stamp their feet and shout. I could barely move. I sat in my pew while Kee went up to the podium to stand as the deputy commissioner came forward to offer the mini-station. He offered to put it in the curacy and renovate the whole building and house a new chapter of the Police Athletic League there, too. The people in church clapped and cheered. Our pride is dust.

Kofi was waiting for me at the back of the church at the recessional. He had the baby in one arm and his quilt in the other.

"You know," he said, "you chose the irrational."

"Yeah," I said. "Now I know why I stayed behind my desk for so long."

"So where do you want to go?"

"With you," I said. "Home. Lemme sit and hold the baby awhile."

His tic today was in his cheek. "Fair enough," he said.

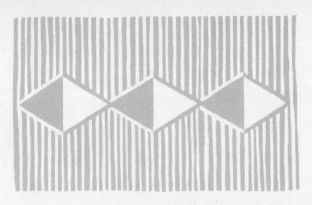

A U D R E Y

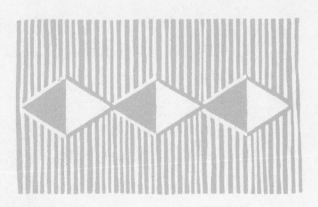

19

I will try not to lie. "Rarely have we seen someone fail who has truly followed our path" is what the AA Big Book says, except for those "few unfortunates" who are constitutionally incapable of telling the truth. But everybody does lie. Tam keeping quiet about Hiram all that time. If that's not lying I'm flying.

Or Roz talking about how we bonded, all four of us, on her twelfth birthday, the day she brought in those cookies that nobody would eat because they smelled like mothballs, and she went out back and cried and puked, and we felt so bad for her we gave her some water. We fought half the time for the first few years. Roz, especially. She'd hit you in a minute. Tam was a smart-ass, always in your face and in somebody's shit. I came out of my crazy-ass house every morning like somebody shot out of a gun, and *I* didn't even know who I was gonna be that day. But before Roz, we never really fought, and then, after she became part of the group, we fought all the time up until she got married.

But even Arneatha hasn't always been rigorously honest. After Larry died, she'd always say how church and the school filled her life. And she couldn't ask for more. Couldn't imagine being happier than she was, blah, blah, blah. Mostly she looked like she'd been punched in the gut—for years. She was on missionary autopilot. How she could deny it, I'll never know. To see her now with that jumpy-eye African and the baby who looks like an old man is amazing. Arneatha is a marrying kind of woman. That's just how she is.

And then, speaking of denial, there's me saying my first time being sober was so wonderful and I was so grateful. I was miserable as shit. And the worst part is I didn't even know it. How to keep from lying when you don't even know the truth? That's the trick.

Rigorous honesty? It already *had* happened. At Odunde. I stopped in at Tam's when I left Roz and the baby at the bookstall. Tam gave me the key. I waded through the people downstairs who'd had a death in the family, and went right to the freezer to get some ice for ice water. And, *boom,* there this bottle of Absolut is staring me in the face. Like a fantasy. *Drink me.* She even had a shot glass next to the bottle, frosted.

I stood there and watched my hand, which, at that point, had no connection to my head, pour the vodka into the shot glass. Next thing I knew that shit was tossed down my throat. Then I watched as it happened again. Just three little shots. I didn't want her to notice. Wouldn't want to notice my damn self.

All I could do was go lie down in her bedroom. She had the air-conditioning on low cool and the shades drawn. Because she is who she is, her bedroom always feels like you done stepped into the Casbah, and I don't even like sex, to tell the truth. So I laid down and let that vodka make its way through me like the white damn lightning that it is.

They say that while you're inside staying sober, your disease is out there doing push-ups. And I'm here to tell you that's the truth. Toward the end of my drinking, I got so that I could never tell anymore how much would tear me up. Could be ten drinks, could be one. Well, those three shots had me lit the fuck up.

My dad was a drunk. And I caught so much hell from his drinking that in high school, when everybody else was getting into beer and rum and Cokes and seven-and-sevens and all that nonsense, I wouldn't touch a drop. I started drinking in nursing school with a girl named Molly. A couple years ago I was sitting in the McDonald's on Oregon Avenue when they called the cops on a woman who looked like her, only fifty pounds heavier and a hundred years older. Her T-shirt said: 100% IRISH (JUST ADD ALCOHOL). I'm almost sure it was her, fighting and cussing her boyfriend so bad they had to carry them both away. Bloated up, looked like a pig.

Rigorous honesty? I probably did, too. Which is why I started the diet pills and why I went back to smoking. A hundred and eighty-two damn pounds. More than I weighed with either of my kids. I saw Molly, and my mind didn't say—Whoa, better let up on the moonshine. No, what I said was: Quitting smoking put fifteen pounds on me. Hey, get me some Marlboro Lights, quick.

When I first started drinking it was real sociable. Nice and ladylike. No fights, no puking, no peeing myself. All that good stuff came later. But I did start. Make no mistake. Birds gotta fly. Fish gotta swim. I had to stay black, pay taxes, die—and drink. Basically, what I know now is that I had been playing in the key of booze all my life. The first drink of the evening was like somebody filled in the bottom note of a chord. For the first time in nineteen years of life, I could sit back and relax. I'd go to classes, go to work at this place where all the junkies and the poor folk came to give blood for cash, and then I'd knock off with a couple guys from the blood bank, or I'd meet Molly. She'd say shit like: "You know your problem? Too much god-damn blood in your alcohol."

She'd say it in this Irish lilt like her granddaddy. Pretty accent.

We went to this one bar all the time. I ate the same dinner for four years: two quarts of Genessee Cream Ale, a roast beef sandwich on a kaiser roll, and a bag of barbecue potato chips. A pickle if they had it. The bar had a sad-ass piano in the corner. Molly and the guys played pool. I played the piano. Lounge music and boogie-woogie. Basic. Some blues. Just a rocking bass'd be enough to keep those people happy for a long time. For one whole week, all I played was "Four O'Clock Blues." Just that. Happy blues. Up blues. All major scale with a little Yancey Bass underneath.

They liked it so much, they started giving me beer and my sandwich free whenever I played for an hour. My mother's piano had been repossessed years before. I told myself I was keeping up with my music. I read the papers and trade publications and went on calls now and then for pianists. I started playing for funeral homes and eventually quit the blood bank. But I was buzzed every night. The only way I got through nursing school was I got up every morning at four and studied. Back then I thought I had an internal alarm clock. Now I know that that's when the booze wore off.

We said we were programmed for success by these parents who stayed on us like a steady beat. All except Roz. She programmed her own self. Of all of us, hers was the straightest line from point A to point B, and God help you if you got in her way. But my programming was complicated. I tried to learn from them. I tried to raise myself, but I was still an egomaniac with an inferiority complex. Bad combo.

But see, the thing about the vodka at Tam's apartment on Odunde was this: Nobody knew. Odunde means New Year. Well, it was a bad New Year for me. Even had the nerve to go out later, get a great, big old cheese steak with everything and some fries and eat them all up. Funny, all the stuff I lost in blackouts and the stuff that remains. I will never forget that cheese steak. That was just about the best fucking cheese steak I ever ate, before or since. That's what they mean when they say this disease is cunning, baffling, and powerful. After I finished, I put on a pot of coffee to perk while I took a bath. Went whole hog. Turned on Tam's CD, cranked up a double CD of Frank Sinatra ballads. What they call suicide music. Just as nice. People downstairs grieving for their grandson, and I'm up there, isolating, and spinning "Only the Lonely."

It was playing house. Like, let's make pretend I'm a normal drinker. Let's pretend I can come in, relax in my girlfriend's apartment (since I don't have a crib of my own), do a few shots to chill out, eat some dinner, and then have a cup of coffee and go to work. That's what I did. I went to work. And all the rest of June, I'm working setting up this after work program at St. Auggie's, trying to learn how to write grant proposals, talking to city officials, visiting other rehabs and group therapy facilitators, talking to shrinks, carrying my damn briefcase like Ms. Sober U.S.A., Ms. Black Recovery—"Yes, hello, right, I am Reverend Thomas's friend. Yes, Representative Hiram Prettyman did call you on my behalf. Yes, well, we want the kind of program you have downtown available right here in the community, yep, right in south Philly. Right! Where the sickness is, the healing begins." All the while, that sneaky drunk within was waiting for our next interlude. They say you're as sick as your secrets, and for me—I'm just talking about for me now—that is about as true as the Ace of Spades.

It didn't kick in right away. Sneaky.

After the community-policing meeting, I went home, and I didn't even get my key out before my mother started. Talking about: "You never did have any consideration for anybody except yourself. Never. What's the point of all this big sobriety if you're still gonna waltz out of here and leave me all alone with a bag to change? This stuff can back up, you know."

I had promised myself I wasn't even going to feed into it. Roz had been on the phone every other day threatening to drive up to Coatesville herself and pick the lock off Buddha's garage and go into his trunk to get her gun, and I kept pushing her back with the phrase "breaking and entering." But Buddha and Mimi had just returned from their trailer-park paradise up in Donegal, Pennsylvania, so I was on my way up there that afternoon.

"I went to work yesterday at three. I did a double shift till seven. Then I went to church, changed clothes in those pissy bathrooms they have, and attended the service, because I promised Neesie I'd be there. She needs the people, Mom. OK?

"Now I'm here to change your bag and fix you some food and get myself a bath. Then I'm going back out to the train, and I'ma go up to Coatesville 'cause Roz is up my butt about something of hers I left in his car, and maybe I can even con him into letting me have something to drive for a few weeks now that he's home. Like it would have killed him to let me have it while he was away . . ."

Out of all my sisters and brothers, Buddha's my favorite, which is good, since he is the only one living nearby. Everybody else got out of Dodge as soon as they could buy a damn bus ticket or hook up with somebody who had a bus ticket.

The reason I was pulling so many doubles was because Mom had no health insurance and wouldn't get a medical card. She said that she had seven children, and they all had good jobs, so why should she have to go on welfare to be able to go to the doctor? Which, you got to agree, does make some sense. Over the year Mom's health went down, and I called around to try to get everybody to chip in, either to pay her bills—'cause not having insurance sure as shit didn't keep her out the doctor's office and she was already five grand in debt—or else, so we could go in on a policy together until the Medicare kicks in. But no. That must have been too much like right.

They gave me a whole crapload of alternatives, including the ever-popular get Dad to do it. Mom and Dad never divorced (like the Catholic Church would close its doors if they did), so technically, they said, his insurance should cover her. My brother Kevin, the big-deal lawyer in Los Angeles who's never taken a drink in his perfect little life and lives with the perfect little light-bright wife who he backhands on occasion—I know 'cause his kids will call and tell me—Kevin had the nerve to give me the Fed Ex number at his job in case there were any papers to read and figure out once I—me, *moi*—convinced Dad to put her on.

I said to him, I said: "Hello, Kevin, I need some fuckin' help here. You know they don't talk. Dad's a drunk. The man's delusional half the time. He'll listen to a man better. You talk to him."

He gave me some bullshit about being swamped at work and the time difference. *The time difference?* We were talking, on my dime, I might add, from sea to shining damn sea.

"Motherfuck the time difference," I said.

But then I was the crazy bitch, going off again. And Kevin started talking real slow and quiet, like he had a Looney Tunes on the wire. He suggested I tell Dad to consider that we'd all chip in to defray any extra co-pay costs, and I hung up on him.

I'll tell you what I did consider. I considered putting Mom's urine bag in the freezer and Fed Exing him a sample of that in a Little Playmate with some ice packs on either end, but I didn't do it.

The subtext, as Tam likes to say, of these conversations is that I've been an irresponsible drunk like Dad, so I owe them everything forever and ever without complaint. Nobody says it, but that's what they're all thinking.

My Plan B was that sometime soon I'd save, borrow, or steal enough money to send Mommy on a magic mystery tour to spend a month or two with all the successful children she liked to brag about at Bingo and give me and Buddha a well-deserved break. So, that's another reason I was pulling so many doubles. Always a secret agenda.

At any rate, though, I damn sure was going to Coatesville to get the gun—and the car—as soon as it was available. I hate not having a car. I crashed the last one.

"What am I supposed to do when you leave me in a lurch like that? My bag was full. I couldn't even change my bag."

"You were supposed to call Katie Carter up the street. The money's all taken care of. You're supposed to call her."

"Why should I have to call Katie Carter? You made that arrangement. I didn't."

"So she can change the bag, help you get washed, and take out the dog."

The dog had peed on the mat by the back door. The whole goddamned house was a pisspot. If I didn't get out of there I thought I would die of urinary overload.

I let the dog out the back door into the yard, changed my mother, washed her down with Skin-So-Soft in a basin, put the mat into the washing machine with detergent and bleach, mopped the floor with vinegar water to try to keep the fool dog chilled out. I opened the windows, but Mom said her rose fever was going, so I closed the place back up like a tomb, fixed her a plate of food and set it on the stove, and made her a snack and put it in the fridge. I wrote Katie Carter's name and number in black marker on a piece of cardboard and propped it up on the telephone by her chair.

"What about the dog's pills? I got enough trouble trying to keep up with my own."

"All she needs is the heartworm pill."

"Well, I see she needs something. You got the heart decal up on the calendar for day before yesterday, but if nobody's here, what can I do? I don't know which pill is which."

I let the dog in, and went upstairs for a new pack of cigarettes and the dog's heartworm pill. Behind me my mother was griping about how if the dog had somehow contracted a heartworm in the two days since the last pill had worn off, she'd heard that the medicine could kill her, and was I willing to risk that?

"Sure," I said.

"Well, all right, then," she said. "On your head be it. . . . I'm sure, though, that the vet would take a call on a Sunday. If the dog's life is in danger."

"I'ma feed her the pill," I said. "If she dies, call Katie Carter and get her to come put her out on the trash. I'll put the trash out before I go. Give 'er a garbage bag. Ida'll fit right into the lawn and leaf bag, no problem."

"Go ahead. Laugh at me. Why are you putting out the trash? Aren't you coming home tonight again? Answer me!"

In my closet, on the shelf, next to the tangle of winter sweaters and my shoe boxes full of papers and old crap were manila envelopes the size of pay packets with medicine from the vet: her heartworm pills, her flea repellent pills, and the leftover tranquilizers from the trip I took her on to Chicago.

I called her, gave her a heartworm pill, and went to the bathroom to wash my hands. Then I realized I had one of the envelopes tucked under my arm. The tranqs. My heart was banging around in my chest like somebody trying to escape. I filled a Dixie Cup with water and took them all, a couple dozen or so, each measured out for a dog that weighed eight to ten pounds, so I thought that would do me and give me a little extra for insurance. Not like abusing the drug or overdosing. I remember looking at my watch so I could time how long it took them to kick in.

I brushed my teeth and pulled my hair up into a ponytail to get it off my neck.

Then I left the hot, dark house for the hot, bright street and got the hell out of town.

20

I moved out to Coatesville once. That was the first time I started thinking seriously about trying to stop drinking. But mostly, I looked elsewhere for the problem and the solutions. I would get to planning on how I'd find a cheap little place in the woods up above Coatesville and bring Bryant out once I got established, but that was all hot air. What ended up happening was I rented a room from this elderly woman who used to sit up in bed and have her taste and smoke her menthols and watch TV. One night I woke up and the fire trucks had come and the sirens was going and lights everywhere. It was like passing out and coming to in hell. She had fallen asleep smoking, just like the ads tell you not to. She died, too. They were able to get me out.

I moved in with my brother Buddha and his family. Now, nothing says I couldn't have found another place there in Coatesville and gotten a job at the big VA hospital there, maybe, but after six months, I came back to the city. I said the fire was an omen.

Of course my AA sponsors see it differently. My brother Buddha doesn't drink. Teetotaler. He's a lot older than me. There's the three older brothers and sisters, and then a five-year gap, and then there's me. Three kids died in the gap, two in infancy, one of hepatitis as a toddler. Don't ask me how she contracted it.

Rehab counselors always ask me whether I think it was "failure to thrive." How the hell do I know? I made it, that's all I know. My parents split several times, the last time right before she got pregnant with me. I think they went to the priest for counseling. I don't know what he told them, but they got back together, had me, fought for another six or seven years, and then split for good.

For a while my dad, who is part Indian, had this thing about moving to Arizona or New Mexico and living clean in some pueblo built into the mountainside. What AA people call the geographic cure. But we didn't know that back then. At that time, it was part of his rap about how with somebody like my mom and a load a kids hanging around his neck, he had to drink. Who wouldn't?

I half fell for it. Or fell for it enough so that sometimes as a kid I'd daydream that he'd go ahead out to the Southwest and come back tanned red-brown by the sun. I guess I expected the sun would dry him out, too, and make him wise like those Indians in the movies who stare out to the horizon and grunt, and you know that they understand all of nature and the coming tide of white men, and see the future and accept it with sadness for their people but also with dignity. Daddy could've used some of that. He'd come back Chief Ransome and take me, the baby girl who adored him, and we'd live in the pueblo and wear silver and turquoise and I'd cook us dinner out of cornmeal and dried fish.

Buddha laughs about the Arizona talk. As the oldest son, he saw what drinking did in our family—to my dad and my mother's father, too, and I guess he just said: 'I'll take a pass on *that,* thank you very much.' When I lived with them after the fire, I was getting the idea that maybe if I stayed and hung around him and Gloria, who we call Mimi, well, maybe I might have to slow down on the vodka. You don't have to be a rocket scientist to see the handwriting on the wall. No wonder I moved back to the city.

Buddha and Mimi may not drink, but what they do do is eat.

I mean, they go out to those warehouse stores and buy potato chips in boxes as big as a foot locker. They buy peanuts by the bushel and roast 'em themselves. Mimi keeps three or four pounds of hard candy in the car.

As you might expect, Buddha is big—he always was. Great, big fat face, big round belly, little slitty eyes when he laughs. Plus he was happy and easygoing. And Mimi's just huge. There's no other way to say it. I mean, to the point where she can barely get around. And where they live that's terrible, 'cause Buddha collects junk, so the whole lot is littered with crap. He scavenges, and then he sells it or fixes things with it, or, far as I can tell, just keeps it and looks at it and enjoys having it and thinking about it and figuring out what he could do with it if thus-and-so situation ever occurred. But Mimi can't get around there at all. She's got her path from the house to the trailer, which they call their office, and somehow she gets up the steps and turns sideways and sits down at the desk and keeps the books. And then she's worn another path to the garage, although she still doesn't drive.

They've got four boys, and they're big, too, and they all work in the junk business, fixing up cars with their father. I love 'em; whenever I come, they treat me like a queen. Mimi fixes enough food to choke a horse, and we sit around telling stories, listening to Duke Ellington; the boys sing doowop together, and they have their own little world. I said to my nephews once, I said, "So when're y'all going to move away from your mama?"

They just laughed.

"Never." Didn't shame them a bit.

The oldest one, Bear, already had his own trailer up the hill where he'd bring his girlfriend. "What about when you marry?" I asked.

"She'll just move in up there," he said. "And be part of the family."

Well, I sure as shit wasn't going to move into a trailer or a converted hearse or the toolshed my brother rigged up with Christmas twinkle lights when I told him it was too dark for me to sleep out there alone. Like I say, it definitely would have been *The Big and the Restless* if I moved into the dry—emphasis on *dry*—and piney woods back of Buddha's family compound.

In fact, when I moved back from Coatesville is when I started the diet pills. In six months up there I put on twenty pounds. The diet pills made me jumpy, too. Which was the reason I gave myself for starting to take a shot at lunchtime to calm down some. I put it in one of those milkshake vitamin meals. I'd heard a shrink on the radio say that if you could go two or three weeks without a drink, you probably weren't an alcoholic, and in Coatesville, after the fire, I didn't hardly drink much at all for months. So, a little shot in the shake seemed perfectly fine. Yippee.

For a while after I came back, Roz and I tried Weight Watchers, but I resented paying these white women good money after bad just to get weighed and talked at once a week by this smug little bitch in leggings and a chenille tunic. Anybody could tell she was a food addict, which was one of a handful of fuck-ups I told Roz I didn't have. And the black woman who took over for her sometimes was even worse. Roz claimed it was too much food they made you eat, and she couldn't keep up with it. Yeah, right. Anyway, after we finished figuring them out, we quit. I went back to my pills and my shake and she started walking in the morning with Neese.

Since I didn't have any money, Tam bought me a half-year membership at a spa, but I was drinking again, and I knew they could smell it on me in the morning, so I stopped going there, too. I think she ended up transferring the last month or two of my membership to her account to keep it from being a total waste. Which is why I couldn't say but so much about Tam's thing with Hiram. I thought it was just about the shittiest thing she could do, but on the other hand, Tam has been very good to me. And one thing I happen to know about her is this: if you tell her, I don't want to fuck, no, thank you, she'll back off with no hard feelings. I know that for a fact. So, it's not like she had to put a gun to his head.

· · ·

Buddha picked me up in the old Nova, and I had to drive him home before I turned around and came back to the city. When we got to his house, the one thing I did before I let him go was look in the trunk for the gun and the champagne. Sure enough, he had scavenged them. I told him I had to have the gun back because it belonged to Roz, and that I'd promised to sell the champagne to somebody at church for a wedding that week. Otherwise he would've kept them and sold them eventually himself.

Before I left he also gave me a package to take to my father from him and Mimi and the boys—the kind of impossible, two-hundred-piece jigsaw puzzles my father always liked, pictures of coffee beans and licorice. He used to do them dead drunk, and my mother would glue them to a piece of cardboard and hang them on the wall. They're still all over the house. I hate them. Buddha was sending these as a Father's Day present.

"I wish I *would* send him a Father's Day present," I said. In fact, what I really wanted to do was tell Buddha to mail the puzzles his damn self, but I didn't, since he never mailed anything, and he *was* lending me the car. So I took the puzzles.

"How often you talk to the old bastard?" I asked. Like, why mince words?

Buddha shrugged. He reached inside the front pocket of his overalls and pulled out some peanuts. The shells dropped down onto the tops of his work boots. "Every so often," he said.

He and I don't talk about Dad. Buddha was the one who came in on the last fight Mom and Dad had and pulled Dad out of the house. He's the one who reported to us that Dad had retired from Temple University hospital, which is when he dropped her medical benefits. Which, like I said, is why I'm working doubles.

"Next time you talk to him, ask him can he possibly put Mom back on his insurance."

"You're gonna see 'im when you drop off the puzzles."

"Maybe. I might leave 'em with the man next door. Tell 'im Kevin said he'd pay any extra co-pay."

"Kevin's full of shit," Buddha said. "Dad couldn't even put her back on if he wanted to, I don't think. Far as they're concerned, she's not his wife."

"But she is."

If Mom had said it once, she'd said it a hundred times: she didn't believe in divorce. She gave him her best years. She gave him seven babies. That plus the ass-kickings tore up her insides. So now she can't hold her own water. He wasn't getting away with making her into a disposable commodity. Besides, the Church didn't recognize divorce, she said, and the Church was right. What ever happened to women in divorce, except for they got poorer? And ended up taking care of some other loser? And got venereal disease. She had a whole speech. All you had to do was say the word *divorce* and she'd download the whole spiel.

Buddha stuck out his bottom lip and cracked open a few more shells. "She been saying it so long, she probably believe it."

"How could she not be his wife?"

"He divorced her years ago."

"What are you talkin' about?" I popped outside myself and watched my mouth moving slo-mo.

"He divorced her."

"When? How you divorce somebody in secret? Without their consent?"

"Soon as no-fault came to Pennsylvania, he did it."

"Does she know?"

"How I know what Mom knows? She had to be notified, I suppose. That's the law. They gotta let you know you been divorced."

I couldn't believe it.

"I could be standing on my fuckin' head right now," I said. I threw my arms out to the sides and made my eyes go all googly.

Buddha reached into his pocket and cracked some more nuts. "Mimi's frying some liver and onions. You want to come in and have some with me?"

How could I pass up that cholesterol opportunity? "No, thanks, Buddha."

"Couple pork chops I been saving."

"Nah."

We stood on his front lawn a little bit while the sun plopped down behind the rusty washers on the hillside. The junk was everywhere, hunks of bikes and wagons and carts and wheelbarrows—every goddamn thing you could imagine. Last bits of yellow sun reflected off the metal here and there like a crazy field of diamonds.

"Anything you need before you go home, just ask for it. I got most anything you need," he said. "C'mon, I'll send you with a cuppa coffee. You tired, aren't you?"

I followed him into the house. The frying liver smacked me in the face.

Mimi grinned at me. She had two pans working. I swear she'd worn a groove in the floor from the stove to the fridge. Another fifty years she'd be walking around at eye level with the sink.

"You stayin' for dinner?"

And suck down a pile of inner organs big as Rhode Island? Fried potatoes out of a trough? "No, thanks, Mimi."

"I'ma give 'er some coffee," Buddha said. "You know how she likes her coffee."

He poured old coffee from the machine into a twelve-ounce Styrofoam cup and put it into the microwave. He pushed two minutes, full power, which would be way too much, but it was no use arguing, because they drank burnt coffee all the time. I watched the green numbers count down. It beeped. Another two minutes of our lives gone. I felt so tired I could have fallen over.

"You all right to drive?" he asked.

I didn't answer him at first.

"Well," he said, "at least you're nice and calm."

"I'm fucking comatose," I said. "What's the point?"

"Here, drink your coffee. It'll make you feel better."

"I tell you what would make me feel better."

"Don't you start," he said, shaking his finger and smiling nervously.

He always said that. He used to stand behind the bedroom door and whisper it to my father when he'd come in all tore up and begin picking at my mother.

I'll never forget he said it to me when Bryant was a baby, and I'd just put him on the bottle, so I didn't have to worry about alcohol in the milk. Buddha came over and caught me having my first beer in months.

"Don't start."

Two days later they took me to jail, and I didn't have on nothing but my nightgown. It was a man and a woman cop, both white. She was whistling the theme from *M*A*S*H*. The only reason they didn't take my son from me and put him in foster care was that Hiram stepped in and vouched for me.

Mimi turned around and grinned again. She couldn't hear a word we said over the grease. She nodded her head toward the pan and said, "You sure, now?"

You could have sold that shit to the Eritrean militia to make sandals. "Nah, baby, that's all right."

"All right. You missin' somethin' good." She turned back to the counter and started whipping up enough coleslaw dressing to stucco a wall.

"Fresh," she said. "I like my cabbage fresh. Wanna take some in the car? You sure? OK. 'Bye now."

Buddha walked me through the yard to the car. He stopped next to an old bathtub filled with plumbing supplies, reached down, and came up with two chrome guardrails and something else I couldn't see.

"Last time I went to see Mom she had a hard time in the

bathroom. Get Bryant to screw these into the wall by the toilet. And here, these looked like you."

They were crystal spigots.

I put them in the car and kissed him. Less than a quarter of a tank of gas, and I couldn't trust the gauge. Typical. Then I got on the road.

Things went downhill from there.

It was warm that night, and wouldn't cool off when the sun went down. Muggy and close. Smelled like pine and motor oil. Plus the liver and onions steady coming off me. Oppressive. I couldn't hardly breathe.

I remember pulling over to a Wawa convenience store for gas. You go in to pay first. I got ten dollars' worth and stood in the middle of the store gulping the cool air. When the boy asked, "Can I help you?" I ordered a giant Diet Coke. He gave it to me in a plastic cup covered with Power Rangers.

Back in the car, I reached down to take off the brake, and pulled the trunk release instead. So then I let out the brake and drove off. Four or five miles later, I hit a bump in the road and the trunk opened up. I pulled onto the shoulder. It was dark by then, and the cars were zooming by. I was almost scared to get out. Felt like every time one went by, that little piece of car was rocked by the force of it. And so dark. I sat there drinking the soda. Then I had to pee. So I put my bag on my shoulder and went to the trunk and got out the gun and put it into my bag. I don't know what I thought I'd do if somebody came at me while I was in the bushes. Like I'd be there, bare-assed, squatting down, and whip out the revolver, which was in a case, and may or may not have been loaded. But it made me feel safer, so I carried it. I got ten mosquito bites on the ass and wet up my shoe.

Then, back to the car again. I had pushed the trunk to, but not closed all the way. So I take out a bottle of champagne, slam the trunk, and get back in the car. By now, I'm wobbly, breathing heavy. It starts to feel like the anxiety attacks I used to get back in the early eighties. It's just them stupid-ass dog tranqs wearing off, I told myself, so chill.

The dark was taking me the fuck out. So, I said to myself, if I can just turn on the radio and hear somebody's voice, I'll be OK. What I wanted was a baseball game, just to occupy my mind while I drove. And I put the key in the ignition, and turned on the car, and turned on the radio. All I wanted was AM. Radio didn't work.

So here's the insanity. I was like, OK. Now the fuckin' radio don't work? I guess I got no choice but to pour some of this stuff into my Coke.

It was that simple. No nothing in between. Cunning, baffling, and powerful. Like they say, I had no defense against the first drink.

So I opened the foil, opened the wire, and wiggled out the cork. Lotta work to open a bottle of bubbly, and it was like I'd been waiting to do it again. I remember wondering if this is how Mom felt when Daddy moved back. Like when he slipped back into his dent on his side of the mattress, or when he sat back down in his chair at the table or his easy chair in the living room. Right then, when I poured that wine over the ice in my plastic Power Rangers cup, I knew all the hell was coming back, and I didn't care. Not that I didn't care, but that I stopped thinking I could change it. I knew I was stepping back into the life. I knew I'd wake up sick as a dog, in trouble. I knew I was giving up hope and pride and dignity and my Rehab After Work and the trust and respect of my friends and my son. But all those things suddenly seemed impossible anyway, like somebody who's flunking out of school thinking that by doing her homework for a few months, she's going to make the principal's list, go to college, and represent her state in Atlantic City in the Miss Black America contest. Why bother?

And yet at the same time I felt sure it could be different. This time I'd have a few and stop. I wouldn't drink the next day. I'd save the champagne down in the basement, and I'd pull it out on special occasions. I'd have cognac in the wintertime at night. I'd play in the old bar again and nurse two bottles of beer all evening. This'd be like the turnaround in a blues piece to bridge the end of one chorus with the beginning of the next one. This bottle would be like the pick-up notes: C-C-F-F/G-G-Geee. The old "drink-till-you-drop" would go into the turnaround and come out on the other side "drink-drink, rest-rest, not-too-muuuch." I'd sip mimosas at brunches and sherry at teatime, and never, ever drink in the morning.

I let my mind roam around. It stopped at the trap door where I kept my fantasies about what would happen when I won my case against the city. I'd get the money. Then I'd buy a nice place near some mountains for vacations. I'd have a glass of wine with lunch, couple drinks before dinner, something after. I'd eat like Tam and I eat when we cook at her place. Fresh vegetables, steamed, stir-fried. Those big, meaty mushrooms roasted on the hibachi. Paella in a special pan with mussel shells sticking up out of the yellow rice. No wonder Hiram couldn't resist her. When you were around Tam, it felt like the volume was turned up. And I wanted that. Like the carnival truck with wire mesh walls and the Thunderbolt ride when we were kids. Thing flung me around so hard I thought my whole head would pop off. It was noisy-like, gears cranking and the engine roaring. I didn't have a quarter, so Arneatha gave me her quarter to ride, and after the man closed us in, he opened the gate and let her ride, too, for free. He played James Brown loud through speakers shaped like horns. The rhythm section pumped through my head stronger than blood, and the horns were happier than anything, bright, shiny, sound brassy as the trumpets themselves. I stood there afterward just to hear it.

Now, in the dark, I could admit that I hated staying sober. It was so boring and so fucking tedious just to get through the day, I thought I would die. Not drinking was a jail sentence. I just kept thinking: *for the rest of my life,* while everybody else was having fun.

I only drank one glass, because I was driving. Very solid citizen. Then I pulled up in front of my father's house. The lights were out. By this time, it was clear to me that we'd all be better off, Dad included, if he was gone. Period.

Kevin would fly in from L.A. and do the paperwork, and Mom would get Dad's pension. She'd be his wife again, his widow. She took a lot of ass-whippings to be his wife. It was all she had. Now, she'd have it back. He would never again disgrace himself by standing up in front of some white people denying his family. And the rest of us could do a good, Catholic funeral with a hearse where people sit still and dab their eyes and some-body slips off the pew, still drunk from the wake, and has to be carried out.

The ice in my glass had been melted, so now I was reduced to drinking the champagne warm. It was too fizzy. I was sitting in the driver's seat of my car, three cars down from his house, sweating like a pig. The drink didn't help.

Rozzie always said she wanted one of those holy-roller funer-als, where the preacher screams fire and brimstone down on everybody, and tells them that we're all gonna die, and that nobody knows the day or the hour, and people jump up and down and scream and cry and faint. She said she wanted us all to carry tambourines with praying hands painted onto a black background. Her mother had a funeral like that. The only thing good about it was a girl with a tremolo mezzo–type voice who sang "His Eye Is on the Sparrow" a cappella.

> I sing because I'm happy,
> And I sing because I'm free.
> His eye is on the sparrow,
> And I know he's watching over me.

The music in that swoops just like a bird, and you've got to have enough control over your voice to trust it to soar and dive. Pitch. You got to have the pitch perfect. Half the time people mess it up so bad you wish they'd just left it the hell alone, but this girl at this little hole-in-the-wall church did so beautiful it brought tears to every eye in the place. People started talking in tongues. She just kept singing over them, a raspy descant, a counterpoint to the chaos below. I could've cried just thinking about it.

I poured myself another glass of champagne. This one was warmer yet. Made me sweat even more. I wished everything was different. Now I was sorry. I wanted to roll back the time an hour to get another chance. I wanted to go to Tamara's apartment and camp there and let her baby me like she did sometimes, with fancy bath oils and her big white terry-cloth robe and her great sound system.

I also wanted to go to Arneatha so she could hold me like before my first detox, when we stood there under her umbrella in the pouring rain, I'll never forget, and prayed, and she said that God could make a way where there was no way.

And I wanted to go to Roz's house, and be part of the action. Always people coming and going. Things happening. Men making deals, making some goddamned money, not just sitting back talking about it like my father and his sad-ass cronies. Hiram and Roz made things happen, and it was like all you had to do was hang around them and show some little bit of gumption, and they'd hook you up. All I'd had to do was show up. The whole Rehab After Work could've been mine, but I'd fucked it up.

I never really liked it anyway. I didn't want my one chance to do anything to be about a bunch of drunks. Addicts. Crackheads. Dope fiends. Sorry niggers. Like me.

At some point I remembered to check to see if the gun was loaded. I wanted to do it before I got too loaded myself. It struck me funny. Loaded and loaded. That's all I remember.

21

You don't come to consciousness all at once. You go in and out.

First person I saw was this tiny Asian woman who took my temperature one night. Her belly was so big she could barely lean over the side of the bed.

"Whacha got there?" I asked.

"I swallowed a watermelon seed," she said.

Seemed funny as hell. I had no idea what she was talking about.

Then it was dark again, and nothing else. And I could feel where the bullet hit. They say it grazed the side of my head. *Grazed* is a loose term. It gouged in pretty good and dug out some of the optic nerve. But the good news is that the bullet kept going. That's the thing. They didn't have to go in and dig around to get it out. Still, I lost most of my sight on that side. The scar looks like hell. It always will, too.

The people were fuzzy and the dreams were riveting. I had drunk dreams, and sex dreams where I just gave it up to get rid of men, which is what I had mostly done in real life, so what was the point of dreaming?

Then I dreamt I was practicing piano, old "Schirmer Library of Musical Classics" at Tamara's mother's house, because Mom sold our piano. Scales in double thirds. *Sprightly,* Mr. Birnbaum used to say in the old-country accent, and he'd spit on me with every *S* and *P*. The school district gave free lessons. *"Sssppr-rightly*. On top of the keys. Fingers on top of the keys. Attack the notes. Little soldiers marching. Faster. C-major. A-minor. Again, G-minor, E-minor, D-major, B-minor."

I liked the little Russian tunes. "Ah," he said, "dark undertones." He approved.

But then I had to play "His Eye Is on the Sparrow" at my father's funeral. I couldn't play it. Too many flats in the key signature. I couldn't remember them all.

Was he dead? Was Dad really dead? It was just a question, not a big worry. Like: is it raining? Is he dead? It rested over everything, while I obsessed about missing one of those five damn flats in "Sparrow."

I got confused and thought he had drowned my dog. There was water everywhere. Who peed?

I wanted my mother something awful.

Then I remembered the police looking at me through my nightgown that time, and feeling the needle when they stitched up my gum before they wired my jaw after the rape. The rape. Even in my sleep I went blank on that one. It was like everything that ever happened was going on all at once, and I was flying faster than usual, back and forth through the darkness.

The needle pulled. I could feel it punch through. The thread felt like it was dragging through my meat.

Novocain only half worked. If I'd known about alcoholism then, I could've told the doctor that that stuff works on me sometimes, and sometimes not. I could've asked him, like I've learned to do since, to please give me another shot or two more, because one seldom does the job. Or wrote a note or something.

But I didn't know. I was too drunk and ignorant. Bad combo. The doctor was an ER intern or resident maybe. Gave off putrid breath and terrible vibes—a death vibe is what it was. He didn't even consider me as a patient, really. I've seen doctors do that, just turn you off. What he saw was some drunk barfly doing it with niggers "two at a pop, and it got out of hand."

Those are exactly the words he used. The very phrase. Right in front of my face like I didn't even have any feelings. I'll never forget that. I started to cry right then. But my face was too swollen on one side to scrunch up. I could see myself in the glass door. Tears running down this big-ass face like a baseball glove. Looked like Quasimodo.

I hate men. I hate fucking men.

After that Neesie had me on my knees in the sacristy at her church. Even her whispers rolled off the stone like music. Like "Claire de Lune."

"Dear God," she prayed, "relieve your daughter here of the burden of hate. Give her your balm. Grant her enough peace that she'll willingly go to any lengths to get more. Give her your grace.

"For her sake," she whispered, and her eyes were full of tears, "for the sake of her son, lift hate from her. Give her a vision of the kingdom."

Which is when I stopped drinking.

Then nothing. Nothing for a long time. Could've been a commercial break, could've been seven years, could've been a hundred or a thousand. For all I knew I could've been preserved under a glacier since the Ice Age.

Then came the picture we all had in our minds from our parents joking at Christmastime that Santa Claus had took a shotgun out in the alley and committed suicide. Sorry, kids, no presents this year. And they'd laugh their asses off. Hah-hah-hah.

But it seemed so real. I could've sworn I was standing in the backyard next to the shiny black poles that held the clothesline. I was standing out in the cold in my mother's slippers and my sister was trying to knock me over to get them away from me when we heard the *pow*—it was like a deep rumble—of the shotgun going off.

"Come on," Buddha said. "That wasn't no Santa Claus."

Then I felt them rubbing me. They were rubbing my feet and legs, my hands and arms. I felt too warm, sick. My head stabbed with pain, sharp pain rising out of dull pain, burning underneath a dull throb. Sword in the stone. A stake through my eye. I wondered, who did it to me? I tried to ask, but I couldn't talk.

"Did you mean to shoot yourself? Or was it an accident?"

That's what they kept asking me when I came to. The shrinks came and the social workers and the medical doctors and the nurses. *Fuck off.* I wanted to go back to sleep.

When they left, Arneatha and Tamara started up rubbing my legs and feet, too, one on each side.

"Look," I heard Arneatha say. "She's awake."

"Leave me alone," I said.

Tam snorted. "You're supposed to say: 'Why, you were all there. You were the Scarecrow, and you were the Tin Man.'"

"Don't rub. It hurts my head."

"We've been trying to encourage circulation, and bring the toxins to the surface," said Tam.

"Unh-uh."

"I'm rubbing prayers into your skin, sweetiepie, like Buddhists put words of prayers on waterwheels to turn in the water."

I had no idea what she was talking about or what the Buddhists had to do with waterwheels or anything. Her voice was more soothing than her hands.

"Is Daddy dead?" I asked.

"Yes."

The pain shot through my head, through the back of my eye. Arneatha leaned over and hugged me. All I could do was say, "I'm sorry," and "Oh, my God."

Tamara stood over us. "Neese, let go," Tam said. "Stand back."

Arneatha stood up. "What is it?"

"She thinks she killed him." Then to me, "Audrey. Did you go there to shoot him?"

I couldn't answer. I felt like my one eye was in the middle of my forehead.

"Or to shoot yourself?" Arneatha asked.

"Why would she go to his house to shoot herself?" Tamara asked.

"I don't know, Tamara," Arneatha said. "People do sometimes."

Tamara and Neesie stared at each other. Then Neesie said: "Your father was in there, dead. He'd been dead at least a day."

"His lights were off," I said.

"She did mean to shoot him," Tamara said.

"If you don't give up drinking now," Neesie said to me in her gentle, school-principal voice, "you are going to lose your mind completely. I don't know how bad it is for you to go through whatever you need to go through to get sober, but what you're doing to avoid it is much worse."

"So, he was already dead," I said. I couldn't keep my one eye open anymore. I closed it. It was better without the light flooding in.

I couldn't help but think that I had wished death on him. I probably did, I figured.

I heard the fast click-click of heels on the hospital floor, and knew it was Roz. I listened for her voice, and I heard it, raspy and high-pitched, every word very, very clear and still a little Southern. She was asking the nurse for a vase.

Tam leaned over and whispered in my ear, "OK, I'll see you later."

I grabbed her arm. "Don't go. I need all o' y'all." I'd forgotten about their split over Hiram. I wanted the feel of my three girlfriends near me. It was sinking in that I hadn't killed my father, and that I was going to pull through. I wanted my friends.

"Oh, my goodness, is she awake?"

I opened my eyes. Rozzie had brought a huge bouquet of pink roses. Biggest roses you ever saw. Big as a child's fist. She was wearing a pink linen dress and gold sandals with a Capri heel. She came to my right, next to Arneatha.

"Open your eye again, girl. I saw that eye open. Look at me."

I did.

"You yook boodaful," I said. I could smell her perfume.

"I like that," Arneatha said. "Tam stayed the night; I've been here since the crack of dawn; and Mrs. Campaign Trail busts in with roses and she looks beautiful. See how you are?"

"You can buy her off cheap," Tam joked.

"Who's cheap?" Roz said through her teeth.

"Please don't," Arneatha warned.

"Well, darling," Rozzie said to me, bright and false, "like your mother used to say, 'Somebody's got to be the lady.'"

"You gonna stop drinking?" Tamara asked. She looked serious.

"What? Of course she's gonna stop now," Roz said. "My God, she's got Rehab After Work and all—"

"We really fucked things up," I said to Tam. "I'm sorry. I know you are."

"Sorry didn't do it," Roz said.

Neesie started to say something, then brought her bottom lip up around the top lip. "You're alive," she said, "and we're together."

Tam snorted. She kissed me lightly on the top of the head and left.

Later Roz left, too. I remember Arneatha on the chair between the bed and the window, wearing new granny glasses, sewing. She looked like her mother. I asked her what she was doing.

"I'm learning how to make a quilt. And I'm thinking about what women have thought about for hundreds of years while they make quilts."

"I can't see on this side."

"They've got a bandage on."

"What's under the bandage?"

"You damaged the nerve that lets you see."

"I made a mess."

She kept stitching.

"I made myself blind."

"Word game," Arneatha said. She always loved word games.

We'd make them up walking home from school. Starting with a word and then making up rules for what to do with the word as we went along. Like making very simple rap. I didn't feel like it, though. I didn't want to be cheered up.

"Make mess, make blind, make quilts, make shift, make work," she said.

"Leave me alone," I said.

"Make me."

"Make me a drink," I said to shut her up, and because I wanted one the minute the words formed in my head, a nice one, vodka ice-cold in a frosted shot glass or Tennessee bourbon right out of the jug or rotgut wine in a jelly jar from the wino lady across the street.

"Make sense," she said, as if anything made more sense right then than having a taste.

I tried. "Make it better."

She looked at me hard. "Make friends."

"Make it go away."

22

I been drinking, I got drunk before.
Said I been drinking, got so drunk before.
Crawled up in my bedroom, didn't lock my front door.

I heard Roz and Arneatha whispering in the corner of my room, as near to an argument as I'd ever heard between them. Roz wanted to know what another rehab would teach me that I didn't already know.

"She shouldn't be in the doggone drunk tank when Bryant's baby is born. Chief Ransome fallin' over dead in his chair, her doing this thing *with my gun* . . . It casts a pall over the baby's birth, I tell you."

"That's superstitious nonsense. What could be better for the baby than to have a grandmother who is really getting sober?"

"Having a grandmother who gets sober quietly, at home, without stealing the limelight from everybody."

"Including Hiram's election coming up? Is this part of it?"

"Look, we can argue and get mad, but the fact is, Audrey ain't got no insurance anyway, so what's the point? She'll get it from experience or she won't get it."

"But going back to her mother's is like sabotage."

"Hard head makes soft behind. You gonna take 'er?"

"Sure."

She didn't. Tamara volunteered her apartment. The shrinks liked that solution, and so did I. Living with Arneatha might have been too much work for everybody.

The first week I slept a lot. I felt like I'd been beat up. When I awoke I never knew whether it would be night or day. It was July and hotter than hell so Tam kept the air-conditioning on. I stayed under the covers, never quite warm enough. Then I'd go back to sleep. I didn't dream, but I kept waking with a start, thinking I was in my old house on Catherine Street, before my husband left and Bryant was a baby, and all I could think was that I'd passed out and forgot to lock the door and bring up our keys.

One night I awoke, sure that my father's card-playing buddies had come to our house, and that they'd sat my sister and I on their laps and run their hands up under our dresses and gave us a quarter. I lay in the bed not able to decide whether it really had happened or I'd dreamt it up. It worried me so bad that the next day I called my sister, Regina, in Dallas and asked her.

"Oh, Audrey," she said, "please, please do not call up here so you can drag everybody into these alcoholic recovered memories with you.

"How could I have sat on anybody's lap? When you were seven I was twelve or thirteen, and I was big for my age, too. Don't call me with this garbage. Call me with some good news. Call and tell me you got a new job or something."

I'd forgotten how bad Regina could work my nerves. I did not call her back.

Arneatha and Roz saw to my mother, who told me on the phone that she was doing fine without me and hadn't realized how much she liked living alone, after all those years with a house full of children. Katie Carter was coming regularly to change the bag and help her out. I should just stay where I was and get better. She couldn't take care of us forever.

I got off the phone ready to spit nails, but Tamara just laughed. I was anemic, so she fed me a strict diet of fruit and grains and spinach, raisins, currants, cabbage, potatoes, tiny cen-ter-cut lamb chops, broiled salmon, and thinly sliced rare roast beef. We ate couscous and India-style chickpeas. She floated me away in spring water.

When I went to the freezer, the Absolut was gone. First it felt like an insult; then I was relieved.

Crystal had the baby in July. She weighed eight and a half pounds. Arneatha drove me to the hospital to see them. Crystal hesitated when I held my arms out to take the baby, and that thing hurt me for real. Junior was there, too, Mr. Ebony Eligible Bachelor of the Year, looking great and calling himself Uncle Junie. He took the baby, handed her to me, winked at Crystal, and said: "I got my eye on 'em; don't worry, sister-in-law."

I was this far from slugging her in her big face.

The baby was so beautiful, though, and so alert, she captured our attention. All I could do was stare at her.

"OK, time's up," Junior said. He handed the baby back to Bryant, who was leaning on the radiator and must have given him the high sign.

Arneatha cut the visit short because she had to fetch Kintu from her father's and go meet Kofi for their standing Thursday night dessert date at the Pink Rose pastry shop down on Bainbridge Street. They did everything according to schedule, like the army or like old people. I commented on it, and she said: "We both need structure. Nothin' wrong with that as long as you get humble about it and act accordingly."

" 'Scuse me," I said.

"Certainly," she said.

Then I made some crack about how Crystal turned out to be the brood mare we always thought she was, and Arneatha turned to me and said, "Audrey, why don't you just shut your mouth about that girl? Just shut up and get better, and get *on* with it."

Made me glad to be living with old two-timing Tamara.

But when they removed the bandage, Tam got it into her head to take me down to her gym at six every morning. I could barely do a thing. She had this little black Barbie type watch over me, so damn perky I wanted to slug her. She put me on the Skywalker and three or four other machines. At seven-fifteen Tam dropped me at the early morning meeting in town while she drove down to the cable-TV studio to tape her segments of *Food for Thought,* a show started by this big-hipped woman we went to Girls' High with. Tam's role was to talk to community people about food and herbs. My mom watched the one about garlic and swore that the garlic pills had brought down her blood pressure. Tam tried to make her go to her doctor, but Mom just let her prescription lapse and used the garlic pills instead.

"Now, laugh about that," I said to Tam.

I was not fun to live with those first few months.

"I don't feel like going to your gym in the morning," I announced one day when Tam woke me.

"Too bad," she said. "You're going. Exercise is the one thing standing between you and murder, and I don't want to be your next victim."

She put down our tray of green tea. "I didn't mean *next* victim."

"Yes, you did. You know you did."

There was no funeral for him. No memorial service. At the morning meeting I said that I needed closure, and some wise-ass rock musician, so-called, who shared about doing cocaine in the back of a limousine, came up to tell me: "Think about it. He's dead. That's pretty much closure."

Another time I said that I had wished him dead, and a black woman wearing bright blue eye shadow came up afterward to remind me that everyone, no matter how loved and adored, dies sometime. She held my hands and did all this eye-contact shit like out of a manual and offered to be my temporary sponsor. No, thank you.

And as I came out the door, a fat white girl, sixteen at most, practically jumped out of the shadows to tell me that she, too, had wished death on her parent. "That's, like, why I came into the program."

"Lemme guess," I said, "you wanted to use this power for good and not for evil."

"Uh-huh," she said. "Will you be my sponsor?"

The nursing temps had let me go, so I had to keep busy. At first I visited my mother every day, thinking I owed her amends, but she no longer believed in my ability to stay sober. I don't know if she ever did. I don't even know whether she thought abstaining from alcohol was the thing to do. She passed on my brother Kevin's interest in a group called Rational Recovery. She told me that from his account it sounded "less kooky" than AA. And once, when I came in the evening, she offered me a bottle of beer, which she found when she cleaned out the fridge.

"It's only a light beer," Mom said. "Is that bad, too? I mean like whiskey? Your father could have a light beer."

I ran out of there like the place was full of gremlins and into a meeting a few blocks away. The meeting was half over. I didn't care that I was late. I wagged my arm in the chairman's face until he called on me. That beer was still calling to me, I said. It was so close, so easy.

Might as well take off your pants in prison. They were all over me.

"No drink is going to jump down your throat unless you bend your elbow."

"Just remember it's the first drink that gets you drunk."

"Don't remember your first drink, remember your last drunk."

"Get some phone numbers and use them."

"Find a sponsor."

"Stick with the winners."

"Why go to your mother every day if she said she's OK on her own? What do you want from her?"

"Stop going to the hardware store asking for apple pie."

"Insanity is doing the same thing, expecting different results."

The next morning, after my early meeting, I did not go to my mother's. I took the bus to St. A's church for prayer meeting, thinking that Neesie would still be running it. She wasn't. Summer school was in session, and Neese only came in in the afternoons to prepare for school in the fall.

"But I'd love to have you stay and pray with us anyway," Father Cherokee said.

I had been looking forward to seeing Neese, and I felt cheated.

"Please stay," he said. *"I've* missed you, too."

"How's Rehab After Work?" I figured I might as well state the obvious.

"We're going ahead with your plans. You left a marvelous design for us to work with."

"I gotta go," I said.

Behind him somebody had covered a bulletin board with teeny, tiny writing that made no sense whatsoever. Covered the whole bulletin board. A cockroach dropped off the ceiling and hit the radiator and kept on trucking. The prayer meeting people were shuffling in.

"I can't stay here," I said. Everything ached. My eye ached when I woke in the morning, and by the time I'd dragged through my half a workout and listened to people at the meeting, the pain proceeded to the back of my head, down my neck, and into my shoulders. The only reason my feet didn't hurt was because Tam insisted I wear her size nine-and-a-half sneakers, and I hated admitting I took a damn nine and a half.

"We need you," Cherokee said, smiling. "Come on. Have a cup of coffee at least."

What made it so bad was I'd seen him do this to other people. We'd talked about it in meetings: radical respect because, they always said, Jesus told us that whatever you do to the least of his people, you do to him.

"I look that bad?"

He cocked his head to the side. "Like you could stand a cup of coffee. And, hey, prayer never hurt nobody."

I took off the sunglasses. The eye was still black-and-blue and mostly shut. My face was puffy.

My mother used to always wear sunglasses. Cat's-eyes with little holes where the rhinestones used to be.

"May I?" He put one arm out to hold me.

I did not want to be touched. "Unh-uh," I said. "No thanks."

"Well, come on out here and sneak a smoke with me. You'll keep me company, won't you?" he asked.

We stood in the courtyard in the sunlight. It was just getting hot. I could feel the sweat starting to run. We didn't talk. The cigarettes smoked nice and quiet. I could hear us blowing out and a few sparrows cheeping.

There's this autistic woman who built herself a hug machine: a box she could climb into to apply even pressure to her body without the stimulation of having a real, live person hug her. That's what Cherokee was like for me: a man machine.

I never did go to prayers, but that summer I did get into the habit of catching the bus down to St. A's after my early morning meeting. Sure enough Cherokee would come out into the courtyard and have a smoke with me. Sometimes he'd ask my advice about the rehab, and I knew he was just building up my ego, but I considered carefully and answered as best I could. Mostly we just stood in the courtyard in the sun and smoked and sipped our coffee. Then the kids would begin to arrive for summer camp, and I'd get out my transpass and get back on the bus, and go to the apartment.

My face still looked like hell. The scar tissue on the side was shiny and pink. I tried to comb my hair over it and looked like an old-ass, fat black Veronica Lake wannabe. Saddest, oldest niggers in Philadelphia wanted to get next to me, asking if my hair was real. Old men in high-water pants. Was that the best I could do? Between them and the program beating on me, if I had had any pride to begin with, that summer would have stripped it away. If you don't get humble, they told me, life will humiliate you.

I upped my meetings to three a day, like meals. I stayed in meetings. For a while they were the real world and everything else was backdrop. I couldn't get enough. I took in the clichés: *Meeting makers make it.* I went to more meetings.

HALT: Don't get too hungry, angry, lonely, or tired. When had I not been all those, all at once?

First things first. I began small changes. Embarrassing to discover. I fished out my transpass *before* the bus arrived at the stop. I urinated *before* the meeting, so I wouldn't have to go in the middle or hold it for forty minutes. Twenty times a day I asked myself: What's the first step? and Do I have to *do* anything?

I tried to make new friends. I asked a woman to be my sponsor, and then, when she insisted that I should move out of Tam's apartment into her own recovery house for three hundred clams a month, I unasked her. Next time I went for an older man named Lucky with round eyes and cheeks who always said when I called: "I don't have nothing more important to do right now than to listen to you."

Lucky liked to garden, and he gave us tomatoes, zucchini, and eggplants from his community plot. He ground eggshells and shoved them down into the ground next to the roots of his plants, and he made compost in the back of his house in dented trash cans with holes punched in the sides and set up on bricks. He was one of those elderly Philadelphians who act like they left North Carolina only last week. He put cut potatoes on his forehead and belly to draw out fever, drank vinegar to cure a cold, and raised a couple of scrawny tobacco plants each year as a reminder of the old country. I checked out the garlic pill business with him, and he said he'd been taking them for high blood pressure for fifteen years.

But while we had nice conversations about the daily meditation or ginger root tea, I kept thinking how I had driven to my own father's house with every intention of blowing him away. It swam around in my head. I'd get to the meeting, go pee, settle down to listen, and I couldn't hear anything, because it would come up again. When I told Lucky something was driving me crazy, he said I should write about it.

So I wrote what I could, first tiny notes on the bookmark I kept in my AA Big Book, then a ring-binder full of dredged-up shit from a hundred years ago. Daddy took my birthday money one year and never paid me back. Six dollars and forty-five fucking cents. I saved my favorite cookie for last at Christmas dinner and he ate it. Shit like that was right up there with the time he knocked my mother out the shed kitchen and broke her finger. Or the fact that I ate humble pie and invited his sorry ass to Bryant's wedding, and he called Bryant to say he had a mother-fucking "previous engagement." Then nothing. Not even ten dollars in a card. Some men would have done anything to have a fine grandson like Bryant invite them to his wedding. Take Tam's neighbor Mr. Hendricks. What wouldn't he have given? And old Chief couldn't be bothered to show up.

Sick. I was so sick with this shit I couldn't stand it. This, I thought, must be what they mean by being sick and tired of being sick and tired. I was ready to drop the load. The resentments seeped out of me. I felt like I was swollen with pus.

It's what my father's buddy Buster used to say if I tried to wriggle away when his hand went up my dress. I had little buds early under there, got my period at ten, and he'd run those big, horny goddamn fingers over my nipples. What I couldn't remember was whether the men were in the kitchen and he took me down to the basement with him, supposedly to get beer out of the icebox down there, or if they were playing in the basement and we went up to the fridge in the kitchen. Seems like I can see it both ways in my mind. But I know I'd squirm to get away when I felt his fingers, and he'd say, "Don't get so pus-sie, little girl. Here, I'ma give you your quarter."

Like I wanted his fucking quarter.

Then he'd reach in his pocket and give me a coin or two and let me slide down, and hit me on the butt as I ran away.

I do not recall what was going on at the meeting to unearth that little gem, but I shared it, and was sorry I did. Every wounded child in the place brought out his or her sore for us to admire. Thank God Lucky waited to walk me home.

"How could a man let his friend do that to his kids?" I asked.

"Could be he didn't know," Lucky said. He held up his hand to keep me from jumping on that, and said, "But he drank is the real answer, and alcohol makes parents careless. Sorry. That's just how it is. You still got a problem with that—and you're entitled—go to Al-Anon."

I didn't even answer.

"Is this something you gonna drink over?" he asked. " 'Cause if so, you might want to do a Fourth and a Fifth Step on it right away. Doesn't say anywhere you have to wait to do the steps."

"Write down my resentments and what I did wrong and then talk to somebody about them? Boy, this get funner and funner every day."

"Go talk to your priest friend, the lady. Somebody you feel comfortable with."

"No," I said. I did not want to face Arneatha talking to me about forgiveness again. "I want to talk to you."

"Suit yourself."

The night before my Fifth Step I took a long bath. I felt like I was losing it. Somebody took my head and put it on a record album, and the DJ pushed it backward like back in the old days of turntable. Static. *Roo-gah. Roo-gah. What's the four-one-one, hon? Don't push me*—I was close to the *eeeedge.*

I washed my hair and clipped my toenails. Then, I did something I haven't done since high school. I picked out my clothes, ironed them, and laid them out—stockings, shoes, the works.

"So where you goin'? To a prom or a funeral?" Tam asked.

"I don't know," I said. "I'll tell you when I get back."

. . .

Lucky lived in the first floor of an old house just barely held together with coats of paint and recycled nails. When the lights went out, he put a penny in the fuse until he could get to the hardware store. I had only been to his house once before. Usually I'd see him at meetings, and we'd go for coffee after, or I'd hunt him down at his community garden plot.

He walked me through his living room, then his bedroom to the kitchen. The floorboards were painted a dark gray. Just beyond the back door, in a yard no bigger than a mid-size sedan, he grew plum tomatoes and greens. A trumpet vine hung so heavy that the wooden fence sagged in the middle. Lucky said that the bright yellow flowers attracted butterflies. He claimed that some years he even had seen hummingbirds.

We sat down at his kitchen table. He poured us some of his watery ice tea and plopped one sad-ass ice cube into each glass. I set my notes on the table, and he launched into his speech. The ice cubes melted before he finished talking.

"Most spiritual disciplines have some sort of confession built into them," he said. "This is something that the human animal seems to need. So, we do it in our program. And we do it, like we do everything in AA, not because we are good and virtuous people striving for spiritual enlightenment, in case we get too highfalutin' here, but just so we won't get drunk. It's that simple. That's the bottom line. That's the big picture."

Then he opened the Step Book and read the first paragraph slowly: " '. . . When it comes to ego deflation, few steps are harder to take than Five. But scarcely any Step is more necessary to longtime sobriety and peace of mind than this one.' "

He handed the book to me. We read like that, pushing the book back and forth across the table, until the end, which was mine to read:

"This feeling of being at one with God and man, this emerging from isolation through open and honest sharing of our terrible burden of guilt, brings us to a resting place where we may prepare ourselves for the following steps toward a full and meaningful sobriety."

I had meant to say many things, but I ended up telling Lucky that I'd left my son with other people, and that I'd gone to my father's house with a gun wanting to kill him.

"But what?"

"But he was already dead."

"Hah!" The room had been so quiet and Lucky laughed so loud and long that he had a coughing fit. "Oh, dear," he said when he finally got himself back together. "Honey, I don't mean to laugh, but that is just too funny."

Then he got real serious. "I bet somethin' in you knew he was dead. It disturbed you. You talk about him and I feel sparks comin' out. Like it or not, y'all had a powerful connection. That's why you went there. That's why you got that thirst, and, of course, we know that you had no defense against the first drink.

"But I'ma bet that's why you was scared when you was on the road. I'ma bet that's why you took out the gun in the first place."

It occurred to me that Lucky might be stone crazy and that what I had always thought about AA was true—that it was a haven for wacko ex-drunks who might as well be drinking for all their connection to reality. Nobody in AA was happy until they got down to some crazy, weird shit. That's where they lived, and that's where they liked it. They wanted God to come down personally in white robes with gold trim and open up parking spaces for them right outside the meeting, and preferably with money in the meter. They wanted Jesus Christ to do their Fifth Steps and, when they finally got up the balls to go back to school, they wanted Confucius to help them write their papers.

I found myself wondering whether my case would ever come through. When I got old enough I could start drinking again and hire me a home-duty nurse to scrape me off the floor, slap on a new Depend, and shovel me into the bed.

"I'ma give you two pieces of advice to take with you now," he said. "Don't throw it away; stow it away, y'hear? One is: 'There are more things in heaven an' earth than are dreamt of in your philosophy.' That's one. And the other is: 'If thine eye offends thee, pluck it out.' "

My hand flew up to touch my eye. My sunglasses were on the table, where I'd laid them. I'd already given some thought to whether or not I'd keep wearing them throughout the winter. My hair mostly covered the stitches and the scar, but the eye itself wandered. I could see people looking at it. I hated looking like a damn fish. If my goddamn case would come through, I thought, I could go see about some surgery to get rid of the scar tissue, and maybe something to keep the eye from floating around so bad.

"And listen to this, too, my dear—"

I was ready to get out of Lucky's nasty little house that smelled like garlic and cabbage and Pine-Sol and old age. The sky was darkening.

"It's gonna rain soon," I said.

"You gonna melt to brown sugar?" he asked, smiling, oblivious, it seemed, to my desire to go. I mean, I was practically out of my skin and at the door.

"I'm telling you, if you can't stand to hear it now, stow it away. Now, you done done Step Five—'the beginning of the end of isolation from God and man.' I didn't mean to laugh at you, but I tell you, we all have wanted to kill. I tried to back my car up and run over my wife."

"Oh, my God. Did you?"

"Nope. There was a gate behind her, and she fell back against it and the gate gave way, so she fell back where I couldn't run over her.

"I was supposed to have fixed the gate, but since I was drinking, I never got to it."

"Did you all have children?"

"Nope. Never did."

"Did you get back together?"

"Stayed together till she died five years ago. A very unhappy marriage, I'd have to say. The last twenty years warn't as bad as the first. See, this the thing, and you're getting it so young, it ain't funny. See, the thing is you're gonna have to give what you did not get. And until you're willing to do that, well, you will always be standing on the threshold wondering why the caravan is movin' on, see? Talkin' 'bout: Why do the parade keep passin' me by?"

Of course that was how I felt, and I hated him for knowing and saying it. So this was the beginning of the end of isolation, hating my dear sponsor? What was it, I wondered, that he wanted me to give? What the hell did I have?

"What I'm meaning is that you are a miracle. And you are gonna do miraculous things. You're gonna learn to *give* what you didn't even *get*."

Tamara was not home when I returned. Seldom was anymore. Somebody on the Health Network was using an excerpt of her crazy cable show on his weekly program. Her book was coming out from the publisher in Atlanta under a new title: *Each One Teach One: A Home Study Guide to African-American Arts and Letters*. And the Painted Bride asked her to curate a series of small multidisciplinary shows for them. Then there were her workouts, and then there was Bill Williams.

I tried not to compare my life with hers. I made myself think of this time as a rent-free opportunity to sit in Tam's black leather chair, put my feet up on her embroidered ottoman, set my seltzer water on her brass table with the Arabic carving, and develop the still, small voice of intuition and sobriety that would guide me through Steps Six and Seven, when I would pray to become *entirely* willing to have my defects of character removed and then ask God to remove them.

What a transformation I would accomplish. Here Arneatha

had been limping along with her faith issues all this time—to preach or not to preach—while I would *become* Paul on the road to Damascus. Didn't Jesus say the last would be first? Weren't we sinners, the drunks and the prostitutes, the people who knew the depths, the ones who'd be catapulted to the heights?

I put down the Step Book and rubbed my eye. The voice within spoke to me. "Audrey," it said, "leave me the fuck alone."

I felt a tingling at the back of my mouth, right at the top of my jaw, like the salivary glands were getting ready to secrete me some ice-cold vodka.

23

After having left me alone through the early part of my sobriety, the urges were on me again. Not just urges coming, but defenses running out the back door at the same time. Like "I want a drink," and instead of my head saying: "Get out of here," it said, like: "Yeah, me, too." Or, "Well, this time, go to the bar at the Ritz Carlton and order something nice, not that cheap crap you was drinking before. No wonder you overdid it."

I read ahead in the Step Book about amends and convinced myself that I'd feel better if I knocked out a few. So I jumped on the horn and told Bryant I knew I should have bought him that bike he asked for that time, and I was sorry. Then I told him to come on over to Tam's some evening, because I had the money and I wanted him to have it. I'm on the cordless, chillin' in Tam's leather recliner, getting ready for the big reunion, when, without missing a beat, my son lets me know, very politely, that between work and school and a new baby, her really does not have the time.

"Keep your money," he said. "Or put it away for Keesha so you'll have it to give her when she's old enough to come ask you for something."

That's the kind of shit his father would do. Mind games.

I told Lucky. "I'm trying," I said. "But some people won't *let* you change."

I went on to say some things I can't remember now about the needs of my inner child. Lucky seemed to think that it was not my inner child that needed further development at that point, but my inner grown-up. Typical AA bait and switch, I told him. They say find your inner child, and I find her, and now it's time to drop her and grow up. He suggested that I find a second sponsor, a woman.

I wanted someone I could trust. But trust was part of the problem. I went back to Lucky and told him I couldn't find anybody I trusted. He asked me to name somebody I did trust, and I told him that the one person I could always trust was Arneatha.

"So look for somebody reminds you of her," he said. "Stick with the winners."

Jewell had none of Neesie's bearing or education, but she seemed patient and honest. Actually, I couldn't imagine her drunk. She said she tended to the depressive side. I wanted to know how depressed.

"Suicidal," she said dryly. Once she walked off the riverbank into the Schuylkill, and a Temple student jogging past dove in and pulled her out. "Wet brain."

I did another fifth step with Jewell. I told her about the rape and how they wired my jaw shut and how my first year without alcohol began silently, hungrily, which was when I started going over to Tam's mother's house to practice piano again. Stuff came up I hadn't thought about, like this girl I used to terrorize on the way to music lessons at Settlement when I was a kid; or the girl from the Curtis Institute who moved in on the small street behind my mother's house last year and started practicing Rachmaninoff every night, the Third Concerto. She practiced five and six hours a day to my one, and she worked that concerto; I mean she worked that shit until she nailed it. I kept my window open from early spring all the way through till the winter just to listen, sometimes loving it, sometimes so jealous I could just—and while I'm talking to Jewell the words just

popped out of my mouth before I could take them back—
"shoot myself."

Jewell said nothing. She's got these little drawn-on eyebrows,
and she worked them up and down, and then lit two cigarettes
and passed me one. My husband used to do that, and then here
come a whole 'nother flood of memories.

I told Jewell about my momentary marriage and my son.

"Your girlfriend, Roz," she asked, "did you resent her callin'
herself Bryant's other mother?"

I shrugged. "He had another father, at least. That was good.
And a brother and sister, a play brother and sister."

"Uh-huh. What happened to their father?"

"Skeet moved to Canada and disappeared."

"You don't see 'im? He don't see 'im?"

"No. What is this, a Fifth Step or *The People's Court?*"

"And what about your own father?" she asked. "Did you love
him?"

I couldn't answer, but my eyes filled up. What kind of fool
would love him? I mean, it took somebody with no fucking
pride at all to keep loving a man who didn't return a phone call
or a postcard for twenty years. A bully who hit women and
children and made fun of us.

"He'd get drunk on Friday into Saturday," I said. "Then no
matter how bad they'd fought he would always drive my mother
and us children to Mass on Sunday morning. I couldn't sit still in
church, so Mom would leave me in the car with him. He'd turn
on the radio to the jazz station, and pull out a beer and a bag of
peanuts. If his hands were too shaky from the night before, I'd
crack the shells for us, and he'd eat them from my fingers. The
whole time he'd be humming the bass line. Then I'd hum it
with him—I'd mock him—and he'd laugh."

"You loved 'im."

"I adored him."

I cocked my head at Jewell like a bird trying to look at something from different angles. I'd been trying to hold it together for

so long. I felt unreal, like I was falling apart. Or like I was sitting up in the corner of her kitchen, in the greasy, black hole where the pressed tin had rotted away, watching myself melt and seep into the cracks where the linoleum curled up from the floor.

Or I'd see myself burn up like the ash on a cigarette. Like some giant would light me down at my feet and draw all the life out of me and I'd glow for a minute and then scatter like ash and blow out the window to the *clickety-clack* of the big kitchen fan.

Jewell and I finished our cigarettes. She didn't say anything for a long time. Her grandchildren's show on the TV in the living room was going off.

"You know you could drink over this," she said.

More than anything I wanted to slap her face at that moment. She saw it in my eyes. Didn't faze her.

"Why don't you write your father's name on a piece of paper and write the word *amends?* Then start prayin' for him."

"I don't pray. I can't pray. And I certainly can't pray for him."

Her grandchildren came tearing into the kitchen.

"Hold up," she told me. She reached her hands out and grabbed each child by the arm. "Hey! Didn't I tell you I wanted to talk to Ms. Audrey?"

I was still trying to get a grip on my face. I hated when AA people threatened me with a drink.

She pursed her lips, reached into her pocket, took out a half dozen pieces of hard candy, and put them on the table. The children started to bounce. From the other pocket Jewell pulled two balloons. The children squealed. She pushed three candies into each balloon. The kids were hollering color preferences.

"You gone take what you get."

Then she blew the balloons to about half their capacity, tied them, got up, and excused herself. "I'll be right back soon's I get them settled," she said. To them she said, "Now I'ma put yours on your hook, and yours on your hook out back. Anybody hit the other one's balloon, I'ma take 'em both away. And anybody hit the other with a stick, *I'ma* take the sticks and start swinging. You got it?"

They followed her outside. When she came back in I could hear their sticks banging on the wooden fence.

"Long's you don't blow 'em up too full and you wrap the ends of the sticks with a rag, they can go to town," she said.

"My girlfriend used to make those for the boys' birthdays," I said. "Out of papier-mâché. She'd do 'em in shapes and paint them. They were great."

"That's nice," Jewell said. "Why can't you pray?"

"Well, if I don't believe in Him, what's the point?"

"Lemme tell you like this: I don't know what to do for your father. I didn't even have a father—you hear me what I'm sayin'?—but this what I'm telling you is something it was suggested to me that I do about my husband to relieve me of the burden of hate toward him.

"The way it was put to me was: do you want some mother's son down in Atlantic City rentin' free space up in your head here in Philadelphia? My answer was no. I do not. They asked me if I had a better idea. I did not."

"You used to live in Atlantic City?"

"Lived all over. When he was in the service we lived in Alaska."

The kids popped their balloons at the same time. They were quiet as they ate their candy.

"About your son," she said. "Maybe you're ready to make some more amends. He sounds like he needs you."

"I tried that already."

"Well, keep it in mind. You could try something different. Maybe something'll come to you."

That night I wrote a note for Tamara, since she was out with Bill Williams, as per usual. I wanted her to show me how to do the papier-mâché piñatas.

z   z   z

I fell asleep hard and dreamt I was supposed to be driving a
vanful of people to the ocean, and we were late, but we were just
sitting in a circle in the woods by the side of the parking lot
smoking hash out of a little metal pipe. I could practically feel it
burning my throat. Funny thing was, I never did smoke hash
except once or twice in nursing school, and it never did do
much for me. But in this dream, the high was so nice I couldn't
believe it.

Tam woke me early so she could show me strips of paper and
the flour-and-water technique.

"You don't want to glop it on too thick," she said, "or else
the kids'll need a sledgehammer to break it. I did a pig one year,
and the belly of that old sow was like rock. Roz had a bird. The
kids had to hit so hard she thought we'd have an accidental
homicide. Nicki went wild, of course."

"I remember that year. Rozzie was, like, into pigs. What the
hell was it with pigs?"

"Miss Piggy. Rozzie loved her. 'Member she used to say *moi*
this and *moi* that all the time?"

Tam took a big breath and put on her ironic look.

"You know," I said, "that I am in no position to cast any
stones. You know that."

"But how could I? Is that what you're thinking?" Tam asked.

"It's not how could you do it—I bet Hiram, way he is, he
probably *needs* two women. And we're not even gonna talk
about what you need. I don't think I'm quite ready to go into all
that. . . ."

"But Rozzie, Tam. You *knew* her."

"Roz'll be fine, Audrey."

Tam got up from the table and took the dish mop off its hook
over the sink.

"Hold this in your right hand," she said. "OK? Move your
arm to the right. Now stop when you can't see the mop part.
Like your blind spot off the passenger side when you're driving."

I moved my arm, and for a moment the dish mop disappeared. I saw nothing. It was out of my line of sight. But my mind couldn't leave that space blind. Where there'd been nothing, a background around the mop began to fill in. Slowly I could see the stencils Tam had painted onto the red wall: solid shapes of gingko leaves in white. I couldn't see them, really. I knew that, but the filled-in illusion was so convincing that I had to turn my head to check. The stencils were there, all right, but different from the picture my mind's eye had conjured up in lieu of real eyesight.

"It's all in how you look at it," she said. "I never stopped being Roz's friend, just like I never stopped being yours."

"What does that mean?"

"It means just that. If she needs me, I'm still her friend. I love Roz. She doesn't need me to help her marriage."

"She didn't need you to tear it up, either."

"I didn't tear it up. She's married and they're falling in love all over again. I've been their angel." She laughed at her joke and left me sitting alone at the table with the flour and water and newspaper.

In October, St. A's fifth and sixth grades took a field trip to the zoo, and Arneatha asked me to come with them. It was the tail end of Indian summer, surprisingly warm. Animals were lying on the ground with their tongues hanging out. We'd eaten lunch and gone to the toilets. Now we were headed back. Next to the marmoset house, Arneatha pulled me aside.

"Do you remember this tree?" she asked.

The teachers and the kids—climbing on a dinosaur statue— were up ahead.

"Are they far enough away now I can have a smoke?"

"I am talkin' about this tree."

"Hold on." I lit up and took a drag. After a whole morning with the kids and lunch in my belly, it tasted so good. "Now I can concentrate on this one tree I'm supposed to remember from second grade. Second grade. OK. What do I remember? I remember John Kennedy got shot. Regina used to pee herself every day and Watson made her sit in it until the janitor came. I started taking piano lessons and they gave me a scholarship. Nope. I do not remember this particular tree."

"There was a black wrought-iron fence along this line," she said, indicating where the ground met the walkway.

"You just don't give up," I said. "Like water on a damn rock. No. I do not remember a stupid tree at the zoo. Try a tree on our block. We had trees, didn't we? Did we have trees?"

"Around the trunk of the tree the fence made a circle. The tree had obviously grown since the fence was put in, because the tips of it were just beginning to dig into the trunk. I thought that that fence would keep the tree from growing," she said. "But look at it."

We could see the shape of the fence in the trunk. Clearly. It reminded me of snakes in the reptile house next door after they'd swallowed their mice.

I did remember. Who would have thought that such a mild-mannered maple would completely consume a wrought-iron fence like the eggplant that ate Cincinnati? The sides of the trunk had grown out where the straight, high rail must have been, too. They pointed in triangular flaps like elbows, as if the tree had its hands on its hips.

"And here we are, thirty years later," Arneatha said, "and the tree is standing there, looking at us like—"

"Like a girlfriend," I said.

I wanted to bring Tam, but she'd gone to Florida with Bill to check out their winter quarters, and Roz was visiting Hiram in D.C.

Suddenly I heard a loud *clack-clack-clack* and hoarse animal grunts.

"Oh, Lord," Arneatha said. "The turtles."

She marched, with me puffing behind, to the children, who were strung along the rock wall separating them from a muddy yard for the Galápagos turtles. The kids were laughing hysterically and slapping one another on the back.

"What's that noise?" I asked.

Arneatha pressed her lips together flat. "Their shells."

"But what the hell are they doing?"

We rounded the bend, and there, up against the wall, a male tortoise had mounted a female and was banging away, shell to shell, for all he was worth. I couldn't help it. I yelled with laughter.

"You're worse than the kids."

"That's 'cause the kids and me ain't gettin' none." It got funnier and funnier.

"What they doin', Reverend?"

"They're making eggs," Arneatha said.

"Ah, sookie-sookie!"

"Oh, shuckie-duckie!"

"They're makin' love," screamed a kid. Three others turned and pummeled him for saying such a riotous thing in front of the adults.

"Sugarpie," Arneatha said, pulling the boys up by their collars. "Those poor tortoises should be in the Galápagos Islands, on a sunlit beach with nobody to bother them. But here they are, in Philadelphia, cooped up in a muddy little pen where schoolchildren come laugh at them every day. They are not making love, honey. They are making do. *People* make love. *Some* people make love. Some people just have sex, like those turtles."

They laughed harder. Three boys fell off the wall and rolled on the sidewalk again.

"Go on, Reverend," one of the young teachers said, laughing. "You sure are setting them straight."

"I'm doing real good, aren't I? See can I make it worse now.

"So, the sex can happen by itself, but the love comes from God. You've got to *make* the love from God *happen* in your life. I certainly try to. Your teachers do. Your parents do. Some of you do, too. I've seen you."

They went into orbit. Two of the boys did flips in the air. They slapped five and shouted. The girls jumped up and down and bent low and laughed with their heads down between their knees.

"OK, now that that's settled, let's move 'em out."

Nobody came right away but me. At the front gate Arneatha and I had to stop and wait for the group to catch us. A youngish, black volunteer approached with a big smile wanting to sell us a membership.

"Not for me," Arneatha said.

"We're going to have the white tigers again next year."

"I am so sick of white animals," I said. "What's so special about white animals, I would like to know? Everything white this zoo gotta run out and get. What else you have to offer?" I asked.

"Don't even tell her, miss," Arneatha said through her crooked smile. "She's not buying a membership."

"Well, what are you interested in? What kind of work do you do?"

The impertinent little fake-hair hussy was determined to make me look bad.

"Nursing," I said.

"What kind of nursing?"

Now I just didn't give a fuck. It's amazing how angry early sobriety can be. "Mostly," I said, "I've nursed a lot of beers and an astonishing number of grudges. I'm gettin' one now, you keep askin' me my damn business."

"Please don't mind her," Arneatha said. "She's the kind of person who makes friends by engaging you in conflict. Some of my schoolboys do that. Their idea of making friends is to butt heads."

"For Christmas," the girl said, looking at Arneatha, "we will be featuring the annual tree-lighting ceremony and Members Only Night. That's a beautiful evening. Maybe you two will want to come."

"She's signifying," Arneatha said as she walked away. "She's telling you something dark. Nighttime. You want black? Come at night."

I heard the familiar chords of resentment playing in my head against the volunteer. I made fun of her weave sticking up off the back of her head like a hoop skirt.

"Oh, leave the child alone," Arneatha said.

"You so good. You always was so good."

"I was not."

"Oh, I forgot. There was that time you left the tops off all Tamara's markers. Oh, that was bad, very bad."

"If you want a cigarette before the children catch up to us, you'd better have it now," she said, "and stop running your mouth."

I lit the cigarette. I could see just our family dressed in matching blue coats and fur-trimmed hats, holding hands, holding our breath as the twinkling lights above our heads switched on and horn players in red Santa caps blew carols into the cold air. I love that sound.

Of course it would never have happened like that. My father wouldn't have come; my mother would have brought us late. We never had matching coats and lost every hat people gave us. Or, we'd all have been fighting.

Back at school, we saw the teachers and children off the bus. Arneatha asked me to wait with her and go into the sanctuary. She hauled out her ring of keys and opened the heavy red door.

"You gonna make me pray?"

"Unh-uh."

It was cool inside. Our feet made an easy beat on the stone. Sometimes in St. A's the vibes are too much to handle. But that afternoon they were peaceful. I stood in the center listening to Arneatha's footsteps and jangling keys go back to the priests' office. I took off my flip-flops. The floor felt cool and dusty as I walked over to the organ. It's a smooth console, good proportions, beautiful maple-colored wood. I did not turn the organ on, but I let my feet play on the foot pedals. I could hear them in my head going lower and lower, deep and round, deep, dark sound, farty bass, grand and loud, like shaking the roots of a big, old tree.

Arneatha finished her business in the office and came out carrying a small shopping bag.

"If I don't believe in God," I said, "how do I pray?"

"Ask for the question. Leave God out of it for the time being. Get a dialogue going with your truest inner self."

I looked at her. My feet played D-flat-major scale. I'd had such a hard time with that key signature.

"Ask," she said.

"Now?"

"Sure," she said. "Close your eyes. Make your feet be quiet. I can't think."

"Christ."

"Shhh."

Into my head came the bottom three notes of the organ. E-D-C. No lower. Nothing more. I know there are lower notes. I could see them in my head, like a cartoon drawing them in below the bass clef. But I couldn't hear them in my head because the organ doesn't go there.

I heard the Peggy Lee song, with a little oompah band in the background: "Is That All There Is?"

I opened my eyes. Arneatha was sitting next to me on the organ bench. Her smile looked tired. I was touched to see how much effort she was making for me.

"You beat?" I asked her.

"Must be a low-grade bug of some kind. Maybe I need to take some of Tam's high-protein diet, or iron tabs or whatever she used on you."

I did feel strong again. It had happened so gradually I almost hadn't noticed. And my mind was clear.

"How do your breasts feel?" I asked.

She thought for a minute. "Tender."

"Do you keep good track of your periods?"

"No. I never bother," she said.

" 'Cause you could be pregnant."

"Nah." She frowned. I could see her putting together all the information her body had been giving her.

"You due? Overdue, maybe?"

She nodded her head. She looked dazed.

"So. What's in the bag?" I asked.

She took out a square cardboard container. The line sprang into my mind from the old game shows: "Is it bigger than a bread box?"

"It's your father's ashes. It's time I gave them to you."

Now it was my turn to go tongue-tied.

"Your mother asked me to keep them," she said.

"What the hell do I do with them?"

"That's up to you, unless he made any specific requests."

In November, Hiram won his election and a full two-year term in the seat the governor had appointed him to in the spring. He'd been ahead the whole campaign, and won by a healthy margin, as they kept saying on the radio. None of us went to the headquarters that night. Tam didn't, of course. Arneatha made her excuses about being tired and having the baby, but she would have been there if he'd stayed Democrat, I'm sure. Rozzie leaned on me pretty hard to come and hold down the fort with her, but I told her they'd have to pop all them corks without this recovering alcoholic. When she started whining, I reminded her what had happened in my last run-in with champagne.

On the night of the election, Rozzie announced that she had found the perfect house in Georgetown. For the benefit of those who weren't there, she called us personally to let us know.

"Isn't it like a dream come true?" she screamed into the phone at me. I hadn't known that she'd been looking.

When Nicki protested that she wanted to finish out high

school with her old friends, and Hiram said, "Yeah, what about that?" Roz called to ask me to move into their place and stay with her.

Roz didn't say it, but we both knew that I owed them. I mean, she raised my kid his whole childhood. I did not particularly want to move back in with my mother and she didn't want me either—we'd finally come to some clarity and some honesty about that. So I said yes, gladly. I gave Tamara back the run of her funny little apartment, with its statues and pictures and prints, and went back to work, not as a temp this time, but as a hospice nurse. It was time to stop star-gazing down my own belly button and sponging off my oldest and dearest friends. Hospice nursing might not heal the world, but I'm suited to it in a funny way, and it does pay the bills.

24

I went back to the zoo and bought a family membership. Just after Thanksgiving, I shoehorned Bryant, Crystal, and Keesha into Tamara's Karmann Ghia and drove us all together. I took direction from my various advisers. I had wanted the trip to be a surprise, but Lucky and Jewell agreed that it was disrespectful to try to take grown-ups to places without their consent. So I asked ahead of time if they minded and used a car seat for the baby.

I also started out half an hour earlier than I normally would have. We didn't rush. It was a cold night with no moon. No rain. We didn't talk much in the car, except for Crystal, who blabbed about how much she used to love the clowns who poured out of circus cars. The baby took a dump and stunk up the car. We opened the window. I felt very tense and sort of ridiculous, too. It wasn't like Bing Crosby and Ginger Rogers in *Holiday Inn,* but nobody argued, and we arrived on time.

When we got to the zoo, we parked in the lot with the other members and walked in. I had my receipt out—the card hadn't come—ready to duke it out with anybody who would not believe us, but nobody checked. The volunteer at the door was the same girl I'd bought the membership from. She said hi to me like we were old pals and asked if this was my family. I said yes. It felt good to say.

Dressed-up people were jammed onto the patio outside the rare-mammal house. Volunteers in Santa hats pushed through to give children endangered species stickers. Several helpers and a dozen and a half kids were wearing hats made out of balloons tied up to look like animals. A clown tried to make his way through to do a few tricks every ten yards or so. When he got to us, Crystal asked if he knew how to make animals out of balloons. He was one of those clowns who doesn't talk, so he pantomimed. He put his arms real wide to say: a big one? And then made a two-inch space between his finger and thumb: or a tiny one?

"No," she said, laughing. "Like thith—" She spread her hands about a foot apart. "You know, like the kind they be makin' at birfday partieth."

Need I say most of these people were white? And the clown was white. He started scratching his bald white head with the red hair sticking out on either side and putting his hand under his chin like he was thinking, and the people around us started to titter a little bit. I felt Bryant stiffen next to me, and I thought to myself: This clown is getting a fucking laugh off the girl in front of these white folks. The lights hadn't gone on yet. My stomach started to flop. Everything had been so nice up till then. And he's getting ready to ruin it all. That's all I could think. He's going to ruin it.

I could feel myself start to withdraw. It was like somebody was pulling down the shade. I could tell. I was in there pulling down the shade, turning off the damn lights, getting ready to go down the cellar and act like I wasn't home so the meterman couldn't get in and turn off the water. I hadn't brought my kids out for another fucked-up occasion. That was the whole point.

Then it came to me—while he's doing all this shit—to maneuver myself behind him. I eased around to where I was directly behind his ear and I whispered: "Just do a dog or a cat, and then move on and make fun of somebody else. 'Cause I stopped drinking not long ago and I swear it don't take much more than you just did to set me the fuck off."

Well, his eyes flew open and he nodded real big like he just got it, and then, sure enough, he found himself some balloons and made one long hot doggie and then another one and wrapped them together to make a hat. Crystal was thrilled. The clown turned away from me and made hat-doggies for some children behind him.

Then over our heads the lights came on. Mostly small and white, they covered the trunks of the trees in perfect rows no more than an inch or two apart and covered the bare branches out so far to the ends that it looked like the trees had pointed fingertips to touch the night sky. One tree was covered in green lights and one in red. Out on the lawn we saw lit-up animal shapes, and in the middle, the twinkling outline of an old building called Solitude in the middle of the zoo. The people in the crowd let out oohs and aahs the moment the lights went on. We'd been in darkness. Suddenly we were under a canopy of twinkle lights. We could see one another's faces in the glow.

Crystal oohed louder than anybody—she really is spontaneous—threw her arm around my neck, pulled my whole head to her, and gave me a big, wet kiss on the cheek.

"Mewwy Chrithmath, Mom!"

"Come over on my good side," I said to Bryant. He stood back and aloof, as usual, it felt like to me, holding Keesha. "I can't see you."

"I'm showing the baby the lights," he said.

"He's all choked up," Crystal said. "He don't want you to see. He wanna be the man."

"You man enough to walk down that dark pathway over there?" I asked. "I want to show you something."

We walked to Arneatha's and my tree that had grown around its fence. We were standing under a lamppost.

Crystal walked up to the tree and felt its gnarled trunk.

"It' th'pooky," Crystal said.

Bryant put his ear to the trunk. "Aw, shit. I hear a heartbeat. Listen here. *Ba-boom. Ba-boom. Ba-boom.*"

I hadn't seen him joke around since the wedding. I told him

so. As we walked back to the lighted trees, Bryant said quietly, "She makes me joke, you know. She really loves to live."

Bryant touched the dent on the side of my head, the one I'm always telling myself nobody can see, and traced his finger over the spiderweb scar tissue that comes out of it.

"I'm trying to learn how to make amends," I said.

"Good," he said. "I'm trying to learn how to accept them."

I drove home to my new digs at Roz's, keeping the Karmann Ghia, as Tam and I had agreed, for an errand I promised myself I'd make the next day.

When I got home Nicki was in bed, but she'd left the radio playing. I turned to Temple's jazz station. A young white boy with an upstate Pennsylvania accent was talking about Louis Armstrong. He played several cuts in a row of Armstrong doing W. C. Handy. It had spring and jump on the surface of the music and enough blues underneath to make you moan. I was glad that Dad had had the radio on when he died.

The next day, after hemming and hawing and doing half a dozen chores around the house, I put the box of ashes and my checkbook in the canvas bag Roz kept hanging on her Peg-Board in the kitchen. I double-checked to make sure I had the address of the cemetery where I could buy a bronze memorial plaque for two hundred and fifty dollars instead of a plot and stone for a thousand. In recovery I felt a little bit like a retarded child going off to school each day with my lists and my bags and following directions to a *T*. But I was determined not to pull some dysfunctional shit like drive to the wrong damn cemetery and not be able to afford the plaque and end up sitting in Tam's car pissed off and starting to hyperventilate.

The bag had been a premium for supporting Temple's jazz station. Hiram's and Roz's house was a constant reminder of all the things I hadn't done. Or all the things I said was wrong with the world, but just sat on my ass complaining about. Hiram had a standard line about all the niggers in Philadelphia always wanting

Bill Cosby and Patti LaBelle to give somebody money. "Before you ask them to give a half a million, why don't *you* give 'em twenty dollars first?"

I got in the car and drove north to Temple. I found a legal parking place on Broad Street, fed the meter, and took my canvas bag with me into the student center, where they directed me to the building where the radio station was. Then I went inside and wrote them out a check for two hundred and fifty dollars in my father's name. They said they keep a record of such things, and that they'd read his name out loud in the next pledge drive. He always said he wanted to give to the station. Well, now he had.

Then I filled the car with gas, and called Tamara to ask if she would drive with me to Atlantic City. By this time it was afternoon. She must have heard something in my voice, because she said yes. She had something planned, but she'd cancel it. No problem.

I don't know who else I would have called. Tamara was the only one of my friends who ever liked my father, despite the fact that she, like the rest of us, stayed out of his way when she was small.

"I want to pour my father's ashes into the ocean," I said.

"Well, it's about time somebody did," she said. "And who could resist an invitation to such a happenin' good time?"

Tamara convinced me to drive the extra thirty miles to Cape May Point instead, right to the southern tip of New Jersey, where the Delaware Bay meets the Atlantic Ocean. She said that it added the necessary symmetry.

It took more than two hours to reach the point. When we arrived, we parked the car and walked out onto the sand. The ocean was louder than I remembered and black. The waves crashed and rumbled deep like a timpani.

I had the idea that I wanted to scatter the ashes from a jetty, but the water was at high tide, and the jetty was submerged.

Tamara looked at the jetty and laughed. "Plan B, Audrey. What's your Plan B?"

"I could get up there," I said, pointing to the section of the jetty closest to us, "and throw in the whole box."

"What, just chuck him over the side?" She started to laugh again.

"Shit." The waves were crashing. I mean hard. I was getting fed up. Here I'd gotten this great big goddamn idea, and everything had gone so good, and now it was starting to look ridiculous.

"The box'll crash against the rock and the ashes will scatter. Same difference," I said.

"No, no, no. You brought me because you wanted a nonreligious artistic consultation. I know you did. And dumpin' a box onto the rocks does not cut it. You didn't come all the way down here for an anticlimax. Think."

I tried to imagine standing on the jetty and pouring the ashes out, but the wind was blowing, and I was afraid they'd cover me. Tamara agreed and added that I might have the misfortune to breathe him in or blind myself by getting some of him in my good eye.

"Aw, man. I give up."

I thought of walking along the jetty as far as I felt safe and leaving the box there for the tide to take out, but she said that the jetty was too slippery.

By this time we were chilled through. I was scared, too. The ocean lets you know how strong it is. When I saw the big waves crash over the jetty, I wondered how I could even have entertained the idea of climbing up onto it.

The lighthouse beam slipped through the air and floated on top of the black water. All the energy that had carried me through the day was gone. Tamara had laughed at me so much I felt stupid, and angry that I'd asked her.

"Come on," she said again, in that amused tone of voice. "We've got to think."

"Oh, screw it," I said. "I'm tired." I started to walk away from her along the water's edge. Sand was seeping into my half boots.

I took the box out of the bag I'd been dragging around with me since morning and used a seashell to cut the packing tape around the edges. I dropped the shell into the bag as a keepsake and poured the ashes in a steady stream onto the sand along the water's edge. I spread them very thin so he'd be along as much beach as possible, and so that the ash would be incorporated quickly into the ocean. Black sea water slapped against the beach. I loved that sound. Silent foamy wavelets lapped higher onto the shore to wash down Dad's ashes. The ocean gargled and swished and licked its lips.

Dad was gone.

I thought of how I'd sat outside his apartment wanting him dead. Now he was. There was no sign of the line of ashes on the sand. I walked back to Tamara, who was standing back away from the sea next to the dunes. She put her arm around my shoulder.

"There. You did it."

If she hadn't been there, I might not have believed it had happened.

We climbed the wooden pathway over the dunes, and immediately, the crashing, drumming, pounding waves were muffled. I felt safe again, neither threatened by the ocean nor tempted by it.

Tamara got into the driver's seat. She handed me a present wrapped in the funnies from the Sunday paper and tied in a blue ribbon. It was a tape of a traditional Dixieland band. I saved it until we'd driven out of town, and the sad-ass heater in the Karmann Ghia had cranked up. We bought coffees and sandwiches. When we were on the highway, I played the tape. Happy sad music. I'd never played like that. Never had the craft or the art or the discipline to practice. Never let myself be sad enough. Never known the happiness. Never accepted that they'd both come and roll over you like the ocean. Lap you up, drink you down. Better hold a parasol and dance about it. Better practice your scales so your E flat comes out pretty enough to make people cry.

I didn't say anything. Tamara let me be quiet until the end. No big pronouncement, no demands for feelings or reactions. I felt a little crazy and dreamy. But the coffee was hot and strong, the ham-and-cheese sandwich was fresh, and the music played fine.

"So, do your program people have the next step toward creative self-improvement and emotional and spiritual wholeness ready for you?"

"I got big fun to look forward to," I said. "Rape counseling is next."

"Now I feel bad saying it."

"Say it. You can have a life. Don't mind me."

"Florida. Bill goes down in the winter to do personal training for some Hollywood types and some rich old New Yorkers who're keeping up with their third wives. Soon as Arneatha gets married, we'll go down."

"I have to admit something about this wedding," I said. "It makes me sadder to think of her getting married than it did to scatter my father's ashes. All my friends are leaving, just when I'm comin' back to life."

"Ninety-nine dollars to Florida."

"What about Ghana?"

"You think she's really going to go?"

I did. But I couldn't say it without starting to cry, so I shook my head.

Arneatha's wedding to Kofi, I figured, was the last time we were going to be together for a long time. Arneatha was worried about looking pregnant, but she didn't. After all, she wasn't quite three months gone. All you could tell, and only if you were looking for it, was that she was a little hippier. It helped her fill out her mother's dress, a form-fitting cream-colored gown with a matching, beaded jacket that Mrs. Bell wore to her last formal. I'm glad Arneatha found it. Her alternative was this beige-colored business suit that you wouldn't wish on your evil step-sister.

She was getting clumsier, though, and that looked like it could be a problem. Instead of a red carpet, Tam said maybe she needed a conveyor belt.

They threw together a ceremony and reception aimed at the church and the kids from her school. They ordered all-beef hot dogs, mini-hoagies, buckets of macaroni and cheese, a cake the size of a bandstand, and ten gallons of ice cream with a half-gallon container of chocolate sprinkles. On either end of the parish hall, four one-hundred-year-old church ladies were assigned to serve tea from silver urns. Throughout the hall Arneatha arranged for kiddie snack stations: half-bushel baskets of goldfish crackers and soft pretzels, fountains spouting punch in purple and red and green and blue, and self-serve gallons of water ice set in ice-filled kitchen trash containers with linen tablecloths tucked around them to make skirts. She only got lemon, so it wouldn't stain.

As fast as they threw the wedding together, that's just how long the ceremony was, too. Cherokee Jones had to tell a story. This one was about the blind man and the lame man who wanted to attend the wedding feast of the daughter of a wealthy man in an ancient village, but the blind man couldn't see to get there and the lame man couldn't walk. So the lame man hitched up on the blind man's shoulders, and the one walked and the other told him the way. When they arrived, they ate their fill and danced and had a ball.

"Just like we, too, will do tonight," he said, "having brought our animal body and our spiritual body together to worship and experience the love we share in this world that comes from and continues into eternity."

At least a dozen groups of kids from St. A's school sang songs and recited poems. Then the glee club and the madrigal and the fourth-grade chorus, and like that. Went from "Getting to Know You" and the theme from *Family Matters* to *The Magic*

Flute and, from a teenaged alumni reggae band, Bob Marley's "Redemption Song."

OK. Kids I could understand. But everybody in the damn church had a solo, too. One solid hour and fifteen minutes. Tam whispered in my ear that we'd entered The Wedding Zone, where children celebrated joy and happiness forever, and we'd never get back to the real world. We're way over the scheduled time; I'm starving. Then Sister Somebody, who was not on the program, felt moved to throw down a couple verses of "He Is Real," and I was like: Jump the broomstick, pul-lease.

Then the drums began for the final prelude to "Repeat after me . . ." The choreographer in the congregation organized the teenagers into this dance that they did down the aisle to drums, flashing banners and carrying petals. That part was spectacular. In the middle of it this group of Pentecostal parents got hit by the spirit and two of them jumped up and started talking in tongues. Somebody fell out; things went totally out of control.

And the drums keep pounding like I love them. No words. No talk. Melodies under and over the rhythm. In the rhythm, but secondary. Rhythm the same until it's perfect, then they change to a new one that's unexpected, but practically clairvoy-ant, as if they could tell what we needed next. Go from quarters to thirds to eighths.

Next thing I know I'm standing up. Several people are danc-ing with the kids. It's a simple dance, repetitive, like blues and church songs. I could do the dance, but I don't want to distract myself from the sound, or from the view I have of Arneatha, smiling, rocking, holding hands with Kofi.

"You want to dance?" Tamara and Bill moved their legs for me to let me by, but I shook my head. Something stood me up, but I didn't feel the *need* to dance. It wasn't want and it wasn't need. For once in my life I felt no need, but the opposite of need. It was plenty, like the music was plenty. Enough for me to sit. Then, so full up I had to stand to make room. Enough, more than enough, so full, it splashed over my sides and poured over me and out of me and I felt my arms reaching up and the top of my head softening, opening to receive it. The sound carried strength. It brought me hope where I had no idea I'd been hopeless. Waves of sound and the hopefulness of this wedding, this love they'd made, our years together and the coming years apart went through me like radio waves, and my fingers let them in. I was going to be flapped in the wind like a rag on the line.

I opened my fingers because I knew I could take it. I was elastic and supple and strong. Where I fell on my back I could twist like a snake; the jaw that they wired was not stiff, but wide open and laughing; the knees that I banged and fell on were nimble and painless; the hole where they scooped out my uterus was not empty but quiet, finished, satisfied; I could take what would come without tensing. I did not have to run away and hide. This was no ass-kicking coming down, no pain, no trick, no bait-and-switch. Not this once.

The joy seeped into my fingertips. Not crazy, wild, *Hallelujah!* ecstasy. Simpler. Plain as sweat. A sweetness. A breath. Plain as watching a baby sleep. Such sweetness. But tough. Plain as fresh water. Clear. Plain as breathing air.

I knew where I was when I fell. I knew they'd catch me. I knew I'd come back, not changed like Moses down from the mountain, but changed for having known a moment without need or fear.

Tamara was sitting next to me, regarding me with her usual ironic amusement.

"Born again?" she asked.

I shook my head. I had not sprouted wings, not traveled anywhere, not seen visions or heard new songs, or felt the presence of other beings. But I did feel grounded. If I let go the side of the mountain, I would not fall off the earth and tumble into a loveless sky. I was not reborn, but set free to do ordinary miracles. I could let go the side of the cave and walk out into birdsong and sun. I could bear sudden heat and the threat of rain. I hadn't been born again, but I nearly had to squint my eye and cover my ears against the intensity of the world that came at me as the sweetness receded.

After the service Arneatha pulled me by the arm into the bathroom and asked me what I had felt. I tried to explain it to her. She told me that sweetness was the word the old people used.

"This is not the pearly gates," I said.

She smiled. "No, I shouldn't think so."

"I didn't want you to marry him," I said. "I didn't want you to go away."

"To Ghana?"

"Sure, to Ghana, but even before that, even if you stay here, I didn't want you to go behind that wall. Marriage is a wall."

"Can you stand it now, you think? Because I am going. I love being in there with him. It's like a garden."

"You love him like you loved Larry?"

"Different. The love is less . . . all-encompassing, I think. More organized."

"Only you would say something like that about the love of your life."

"Well, you make it sound like we're being sealed alive in a tomb."

We laughed, and she leaned against the wall.

"Stand away from that nasty wall," I said.

"What you felt tonight," she said, "does that make it any easier to see us kind of drift apart?"

"I guess. Maybe I'm cured. You think so?"

"You mean, do I want to take you out for a drink?"

We said together in imitation of Tamara's Daffy voice: "Not this little black duck."

"I wish you could find a way to be happy for me," she said seriously. She ran her hand along my face. I felt her fingers touch the bottom of my scar.

"Yeah," I said. "I can. It's just that it seems like I only just got all of you back, and now you're gone so soon."

"Almost missed it, eh?"

"Yeah. I almost did."

She went back to her guests, the tall and the small. The reception lasted three times as long as the wedding. After an hour Hiram and Rozzie's car and driver arrived, and while Hiram finished working the room, at Neesie's insistence, we four went outside together. We hugged and kissed, except for Roz and Tam, and I cried because we'd never be like we were before.

"Don't cry," Tamara said.

"She can cry," said Arneatha. "Probably good for her."

Rozzie rubbed my face between her two tiny perfumed hands. "Well, I'm just glad it ain't me bawlin' this time. I want y'all to remember that."

Then Hiram came out of the parish hall, and they drove away.

Later in the week Arneatha and Kofi left for their honeymoon in Ghana. After Christmas, Tam joined Bill in Florida. There she dredged up the oldest living Negroes she could find to cook alligator and cornbread with sorghum for her show.

On New Year's Eve Nicki went to Washington with her parents, and I cooked pigs' feet and greens and black-eyed peas and took some to Bryant and Crystal. Keesha came home with me, and we fell asleep in the TV room before the ball even dropped.

I'll stay here on Christian Street awhile and hold the fort. Having only recently come home, I have no desire, for the time being, to leave.

ABOUT THE AUTHOR

LORENE CARY is the author of *Black Ice,* a memoir, and *The Price of a Child,* a historical novel. She teaches writing at the University of Pennsylvania and lives in Philadelphia with her husband and two children.